ECHOES OF THE ETHERSTONE

LUCY A. MCLAREN

First paperback edition October 2025

Cover design by Matisse Luisa Designs

OWL TALYN PRESS

First published in the United States by Owl Talyn Press in the United States

www.owltalynpress.com

For anyone fighting to make the world a better place—we're in this together.

CONTENT WARNING

Thank you so much for picking up *Echoes of the EtherStone*, it means so much to me. The world can be a dark and scary place, and I tend to explore some of the dark and scary things we see in real life within my writing—and that's certainly true for this story. *Echoes of the EtherStone* includes depictions of murder and violence, descriptions of gore, religious and patriarchal oppression, mentions of historic child abuse, as well as explorations of mental illness, including grief and trauma. As such, please take care of yourself first and foremost and set the book aside if any of these aspects are likely to be tough for you to read right now.

THE FIRST

DAISY

I had been watching her for a while before I approached her. The stench of the docks was heavy in my nostrils—fish and filth, the rotten odor of the decaying streets of the Workers' District—while the cobblestones were slick beneath my feet. The streetlamps had been lit what felt like hours ago, and I was sheltered in a doorway hidden from the flickering gas flame of the nearest one.

Daisy stood beneath her usual streetlamp on the opposite side of the street—a place I had observed her parade herself many times before. I wanted to bide my time before striking. She leaned against the tall, metal pole, doing her best to seem appealing. Her skinny ankles were bared and her modest cleavage was pushed up within her hand-me-down corset. Despite this, she was unable to hide the occasional shiver when a chill breeze gusted down the street. It may also have been due to the fact that as a young woman barely past her sixteenth year, she couldn't possibly know much about the pleasures she purportedly offered to passersby who glanced her way.

I knew she was the one; had the moment I first laid eyes on her. I knew too what must be done. I simply had to commit. For weeks now, the voice in my head had been urging me on, imparting the urgency of my mission.

My savior, it said, *why do you hesitate? What is one life, one sacrifice, to maintain the sanctity of my reign? What is one life compared to my protection over this beloved city of yours, over the very Kingdom of Estra?*

As the days passed, the voice—He, I should say—had grown louder and louder until it was all I could do not to scream.

I had to act. Only then would He leave me in peace. He had promised.

My palm, slick with sweat, rested on the hilt of the knife sheathed at my waist. As I drew near, she turned to me and smiled, her pale blue eyes flitting up my body, lingering on my hooded face. There was no recognition in her expression as she tilted a bare, pale shoulder towards me. Momentarily forgetting myself, there was a stirring of excitement in my loins. She certainly was not unattractive with her slim waist, full lips, and long, chestnut locks.

"Lookin' for a good time, mister?" she asked, her voice slurring slightly. Intoxicated.

My lip curled with disgust, even as I knew alcohol was likely an attempt at self-medicating against her condition.

"How much?" I asked.

Her eyes gleamed with reflected lamp light as she looked me up and down once more. "A gold crown."

I bit my tongue, knowing this price to be far too high, yet fully aware I could reclaim my coin once the deed was done if I so wished. "Of course," I said, reaching into the leather purse at my belt. I retrieved the crown and held it up, letting it glint in the light.

She gasped. Given her background, I doubted she'd ever seen a gold crown before. Daisy stepped forward, lifting her chin and proffering a dirty palm. "Payment up front."

I admired her tenacity and held the coin out for her to take. She reached for it hesitantly, as though expecting it to be snatched away. Once it was in her grasp, she stowed it in a shabby, limp purse tied to the tattered belt at her waist.

"Well then, sir," she said, running a finger down my front, "where d'you want me?" She gave what she must have believed to be an alluring smile.

It wasn't bad, not really. I was just impatient to be at my work. To be done and away from this wretched place.

I peered around, pointing behind her to a darkened alley. "There."

She winked. "A shy boy, I see."

"I'm not a boy," I snapped. Seeing a glimmer of fear in her eyes, I said more gently, "I simply do not like to be on display." I leaned in close to her ear. "Who I lay with is my business and no one else's."

My words had the desired effect and she appeared to relax. "'Course, sir." She took my hand and led me to the alley.

Around us, the streets were quiet. The Scrubbers were tucked away in their meager, run-down homes or cradling a cup of EtherAle in the local drinking hole. Either way, it worked in my favor. The light from the lamps faded as we moved away from them. The alley was damp and cold, but was sheltered. Here I could carry out my work in peace.

As she turned to me, I rushed forward, pressing her against the wall. I will admit there was an air of arousal being so close to her body, malnourished as it was. A woman's scent has always driven me to a kind of madness. Yet I had been able to resist its allure thus far in life. Now would be no exception—my mind would stay focused.

"You're an eager one, ain't ya?" she said huskily. She pulled at my cloak, causing the hood to fall, and let out a gasp. "Oh! I know you! You're—"

I pressed my mouth to hers to stop her next words. *Shit.* She wasn't supposed to see my face. Somehow my task was made harder by her knowing who was taking her life.

When I pulled back, she grinned. "Well, I'd've never

suspected one such as you'd be down here. You was awful proud, arrogant even, when you was at my house." She gave an awkward smile. "Not my words, you understand. Jus' what me ma said." She tugged at my belt, undoing it with deft fingers, and slid her hand inside my trousers. "But it seems you weren't too proud t' come back for what you wanted."

My savior, remember your mission, the voice in my mind said.

Yes, Father. The servant of the EtherMother must die. I gritted my teeth against the waves of pleasure building at Daisy's touch.

"Stop," I said sharply.

Her eyes snapped up to meet mine. "My lord?"

I exhaled, wishing she hadn't said that—hadn't acknowledged my title or that she knew me. I had to be done with this.

I leaned in to kiss her neck and she moaned. As I distracted her, I slipped my knife from its sheath; a fine, silver blade with a gold gilt handle, a sacred blade passed down in my family. In one deft movement, I lifted it up, stepping back and slashing at her neck.

Her eyes widened, a moment of shock as she registered what was happening before her hands flew up to stem the gush of blood.

But something was wrong. There wasn't enough blood. I hadn't hit the artery as planned. She could survive this.

Fuck.

In that split second of hesitation, she turned to flee.

"No!" I cried, leaping for her.

"Help me!" she called out, though it came out weak and wheezy.

Hot, burning rage coursed through me at her audacity to attempt escape. "Whore," I spat, dragging her backwards into the alley. "Where is your EtherMother now?"

Her only response was a gurgled whimper. I held her from behind, keeping her in place as I stabbed at her throat. I had to be sure this time. My lips peeled back in a grimace, and I entered a trance-like state, my arm moving back and forth, stabbing and slashing, blood splattering my face and clothing.

Eventually, I came back to myself. She was limp, silent.

Dead.

I let her slump to the ground, her body thudding dully against the cobblestones. Looking down at her, at the blood pooling around her head, my breaths came hard and fast. I was sickened by the sight of what I had done. The knife was still in my hand, and I held it up, watching the dark red liquid trickling down the blade. I wanted to laugh and vomit simultaneously. I did the first and a strangely high-pitched sound burst from me, echoing in the oppressive darkness of the alley.

I glanced down at the whore's body once more. "Daisy," I whispered.

A sense of relief flooded through me as I took in the ragged, torn flesh of her neck, at the blood trickling from her wounds.

There could be no judgment of what I had done here; I was a loyal servant of the EtherFather.

I was the savior of Alpinside.

PART I
THE MISSION

The EtherFather decrees that all have their place in this world. There are those born to rule and those born to serve. It is the way of life and shall be preserved at all costs.

-- **The EtherFather's Sacred Doctrine**, *On the Social Order of Estra*

Stalker Strikes Again!

The mysterious killer known as the Scrubbers' Stalker has once more taken life and our beloved Alpinside weeps. Six months after the first murder—a prostitute by the name of Daisy—another young woman, also a prostitute, has been brutally killed. Penny Sparrow's body was found alongside that of Reginald Locke, purported to be her betrothed, in a rundown factory located in the Dockside quarter of the Workers' District. A man in black was seen fleeing the scene. The City Guard continues their hunt for the monster who has now slain five people, though they have no leads, and the trail runs ever colder. It is requested that any individuals with information that might assist the Guard in their investigations should attend their offices in the Workers' District without delay.

--The Workers' Tribune

Ghastly Murders Mire City in Fear

A prostitute and her illicit lover, Penny Sparrow and Reginald Locke, have been named the fourth and fifth victims of the so-called Scrubbers' Stalker. The City Guard have been valiant in their attempts to track down the killer who, it is believed, must be known to the victims given their proximity to each other as residents of the Workers' District of Alpinside. With limited resources and a city already under strain from the recent mining shortages, these murders are a distraction the citizens of Alpinside can scarcely afford. May the EtherFather guide the brave City Guardsmen in their quest to find and imprison this killer once and for all.

-- The Alpinside Journal

CHAPTER 1

THE FAIRYTALE

The day was fast drawing to a close in Alpinside. The air was cold enough to freeze while the sky was colored like an old bruise, threatening fresh snowfall, and the nearby mountains were a ghostly shadow on the horizon.

Nobles walked the streets. Women were warmed by fine furs over corseted, multi-layered dresses. Men wore thick woolen cloaks over velvet jackets and waistcoats, silk shirts tucked into their woolen trousers. Both had on thick, well-polished leather boots. As they walked, they sipped casually from wooden mugs of hot cocoa or spiced winter wine. As they sipped at their warming drinks, they admired the flickering candles on display in shop windows and took in the scent of roasting chestnuts. Many were deciding what shop they might visit next as they loaded their already overburdened servants with boxes and bulging bags. There was always cause for celebration for a noble. This wedding or that ball must be prepared for, for none could be outdone by their fellows in their displays of wealth and finery.

So absorbed were the nobles in their talk of upcoming festivities and parties, or busy gossiping about Lord so and so and Lady such and such behind jeweled hands and doeskin gloves, that they scarcely turned their heads towards the two peasants darting through the thrumming crowd, a boy and a young woman.

Both wore thin leather shoes which slapped against the cobblestoned streets, wet from recent snowmelt. Their thread-bare clothes could've hardly kept the chill from their undernourished bodies on a warmer day, let alone as the winter night set in.

But Ellana Stone had more on her mind than the scant dress she wore, stained with mud and repaired in so many places it was almost more patch than original dress, or the too-short trousers that hung about her younger brother's calves. They were late returning home, and she knew all too well what that would mean.

"Quickly," she called over her shoulder. "Da will be—" She stopped. "Ren?"

El turned, seeking out the cold reddened cheeks and blond hair of her brother. He *should* have stuck out like a sore thumb yet was nowhere to be seen.

Fear crumpled her stomach into a knot.

"Garen?" she called, using his full name. She cast about, blood rushing in her ears, her mouth dry. *I'm gonna bloody kill 'im. Little bugger don't know—*

"Here, El!" Ren leapt out from behind a nearby crate, giggling.

El flitted from worried to furious in an instant. "Ren, don't do that!" she cried, not caring about the gasps of shock or sneers of disgust around them. Even as Ren's face dropped, eyes filling with tears, El couldn't hold back her fury. "I thought I'd lost you! You've gotta stay close to me."

She exhaled, her breath a white puff in the darkening air. How could he understand? She'd shielded him as best she could from the news spreading throughout Alpinside—the horror stalking these very streets, the young women found dead just doors away from their own home.

"Don't bloody do that again. I can't—"

"Watch it!" an angry voice called as a steam carriage rumbled past, affording them barely a second to leap clear of its path. "Bloody Scrubbers," the driver snapped.

In her desperation to pull her brother away from the speeding carriage, she lunged towards a nearby gate, turning away from the speeding vehicle. She remained leaning against the black iron bars, eyes drawn towards the imposing, red-bricked mansion beyond even as the carriage rattled away.

"I'll tell you what, little brother," El said, her voice sounding faraway and wistful even to her own ears, "we're gonna live somewhere like that one day. I'm gonna take us away from 'ere. Away from Da. From this stinkin' city, these filthy, shit-stained streets. Mark my words. It'll 'appen afore—"

A horse-drawn cart drove by, splashing the back of her legs with the very shit she spoke of. Brought back to reality with foul-smelling abruptness, El grimaced.

Ren let out a raucous laugh.

"Shut up," El muttered, giving him a hard glare. She scanned the sky, inhaling deeply. "Come on, Da's waitin'. He'll be angry if we don't hurry."

He'll be angry no matter what. She shook the thought away. One problem at a time, that was how she'd learned to live.

As they walked away from the great house, El looked back at it one last time. In one of the second-floor windows, she saw the twitch of curtains, hinting at the occupants within.

Ren tugged at her sleeve. "Won't Da punish us anyway 'cos it's dark?"

El let out a bone-weary sigh, conscious of the fading bruises on her back and ribs from the last time Da had been displeased. *He knows to hit me somewhere hidden,* she thought bitterly. *The EtherAle don't rid 'im of that awareness.*

"I'll talk to 'im," she said. "I won't let 'im hurt you."

Ren nodded up at her, blue eyes glistening, and she knew she'd take any number of punches, slaps, or kicks if it meant protecting him.

Eager to change the subject, she flashed him a grin. "Race you."

Before Ren could respond, El darted away. She let out a giggle as he caught up with her and then swiftly overtook her, throwing a smug glance over his shoulder. For a time, she wanted him to be as he was: a child. He should get to enjoy the twists and turns of the mountainside city and ignore the shouts and cries of other citizens, carriage drivers, and merchants. For a moment, even El was able to forget what awaited them when they reached home—a reality perhaps even more dangerous than the killer stalking the streets.

As their run-down home came into view, nestled at the bottom of Scrubbers' Hill between other houses much the same, her stomach clenched into a knot of apprehension.

"Slow down," she called to Ren. "Don't go in without me."

Her brother pulled to a stop midway down the hill, turning to look at her with his sweet eyes. When she caught up, heart pounding and lungs burning, a tiny part of her mind acknowledged with pride that her brother was barely out of breath.

With no coin to pay for food, Ren had learned at a young age he could use his skills to their advantage and had eagerly offered to do so, keen to test himself and help his sister besides. Over the years, she'd acted as watcher or a distraction as he'd taken hot pies from local stalls, fruit from the farmers' market, roasted nuts, salted fish and even, once, a whole cooked chicken from the open kitchen door of an inn. She loathed allowing her baby brother to become a thief. The punishment if caught was loss of a finger, then a hand, then a head, but damn it, he *was* fast. With Da drinking away all his wages and leaving them near starving, their options were limited.

What choice do we 'ave? As the thought crossed her mind, it solidified the burning hatred she felt for their Da. "Bastard," she muttered under her breath, hands clenching into fists.

"What's wrong?" Ren asked, frowning.

Such innocence, she thought with a pang. He still loved their Da, still hoped he might change, redeem himself, become the man he should've been after Ma's death. If Ren didn't feel that way, El would've killed the man long ago.

"Nothing," she said, giving him a weak smile. "Come on." She touched a hand to her belt, checking the package was still safely secured in its pouch, and together they walked the last few steps to their home. The air, as always, was rank with the smells of rotten food, feces, and disease. Misery, she'd realized long ago. Misery and despair, that was this place.

Outside the front door, El squeezed her brother's hand. She reached for the rusting door handle and turned it, expecting a spout of abuse and vitriol as they stepped over the threshold. It was because of this expectation that the ensuing silence was so jarring.

And then the smell hit her nostrils.

Blood.

Once, before Ren was born, Ma had taken her to a butchering festival. It was supposed to be a celebration of life, of a bountiful, unduly warm Springtime that had brought with it a flourish in livestock numbers. Of course, the nobles had praised their gods—Ether... something or other, El didn't care to remember. All Ma had cared about was the lamb stew they would have for dinner that night—Da's favorite. All El had been able to focus on were the dark pools of blood, the hanging carcasses, the death that seemed to scream at her wherever she turned, leaving her with an awful, foreboding emptiness that had stayed with her for days afterwards.

She felt the same sense of hollowness now.

With Ren at her back, she peered into the darkness and swallowed back rising bile. "Da?"

No response.

"What's wrong, El?" Ren whispered. "What's that smell?"

She drew herself up; she had to be strong for him. She was eighteen, a woman grown, the same age her mother had been when she'd had El—old enough to shield her brother from whatever dangers lurked before them. "Nothing, Ren. I'm sure he's jus' fallen asleep an' not stoked the fire." She turned and placed a hand on his shoulder. "I'll go an' check on 'im. You stay outside. Okay?"

Ren hesitated, so she gave him a gentle nudge back over the threshold. El took a deep breath and, ignoring the tightness spreading across her chest, she moved into the kitchen.

Da's worn armchair was in front of the smoldering fire as usual, but even from behind she could see it was unoccupied; his thick mop of greasy, blond hair wasn't on show, nor could she hear his heavy, wheezing breaths. The back door, leading to the shared outhouse, gently breezed open, then clunked into its frame, not quite closing. She frowned at it. If Da was outside, she'd have expected at least some sign of life in their home. But there was nothing, no half-drunk cup of EtherAle or shoes by his chair.

She glanced around at the rest of the room, at the herbs she'd so carefully arranged into jars on the crooked shelves, the pots and pans she scrubbed and scrubbed but never truly got clean, the splintered broom she used to sweep, the crooked table upon which she served dinner. Everything was out of place, scattered, as though someone had been frantically searching for... what? Something niggled at the back of her mind, though she was too anxious to pay it any heed.

Stomach fluttering, El made her way to the only other room in the house—the small bedroom she shared with Ren. It was unusual for Da to venture away from his chair and even more so for him to enter their room. Despite his vicious temper, he afforded them the bedroom as a kind of sanctuary—as though he believed himself a good man as long as he gave them some refuge from his fists.

With a quivering hand, El pushed at the door, sending a silent, useless prayer to gods she didn't believe in. She hoped she'd simply find an empty sleeping pallet, but a part of her already knew that wouldn't be the case by the smell which grew stronger by the moment. As the door creaked open, she was overwhelmed by the stench and gagged. She held back the wave of vomit that threatened to pass her lips, leaning against the door frame to regain her composure. She blinked back tears, trembling breaths acting to give her some small measure of strength.

"S'alright," she whispered to herself, as if useless reassurances could change what was before her eyes. "Everything's fine, everything's fine." She took in the scene with a cold sort of disconnection, numb from head to toe.

Da was dead.

The Scrubbers' Stalker. The thought entered her mind without hesitation, for it seemed to be the only answer that made sense.

Da had been ravaged, stabbed and chopped, limbs detached and haphazardly strewn across their sleeping pallet, hunks of flesh that no longer seemed to belong to a person. In the killer's deadly strokes, Da's blood had been splattered over the walls and ceiling, pooling on the floor and dripping between the cracks in the floorboards. The sight should've meant more to her, made her feel *something*. Instead, her mind seemed to detach from itself and float above the room, observing the scene from outside her body.

A clattering from the direction of the kitchen brought her back to herself in an instant. On quaking legs, she turned as though in a trance and went back down the short hallway. A flash of movement was all she saw before she was pinned to the wall, bony fingers digging into her shoulders.

"Get off me!" she cried, struggling to free herself.

When the figure leaned closer, she froze. The lower half of his face was covered with a black scarf, and a top hat pulled low darkened the rest, but his eyes... even in the dark room, they glowed with an ethereal, otherworldly light—deep red, the color of blood.

An icy chill coursed through El. She scrunched her eyes, afraid this monster could see into her very soul.

The newsboys hadn't mentioned those eyes—but, really, how could they have known? The Scrubbers' Stalker had evaded the City Guard at every turn, seeming to melt into the very night through which he crept. And now here he was, in their home, Da murdered by his very hand.

"Where is it?" the Stalker growled, pressing her harder into the wall, forcing her to look at him.

Despite her trepidation, El's face creased with confusion. "What? I dunno what you—"

The Stalker shoved his weight against her, pressing his fingers into the tops of her arms so hard she feared her bones would snap.

The dark room swam for a moment as her panic heightened. "Ow! Get the fuck off me!"

The Stalker's face moved closer. "Don't be a fool," he whispered. "I will do to you what I did to *him*." Those awful red eyes flitted towards the bedroom. "But I'll make sure it takes a lot longer."

El swallowed, sure that if he hadn't been holding her against the wall, her trembling legs would have given way. She gritted her teeth against the pain of his clawing hands. She could take it; she'd taken worse from Da.

She forced herself to look into his eyes. "I told you, I dunno what you're talking about," she spat. "How can I give you what I don't—"

The Stalker let out a screech, the sound piercing El's ears like a blade as he released her and collapsed to his knees. For a moment she wondered what had happened, then Ren stepped out of the shadows with bloodied hands and a look of wide-eyed shock.

"Ren? What did you... Oh." El saw the knife protruding from the Stalker's upper back.

"Quick, El!" Ren grabbed her hand and headed for the open rear door.

She stumbled after him, giving a final glance towards the groaning Stalker before they were outside. After the cloying stench of death in their home, the cold night air was shockingly cold. She gasped in deep breaths as they ran, fearing they would be followed before long.

The rear of their home opened onto a small, shared courtyard where the outhouse for that block of houses was located. Ren often played in the warren-like system that ran between the streets and he dragged her onward, darting down alleys and crouching into tunnels until she couldn't have found her way home if she'd wanted to. It was only when they stopped for breath that El noticed they weren't being followed; there were no sounds of pounding footsteps, no shouts of anger, no mysterious masked man on their tail. They'd lost the Stalker. She even dared to hope Ren's lucky strike had killed him.

"I think we can stop," El gasped, leaning forward and gulping mouthfuls of air.

Ren squinted into the darkness behind them. "Who was that, El? An' what happened t' Da?"

El's stomach lurched and she glanced towards her brother, chewing her lip. "Da..."

Ren's eyes were shining, face eerily pale in the stray beams of moonlight that filtered through the latticework of wood lying across the alley.

"It's just me an' you now, Ren. I'll protect you, no matter what. I promise." She placed a hand on his shoulder and squeezed, doing her best to sound confident. When his lip began to tremble and tears trickled down his cheeks, she was almost surprised.

"Da's gone?" he asked, voice quivering.

Ren's question drove the realization of what had happened into her heart like a stake. They were alone, homeless. Orphans. At least Da had given them a roof, a room they could call their own, the warmth of a fire. He was a ruthless, cruel man but he had been kind in his own way.

He was p'raps even a good man once, afore Ma... She closed her eyes the pain still too much to bear even after eleven years.

"Shit," she muttered, swallowing a lump in her throat. "Come 'ere." She drew Ren into a hug and felt the sobs shaking his body.

El held her brother until he quieted, sniffing and wiping his nose on his tunic. She turned her attention to their most immediate concerns; they had to find somewhere to sleep—preferably a place that wasn't exposed to the freezing night air. Alongside this, El feared being found by any of the men who roamed the streets of the Workers' District at night, drunk on EtherAle and seeking some distraction from their own wretched lives.

She looked into Ren's blotchy face. "Is there anywhere we can go? Anywhere you've used as a hidin' place wi' your friends?"

He hiccoughed, giving a brief nod. She could tell he was holding back his devastation as he led her further into the network of streets, tunnels, and alleys between the close-built houses in the Workers' District.

When Ren held up his hand for them to stop, El noted the smell of rotten fish. They were close to the docks and fish market which skirted the outer walls of the city alongside the Flow River.

"'Ere," Ren said, directing them to a nearby factory. "It's empty. I've played 'ere sometimes. Others use it, too." A rat scurried away as he pulled aside a wooden board covering a hole in the bottom corner of the building. Without looking back, Ren crawled inside.

El took a final glance about before following him through the gap.

It was clear the factory had long been abandoned—at least as a place of work. There was evidence of people living amongst the old and rusted machinery in the form of shards of glass and empty EtherAle bottles. The air was musty and stale, heavy with the stench of the unwashed and the desperate.

Better than outside, El reasoned. "You play 'ere?" she asked Ren.

He glanced back at her. "I used to. There were a fire. It weren't too safe after that."

"A fire?" El let out a deep exhale and took his hand, too tired to even think of leaving despite her misgivings. "Let's try an' get some sleep. We might feel better in the morning."

She could tell from Ren's pinched face he didn't believe her. He led her past occupied areas of the factory, a few people giving them grunts or nods, while others ignored them altogether. Eventually, they reached a back room that remained, to El's relief, uninhabited. Inside, there was an old leather armchair, a fireplace stacked with wood from a nearby broken desk, and a scattering of old newspapers.

"Well, there's plenty to burn," El said, smiling weakly.

Ren was staring at the wall with glazed eyes. She'd get no more talk from him tonight; when he was upset, angry, or afraid, he had a habit of receding into himself, his usually flushed cheeks growing pale, his lips downturned. And right then, he was likely to be feeling all three and more.

"Get yourself comfortable," she told Ren. "I'll see if I can start a fire."

El heard him arrange himself in the ragged armchair as she began searching for something to light said fire. To her relief, inside one of the drawers of the broken desk was a box of matches.

"Some luck at last," she murmured.

She screwed up some newspaper, tucking it between the wood before lighting a match over it. El held her hands out as the flames took hold, grateful for the warmth that seeped into her fingers and spread through her body. She found a stoker and prodded the wood, shifting it to maximize the heat.

"Tomorrow we can— Oh." El turned and found Ren fast asleep, head resting on the arm of the chair, curled into himself. She stroked his hair back from his face, lightly kissing his forehead. "It's jus' us now, Ren."

She retrieved some of the newspapers and cleared an area of the floor as best she could, fanning dust, debris, and old bits of metal aside. Laying the newspapers flat, she made a makeshift sleeping area. El imagined the pages she laid on told of the Scrubbers' Stalker and his latest victims. Da had never wanted his children to learn to read—"A waste of bloody time an' my hard-earned coin," he'd always said—so she could only guess at what the pages said. More about the other victims, perhaps—all women, she'd heard. Some that she and Ren had even known.

Why did 'e kill Da after all those young women? El wondered. *An' did Ren jus' finish the Stalker's reign of terror? Could it be so easy? Should I go back an' see if there's a body?*

Lying down, she pulled some of the newspaper sheets over herself, using her arms as a pillow as she tried to push away the flashbacks of the scene in their bedroom.

When sleep didn't come, she recalled the fairytale Ma used to tell her. It had been some years since she'd heard it, but, in that moment, she found the words returning with a strange familiarity.

There had been a princess, alone and afraid, her kingdom betrayed, and a prince who would rescue her, brave and kind. Then the kiss that brought them together in true love and the happiness that shielded them forevermore. The story had always excited her, the possibilities of finding such a life for herself still tangible in her childish mind.

Now, years later, she knew she would never be that princess. No prince would rescue her, no kiss could bring her true love. Happiness was a distant dream. Her Ma was long dead and her Da had been torn to pieces—and she could scarce bring herself to feel upset about the latter.

No more cruelty, no more living in fear, no more beatings. But why the fuck would the Stalker kill Da? An' what am I gonna tell Ren, when he begins to wonder?

She forced her eyes shut and eventually drifted into a restless sleep, her mind flooding with images of blood and limbless bodies and death.

CHAPTER 2

THE SCREAM

Beth twitched the curtain open, curious at the shout she'd heard from the busy street. A steam carriage clattered past, the driver glaring back towards two people who clung to the mansion's gate, a young woman and a boy, their blonde hair bright even in the growing darkness of late afternoon. She watched as they stayed there for a moment and imagined what they must be saying.

Then they turned and were gone, free to roam the city. A stab of jealously knifed into her gut. She was an unmarried young woman and, as such, she must abide her parents' wishes. Sighing, Beth released her hold on the curtain as her father cleared his throat behind her.

"Are you listening, Elizabetha?" he asked.

Beth rolled her eyes before turning back to him. "Yes, father."

"I'll thank you to lose that attitude, young lady. A woman betrothed and you're acting like a petulant child. What will Lord Branton think when he meets you again? I'll not have you—"

"I'm sure he'll think exactly what you want him to, Father," Beth said, moving to take her seat by the fire. "I'm sure you and Lord Aberforth have him well under your... *wing*."

She picked up the embroidery she'd been working on and continued stitching the intricate pattern, hoping her father would take the hint and leave her alone. Instead, he came to stand beside her, casting a shadow over her work. She could smell the tang of liquor on him.

I shouldn't have said that. What has come over me? Beth thought. But she knew what it was—the news of her marriage to Lord Ashford Branton had left her with a suffocating level of anxiety and she was lashing out because of it. *Ashford Branton. How, by the Mother, am I to be a good enough wife for* him?

She blinked up at her father innocently, trying to appease him.

He moved his face close, his breath hot on her face. "No daughter of mine will speak to me in such a way," he said, spittle glimmering on his lip beneath a salt and pepper mustache. He pulled back, lips tight with irritation. "And you know full well Artavius and I are no longer—" He snapped his mouth shut.

She frowned, suddenly feeling guilty for her behavior.

"Well, that *bastard* has only gone and—"

The bell above the fireplace rang out, alerting them to the readiness of supper in the dining room.

Her father ran a hand through his slick, gray hair and let out a long exhale. "Come, Elizabetha. Your mother won't be kept waiting."

Beth set the embroidery in the chair and followed him from the room. Her long skirts rustled about her as they walked in silence down the dim corridor. She purposefully stared at the back of her father's dark jacket, for the portraits lining the hallways had always left her with a feeling of unease. All depicted male members of the family, of course, for the noble women had done their most important work in producing the male heirs; there could be no greater honor, as per the EtherFather's doctrine.

Her mother was seated in the dining room and gave Beth a wide smile as she took her usual seat. Father sat at the head of the table and for a tense, drawn-out moment, the room was quiet, awaiting his permission for supper to be served.

Her mother reached a hand towards her father's arm. "My dear, I don't think Edward will be joining us."

Her father snatched his arm free, face reddening. "Where is he, Oren?"

Beth flinched, sharing a nervous glance with her mother.

"There is no need for anger, Landrum," Oren said. "He went to get some fresh air. He's a grown man, surely a simple walk can't be—"

"I left strict instructions for his care. Don't pretend to be ignorant to them," Landrum said. He flashed Beth a glance. "That is to say, he must be careful in his condition."

Beth frowned. She knew little of her brother's ailment and it certainly was not her place to enquire further. Instead, she said, "Father, perhaps we can speak to Mother about the wedding. Start making plans."

Her father's brow furrowed and he opened his mouth to speak. Before he could say anything, her mother, seeming to understand her intent, nodded eagerly and reached a jeweled hand out for her husband. "Oh, yes, let's do that, Landrum."

Her father rubbed his forehead agitatedly. "Very well. I suppose Edward will be safe enough. I'm sorry, it's all this business with Artavius. It really has—"

"Come now, my dear," Oren said. "Such talk is not necessary at the dinner table." She turned to Beth, her lips twitching into a smile. "So, Lord Ashford Branton."

For the thousandth time since Beth had learned of the betrothal, her stomach flipped.

"A good match," Landrum said proudly. "We couldn't have asked for better, especially given—" He cleared his throat, glancing at his wife, whose face was unreadable. "Anyway. He inherited a fortune when his parents perished in that unfortunate accident. I've worked tirelessly to ensure he is agreeable. Some gratitude wouldn't go amiss, child. I haven't even received a thank you."

Perhaps it was because of the delicate tension in the air—the undercurrent of knowledge that her father's mood could change in an instant—that made Beth smile brightly. Perhaps she'd realized, as those butterflies fluttered in her gut once again, that marrying Lord Ashford *could* be a source of happiness and excitement... if she really fought against the self-doubts and anxiety clouding her every thought.

"I'm sorry, Father," she said. "I truly am grateful for the match. I am sure you worked hard to secure it." She bowed her head. "Thank you."

Her father's face softened as he leaned across the corner of the table to pat her arm. "That's just as well, for the marriage contract is all but signed," he said, picking up his empty wine glass, ringing a fork against it. The room filled with a high-pitched *ding, ding, ding*. "Well then, supper!"

Servants poured into the room, silver trays laden with food that filled the air with the smell of rich meat and gravy, fresh bread, and roasted vegetables. Beth's stomach grumbled as she watched food being piled onto her plate.

Things are not so bad after all, she thought.

Tomorrow, she would meet Lord Ashford for the first time since that summer dance two years ago. She almost giggled at the memory. The Branton Ball was an established tradition in the Noble District of Alpinside, a yearly exhibition where all could flaunt their finest dress, share a tipple and the latest gossip, and rove their eyes over the city's most eligible.

And who could be more eligible than young Lord Ashford Branton himself? It had been the first ball since his parents had so tragically perished the previous winter. Despite the tragedy that had befallen him at just eighteen, he had bravely stepped into his title and taken up his father's mantle. All eyes had been on him at that summer ball, so handsome in the glow of the great crystal and gold chandelier hanging above the ballroom, dappling them with its soft light.

Beth, just sixteen at the time, remembered the way her breath caught at the sight of him, her heart hammering and vision swimming. He was *perfect*. Everyone agreed. He was rich, lean and fit, an adept huntsman, a fine dancer, and with a growing interest and knowledge in the field of medicine; he was a gentleman in every sense of the word. But for Beth, it was the brightness of his blue eyes that had struck her the most, and the fullness of his lips, tinted red by the glass of Blood Whiskey from which he sipped.

Of course, he'd never be interested in her; plump Beth, with her unruly black curls and round hips, so often the scorn of the other noble girls. Nevertheless, she'd imagined kissing those lips for months afterwards... and now she would kiss them for the rest of her life! The thought sent a flurry of anticipation through her whole body, the hairs on her arms standing on end.

"Are you listening, dear?" her mother asked, bursting Beth's reverie.

She flushed with embarrassment. "Yes, Mother," she said. "We can shop for my dress as soon as you'd like."

"That would be lovely," Oren said, a hand placed on her chest as she beamed between her husband and daughter. "Only the best for you, Elizabetha. You'll be the talk of all Alpinside, I have no doubt." Her eyes roved across her daughter's ample bosom, then down towards her stomach. "Though we might need to discuss your diet before the wedding, hmm? Less of the sweet cakes, I think. And you, you may stop serving my daughter now." She stared at the maid who had been loading Beth's plate with potatoes.

The maid nodded and stepped back without a word.

Beth rolled her eyes as soon as her mother's gaze dropped to her own plate. She was used to such criticisms and knew it was useless to argue against them.

As they ate, her mother and father spoke of news from Alpinside while Beth daydreamed about the beautiful lips of her husband-to-be. The pleasant conversation was interrupted when the dining room door burst open.

"My lord!"

"How dare you, boy!" Landrum roared. "You'd better have a damned good reason for interrupting our meal or I will see you whipped."

The boy in question, a young servant who hadn't been with the family long, visibly shuddered though remained rooted where he stood. "I- I- I'm sorry, Lord Estamore, sir, it's just—I was sent to fetch you right away. It's Master Edward, my lord, he's—"

Her father's demeanor changed in an instant. "Edward?" His cutlery clattered onto his plate and his chair scraped across the wooden floor. "Where is he, boy?"

"He just returned, my lord. This way, this way," the servant said, leading her father from the dining room.

Beth glanced at her mother, seeing in her face the same fear that was clenching at her own heart. She made to stand, thinking to follow her father and find out what had happened.

"No, Elizabetha." Her mother dabbed a napkin to her lips as she eased herself from her chair. "Finish your supper and then retire to your bedroom." She patted Beth's shoulder before leaving.

With the gentle closing of the door, Beth was alone.

She found that her appetite was gone, so placed her cutlery down and finished off her wine. Resigning herself to an early night, she made her way from the dining room towards the rear staircase, thinking she might sneak a glance into her brother's bedroom. It would go a long way towards learning what had happened. But she wasn't halfway up the stairs when a piercing scream resonated through the house, seeming to echo through the dim hallways. Her gaze flitted back the way she had come.

Edward?

Without thinking, she hitched up her skirts and darted back down the corridor, heading for the source of the sound, which she instinctively knew was her father's study. Something must be seriously wrong. When she reached the study, the door was cracked open, the sound of voices drawing her closer, even if it risked her father's wrath.

What she found left her weak at the knees. Her mother was leaning over Edward, who had been laid out across Father's desk, her face creased with concern. Edward's face was down and much of his body was obscured. His breathing was strained as he let out low groans of pain. Her father was standing to one side speaking with ill-concealed desperation to the doctor, who was employed as a full-time staff member because of her brother's ongoing health concerns.

Landrum was ashen-faced as he glanced over his shoulder towards his son, oblivious to Beth's appearance. "Do we need more EtherStone, Doctor Morgan?" he asked, voice strained. "Will that cure him faster? His health has been... impacted of late, with the waning supplies."

EtherStone? As a cure? Beth knew of the sacred stone. It was distilled in tiny amounts within the Blood Whiskey all noblemen consumed to be connected to the EtherFather and was worn by the noblewomen as a sign of loyalty to the EtherMother—but the idea of it being used as a sort of medicine surprised her.

The doctor gave a non-committal shrug, eyebrows drawn into a frown. He cleared his throat before he spoke. "Edward will recover from the wound, my lord, likely without the need for such treatment. Once my assistant has arrived, we will prepare him for surgery. Besides, with the shortages, I would advise caution in using it quite so... frivolously. We must save it for more urgent incidents."

"*More* urgent? Damn it, man, what could be more urgent than this?" Landrum waved his hand towards Edward.

Beth turned her gaze back to her brother, though still couldn't see him properly with her mother standing over him.

Doctor Morgan cleared his throat as though hesitant to speak. "My worry is that there's more at play here." He ran a hand over his beard, then dropped his eyes to the bloodied white shirt discarded on the floor beside her brother's cloak and hat. "Some of the blood on Edward's clothing, my lord, it, um, well... what I mean to say is, it can't all be—"

"Beth!" Her father had noticed her presence at last. He hurried towards her, roughly grasping her arm. "You can't be here, girl. Your brother is not well."

"But, Father—" She let out a gasp of pain as he dragged her away from the door. "You're hurting me!"

Her father ignored her cry and pushed her out of the study. "Go to your room," he snapped. "I don't want to see you again before morning."

"Father, how could EtherStone cure Edward?" she tried. "And whose- whose blood is that?"

Her father froze, his face dropping, sweat glistening on his brow. "You will not speak of this again. It does not concern you," he whispered fiercely. He moved to close the door.

Desperate to delay him, to try and understand what was going on, Beth held out a hand to stop it from slamming in her face. "Please, Father. I just want to know if Edward will be..." She peered over his shoulder. Her mother had moved aside, and her hands flew to her mouth as she saw the truth of the matter. "Oh."

Her father stepped to block her view. "Don't make me tell you again, Elizabetha," he said. He didn't shout, he didn't need to; Beth was numb with shock.

The door to the study closed, and she stood for a while, trying to comprehend who could have done such a thing to Edward. She closed her eyes and saw the scene within as clearly as if she were still looking upon it. The firelight played over her brother's bare upper body, highlighting his ragged breaths. The sweat sheening on his forehead gave a pale glow to his dark brown skin. Her eyes traced a line of blood up around his ribs... and locked onto the dark handle of a knife protruding from his upper back.

She took herself to her bedroom in a daze, unable to push the image from her mind.

Who would want to hurt Edward? Why did Father not seem concerned about finding them? And why does he always *dismiss me?*

And then a thought struck her. She could help; she could discover the truth, take away the stress of doing so from Mother and Father, *and* prove that she was capable of dealing with such upsetting matters. Mind made up, she determined she would do everything she could to discover the truth.

CHAPTER 3

THE POUCH

Ellana awoke with a stiffness in her limbs and a coldness in her heart that she sensed wouldn't be melted away with mere physical heat. Nonetheless, she sat up and moved to restart the fire. It was a new day. She would need to find a way for them to survive.

As she stoked the newly kindled flames, she heard a shuffling behind her. She turned to give her brother a weak smile, hoping he couldn't sense the doubt that weighed heavy on her shoulders.

"Good mornin'," she said, forcefully cheerful. "Did you sleep well?"

Ren was paler than usual, his blue eyes underlined with bruise-like smudges. He nodded, remaining curled up on the armchair like a wounded animal.

El put the fire iron down and moved to comfort him, placing a hand on his back and gently stroking. "It'll be a'right," she whispered. "You'll see. I won't let anythin' happen to us."

"Why was Da killed?" Ren asked, surprising her with his bluntness. He stared up at her with wide eyes and she wished she could give him a reassuring or helpful answer.

Instead, she let out a deep sigh, pushing his blond hair back from his face. "I dunno. That man, the one you hurt, he's been killing a lot o' people. We can't ever understand why someone like that would—"

Ren jolted upright, mouth agape. "You mean *that* was the Stalker? *I stabbed* the Stalker?"

El blanched; she'd thought she'd kept her brother shielded from the news, though, she reasoned, he'd likely heard gossip from his friends. Scowling, she asked, "What d'you know about the Stalker?"

Ren glanced away. "Oh, I dunno. Not much. Just what the other kids told me when we was playin'. Sometimes one of 'em wanted to be the Stalker, chasing us through the tunnels..."

El crossed her arms and said disapprovingly, "You realize that makin' a game out of something like that is..." She waved her hand in the air, grasping for a suitable word. "Well, not right."

"I know," Ren mumbled into his lap. "Still, it was fun." When he looked up, his eyes gleamed with mischief and El's heart leapt to see her brother back to his normal self. But the joy melted away in an instant and his features became serious again, his mouth pinching tight. "You *really* think that was the Stalker?"

She ran a hand through the knots in her hair, thinking back to the man's terrifying red eyes. "I can't be sure," she admitted. "But... who else could it be? Whoever he was, I dunno why he—" She stopped mid-sentence, realization hitting her like a blow to the head.

"What?" Ren sat forward. "What is it El?"

El returned to the moment the man had pinned her to the wall, to the vehemence of his voice—and the words he spoke. "Where is it?" he had asked.

He'd been looking for something. Been searching their home for that something. And he hadn't found what he was looking for.

He wanted the pouch!

El smacked herself in the forehead for her foolishness, for it seemed so obvious in the light of day. After all that had happened last night, she'd forgotten about it. Now it seemed to almost tug on her belt, near-pulsating with the possibility of answers. Her hand drifted to it.

"You 'ave to be careful not to be seen," Da had said, words already slurring from the EtherAle he'd started drinking before noon. "This is important. My associate 'as gone to great lengths to conceal it for me. This'll make us rich, you'll see." He'd laughed then; a strange, unnatural sound from a man so used to allowing rage to dictate his actions. "We'll make the bastards pay."

"What could be so important about this?" El asked herself aloud, untying the pouch and holding it up.

"D'you think the Stalker wanted that?" Ren said, reaching up as if to touch it.

El snatched it back, giving him a glare. "Be careful! We dunno what it is. If Da *was* killed for it..."

She studied the pouch; it was ordinary enough, black leather, soft and supple, with a golden crest stamped on its front. She ran a finger over the crest—a shield emblazoned with a great owl, two spears interlocking beneath it. "I wonder what this means."

"Lemme see," Ren said, leaning closer.

"Fine, but don't touch it. It might be dangerous... or precious. If it's not, why was Da murdered for it?"

Ren studied the crest with interest before giving a decisive nod. "I've seen that afore," he declared.

El raised her eyebrows. "You 'ave? Where?"

His face flashed with guilt. "Oh, um," he said, playing with a ragged patch on his trousers.

"Ren," she said sternly, "tell me. You won't get in trouble."

He glanced up at her from beneath long, dark lashes and chewed his lip. "Well, uh, one time, me an' Gobby, we was playin', an' we... ended up in the Noble District."

"Garen! You should never've gone there without—"

"Hey, you said I wouldn't get in trouble!"

El rolled her eyes, reluctantly nodding him on.

"We were seein' how far we could get without the Guard spottin' us. We did quite well, we..." Ren trailed off as he met his sister's impatient stare. "But there were this carriage. Big an' black an' shiny, a really grand steam carriage it was."

"What's that got t' do with this?" El asked, raising the pouch.

"That shield thing," Ren said, pointing to the crest. "It were on the carriage door."

El's heart skipped a beat. "You sure?"

Her brother nodded emphatically. "Me an' Gobby followed it for a while. Wanted to see where it went."

"And did you?"

"Did we what?"

El flicked his leg. "See where it went!"

"Ow!" Ren rubbed furiously at his thigh. "Yeah. It were that big mansion you was lookin' at yesterday when we was nearly hit by that—"

"You're sure?" she asked, her heartbeat a thunderous roar in her ears.

"El, stop askin' me that," Ren said, brow furrowing. "'Course I'm sure. That's where the Guard caught us anyway, outside that big 'ouse. Marched us back t' the Workers' District with a stern warning and a smack t' the head."

"Shit," she muttered. "This can't be good."

"Maybe we should see what it is," Ren said, fingers creeping towards the pouch in her lap. "If the Stalker wanted it, might be it could give us answers."

She knew he was right; they had to know what it contained, had to try to understand what had happened. Why their Da had been murdered.

She gave her brother a grim nod and, with fumbling fingers, untied the strings. Tipping the pouch, she emptied some of the contents into her palm.

"What are they?" Ren asked.

"I... I dunno," El said, shoulders slumping with disappointment.

The stones were tiny shards of deep red, like solidified blood. As a stray beam of sunlight hit them, she was reminded of the

Stalker's eyes and almost dropped them. Instead, she pursed her lips and put them back inside the pouch, careful not to allow any to fall.

"Let's go," she said, attaching the pouch to her belt once more and standing with far more decisiveness than she truly felt.

"What we gonna do?" Ren said as he stood and stretched.

El was glad to see some color had returned to his cheeks; having something else to focus on was clearly helping distract him from his devastation over Da. With that in mind, she rubbed a hand over her grumbling stomach and gave him a pointed look.

"First of all, we're gonna use the outhouse," she said. "And then you're gonna steal us some food."

Ren grinned; stealing food was his forte.

As they prepared to leave their shelter, El found her mind drawn to the pouch and the mysterious stones it contained. *How are they linked to the Stalker? Was Da really killed for 'em? What do we do with 'em?*

It seemed the pouch hadn't given them any answers, only further questions. Questions, she decided, she would find the answers to no matter what.

CHAPTER 4

THE KNIFE

Beth slept fitfully that night, waking several times only to recall the sight of the knife in her brother's back. She wanted desperately to know if he would recover. What if the worst happened and she'd allowed herself to sleep through it? She and Edward had never been the closest of siblings. Father often kept him shielded away due to his lifelong illnesses, even from other family members, but he was her brother, and she was fiercely protective of him.

A knock on her door alerted Beth that her maid had come to help her dress for the day.

She sighed and stretched, taking a deep, jaw-cracking yawn before calling, "Yes, Peggy."

The maid shuffled in and gave a brief curtsy. "Good mornin', mistress." She carried a bucket of warmed water, which she emptied into the washbasin. A well-rehearsed routine, Beth stood so Peggy could wash her, diligently moving over her body with a cloth to refresh her for the day ahead.

Once she was clean and laced into her corset, Beth sat on the stool before the vanity so Peggy could set to work on her long black curls. The young maid started by removing the braids she had worn to bed. Beth shuffled and fidgeted, watching the maid from the corner of her eye.

Finally, she could stand the silence no longer and asked as casually as she could, "Peggy, what news of my brother this morning?" Beth watched her maid blanch in the mirror.

She continued arranging Beth's hair for a moment before speaking. "He's well, mistress," she said unconvincingly, dark eyes darting towards the door.

"Is it true he was stabbed?" Beth asked, fiddling with a decorative feather on her dressing table.

"Oh, uh, I- I don't know, mistress. I mean, I've not been told much..."

Beth almost felt bad for making Peggy so uncomfortable. Still, she was determined to find out as much as possible. She inhaled sharply and turned to look her maid in the eye. "I won't tell anyone. It's just that... well, I'm worried. Please, Peggy." She took ahold of the woman's hands and squeezed.

If Peggy was shocked by the physical contact—such an intimate gesture was frowned upon and meant possible punishment, whether she'd instigated it or not—she didn't show it. She looked at Beth for a heartbeat, then let out a soft sigh. "It's as you say, Mistress Elizabetha," she whispered. "The young master was stabbed. But the doctor did what he could and has been with 'im all night and I heard he's expected to recover, though he's like to be abed for some days yet."

Beth closed her eyes, seeing the knife handle protruding from Edward's back once more. "Thank you," she said, squeezing the maid's hand again as relief washed over her.

This time, Peggy flinched, as though only just registering the contact between them. "Come, mistress," she said, beginning to pin Beth's hair once more. "Your mother will be waitin' for you."

"Mother?" Beth's brows shot up. "I did not realize we had plans today."

"She's waitin' in the dinin' room, mistress. Weddin' organization to be attended to, I believe." She cast Beth a brief smile in the mirror before returning to her work.

A short while later, with her hair intricately braided and arranged neatly around her head, Beth strode through the dining room door with as much confidence as she could muster. If she trod carefully, she might be able to learn more about Edward from her mother.

That idea was blown away like a wisp of steam, however, when she saw the puffiness around Oren's usually bright and clear eyes.

"Good morning, Elizabetha."

"Morning, Mother," Beth said, taking a seat opposite her and beginning to pile her plate with food she had no appetite for.

Her mother frowned. "Be sure to watch what you eat. Remember what I said last night."

Beth nodded, not meeting her gaze, and continued to reach for the platters before her.

Oren sniffed. "Your father has arranged a visit to see Lord Ashford this morning and has instructed me to accompany you."

Beth narrowed her eyes. "Why isn't Father taking me?"

"He is attending to urgent business." Her mother's expression was hard, brooking no argument.

Beth put her cutlery down and leaned forward. "Is it about Edward? Is he going to find out who stabb—"

"Enough, Elizabetha," her mother snapped, eyes flashing with irritation. "*I* will be taking you. That is all. We leave after breakfast."

Beth didn't dare say anything more; if her mother was speaking to her in such a way, Edward must be worse than Peggy had said. There was more to learn, Beth was certain of that, but she could think of no way she might go about discovering anything yet with Mother in such a mood. She would bide her time, do as she was bid, meet her future husband, and hope things became clearer in time.

After a short while, her mother cleared her throat, dabbed her lips delicately with a napkin, and said, "Are you ready?"

"Yes, Mother," she said, taking a final sip of tea before standing.

Her mother eyed her breakfast plate and gave a nod, seemingly pleased Beth had barely eaten any of it.

They left the house and entered the awaiting carriage in silence. The journey through Alpinside's Noble District would be short but, even so, noblewomen of their status could hardly be seen walking the streets like Scrubbers. Beth leaned forward to observe the streets as the carriage rumbled along, waving or giving a courteous nod to those who she recognized.

She was about to close the curtain when she saw them, her stomach lurching with recognition at the sight of the two Scrubbers, distinguishable by their ragged clothing amongst the finery of the Noble District. A young woman and a boy, each with light hair. Yes, she was sure it was these two who had clung to the wrought iron gate in front of her home the night before, staring towards the house with an almost palpable hunger. Beth's eyes locked with the young woman's, and she saw her say something to the boy—her brother Beth assumed from the similarity in their appearance. The boy looked towards the carriage, brows furrowed. It seemed they had a keen interest in it, though before Beth could work out what was said, they were lost in the crowd.

She wondered what it could mean, given how unusual it was for Scrubbers to be freely wandering the Noble District. *Are they following us?* she wondered with a frown.

She didn't have time to dwell on it before they were pulling into the driveway of Lord Ashford's home. The Branton family was generations old, much like her own, and their home was an impressive, white-stoned manse on the outskirts of the Noble District, the vast Alpin Mountain range sitting at its back. As their carriage came to a halt, the front door of the house opened, and Lord Ashford stepped out.

Beth's breath caught as it had two years ago at the summer ball.

Lord Ashford smiled widely and held his arms out in greeting as she and her mother climbed from the carriage. "Good morning, ladies," he said, moving forward but stopping short of touching them. It wouldn't be polite with her father not present and in view of the other nobles of Alpinside.

Still, her cheeks flushed as his piercing eyes met hers. Beth glanced down at the ground, suddenly overcome by a shyness she'd never experienced before.

"Answer Lord Ashford, Elizabetha," her mother said softly, giving a gentle nudge with her elbow.

"Oh," Beth said, smiling up at him. "I- I'm sorry, I didn't hear you, my lord."

Lord Ashford laughed and began to lead them towards the house. "I asked whether you prefer lemon or honey cakes."

"Oh," she said, daring to meet his eyes for a moment. "Lemon cakes, Lord Ashford. Though both are delicious."

He nodded with mock seriousness. "Of course," he said. "I had my cook make both, to be on the safe side." He flashed her a grin. "And none of this Lord Ashford business, please. We're to be married. Ash will be fine. Or, if you must, Ashford." He winked.

Beth thought her legs might buckle. "Yes, Lord Ash— I mean, Ashford."

"That's better," he said jovially. "Come, my study has been warmed and the tea and cakes will not stay hot for long."

When he turned away to lead them down the hallway, her mother tapped her on the arm and widened her eyes, shaking her head in disbelief. Beth ignored her; she felt a fool as it was and didn't need her mother's reprimanding to feel any worse.

Inside the study, the fire was, as promised, blazing, and the room pleasantly heated. Beth removed her fur stole and took a seat opposite a man she didn't know.

Sitting next to him, Ashford said, "This is Lord Denys Winborn. His family moved to Alpinside from the southern regions some years ago. We've been friends ever since, so it seemed only right that he should become my Companion when his father unfortunately passed away, leaving little to his name. He has no other family, like me. We have become each other's family." He flashed a smile and Lord Denys' face lit up.

Beth prickled hotly with jealousy, though she couldn't fathom why.

Oren bowed her head. "It is wonderful to meet you, Lord Winborn."

Beth copied her mother. "Nice to meet you, my lord." She studied him from beneath her lashes, finding herself overcome with curiosity for the stranger whom Ashford deemed his family —and who, in turn, looked at Ashford with such warmth.

"Winborn," her mother said thoughtfully. "There was a Winborn family in Alpinside some years back. Are you related, Lord Denys?"

"Distant relations on my father's side," Lord Denys answered. "They have little association with my family and gave no assistance when my papa and I moved here." He gave a weak smile. "But of course, my lady, you are from the southern regions yourself, are you not?"

Oren nodded politely. "I am, my lord. Though I haven't returned since I was a child. Alpinside is my home." She lifted her teacup and sipped before glancing around the room. "I recall the city was quite intimidating when first I arrived. It is kind of Lord Ashford to offer you his home."

Denys turned to Ashford, and they shared a brief, unreadable glance. "It is. Most kind. But soon he will have less time for me, what with a new bride to entertain," Denys said. Though he spoke with an air of amusement, Beth was sure she saw a glimmer of unspoken resentment in his eyes when he looked at her.

Ashford laughed and patted his friend on the arm. "Nonsense, Denys. I'll have time enough for the both of you, of that I can assure you."

Denys raised an eyebrow and nodded, saying no more.

Beth could only smile, unsure what the exchange meant.

"And now, let us celebrate," Lord Ashford said, holding his cup out. "To my future wife, the beautiful Elizabetha Estamore." He beamed at her. "To our long and happy life together."

Lord Denys and her mother followed suit, emptying their cups as though drinking the finest champagne.

Conversation soon moved on to other matters. Ashford spoke of the success of his mines and his ongoing studies in medicine. "Not something my father would ever have allowed, Father rest his soul, but a pursuit I couldn't resist once I had the freedom for it. Denys has joined me in it too, though his stomach isn't as strong. He struggles with some of the... gorier injuries we have attended to."

Despite Ashford's easy manner and smiles, Beth couldn't shift the nervous fluttering in her stomach. When she dared to glance towards Lord Denys, he was serious faced, seemingly entranced by Ashford's words, sitting so close to him that their shoulders were almost touching. She had the odd feeling this man believed her to be beneath the arranged marriage, that Ashford deserved better, that she was getting in the way of their companionship.

Lord Ashford finished his tea and set the cup down with a gentle clatter before turning his attention to Beth and her mother. "Of course, you're not here to speak of business. Please, forgive my excitement at discussing my personal interests," he said. "The wedding. I understand your father has it much in hand, Elizabetha. The ceremony will be in the EtherTemple, our words spoken before the EtherFather. And then I plan to hold a ball here afterwards, bigger even than the annual Branton Ball."

"Oh, Lord Ashford," Oren said. "You are most generous." She leaned over and squeezed her daughter's hand.

"Yes, thank you, Lord, uh, Ashford," Beth said.

"It's the least I can do," Ashford said. "After all, Alpinside needs an occasion to look forward to, what with those awful killings in the Workers' District, hmm?"

"Another two murders," Lord Denys said. "Heard the newsboy this morning." He fiddled with the sleeve of his jacket, eyes downcast.

"*Two?* Getting cocky, isn't he?" Lord Ashford shook his head. "But truly, awful news."

He must really care, Beth thought admiringly.

"Oh, how tragic," her mother said, fanning her face with her hand as though she might shed a tear for people she'd never met and Beth knew all too well she cared nothing for. "You are quite right, Lord Ashford, the ball will be just the thing to take everyone's mind off such terror."

"What is it they call him?" Ashford asked. "The Scrubbers' Stalker?" He smiled at his guests, raising an eyebrow when they didn't seem to share in his amusement. "An apt name, don't you think? Stalking through the streets of the Workers' District, and yet they say the City Guard scratch their heads—that he melts into the shadows without a trace." He examined his fingernails casually. "Well... anyway, let's hope he's captured before more of our workers are lost."

"Yes, Lord Ashford," her mother said, "it is certainly a tragedy for the whole city that he has yet to be brought to the King's justice."

"A toast to that, Lady Oren," Lord Ashford said, refilling their teacups and holding his aloft once more.

"Ashford, is it not time we..." Lord Denys trailed off.

"Oh, yes, yes. Quite right." Ashford stood, brushed down the front of his pristine, navy waistcoat, and cleared his throat. Coming forward, he knelt and clasped Beth's hands. "Mistress Elizabetha, please forgive me for cutting our time short." He raised her hand to his lips and Beth's heart pounded in a fierce beat of excitement.

This is real. He is marrying me. It was all Beth could do not to let out a shriek of delight.

She inhaled his scent, admired his long fingers and his smooth, white skin. She noticed how the billowing sleeves of his silk shirt draped across her leg, how his waistcoat nipped in his slim waist.

"It would be my honor to have you by my side. As my wife."

He pulled a small box from his pocket. "Will you permit me that honor?" He opened the box to reveal a simple gold band.

Beth let out a joyous gasp. "Yes," she whispered, a lump rising in her throat. Lord Ashford wasn't expected to propose—not with the marriage arranged—and in that moment she loved him already. "Yes."

Lord Ashford removed the ring from the box and placed it on her right hand. It was a symbol that she was his betrothed, that she would be his wife—and no other's.

"Thank you, Lord Ashford!" Beth unthinkingly clasped for Ashford's hand in her excitement, then realized her mistake and, embarrassed, made to pull back. As she did so, she snapped her hand upwards and bashed his wrist. He winced and pulled back, rubbing at his arm. "Oh, my lo- Ashford, I am sorry. Please, I—"

"Think nothing of it," he said, pulling sharply at his shirt sleeve and flashing her a smile. He reached for her hand, lifting it for her mother and Denys to see. "A perfect fit. It was my mother's. I trust you will step up to your role as Lady Branton, Elizabetha, much as she did." For a moment, his expression was serious, his thick brows creased and his blue eyes affixed to hers.

Then his face softened, and his full lips turned upwards. Beth smiled back at her future husband. When she looked towards Lord Denys, wanting to include him in the joyous moment—to show he would still have a place in Ashford's life—he simply gave her a hard stare. She sniffed and turned away, refusing to let his dourness spoil her mood.

She still couldn't believe she was getting married! And to such a handsome, accomplished man. If only the other girls from the Temple could see her now. They could hardly mock her for her overly round hips and stomach anymore, not when *she* was engaged to the city's finest bachelor. She couldn't wait to see their faces at the ball—foolish young girls whose fathers could only dream of such a match.

She tried out her name to be, *Lady Elizabetha Branton. Beth Branton.*

Ashford led them to the front door. Before opening it, he leant down to brush his lips against her hand again.

"Until our wedding day," he said, smiling.

She shivered, knowing she'd be reminiscing on the touch for days to come.

As their carriage drove away, Beth held her hand up to the daylight, studying the ring now gracing her finger. It was a simple gold band but it meant more to her than anything she'd owned before, for it signified she would become a Lady in her own right. The next stage of her life would begin the day she married Ashford Branton.

For the briefest time, she allowed herself to be consumed by thoughts of her upcoming nuptials. Her brother, the knife, the secrets that were being kept from her, she pushed them all to the back of her mind as she twirled the ring around her finger.

Lady Elizabetha Branton. Yes, her father had certainly found her the perfect match.

CHAPTER 5

THE SICKNESS

For days after the first sacrifice, I was sick in both body and mind. A sort of fever overcame me, my body aching and my thoughts a-whir with flashbacks of the moments before and after I had taken Daisy's life.

It's a curious feeling, knowing, as I do, that the killing was important. It was essential for this city to continue to thrive under the EtherFather's benevolent wisdom, yet I was overcome with a sense of shock at my own actions.

And then, when I was casting off my sickness and focusing ahead, prepared to leave what I had done behind me, the voice returned.

The EtherFather was not done with me. Or, I should say, my work was not complete.

Daisy was not the only one I had to slay. There would be more young women, more pawns of the EtherMother, whose ruthlessness in Her endeavor to destroy the EtherFather had become all too clear.

One truth I knew—I must do all that was asked of me.

I was the EtherFather's savior, and I would kill any who posed a threat to His might.

CHAPTER 6

THE CARRIAGE

E l needed to see the red-bricked mansion again in the light of day. She hoped to catch a glimpse of the crest from the pouch; to try and understand what their Da had been doing with such an object, for she was becoming more and more certain it had caused his death.

An' what are those red shards? she wondered repeatedly. She prayed she could find answers, and shield Ren from any danger they might bring.

And so, with a loose plan to learn more about the crest, they left the shelter of the rundown factory.

Not long later, bellies filled with stolen apple pies—Ren's favorite—they made their way to the Noble District. El's heart thrummed as they approached the house. She glanced around, checking for City Guard who would escort them back to the Workers' District—or far worse, depending on the Guard's propensity for cruelty.

"You're sure you saw the carriage here?" she asked Ren as they stood side by side, looking through the iron bars of the gate.

"It was—" He narrowed his eyes. "Oh, look!" Her brother pointed through the gate at a black carriage rumbling around the side of the house. A cloud of smoke puffed from its exhaust as a black-suited, pale-faced man steered it to the front door where it pulled to a stop.

El watched as the door was opened and two finely-dressed women—mother and daughter, she guessed—walked out. They each had gleaming black hair braided atop their heads in intricate styles, dark brown skin, and white fur stoles around their shoulders to protect them from the growing cold. El became aware of her own threadbare garments and her filthy, mud-spattered arms. The older woman stepped inside the carriage with the help of the black-suited man. The young woman picked up her deep blue, multi-layered skirts and followed behind her.

"Open the gates!" called the carriage driver.

El dragged Ren to the side as another black-suited servant stepped forward to unlock and open the iron gates. The gates moved on their hinges with barely a sound and the steam-carriage rattled past. As it did, the gold crest could plainly be seen against the smooth, inky blackness of the carriage door.

"Come on," El said, tugging her brother's tunic and making to follow the carriage through the mid-morning crowds.

The smell of roasting chestnuts filled the air as they darted and weaved around people, trying to keep close to the carriage without alerting the driver or passengers—not that she thought the passengers would bother to pay attention to two Scrubbers. El was curious to see where the carriage went. As it turned down a street to the right, she saw the face of a young woman peering out of the window. Below her, the crest was visible once more.

"That *is* the same crest, isn't it?" she said to Ren, holding the pouch up. They stood still as the carriage pulled away.

He followed her gaze, squinted against the bright grey of the sky. "It is," Ren said. "What we gonna do, El?"

As El muddled through her thoughts, a newsboy called out from the corner, "Stalker Strikes Again! Man found dead!"

She glanced down at Ren, noticing his pale face.

"They found Da," he whispered.

El pursed her lips and nodded. "It was only a matter of time."

"But the Stalker... there's no mention of 'im bein' dead... of his body. I din't kill 'im, did I?" Her brother's words echoed her thoughts. "They ain't found a body."

"Don't seem like it," she said. "Sorry, Ren. We was lucky you did enough t' help us get away. Would've been a lot t' ask that you was also lucky enough t' kill him."

"D'you think he'll..." Ren swallowed. "D'you think we're in danger?"

Despite the fear nestling in her heart, El puffed herself up and placed a hand on her brother's shoulder, squeezing gently. "We're not in danger, Ren. I'm here t' protect you, got it? Besides, I promised, din't I?"

He cast his gaze downwards. "Yeh. I know, El."

El glanced ahead. "Right then. We've lost that carriage." Suddenly very conscious of how conspicuous they were amongst the nobles, she said, "Best leave, afore we're noticed."

Ren wiped a hand across his eyes before looking up at her. "Where we goin', El?"

"Home. We can get some supplies. Decide what t' do from there."

Without a word, Ren followed her.

In the harsh light of the winter morning, their home looked much as it always had: in a state of disrepair, windows covered in filth, the door hanging on rusted hinges. Looking down the street, all the houses in the row were much the same. It was just the way of things in the Workers' District, as El had been told by Da many times.

As they approached the house, she felt a stab of sadness knowing this would be their last time here, despite all that had happened within its walls. For El, the memory of what had been done to their Da sat too fresh in her mind, images that infil-trated her thoughts like the Stalker himself, sudden and sharp and all too clear. Their Da had been a brute, cold and uncaring, but no one deserved to die in such a horrific way, butchered and torn apart until his body was barely recognizable. And for Ren, the grief at losing Da was likely too much to bear. She couldn't let him sleep in their room, knowing that was where the man he'd loved and feared in equal measure had been killed so brutally.

"Right, you remember the plan?" El said, turning to Ren. "You stay out here. Keep watch. Keep hidden. I'll be quick as I can."

"But El," he said, "you usually keep watch... I- I'm not sure I can."

She gave him a gentle cuff on the chin. "'Course you can. Just keep lookin' all 'round. Watch out for anyone suspicious. Anyone who might be showin' the house a little too much interest. An' if you see that, come an' get me."

Ren gave a weak nod, eyes darting about as though expecting an ambush at any moment. "El?" he called out as she moved towards the door.

She glanced over her shoulder to find him fiddling with the bottom of his tunic.

"Can you- can you get Da's cloak for me?" He gulped and guilt nestled in El's gut; he thought she'd be angry.

El smiled. "'Course."

She inhaled deeply, reaching for the door. Some small part of her still expected a scornful shout from Da as soon as she stepped over the threshold and her body tensed out of habit.

"Where've you been? What took so bloody long? Ungrateful little bastards, the both o' you," he would yell. Then would come the fists and kicks.

But the room was cold, the fire long since burnt out, the back door swinging on its hinges with an incessant *bang, bang, bang* that beat in time with El's heart. She moved to close it, as much to keep the icy chill at bay as to secure her home against the outside world—for now, at least, for it wouldn't remain so for long. Da's body had been found, then would've been cleared out by the City Guard. Soon word would be out about an empty house on Scrubbers' Hill. The squatters would move in. Homeless, beggars, drunkards who'd lost their minds to EtherAle—just like Da. It would be a free for all until someone asserted their dominance and claimed their home like a prize.

They're welcome to it, El thought bitterly. Too many bad memories had been created here—mostly by Da—drowning out the good like a great, smothering shadow. Though he hadn't been able to make her forget her Ma, much as he'd tried.

Ma was locked away in El's heart, a golden light that held her up when she felt as though she couldn't go on. It glimmered in that moment, lending her strength as she began her methodical search of the house.

She wondered who had alerted the City Guard about Da. Another miner perhaps, come to check why he hadn't turned up for his shift? Or a neighbor who had seen the open back door?

The Guardsmen had, as always, ransacked the house in their search. They cared little for the Scrubbers, and their so-called investigations of the Stalker's killings were little more than clean-ups of the bodies left behind. It was as well there had been nothing of real value for them to take—they would've done so without a doubt.

She found an empty waterskin, two over-ripe apples and a palm-sized square of cheese she could only assume Da had stashed away for his personal consumption—she and Ren certainly wouldn't have been allowed such a luxury. There was also a semi-blunt knife which might come in handy. At the very least, she felt better knowing they had some form of weaponry.

El stashed everything inside Da's worn, brown satchel, stowed roughly beneath his armchair as it always had been when he was home, and looked around with an exasperated sigh. *A measly fare but it's better than nothing,* she told herself. She looped the satchel over her shoulder and clutched it to her side.

Finally, she edged down the short hallway leading to the bedroom. Goosebumps sprang up on her arms. She couldn't help but wonder, *What if Da haunts that room?*

The old tales spoke of the phantoms that remained behind if one's death had been particularly gruesome or torturous. She and

Ren had sometimes taunted each other with stories of ghouls and geists, and images of such horrors crept into her mind.

She chided herself for being a fool and curled her hands into fists, marching forward with a clenched jaw. "Ghosts," she muttered. "Childish superstitions, nothin' more. Get yourself together, El."

But as the door creaked open, and the rotten smell of death and decay hit her nose, a movement from her left caught her eye and she leapt backwards with a shriek. Sweat sprung up on her forehead and ran down her back.

"Don't be stupid," she whispered. "Nothin' there, Da's dead. Nothin' bloody there."

With a trembling breath, she crept forward again to peer around the door frame, all the while trying to convince herself the stories weren't real. When she saw what had caused her fright, she almost laughed. A white sheet was draped over the wooden chair that father had proudly presented them with one Winter's Fest. "You'll 'ave to share it," he'd said. "I ain't the time to make another. Nor the inclination for such thankless brats as you."

Walking past the blood-stained sleeping pallet and across the crimson-splattered floorboards, she moved to retrieve the sheet. It would come in handy if they had to sleep in the factory again. As she pulled the fabric free, the chair toppled to the ground with a clatter. The sheet safely folded into the now bulging satchel, she bent to pick the chair up, strangely unwilling to leave it in such a state of disarray.

As she did so, she noticed a floorboard poking up at an odd angle. Perhaps the chair had dislodged it as it fell, or maybe it had been so all along. She pressed a hand to it and found it wiggled with ease, as though lifted regularly.

"What the..." El frowned, pulling the wooden board up to reveal a dark, dust-filled crevice. She reached inside and groped around, at first unable to feel anything. Then her fingers brushed something solid and cold. She had to move closer to the gap, twisting her arm awkwardly, but finally she was able to grab ahold of it. She removed the object with relative ease and sat back on her haunches.

Despite the dirt and dust beneath the floorboards, the item was clean. She ran her finger over the top; the wood was carved with intricate patterns and gleamed as though well-polished.

With a jolt, El realized she'd seen this box before many years ago.

Ma. It had belonged to her. Before Ren. Before she'd died. Before everything had changed.

She remembered asking, "Can I help, Mama?" and a light, tinkling laugh, before the response came, "Yes, my darling. Here, hold this."

The box was as it had been then, with its satisfying weight that told of quality craftsmanship—the kind of thing El could only dream of owning these days. As she opened it, she was hit with the sudden, sweet smell of Ma's perfume. It took her breath away, and a lump to rose in her throat. The box held a tiny glass bottle, empty but still carrying its old scent.

But that wasn't all it held.

Alongside the perfume was something El had forgotten about until that moment. She recalled how Ma had polished it with pride and had never taken it from the box for too long. It had been her most treasured possession.

Gently, El pulled the necklace with its red stone from the box, turning it over. On the back, two words were etched, though she couldn't read them. As she studied the stone, stroking her finger across it, her blood roared in her ears. Her heart thumped and her vision momentarily swam, overwhelmed at the flood of memories. She held the necklace in her palm, feeling the weight of it, and suddenly became aware of a sharp, jabbing unease in her gut. She glanced towards the door.

Ren.

She'd been too long.

She stood and shut the box before carefully concealing it within the sheet in the satchel, then hurried for the front door.

"Ren," she called quietly, stepping outside. "Sorry I took so long, I— Ren?" She glanced up and down the street. *He's gone. Damn it, bloody hidin' again.*

"Garen!" she yelled, seething.

Curious faces turned towards her, but she ignored them, her unease growing. After a moment, she began to consider that perhaps he wasn't hiding after all and her panic spiked all the more. She couldn't lose him, she couldn't be alone—she couldn't survive without him.

El sprinted up the hill. Nothing. Back down towards their home. Nothing. All the while, her cries became more and more frantic. Not knowing what else to do, she slumped to the ground near their front door, tears running freely down her cheeks, despair sitting heavy upon her chest. She didn't know how she would—

"El?"

"Ren?" She rubbed her eyes, looking around for his voice.

"Psst, here, El!" Her brother's face was peering at her from the dark alley directly in front of their home.

"*Garen*, what the— I swear I'm gonna—"

"No time," he said, glancing behind him. "Quick, this way."

Before she could protest, he darted down the alley.

She stood, repositioned the satchel, and followed. *Better be a bloody good explanation.* "Slow down," she puffed, doing her best to follow him as he hurried down the alley.

Ren skidded to a halt, and El stopped behind him. She dropped the sack, and placed her hands on her thighs, huffing in great gasps of air. They were still in an alley but ahead it opened up onto the street.

"What you doin'?" she managed to say. "And what happened t' bloody keepin' watch?"

Ren held a finger up to his lips. "I got a bit bored," he admitted. "But it's a good thing I did 'cos it meant I saw... well, look." He turned his face back to the street.

El glared at the back of his head before following his gaze.

Her heart skipped a beat. It was the carriage. Or at least it was another steam carriage with the same crest emblazoned on the side, a dark-haired man dressed in black at the driver's seat.

"That's—"

"Shh," Ren hissed, easing back against the wall. "There's a man. He looks..." His nose wrinkled. "Rich. Top hat an' that. He's knockin' on doors."

"What?" She frowned and peeked round the edge of the wall, then pulled back just as fast. Ren was right; there *was* a man—a rich looking one.

He was well-dressed in a dark grey, fur-lined coat, black woolen trousers, and shiny black boots, alongside the aforementioned top hat, all of which were far out of place in the run-down street.

"Shit. What's 'e looking for?" El murmured. *No one lookin' like that comes 'round 'ere. Is it somethin' to do with Da? And the pouch?*

Her hand drifted to her belt and Ren's eyes followed the movement.

"D'you think that's what he's looking for?" he asked.

"Seems too much of a coincidence, don't it?" El answered, feeling the weight of the stones inside the pouch.

"What we gonna do, El?"

"I dunno." Then she rested her hand on the satchel, thinking of the wooden box and the red-stoned necklace within, and made a decision. "I 'ave something that might 'elp us find answers."

Ren looked at the satchel, frowning. "What?"

El shook her head. "Come on. I've got some food. Let's find somewhere quiet an' I'll show you." She was all too aware of the nobleman still searching the street. If he was somehow involved, it wouldn't do to be caught here.

They headed back down the alley, soon emerging on Scrubbers' Hill once more.

"El? Did you- did you get it?" Ren asked.

El stopped in her tracks, giving him a confused look before

she abruptly remembered. *The cloak. Shit.* "Oh, Ren. I'm sorry, I—"

"There's still time, ain't there? To get it?"

El's stomach knotted. Something told her they had to get away from here as quickly as possible to avoid being spotted by the man, yet she couldn't bring herself to say no to her brother. He'd been through too much. This one thing she could do for him, and it might give him just a tiny speck of comfort.

"Alright," she said, casting a gaze down the street. She couldn't see the carriage or the man yet. There was time.

She pulled Ren behind some crates in the alley across from their home. "Wait 'ere. Hold this." She bundled the satchel into his arms before making for the door.

Inside, she headed for Da's chair over which the cloak was usually strewn. It wasn't there.

For a dreadful moment she wondered if Da had been wearing it when he was—

No, she told herself, *it's got to be here.*

She looked around frantically. There was no sign of the cloak, and she was sure she could hear a carriage trundling up the road. Towards her brother. Just as she was about to give up, she noticed the end of the cloak peeking from beneath Da's chair. El picked it up, forcing back the well of emotion stirring within her chest as Da's musky scent wafted over her. The thick cloak had been one of Da's prized possessions. Navy in color, it was a fine garment, not meant for the likes of them. For the first time, she wondered where he'd come by it.

Don't matter. Never gonna find out. She bundled up the cloak and hurried towards the door.

Outside, Ren was staring down the street, eyes wide. She followed his gaze and saw the carriage. The man was nowhere to be seen; they still had time.

"Here." She threw the cloak over Garen's shoulders; it was far too big, drowning him in wool and dragging on the ground.

Ren gave a small smile, pulling the cloak tight across himself. "Thanks El."

She nodded. "Let's go." She took the satchel from him and slung the strap over her shoulder before turning him away from the carriage.

"You there!"

Ren gasped. "Are they—"

"Shush," El snapped. "Don't turn 'round." She ushered him onward, head down.

"Stop! You two!"

El risked a glance over her shoulder. It was the rich man, and he was staring directly at them, his driver now standing next to him.

"Shit."

"What? What is it?" Ren peered up at her, eyes gleaming with fear.

"Don't worry, just keep walkin'," El encouraged him. "Hurry now."

But the man had sent his black-suited driver after them. The man was fast and he quickly caught up, appearing in El's periphery. Before she could steer Ren towards a nearby alley, his hand had clamped down on her arm.

"You two need to come wi' me," he growled.

"'Scuse me?" El looked the man up and down, trying to appear incredulous even as his fingers dug into her flesh. "My brother and I are just—"

"There'll be no arguin', Scrubber." He threw her arm down, moved to stand in front of the alley, and nodded towards the rich man and his carriage. "That way. Now."

El gulped. She might have run if it was just her. But, for the first time, she admitted to herself that she was afraid. Besides, fleeing might just make the situation worse than it already was. She nodded numbly, reaching for her brother's hand and giving it a gentle squeeze as the two of them were marched towards the carriage.

CHAPTER 7
THE COMPANION

The rest of the day flew by in a flurry of wedding preparations that so exhausted Beth, she had barely been able to keep her eyes open during dinner. She'd excused herself early and gone to bed. Now, as Peggy braided her hair, her mind whirred at the lengths to which her mother was prepared to go to in order to ensure this would be *the* wedding of the season.

They'd hurried between the local patisserie, dressmaker, and florist, booking appointments and consultations for the coming days. Beth had smiled and nodded where necessary, though it seemed her mother had everything in hand and that her presence was barely even needed. All the while, her mind flitted back to the way Ashford had held her hand, the softness of his lips on her skin, how soon they might be together again.

Her head sank into her feather pillow, a smile playing on her lips, and it was to those thoughts she drifted into a deep sleep. Despite the pleasant feelings with which she'd fallen asleep, Beth's dreams were haunted by her brother, his groans echoing through her head while his eyes shone with pain—and that awful knife protruding from his back like a beacon, a warning, a message.

"Edward, what have you done?" her dreaming mind whispered over and over.

Her father was there, pushing her back, speaking of Ether-Stone, of a cure for her brother.

And then Edward was screaming her name, his eyes screwed shut. He gave a pain-filled cry. "Help me!"

She awoke unrested the next day, body drenched in sweat, hair loose from its braid and sticking to her neck. It was early enough that Peggy hadn't arrived yet. Beth exhaled shakily, sitting up to reach for the jug of water on her nightstand.

With a splash of cold water to the face, her mind cleared, though remnants of her dream lingered at the edges of her mind. She knew she couldn't dwell on it, for there was much to do and her mother would, no doubt, have made arrangements for the day.

"A wedding does not arrange itself, Elizabetha," she'd said pointedly during their carriage ride home yesterday.

Beth resolved, once more, to try and find out more about her brother's condition, and perhaps about what had truly happened to him.

As she stood and stretched, there was a gentle knock on the door. "Come in, Peggy," she called.

Her maid entered, head down as always. "Mornin', mistress. Your mother has asked to see you afore breakfast today."

Beth moved to sit at her dressing table, rolling her eyes. She was excited for the wedding itself, but everything that needed doing to prepare for it was more than a little exasperating. Besides which, it seemed her mother's focus was so keenly on the wedding that the idea of bringing up Edward's condition was becoming less and less plausible.

She chewed her lip in thought as Peggy re-braided her hair and arranged it about her head, wondering how she could bring up Edward. *Perhaps she'll still answer my questions if she's in a light mood. Perhaps I'm overthinking it.*

Once Peggy had finished, Beth hurried to her mother's room.

Mother would see it as eagerness to continue wedding planning, but she was far more driven by her eagerness to continue her thus far unsuccessful investigation into her brother's condition. Any notion of being able to do so, however, were dashed when she saw the look on her mother's face.

"Shut the door, Elizabetha," Oren said plainly, a frown knitting her brow.

Beth did so as gently as she could, not knowing what she'd done to rile her mother but not wanting to give her any more cause for upset.

"Come." Beth was waved forward. "Peggy might have dressed you in something a little more flattering." She scoffed and flapped a dismissive hand in the air. "No matter. Sit."

Beth sat beside her mother on the edge of the bed, smoothing down the long skirts of her dark green linen dress—a favorite of hers, despite the snide remark. "Are you well, Mother?" she asked politely.

Oren snorted, turning her head towards the window that looked out upon the gardens. It was a small green area that Beth was particularly fond of, especially in summer. But today, the sky outside the window was a dark grey, the threat of snowfall heavy in the air. For a moment, Beth was reminded of a winter, years past, when she and Edward had giggled as they threw snowballs at each other, not a care in the world. They'd caught the tiny, precious flakes, delighting in how quickly the snow had melted against their skin. Her heart ached to recall it. Edward's health had declined much since those days, and, by the Mother, how she wished she'd paid more attention to his ailments.

"It's your father," her mother finally said, bringing Beth back to the present.

"Father?" Beth asked, eyebrows creasing.

Her mother shook her head, the black curls hanging loosely around her face swinging slightly. "Foolish man. He's hired two new servants. Scrubbers, of course, and ones that seem fresh from the streets."

Beth could tell she was supposed to be angry though wasn't sure why. Father was master of the house, not to be questioned. She bit her lip and remained silent.

Her mother let out a harsh laugh. "I suppose he thinks he's *helping* them in some way, offering a place to work, a roof over their heads. Of all the times to be charitable! They'll need paying, too. Ever since that damned law. Nonsense about unions and being an essential part of the running of the city. Bah, now they're entitled to a weekly wage—as if they have anything to spend it on!" She turned to Beth as though this made her point clear.

Beth looked into her mother's dark brown eyes and noted a glint of worry within the anger burning there.

"We have a wedding to pay for and I want the best for you. But- but *this*!" She stood and began to pace.

Beth frowned. Surely servant's wages—meager as she believed them to be—weren't enough to threaten her wedding. But... perhaps she'd misunderstood. "Surely Father will have a separate purse for the servants? I'm sure the wedding will be wonderful, Mother."

Her mother froze and turned to face her. There was a sad smile tugging at her lips while her brows pinched together as though she was trying hard to find her next words. "There are some matters... The family mines are not— And that *scoundrel* Lord Aberforth has gone and—" She sighed, mouth working as though chewing on a sour slice of lemon. Finally, she seemed to recover herself and said, "No matter, my dear. The wedding is what's important. Come, let's go to breakfast. Best not to keep your father waiting."

Mother led them towards the door, leaving Beth with the sudden certainty there was much she didn't know, and not just about her brother.

That discomforting thought stayed with Beth as she followed her mother down to the dining room. The house seemed eerily quiet that morning, the usual bustle of servants from the kitchen practically non-existent. Instead, when they walked into the dining room, the table was bare.

Her father stood at the head of it, behind his seat. A blonde young woman and a boy, obviously her brother, stood beside him. These must be the new servants. Beth was surprised to find her father appeared as tetchy as her mother. It immediately put her on edge, and she frowned towards the new servants as though they were directly responsible for her parents' foul moods. Her father clapped his hands, drawing her attention back to him.

"Ah, Beth," he said, his dark expression clearing as he met her gaze.

"Good morning, Father," she said, bowing her head.

Studying the new servants more closely, she jolted with recognition. Though they were dressed in the plain black livery of the other household servants, she was certain she'd seen them before. Both had their faces to the floor, hands clasped behind their backs, and yet—

"No doubt your mother has told you," her father said, eyes narrowing and glancing towards his wife, "of our newest staff acquisitions."

Beth ignored her mother's irritated sigh, casting her father a brief smile. "She has, Father."

"Ellana and Garen Stone will be part of the household henceforth. Garen will be helping in the kitchens, and Ellana will be your Companion. It's about time you had one, Beth."

"Landrum, really! This is hardly *proper.* A Companion should come from a far more respectable background. Is it—"

"Hush, Oren. I am the master of this house. These servants are under my employ, and you will not question me. Their father worked in my mines." There was a flicker of pain across his eyes. He cleared his throat. "I am doing this as a favor to him. I will say no more about it."

Her mother's fists clenched in her skirts, though her voice remained calm as she said, "Yes, my lord."

Landrum exhaled slowly. "Now, Garen, you may send for breakfast."

Garen hesitated, glancing up at Ellana. She nodded at him, lips pursed into a hard line.

"Y-yes, m'lord," Garen said, almost stumbling in his haste to get to the door.

"What will I be doing, m'lord?" The young woman was bold, looking Landrum full in the face without a hint of deference.

It irked Beth to see her so confident; it wasn't polite for a servant to be so. And now, as she looked at the young woman, she was certain that Ellana and her brother were the Scrubbers who had been following the carriage just yesterday. She scowled. Surely something was amiss here.

She stepped forward. "Father, how is it that these—"

Her father held his hand up to Beth, then turned to Ellana, speaking far more gently than she'd expect towards a servant who had been so forthright. "It is as I outlined; you will be my daughter's Companion. This is a great honor." He held his arm out towards Beth, and she frowned towards the over-confident Scrubber.

The fierce intensity of the stare from Ellana's ice blue eyes looking back at her was astounding—who *was* this young woman? She swallowed and looked to her father. "Surely, Father, Peggy will be enough until the wedding. Meaning no offense, but this girl seems... untrained." She jutted her chin out as her mother often did, hoping it conveyed confidence and dignity. "Besides, once I am Lady Branton, I will have new servants from Lord Ashford's household, no doubt including a Companion. One of noble blood, one befitting my new position." Beth wasn't sure where the words came from even as she spoke, though she couldn't deny the pride that prickled up and down her skin. She stood a little taller, her cheeks flushed, lips twitching into the briefest of smiles. Then she met her father's glare and remembered herself.

"Elizabetha," he said sternly, "I have told you what will happen, and it will be so. You are no more able to question me than your mother. Peggy is a *maid*. Ellana will be your *Companion*. You must become acquainted with keeping the company of ladies your own age. I have neglected to provide that for you thus far, and for that I can only apologize. But I believe Ellana will be more than suitable."

She cleared her throat. Though it was unclear why this new servant should be any better than Peggy—indeed, they were both Scrubbers, were they not?—she wouldn't dare to question her father. "Yes, Father."

"Good. Now, breakfast." Landrum pulled his chair out and sat, signaling for Beth and her mother to do the same.

As was often the case, Edward's seat remained empty; he did not usually rise before midday and, even then, all his meals apart from supper—which was eaten as a family—were served in his room. Besides, he was still recovering from his wound. A weight settled on Beth's chest at the thought, the certainty that something was amiss cementing itself in her mind.

"How is Edward, Father?" she asked, already knowing the response she would get.

Her father stiffened. "He continues to recover," he said brusquely, making it clear the matter was not to be discussed further.

Beth nodded, knowing this wasn't the time to push him, for there was a curious tension hanging over the room.

The rest of breakfast was eaten in relative silence, though her parents shared some news regarding other noble families in the city. Beth would've usually listened intently to such gossip, though today she found herself too distracted to follow the conversation. Ellana had taken a seat at the opposite end of the table and was allowed some of the simpler fare being served. The more Beth stared at her, the more she wondered who this strange young woman was, why she had been following their carriage, and how, by the Mother, she'd ended up being offered a position as her *Companion*, no less!

Finally, her father wiped his mouth with a napkin and threw it atop his empty plate. His chair scraped as he stood. "Well, ladies, I must excuse myself. Ellana, you will go with Elizabetha this morning and—"

"Oh, Landrum, we have much to do for the wedding. Elizabetha doesn't have time to be showing a new *servant* how to perform her duties. Surely Peggy—"

"No. Ellana will go with you and learn as she works. It's how I learned as a child, studying my father's business. It's the best way."

Beth looked to her mother across the table, who gave an exasperated shake of her head. "Very well," she said curtly, dabbing her lips with a napkin. "Come, Elizabetha, it is time we made our way into town." Her gaze hardened as she turned to Ellana. "Girl. You will keep quiet and do as you are told. Is that clear?"

"Yes, m'lady," Ellana said. Approaching Beth, she gave a slight bow of her head. "Elizabetha, I'm Ellana. But everyone calls me El, so—"

"We are not friends, Ellana. I do not know how you came to be here, but please be clear on this: it will not be so simply because we're of an age." Part of Beth was surprised at how much she sounded like her mother, though she didn't show it. She sniffed, looking towards Oren, who had an approving gleam in her eyes. "Let's depart. There is, as you said, much to do, Mother."

Beth turned and marched from the room, not sparing Ellana another glance.

CHAPTER 8
THE SERVANT

El was a servant. Ren, too.

It had happened so quickly that she couldn't quite understand how they'd managed to secure such coveted positions. They had little more than the clothes on their backs and the satchel of belongings she'd pilfered from their home, but she felt oddly pleased with herself that she'd managed to negotiate their way to the very place that seemed linked to Da's death. It hadn't been her original plan, but it was a step forward, nonetheless. Besides, it was warm, they had meals provided twice daily, and they were getting a full *ten coppers a week* between them. She could scarce believe their luck, if she was honest with herself.

She and Ren had been shown to a small room and told they were to report to the dining room first thing in the morning, where their positions would be confirmed and their duties would begin.

The room was just large enough to contain two small, feather mattresses on wooden bedframes topped with blankets, with barely a walkway between them. But it was warm and safe—and it was *theirs*. The one thing that concerned her was the lack of places to stow their belongings, especially Ma's necklace. She could wear it, but her gut told her she should keep it hidden.

Besides, to have such a fine item in her possession was begging to be accused of stealing. She decided to hide it underneath her mattress, stored within its box.

That night, as she'd lain on the bed across from Ren, listening to his gentle snores, she'd reflected upon the ease with which she'd been able to manipulate a nobleman.

"Your father, was he?" Lord Landrum had asked.

They were inside the carriage, its motion smoother than El had expected given the uneven road upon which they traveled. Part of her wanted to stare out the window as they were escorted through the Workers' District, to watch the streets she knew so well pass them by, to refuse to give this man the information he so bluntly requested.

Instead, she'd given Lord Landrum a confused look. "My lord?"

The man snorted through his thick, salt and pepper mustache. His next words came slower. "Was it your father who was murdered? Frederich Stone."

Ren nodded before El could respond. She elbowed him, afraid that giving away too much might mean she lost control of the situation.

"You knew 'im, m'lord?" she asked.

Lord Landrum stared out of the carriage window for what felt like minutes. "He worked for me," he said finally.

Da had never confirmed the mines he worked in were the Estamore's—it had never mattered, as long as he got paid... but it explained the crest on the pouch he'd sent her and Ren to fetch.

As if reading her mind, Lord Landrum pointed at her waist, where the pouch was secured. "*That* belongs to me."

Inwardly, she cursed herself for not concealing it, though she had been *somewhat* distracted in trying to ensure Ren wasn't in danger.

Before she could say anything, Lord Landrum held a hand up. "Three things will happen. First, you will hand over that pouch."

El sat forward and opened her mouth.

He shook his head sharply. "No arguments. Second, you and your brother will never speak of the pouch or anything else concerning your father's untimely demise in relation to the Estamore name."

El raised an eyebrow. "So Da's death were—"

"What I mean to say is, there is no guilt on our part, but I'm sure your minds have conjured some nonsense about that pouch. None of which are correct."

"No, m'lord. It hadn't actually," El said flatly.

He harrumphed, pale cheeks flushing. "In any case, leave any such ideas behind. And finally, you will take up positions in my household. That is one way in which I can ensure you behave. And remain safe." He nodded, as though satisfied he'd done the right thing.

El looked to Ren. "And if we refuse?"

There was a lengthy pause. Lord Landrum had once more turned to stare from the window, seeming to have forgotten the conversation altogether. El began to wonder whether he would respond at all.

Finally, he turned back to her, a hardness in his blue eyes that made her flinch. "Then I will have you both arrested for theft and let the City Guard do what they will. They've little mercy for Scrubbers who step out of line. Or so I'm told."

"*Theft?* But we din't—"

"Where do you suppose that pouch came from? I imagine you looked inside, though I'm certain you have no idea of the importance of its contents." He let out a long, weary-sounding sigh. "Suffice to say your father stole what was mine and he lost his life for it. Don't make the same mistake."

He drew himself up, looking down on them. "I will offer you security and safety in my household. I will offer you, Ellana Stone, the coveted position of Companion to my daughter. You will be paid, fed, and sheltered. What more could people of your standing expect?" His mustache twitched. "I am being more than reasonable."

El chewed her lip. "One condition."

Lord Landrum laughed. "You, girl, are bold." He shook his head. "You remind me of my daughter. Go on. What is your *condition?*"

"Tell us why. Why was this pouch so important that our Da," she squeezed Ren's knee, "had to die for it?"

The smile dropped from Lord Landrum's face, his eyes flashing with a dark and dangerous glow—almost red, El thought for the briefest of moments. "I've already told you the contents are important. EtherStone, it's called, and it is the most valuable commodity in Alpinside."

El frowned. It was an answer without giving any real information. "So what if it's valuable? That don't mean our Da deserved to be killed for takin' some of it."

"People have killed and been killed for much less, girl," Lord Landrum snapped. His face softened as he rubbed his brow. "You don't know the ways of this city. Please, trust me on this." He held his hand out, palm looming before her. "Give me the pouch. Secure safety for you and your brother. Surely that is what's important now?"

El bristled, irritated, but didn't want to push him too far. She had no doubt he *would* report them to the City Guard if he sensed she wasn't going to agree to his demands.

She glanced to Ren, pursed her lips, and nodded. "Alright," she said, untying the pouch from her belt. She resisted the urge to nudge the satchel at her feet, lest she bring it under scrutiny; it wouldn't do for the necklace to be discovered. "I'm keepin' everythin' else we own. No questions."

Lord Landrum snorted, his stubby white fingers wrapping around the pouch. "Keep your possessions, girl." He tucked the pouch into his breast pocket. "You've made the right choice."

AND SO IT WAS THE NEXT DAY SHE FOUND HERSELF ALONGSIDE Lady Oren and Mistress Elizabetha Estamore, two women whose beauty seemed second only to their cool disdain towards her. She was clothed in a long, white-collared black dress with woolen tights and shiny black boots, the finest clothes she'd ever worn despite the fact they were servant's garb. Over the top she wore a thick cloak to keep the increasing winter cold at bay. She glanced out the carriage window, not quite believing that just yesterday she and Ren had been on these very streets, watching the carriage rumble past.

She clenched her fists in her skirt pockets, afraid to look up and meet the dark glares of the women before her. Both were fierce in their own way, and both had shown they were all too displeased with her presence. Judgmental of her roots perhaps, or simply suspicious of strangers. Either way, it lent an air of awkwardness to the ride that was near suffocating. El had never liked silence. Silence meant Da was in one of his drunken stupors —lost in the past and dwelling on all he'd lost, building up to an outburst of anger that would only end one way.

In an attempt to break the building tension, she asked. "Where are we goin', m'lady?" El wasn't sure who to look at as she spoke, so she locked her eyes on the wooden seat between them. Even so, she could *sense* the sneering way the women glanced at each other before Lady Oren spoke.

"Since you are... *learning*, I shall ignore the fact you have addressed us without being spoken to. Do not do so again."

El gulped, peering up at the woman from beneath her eyelashes, afraid to make direct eye contact.

"Elizabetha has recently been betrothed to Lord Ashford Branton. A finer match hasn't been seen in Alpinside for some time. Decades, perhaps. As such, there is much planning to do for the wedding." Lady Oren beamed at her daughter, any hint of the hardness with which she'd looked at El melting away. "First stop this morning will be the dressmakers. Keep quiet, watch, and speak only when spoken to. Do you understand?"

"Yes, m'lady," El said dutifully.

She needed to earn their trust so she could learn more about the mysterious EtherStone— which was going to be much harder than she'd thought.

Standing in the corner of the dressmaker's, El watched as Elizabetha was measured and pinned with long strips of material and lace the likes of which she'd never seen before. They were the kinds of fabric she could only dream of wearing, if she'd ever thought to. As it was, she'd never had the luxury of even thinking about it. The conversation was a dull mix of gossip and speculation, and she'd long since tuned it out. With little else to distract her, her mind drifted back to the evening she'd found Da and been attacked by the Stalker. She shuddered recalling the murderer's eyes, red as blood, filled with hatred and rage—the eyes of a monster.

And he's still out there, she reflected. *People are still at risk. And why was Lord Landrum so worried about Ren an' me linkin' the murders to 'is family? I'd never've thought they were involved, even with the crest on the pouch.*

Her gaze washed over Lady Oren and Mistress Elizabetha, the former busy fiddling with the fabric being draped across her daughter. True, they were brusque in manner, but she could hardly imagine them being killers.

But then who else could it be? she wondered. *Unless Lord Landrum were...*

El was brought back to the moment by Lady Oren's sharp tone. "Elizabetha, *really!* I know what's best."

She blinked, focusing on the scene before her.

"You must watch what you eat," Lady Oren punctuated each word with a jabbing finger on her daughter's stomach, "between now and the wedding. We'll take the corset in the smaller size, Jayne."

The dressmaker bowed her head.

El looked to Elizabetha, who rubbed at her stomach where her mother had been prodding—a stomach which was, to El's eyes, perfectly proportioned with the rest of her plump frame. But Elizabetha's face told a different story, her mouth downturned and eyes shining.

"I'm sorry, Mother. I—"

"Hush. We'll speak no more about it. I'll speak to the kitchen staff when we return home and see your diet is amended accordingly."

El furrowed her brow, bewildered by the priorities of those who had no concerns about where their next meal was coming from. *What does it matter how a person's body looks?* she wondered. Surely there were more important things to consider. If she was rich, *she* would celebrate the ability to *enjoy* food, rather than anxiously scoffing down any morsel she and Ren could get their hands on.

"Something to say, girl?" Lady Oren drawled derisively.

El jolted. Pushing her shoulders back, she met the Lady's cold, dark gaze. "Only that Mistress Elizabetha looks... well, beautiful. I see no problem with—"

Lady Oren scoffed. "An unwanted opinion. You are not *educated* on such matters." Her eyes roved up and down El, nose wrinkling. "Keep your thoughts to yourself, Scrubber."

"Yes, m'lady," El mumbled, glancing over the woman's shoulder to Elizabetha, whose lips were turned up in the slightest of smiles. Their eyes met and El felt the tiniest spark of connection between them.

She dropped her eyes to the ground and smiled to herself.

It was a start.

THE SECOND

DELILAH

She was a beautiful young woman, much as Daisy had been —skin perfect and pale, unblemished despite the harshness of her short life, and hair like spun gold, shining in the summer sun that blessed our beloved Alpinside with its heat and light. A blessing from the EtherFather himself. As I watched her pegging a handful of ragged clothes on a line outside her ramshackle home, I could almost believe she was innocent.

Almost.

The EtherFather had assured me she was not; she was the EtherMother's next chosen. I had confirmed it with my own eyes, too. Our paths had crossed for a reason, and she must be removed. Like Daisy before her, she had to be sacrificed for the good of the city—for the kingdom of Estra.

It had taken some time for me to accept my work was not complete, I must admit. Despite my faith in the EtherFather, despite my loyalty and belief in His cause, I had hoped...

But no, there was little point in dwelling on it. Daisy had not been enough.

And it had to be that day—there could be no more delays. Once again, I sensed the EtherFather's impatience building like a raging migraine pounding, pounding, *pounding* against my skull. I had to act, for my own sanity as much as anything else.

As a child, I'd taught myself the value of patience. Of waiting and watching, listening and learning. I had observed Delilah over a number of days, much as I did with Daisy. That evening, as the sun was setting, she left her home and made her way to a nearby tavern—or what the Scrubbers called a tavern, at least. From what I had seen, it could barely be described as more than a hovel, yet it drew a raucous crowd each night. Workers looking to drown their sorrows. Scrubbers whose misery could only be numbed by the voracity of their EtherAle. The whores looking for a John and later something to dull their miserable lives, the usual choice being a mug of EtherAle.

Out of curiosity, I tried EtherAle once. I found it a pathetic homage to the most sacred of objects, EtherStone. The ale the Scrubbers favor is supposedly laced with a small amount, though I cannot imagine any nobleman would be willing to share their limited stocks of the precious commodity, so this is likely false, else the amount is so small as to be rendered powerless—completely removed from the connection to our beloved EtherFather the consumption of Blood Whiskey nurtures.

I had set a plan in my mind to apprehend Delilah as she made her way to the tavern. It was sure to be busy and I could not afford to attract the attention of its patrons, drunk as they might be. Though I had seen no evidence that she was a whore as Daisy had been, I was certain she could be convinced to follow me by the promise of enough coin. Of course, there was a risk she would recognize me as Daisy had and I had planned for that, too. I would not panic—I would explain away my presence as mere professional concern.

Yes, I was satisfied I would succeed without problem.

As the day began to darken, I rolled my shoulders and neck, checked the knife sheathed at my belt, and took several long, deep breaths. Strangely, my heart rate remained steady and my limbs did not tremble. It was curious that I had so quickly accustomed myself to the idea of killing as an acceptable act.

The door to Delilah's home opened and there she was. She called back through the door, her words indecipherable, then set off for the tavern.

"EtherFather guide me," I whispered, moving from the shadow of the alley, following her down the filthy cobblestoned street.

It quickly became clear she was already inebriated, stumbling several times as she made her way towards the tavern. I sped up; perhaps this would be easier than I had anticipated. As I neared, I heard her ragged breaths, and reached out, clamping a hand on her shoulder, turning her to face me.

There was a delayed sense of fear in her dark brown eyes before she blinked up at me and gave a lop-sided grin. "Oh, it's you!" she slurred, immediately recognizing me despite her state.

I cursed inwardly, but quickly recovered myself.

"Delilah," I said quietly, glancing about the street to ensure we were alone. "I came to check on you."

She patted me on the arm. "Din't need t' do that. I'm- I'm fine, mister... mister—what was it?" She sniffed loudly, running her forearm across her nose, quickly forgetting that line of thought. "Was just goin' 'ome, actually."

I smiled at the lie. "I wonder if you might permit me to take you to my carriage first. My satchel is there with my instruments. Perhaps I might find a tincture to ease your mind. I know how it has troubled you of late."

Delilah peered over her shoulder towards the direction she had been heading, then back up to me. There was a measure of unmistakable sadness in her expression as she sighed and said, "Yeh, that sounds... yeh."

"This way." I steered her towards a nearby alley.

As I walked beside her, I reflected on how well built the Workers' District was for concealing oneself. So many small, twisting streets interconnected by alleys, almost warren-like in their darkness. It wouldn't be hard to find a sufficiently hidden place to carry out my work. After we had turned a few times, making it such that we were deep within the network of alleys, I stopped.

Delilah, still so deeply trusting, smiled up at me. "Why we stoppin'? We there?"

If she had not been the EtherMother's pawn, I might have felt sorry for her.

"Oh, yes, Delilah," I said, stepping up behind her and pinning her arms in place. "We are."

She wriggled, instinctive fear kicking in—the urge to survive had always fascinated me, even in the weak, starving, and down-trodden.

"Don't struggle," I whispered in her ear, covering her mouth with my gloved hand and pulling her back against me. "It will be over soon."

The only response I received was a muffled, choking sob.

In one swift movement, I took the knife from its sheath and slit her throat. I was sure this time to cut deep and true. The blood gushed onto my sleeve, warm and thick, and I held her upright as the last tendrils of her life seeped away, her body spasming. When she was finally still, I laid her on the ground. Though my stomach turned at the sight and smell of so much blood, I found I was not nearly so nauseous this time.

"You will have peace now," I told her. "Be with your beloved EtherMother. Be with the one who set you on this path."

Perhaps she would be discovered soon—perhaps not. It did not matter. My work was done.

I wiped the bloodied knife on her ragged dress, noticing for the first time the fresh bruises on her milky wrists, mottling her arms like dark storm clouds in a pale sky. I shook my head, aston-ished at the hidden cruelty prevailing within these streets.

As I walked away, I bowed my head and prayed to the EtherFather.

He would be pleased with me.

CHAPTER 9

THE ETHERMOTHER

The date for the wedding was set. In just a matter of weeks, Beth would become Lady Elizabetha Branton. She giggled to herself, the familiar butterflies fluttering in her stomach. She wasn't due to see Ashford again until the day they would be wed, and she could hardly contain her impatience. She wondered what it would feel like to hold his hand, to kiss him for the first time, to feel his touch upon her.

A knock at her door shattered her daydreaming.

Time to face another day and her mother's endless list of tasks, questions, and incessant chatter. All Beth wanted to do was sleep until the wedding day, when the rest of her life would begin —when she would become a woman in her own right.

"Enter," she called. To her dismay, it was Ellana who walked in. She sat up in bed, frowning. "Where's Peggy?"

The girl gave an awkward curtsy, long black dress hanging loose about her skinny frame while ratty, blonde locks fell about her milky-white face.

She could have neatened up, Beth scoffed. *Looks as though she hasn't even brushed her hair.*

"I'm told I'm t' replace 'er, Mistress. In all 'er duties."

Beth rolled her eyes, recalling that, of course, Ellana would now fill Peggy's role. A Companion was maid, confidante, assistant—anything Beth needed her to be. At first, the urge to snap and shout rose in her gullet, a burning sensation that pushed her to emulate her mother's behavior towards servants. But she swallowed, repressing the urge. She'd never truly felt comfortable when she acted like Mother and spoke bluntly to a servant, a hot flush of guilt often consuming her.

Besides, Ellana had been *kind* to her at the dressmaker's when Mother only sought to criticize. So rare was that occurrence—for no one else had ever acted in her defense, especially against Mother—that it overrode the suspicion she'd felt towards Ellana for seemingly following their carriage. A coincidence, most likely. She had allowed herself to become too much like her mother, seeing the bad in people, expecting the worst.

That was not who she wanted to be.

With that in mind, she pushed back her bedsheets and stood. "Best begin then," she said with a brief smile. She moved to her dressing table, sat on her stool, and waited.

Ellana remained by the door, hands twitching and tugging at her dress.

"You'll need to come over here if you're to prepare me for the day," Beth said, a little sharper than intended.

"Oh," Ellana said, hurrying over with delicate footsteps. "Sorry." She stood at Beth's side, eyes planted onto the floor.

"Well?" Beth was finding it harder and harder to be patient. Who was this strange young woman, and why had Father taken her on as a Companion when she clearly knew nothing of the position, nor how to behave? "You'll want to start with a brush."

Ellana nodded, stepping closer to the dressing table, fingers hovering over the various brushes, clasps, combs, and ribbons strewn across it. She seemed in awe of everything before her, as though she'd never seen such objects.

Initially, Beth felt a stab of anger and impatience and that burning urge to snap returned. But as she watched Ellana's face and the way she gently ran her hand over various items, touching them delicately, her anger dissolved into compassion. *She really has never seen these objects before, has she?*

Then guilt overcame her. This young woman evidently came from a life completely unlike her own. Yesterday, she'd seen a glimmer of who this woman truly was, bold and fearless. That was the only way to describe how she'd stood up for Beth despite barely knowing her.

On top of that, Beth was quickly realizing she never wanted to make another person believe they were worthless, as her mother made her feel. *I must treat her better. I must fight against Mother's influence.*

She let out a slow exhale. For the first time, she properly studied Ellana. She was of a similar age—her father had confirmed as much. Ellana's arms were covered with long black sleeves, yet... Beth's lips turned downwards, her heart clenching. Were those bruises on her delicate wrists?

I must treat her with more kindness than she has received before, she told herself.

Her decision made, she stood, gently taking Ellana by the arm and guiding her onto the stool. She noted the way her Companion flinched away from the touch. "Let me show you."

"But, Mistress Elizabetha, Lady Oren'll be waitin'. There's no time t'—"

"Don't worry about my mother," Beth said. "I can deal with her." She stood back, tilting her head from side to side. "Your hair would look lovely in a braid. Do you mind if I...?" She waved her hand over the bits and bobs on her the dressing table.

Ellana's cheeks flushed a bright crimson. "Oh, o-only if you're sure, Mistress."

"Of course," Beth said. "And... it's Beth. My name. Elizabetha sounds so... formal. My brother always calls me Beth. My parents, too... when they're not angry at me." She grinned at Ellana in the mirror. "I much prefer it."

She began combing gently through Ellana's hair. It was a lighter color than she'd first thought, dirt and dust working loose as she brushed through the lengths. She tried not to wrinkle her nose, thinking how long it might have been since she'd last washed it—if ever. But the more Beth combed, the brighter it looked.

"You have beautiful hair Ellana... or El, wasn't it?" She met the girl's eyes in the mirror and gave another smile.

"El, yeh," she said, lips twitching upwards. "And, um, thanks."

Beth continued to comb El's hair for a short while. The young woman remained still enough, though it was evident from her fidgeting she wasn't used to doing so.

"Braiding is simple enough and will be a passable hairstyle for most occasions." Beth lifted some hair from the side of El's head and separated it into three portions. "You start like this and then you..." Beth began crisscrossing the strands.

El's focus was intent, biting her lip as her eyes followed Beth's every movement in the mirror. When one side of her head was done, she leaned forward to admire the braid. Her eyes shone. "It's like Ma used t' wear hers!" She blinked quickly, as though self-conscious of her emotions. "Um, thanks."

"Not done yet." Beth began the second braid. "It's a simple enough style. I'm surprised your mother did not teach you to do it, if she wore it herself."

El's body stiffened. "Ma died when I were young. I don't remember much of her, though I do remember watchin' her do this for herself. Maybe she would've taught me, if she'd..." El's gaze dropped to her lap, her throat bobbing.

Beth pursed her lips, cursing herself for her blunder. "I- I am so sorry." She continued braiding for a moment, frantically searching for a change of topic. "Your Father, did he— did he petition my father for a place here?"

El shook her head, pulling at the hair that Beth was braiding.

When she didn't say anything, Beth asked, "Where is your father?" She tied off the second braid with a black strand of ribbon and reached for some pins.

After a brief silence, El muttered, "He's dead. Both my parents're dead."

"Oh, El, that's awful," Beth said, touching her Companion's shoulder briefly before pinning the braids around the bottom of her head. "What were their names?"

"Names?" El frowned as though she'd never been asked that. "Ma were called Ariya. Da were Frederich. Stone."

"It must've been incredibly difficult to lose them." Beth's mouth pinched into a line. "Was your father's death... recent?" Though she knew the question to be impertinent, she found she couldn't help but ask it.

El swallowed. "Jus' a few days ago."

Beth gasped. "Oh, by the Mother! What happened?"

El's reflection blinked back at her from the mirror, blue eyes shining. "Murdered. By the Stalker. Ren and I was... Well, we was almost killed by 'im too. Would've been, if Ren hadn't stabbed 'im in the—"

"Elizabetha, what is the delay!"

Beth jolted, dropping the last pin onto the floor. She turned to find her mother in the doorway. She knew how it looked, to be found dressing her *Companion's* hair. Beth floundered to find an excuse that would suitably assuage her mother.

Before she could do so, El stood. "Lady Oren," she said, eyes locked on the floor. "Mistress Elizbetha was jus' showin' me how to braid. So's I can arrange her hair. Was my fault, for bein' uneducated on such things."

Beth watched her mother. Her eyes were dark with anger, her brows furrowed, yet her mouth was relaxed. Maybe she was adjusting to this Scrubber being in their household staff. Maybe she was simply biding her time until she could convince Father to remove Ellana and her brother from their service. Either way, Oren gave a curt nod, running a hand over the large EtherStone around her throat—the necklace she wore only for church.

"See that *Elizabetha's* hair is done, and she's dressed quickly.

Temple service begins in an hour, after which we must speak to the EtherPriest about the wedding ceremony."

Temple. With all the excitement of wedding planning, Beth had quite lost track of the days. Every tenth day she and her mother were required to make their penance to the EtherMother and to prove their continued respect and reverence towards the EtherFather and His ordained order.

"—important we are on time." Beth realized her mother had been speaking and she hadn't been paying attention. "You will attend alongside us, *girl*. You will observe what it means to be within proper society." She fixed El with a patronizing stare. "As a *proper* Companion, I would've expected you to be aware of such important aspects." She scoffed, turned, and briskly left the room without another word, her long, burgundy skirts rustling behind her.

"Sorry," Beth said, casting an apologetic grimace at El as she hurried towards her wardrobe. "She's right though. We can't be late for Temple—the other ladies will gossip."

El's eyes remained focused on the closed door. "That necklace your mother was wearin'..." she whispered.

Beth frowned. "Oh, the necklace of the EtherMother? She wears it for Temple, all noble ladies do—to be closer to the Ether-Father." She held up a dress, wondering whether it would please her mother. Deciding against it, she placed it back and continued to search through her wardrobe. "Come, there's no time to talk, we have to get ready. I can tell you about it later."

At that, El seemed to gather herself. "Am I really comin' with you?"

El seemed unfazed by the way in which Beth's mother had spoken to her, yet there was something unreadable in her stiff tone and stance. Was her face a shade whiter than usual? Hard to tell, with her skin so pale anyway.

"You're my Companion, so, yes, it is expected," Beth said. Inwardly, she wasn't sure it was such a good idea. Ellana didn't seem to understand much about the nobles in Alpinside, and Beth feared there could be some embarrassing mishaps. Regardless, she didn't wish to go against Mother.

She pulled a long, dark grey dress from her wardrobe—simple clothing was best when praying to the EtherMother, humility being one of the most valued virtues a woman could embody. "Help me put this on."

Once they were finished, Beth studied them both in the mirror, side by side. They were the same height, though that was where the similarities ended. El was much slimmer than she, her hair blonde and sleek where Beth's was black and curly. El's skin was pale where Beth's was the dark brown of her mother's heritage. An odd pair to be sure, but a prickling sensation of unexpected fondness bloomed in Beth's chest.

She'd never truly had a friend of her own, not one she'd really felt she could trust or be herself with. Could El be that person? She smiled to herself. *What a thought! What would Mother think?*

She linked her arm through El's. "Let's go," she said. "Mother will be waiting."

El allowed herself to be guided from Beth's room quietly. It was a silence that, somehow, bore the heaviness of unspoken words, and left Beth wondering at its meaning.

༺❀༻

As the carriage pulled to a halt outside the Temple, Beth looked up at it. It was an immense, foreboding building at the heart of the Noble District, wrought of white limestone and topped with a bell tower that reached toward the sky. To her it had always seemed a place to be revered.

Beth turned to El to see how the young woman responded to seeing the Temple for what she assumed was the first time. Instead of respect, Beth saw a mix of confusion and anger. El's mouth worked strangely, as though she was furiously fighting back words.

Beth allowed her mother to exit the carriage before giving El a gentle nudge. She blinked, seeming to come back to the moment. "Time to go," Beth said gently.

El nodded, her face now a blank mask.

Clearly in no mood to wait, Oren had marched ahead. Taking El's arm, Beth pulled her onward. Overhead, the bell tower loomed. She craned her neck to see it, as always marveling at how high it seemed to stretch. She often thought it must be close to touching the EtherFather and EtherMother themselves. As she gazed upwards, the bell began to toll in a great, deafening peal. It would ring three times in total, alerting the city it was the morning of the EtherMother and that all noblewomen should attend their worship.

Ahead, the main doors of the Temple were dark and ominous. Beth's heart quickened like it normally did when she turned her gaze to them. They depicted the EtherFather, sitting upon a great throne, clutching an EtherStone scepter in his hand.

She followed her mother to the side of the building, where a smaller door depicted the EtherMother, head bowed in veneration, an EtherStone necklace glimmering at her chest. At the door, she glanced behind her, noticing El had stopped; her Companion was staring at the EtherFather door, mouth agape.

"El," she hissed, "come on."

The young woman remained frozen.

With a sigh of exasperation, Beth hurried to grab her hand. "Ellana!"

El flinched as if she'd been slapped, and she scowled at Beth.

"Our entrance is over here. We must hurry."

Thankfully, El allowed herself to be led again, though her hands flapped back towards the EtherFather door. "Why aren't we goin' in that one?"

It was Beth's turn to scowl, halting in front of the Ether-Mother entrance. "That door is for men *only*. We women must follow the EtherMother, always." She ran her finger delicately over the EtherMother's likeness on the door before casting El a discerning glare. "Surely you know that?"

"I—"

"Elizabetha!" Her mother's face appeared through the door as it creaked open. "What, by the Mother, do you think you're doing standing out here *chatting*?" She grabbed Beth's wrist and yanked her roughly through the door.

El scurried in behind them, letting the door slam shut in her wake.

Inside the Temple, the voice of the EtherPriest could be heard echoing through the main worship chamber. Beth winced, knowing her mother's anger would be acute when they returned home. To attend Temple was expected of women of their station; they had a duty to the EtherMother. Their lateness showed a lack of respect, and that would be the talk of Alpinside for days. She could only hope the plans for her upcoming nuptials would distract her mother before too long.

Behind her, she could hear El's hurried footsteps. She didn't turn around, frustrated as she was that her Companion had caused them to be delayed. Part of her knew El's curiosity was borne of ignorance, yet that didn't prevent the simmering anger bubbling within her. It would be *she*, not El, who would bear the brunt of the gossip.

As they entered the worship chamber, she kept her head down and followed her mother, cursing to herself that their family seating was so close to the front. She could feel eyes upon them, could almost hear the judgmental whispers, as they took their seats. There was likely curiosity, too, about Ellana's presence. Who was this skinny young woman with the hard blue eyes? Who was this *Scrubber*?

Once they were seated, Beth focused on the EtherPriest. His sermon appeared to be on the value of humility and obedience. As women, it was their responsibility to follow the EtherMother in bowing to the EtherFather—who represented all men within proper society. A small thrill ran through Beth. She would soon be Lord Ashford's wife; she would belong to him, she would obey him, she would perform her wifely duties without question. At that thought, she bit her lip to hold back a smile, warmth filling her stomach. She truly could not wait to call herself Lady Elizabetha Branton. She imagined the looks on the other young women's faces, their acute jealousy that it was she who had married such a fine man.

After the sermon, her mother made the rounds, spreading the word of the wedding plans Beth was sure. Usually she would've joined Mother, but she found she had no desire to after their embarrassingly late entrance. El was staring up at the empty pulpit, apparently deep in thought.

"Do you want to see some more of the temple?" Beth asked.

El jolted from her reverie, eyes widening. "I'm not sure," she whispered. "Is it all that bloody serious?"

Beth laughed. "What do you mean?"

"All that 'bout obeyin' your father, husband, brother."

Beth's brow furrowed. "What of it?"

El mirrored her frown, muttering, "Not sure I like it."

Beth snorted, shaking her head. "I'm sure you must've been taught similar when you attended Temple with your family."

"Temple? No. You think there're places like *this* in the Workers' District?" El's expression hardened. "This is the grandest buildin' I've ever seen. You could fit most of Scrubbers' Hill in 'ere, I reckon. Though there was often men like 'im," she said, waving a hand at the pulpit, "who spoke on the street corners." She scratched at her hair as though irritated. "There were a lot o' talk 'bout punishment an' *wrath of the Father*, whatever that means. Can't say we paid it much attention, if I'm honest. What's punishment from a god you can't see when you already live in fear for lack of food or money or even 'cos o' your own..." She trailed off, lips pinching tight. "Don't matter. You was gonna show me 'round."

Beth decided it was best not to question El's story for now, though it left her with a heavy knot of dread in the pit of her stomach.

"I'd love to," she said, forcing a smile. "Come on, this way."

CHAPTER 10

THE PORTRAIT

El wasn't sure what to make of the Temple. It was impressive, undeniably. The walls were wrought of the finest white stone, polished to a sheen. The golden gilt decorating every oaken bench was beautifully elaborate. Then there were the portraits three times her height and more, the finest artwork she'd ever laid her eyes on.

And yet, she couldn't help but feel sickened by it. Here were the nobles, already rich beyond anything she could imagine. Meanwhile, not so far away, the workers were left to struggle daily on their meager wages, to wonder where the next meal might come from, whether they might still have a home at the end of the week.

On top of which, it seemed everything the EtherPriest had preached to them was wrong—for, if it was true, did that mean Da's actions should have been... *respected*? Or could it be this EtherFather saw fit only to reward those who were lucky enough to be born into fortune? To give them further comfort and blessing in a life that had already blessed them. It seemed a twisted sense of justice, and the thought needled at her as Beth continued to point out this portrait, that tapestry or statue or sacred goblet in the building around them. Her new mistress seemed thrilled to be able to share her knowledge with El—if only it actually mattered.

"This is my favorite place," Beth said, stopping abruptly.

El almost walked into her. She shuffled away awkwardly, glancing around. They were in a long, rectangular room, carpeted in a deep red—for a horrifying moment, El was taken back to the bedroom at home. That awful scene. Da's mutilated body, the blood, so much bloo—

"El?" Beth touched her arm. "You've turned ghostly white."

Before she could try to reply, her mistress was ushering her to a nearby marble bench. As soon as she sat, El hunched over and huffed out a shaky breath. When she was able to straighten up, she gave Beth a strained smile, doing her best to push away the images in her mind.

"I'm a'right," she said ignoring the trembling that had seized her body. "Sorry. Not sure what 'appened." She willed Beth to believe her lie. She couldn't—wouldn't—describe the images that had flooded her mind.

Beth's face was a mask of skepticism. "We can get some food when we leave, that will help. We didn't have breakfast. Though Mother's sure to want to do more wedding shopping..." She pulled at a stray curl, grinning. "Oh! Perhaps we can visit the bakery to arrange the pastries and cake."

El almost laughed. How she wished she could be so carefree. "'Course."

How little Beth knew of what life was like outside of her fine home, fine clothes, fine food. Was she even aware of the Stalker's reign over the workers of Alpinside—of the terror they experienced daily, wondering if another person would be slaughtered.

Beth sat beside her. "As long as you're sure you're well."

"I'm fine," El snapped, suddenly irked at Beth's ignorance. Then, to distract Beth from her irritation, she pointed to the room. "Why's this your favorite place?"

Beth was on her feet in an instant, dragging El up beside her. "Where to begin?" There was a glow about her as she led El to the first of many portraits lining the wall. In it was a short, full-bosomed, pale-skinned woman. No, El realized, looking closer; her skin was more than simply pale, like her own. It was more akin to the color of a pearl, the likes of which her Ma had shown her not long before her death in the form of a precious, golden ring, adorned with a small white sphere. When she held it up to the light, it had glimmered pink and purple and blue and green. El had been fascinated by it and often wondered where it had gone after Ma's death, suspecting Da had pawned it.

"...important to me. To all of us, really." Beth turned to El. "Don't you think so?"

"Uhh—" El peered around, pretending to take in the portraits. "Y-yeh."

"Here, look—this is Lady Gardenia, second martyr to the EtherMother." Beth moved on to the next portrait, seemingly unperturbed by El's lack of a coherent response.

El followed, looking up to where her mistress pointed. This portrait depicted a brown-skinned woman, taller than the first, limbs long and willowy. She, too, had an ethereal sort of glow around her, and a serene expression on her face as though she was *blessed* by the EtherMother herself—which, El supposed, was the point.

What does 'blessed' mean, anyway? she wondered. Then she noticed the necklace around Lady Gardenia's neck and her heart skipped a beat.

Perhaps it was simply coincidence. She looked back at the first portrait and found it bore the same necklace.

How'd I miss that? she chided herself.

She peered down the row of portraits, no longer pretending to listen to Beth's continued monologue about Lady Gardenia. All the women, regardless of skin color, glowed with a pearlescent sheen. And all wore the same necklace.

The very necklace El's Ma had possessed. The one *she* now possessed. A memory came back to her. Ma had shown her the necklace when she was a child and had spoken of it with a distinct air of pride. It reminded her of the necklace Lady Oren wore that morning.

EtherStone. Again. Why does everythin' seem to link back to that bloody stone?

There was only one way to find out more.

"—from the southern regions, like my mother's family."

"Beth," El said, taking an opportunity in the pause in her mistress's speech, "why are they all wearin' the same necklace? EtherStone, ain't it? Is it... is it important?"

Beth's dark brows furrowed, a small line appearing in the middle of them. "EtherStone is very precious."

El nodded. "I were told once that it were," she narrowed her eyes, recalling the conversation with Lord Landrum, "a valuable commodity."

Beth glanced away. "That may be so, but it's not something that I, as a woman, have been permitted to learn much about. I know it's a gift from the EtherFather, granted to all who follow and are loyal to Him. The EtherMother and her martyrs received such a necklace with EtherStone as a mark of their sacrifice in the name of the EtherFather. For without the EtherMother's support and loyalty, the EtherFather's power would dwindle and diminish."

Beth looked up at the portrait, a smile playing on her lips. "It's a true sign of Her strength. Each noble family owns one of the martyrs' necklaces which is passed down through our bloodlines. One day, I'll receive the one Mother's wearing today."

El frowned, deep in thought. *Noble families? Why did Ma have one then?* A thought occurred to her. "Lady Oren doesn't always wear it."

"Oh, no," Beth said. "They're worn only for special occasions, given their value and importance. Mother always wears it to worship. And she'll likely—"

"Elizabetha!" Lady Oren's call was a sharp interruption. "Here you are." She cast El an unduly scathing look. "Come, we have much to do."

"Yes, Mother. Might we attend the bakery first? I've a craving for some sweet pastries." Beth winked at El.

Lady Oren tutted, pointedly gazing up and down her daughter. Then she sighed. "I shall allow it as there was no time for breakfast. But remember what I said at the dress shop. You *must* look your best for the wedding. And that means—"

"Yes, Mother, I must watch what I eat." A light in Beth's dark eyes dimmed and she dropped her gaze to the floor.

El swallowed back the urge to say something.

Lady Oren sniffed. "You'll thank me for it later, darling, when your husband has eyes only for you." Lifting her chin, she turned for the door. "Come."

She marched from the room with the confidence of a woman who knew she'd be followed without question. It was for that reason she missed Beth's eye roll, and the snigger which El failed to repress.

"Better not keep her waiting," Beth said, a glint returning to her eyes as she looped an arm through El's.

Beth's touch sent a tingling sensation over El's body, and she couldn't help but smile. She'd never had a friend before— shielding Ren from Da's ire had been her main focus for as long as she could remember, so she'd never had the time to spend with other girls her age. She was certain, however, that was what Beth was quickly becoming.

THAT EVENING, EXHAUSTED FROM A LONG DAY OF WEDDING preparations and belly aching from eating far too many sweet pastries, El dragged herself to the room she shared with Ren. He was already in bed, though he stirred when she opened the door.

"El," he whispered, rubbing vigorously at his eyes. "Missed you. Been so busy."

She knelt beside his bed and gently kissed him on the cheek.

"I missed you too, Ren." El pulled the blanket up around him and tucked it in. "Go back t' sleep, sorry I woke you."

She eased herself onto her bed, waiting for his breathing to deepen again before moving to retrieve the box from beneath her straw-filled mattress. She pulled it out as quietly as she could and placed it beside her. As her hand rested on it, a bubble of nerves fluttered in her chest, though she couldn't explain why.

She moved it to nestle in her lap, taking a deep breath before lifting the lid. The red stone in Ma's necklace gleamed as though it had its own internal light, dark as blood, mesmerizing in its beauty. Her breath hitched. Had it always done that?

She stroked a finger across it. EtherStone. *Could this really hold all the answers?*

She closed the lid, patting a hand atop it. She felt she had her first solid clue, but so many more questions lay before her. Why did Ma, a commoner, a woman with no family ties El could recall, possess one of these apparently sacred necklaces? What even *was* EtherStone? And why had Da been murdered for it?

Despite the questions swirling in her head, El sensed she was moving closer to the truth. She just had to be patient.

Carefully, she put the box back in its hiding spot. Laying down, she snuffed out the candle Ren had left burning for her.

Her dreams that night were filled with red.

The red of EtherStone.

The red of blood.

PART II
THE MADNESS

The EtherMother was kind and gentle, welcoming all into Her embrace, but the EtherFather saw She was blinded by love. There were those undeserving of the Mother's blessed compassion and grace, those who did not abide by sacred lore and so should not be granted such comfort in death. In His eternal wisdom, He made it so.

--The EtherFather's Sacred Doctrine, *On the EtherFather's Eternal Wisdom*

Wedding Announcement: Lord Ashford Branton and Mistress Elizabetha Estamore

The wedding of the season is upon us! Young Lord Ashford Branton, son and sole heir of the late, esteemed Lord Julius Branton, and Mistress Elizabetha Estamore, daughter of businessman Lord Landrum Estamore, are set to marry within the fortnight. With their wedding celebrations, Alpinside may be provided some brief respite from the murders that have darkened our fair city—and, this writer has no doubt, more than a few young ladies shall weep to see Lord Ashford removed from the market.

--The Alpinside Journal

Landrum,

It is most disappointing you have leveraged the accusation of theft against me. You were fully aware our joint investment in the old Winborn mines were a risk. We split the mines to allow for the clear division of any EtherStone that might have been forthcoming. Alas, I am sorry to hear your half proved unfruitful.

The men I sent into my section were put under great physical danger but agreed to venture into the unstable area only because of the generous fee I promised. They found an untapped vein of EtherStone, evidently undiscovered by Lord Darys before his unfortunate passing.

I will remind you, you were all too happy to allow me to take the half-collapsed section of mines when you believed it would yield little to no reward.

It is unfortunate you have allowed this to come between us, Landrum, after years of friendship and business partnership. If I hear word of any further accusations against me, you will be hearing from my solicitor.

Yours in regret,
Artavius Aberforth

THE THIRD

ROSIE

When the EtherFather first spoke to me, I thought I had finally gone mad. I was young and alone, aside from a dear friend, and my emotions collided like the great, clashing storm clouds that roil above the Alpin Mountains. I moved from despairing grief to burning rage and back again with such speed and force that my head was a muddled fog of pain and misery.

And then, I heard His voice.

My savior, He said, *I have a most important task for you.*

At first, I'd ignored it—Him. It was a madness of the mind, I told myself. A malady of grief that would pass with time.

Yet the voice persisted.

As the weeks and months passed by, I came to realize this was my blessing. I had lost much in my short life, yet the EtherFather saw fit to choose me as His warrior—to bestow upon me His favor, to become His savior of Alpinside. It lifted me from the depths of darkness, this new purpose.

And now, He requires my services once more.

Delilah was not the last.

As with the first two pawns—abominations as I had come to think of them—this one was afflicted with the same madness. At least, if I hadn't known of the EtherMother's influence, that is what I would have put it down to. Indeed, it seemed an answer many were willing to accept.

My attention was brought to Rosie by means of my chosen path. It was meant to be, some might say; I knew the EtherFather watched over us all and guided me towards my destination.

Her hair was a tumble of auburn curls, her eyes the clear blue of the summer sky. Was this a test of sorts, set by the Ether-Mother? An attempt to waver my loyalty to my beloved EtherFather? It was pathetic. She was beautiful, as they all had been in their own way. Beautiful and broken. But I am not a man so easily distracted.

My confidence had been boosted by the ease with which Delilah had been lured in and killed. I had, I reasoned, found my stride. I hadn't been afflicted with sickness after her demise either. This was getting, dare I say, easier.

The Alpinside newspapers all asked the same question: Who is this killer, this monster, this madman who hunts the poor and downtrodden, the impure and sinful? They have even given me a name: The Scrubbers' Stalker. It certainly has appeal; a catchy name for the masses to whisper amongst themselves. I imagine it passing from the lips of nobles as they go about their ignorant lives, unaware of the true reason for my mission. The fools have no idea, thinking me a deranged man—likely a Scrubber—seeking to murder the young women he so desires as a means to feel powerful.

"Thank the EtherFather it's not us," the nobles say to each other as they drink their fine tea and Blood Whiskey. All the while, they glance in the direction of the Workers' District with wrinkled noses and a mixture of relief and arrogance.

"Thank the EtherFather for His protection," they croon.

In that, at least, they are correct.

Yet they misunderstand much, the ignorant masses, for the EtherFather does not protect them from me, His savior, the *Stalker*. No, he uses me to protect them from the far greater threat posed by the EtherMother's attempted rising. It is She who should be judged, not me, for choosing these young women, barely able to look after themselves let alone hold the power She seeks to bestow upon them in Her attempt to challenge the EtherFather.

In a way, I am saving these women.

Rosie stood a short distance in front of me in her usual spot close to the docks. It was not far from where Daisy was killed. She flaunted herself to any who dared to look her way, just like Daisy before her. All these young women were the same. Each had been afflicted with madness. Each had been chosen by the EtherMother.

Each destined to die because of the whims of a careless, selfish goddess.

As I watched, a tall man approached Rosie. I pulled my top hat further down so it tilted across my eyes, edging backwards into the shadows of my shelter, the same darkened doorway from which I had observed Daisy.

A giggle reached my ears. I peered out of my hiding place, noting the man leaning in to whisper in Rosie's ear. I grimaced. Perhaps tonight was not the night after all.

Be patient, a voice whispered in the back of my mind.

I exhaled, watching as Rosie was led away by the man, his broad hand pressing against the bottom of her back as he urged her towards the alley in which I had slain Daisy not two months before. How quickly people forgot and moved on.

I could attack them both, I reasoned. The man would be collateral damage, no great loss. Yet something held me back.

It was not right for her to die there, in the same place as the first, though I couldn't truly have said why.

I closed my eyes, slowed my breathing, and waited.

I don't know how much time passed before I saw the man scurrying away, fiddling with the buckle of his belt, his back hunched as he disappeared along the dimly lit cobblestoned street. It took longer for Rosie to emerge and return to stand beneath the gaslamp marking her territory. I noted her face glistened with tears.

It was time for me to release her from her burdensome existence.

I stepped from the doorway. As I did so, she ran her hands down her skirts, nodded to herself, and began marching down the street. I hurried, not wanting to lose her.

As I neared, I called, "Wait!"

"I'm done for the night," she replied over her shoulder, not slowing. Her hair was a cloak of auburn billowing behind her.

"Please," I said. "I'll pay you a gold crown."

Still, she marched on.

"Two gold crowns."

Nothing.

"Five! Five gold crowns!" A scandalous price, even for one of her beauty.

She stopped and turned, tilting her head to one side. Up close, I could see the freckles dappling her nose and cheeks. "Like 'em young an' unwilling, do ya?"

I snorted, hand pausing mid-way towards my coin purse. "What?"

"Never mind," she said. "Come on then, make it quick."

Hardly the reward for such a generous offer. If I'd truly been here as a customer, I surely would've been angry. As it was, I nodded. "Where?"

She held out her hand. "Coin first."

As I placed the crowns on her palm, I began to wonder how old she was. She couldn't have seen more than sixteen summers, likely less. Why had the EtherMother chosen one so young? What a wretched, cruel goddess she was.

"This way," she said, tilting her head towards a nearby side street.

Once there, she abruptly turned left, where, to my astonishment, was a small, sheltered attempt at a garden. It was pitiful, really—a small scattering of withered trees, some shrubs that might once have been adorned with roses, and a haggard lavender bush, the smell of which filled the air.

She pointed me towards a wooden bench which had almost certainly seen better days. "Sit."

"What is this place?" I asked, strangely bewitched.

She shrugged. "Somewhere nicer than a fuckin' alley. Call it a bonus for your generous fee."

The sound of such harsh language snapped me back to reality. She was mocking me.

I stood back up, towering over her as I removed my top hat.

She gaped, at first angry, then confused. "You!" she said. "I din't put you down as—"

I cut off her words with my knife, plunging it into her heart with one hard thrust. For a few seconds, I was sure I could feel it thumping its final beats where I still clutched the handle.

Rosie's mouth tried to form words, her eyes filled with pain, her brow creased. "W-w-why?" she managed to croak.

And then she slumped backwards, thudding to the ground. Seeing her amongst the wilted flowers, her blood spreading across the front of her dress, pooling on the ground beside her, I felt curiously shaken. I sat with her for a short while, breathing in the scent of the lavender, seeking to calm my body and mind.

When at last I noticed the stench of blood and shit was overtaking the floral fragrance, I made to leave. I gave Rosie one final glance, my heart jolting. She looked almost at peace.

She is at peace now. Remember that, I reminded myself.

I nodded to myself, certain the EtherFather Himself looked upon me then.

I left the garden and Rosie's body behind me. My work was done. For the time being, at least.

CHAPTER 11
THE SUSPICION

The week passed in a blur of wedding arrangements.

As the days flew by, Beth decided she held a responsibility of sorts to educate El on everything about her role as Companion and about the EtherMother, including their duties as women to adhere to Her guidance in life.

Not long after breakfast, she was preparing to discuss this very matter with El when her mother walked in, holding up a scroll with a triumphant gleam in her eye.

"Are you well, Mother?" Beth asked.

"A telegram has arrived." Oren cleared her throat and read aloud, "To my future wife and her family: I would be honored to receive you at Branton Manor this evening for a special dinner in celebration of our upcoming nuptials."

Beth's heart soared.

"It seems Lord Branton has a wish to see you again before the wedding." Her mother gave her a measured stare. "Perhaps we'd best decide upon a more flattering gown. And a hairstyle more becoming a *Lady*."

"Yes, Mother," Beth said, too happy to allow her mother's judgmental comments to jab at her as they might normally.

"You will attend as well, girl," her mother snapped at El. "It is expected that a Companion is alongside her mistress at all times."

"Yes, m'lady," El said, bowing her head.

"Beth, ensure she is presentable, will you? I won't have any more embarrassment such as we had at Temple, do you hear?" Speaking to El, she said, "My husband may have brought you into this household but, believe me, I can send you out of it." With that, Oren turned and marched down the hall towards the drawing room.

Beth sighed. Evidently her mother hadn't forgotten her anger after all. "Don't worry," she told El. "She knows you're here to stay and has no right to fight Father's decision. She's just taking out her frustration at any opportunity she can."

El shrugged, smiling weakly. "Words are nothin'. When Da was alive, he would've..." She rubbed self-consciously at her forearm. "Well, there would've been no words, let's put it that way."

"I'm... sorry," Beth said.

"Nothin' to be sorry for," El assured her. "In a strange way, 'is death was the best thing to 'appen to Ren an' me. Meant we ended up 'ere. A warm house, food in our bellies. All we could've ever asked for, really. I'm not sure what would've happened to us otherwise."

With a rush of embarrassment, Beth saw her foolishness for the excitement she experienced at such frivolous things as an invitation to dinner. She realized then how very sheltered her life had been; how those like El had struggled in ways she could never understand.

"I wanted to show you my father's study," she said after a moment of debate. "Some of his books. Though," she rubbed the back of her neck, "that seems a little silly now."

El's face lit up. "Books? That'd be somethin'." Her lips twisted, half happiness, half anxiety. "I- I can't read though."

"By the Mother! El, I'm sorry. I- I didn't think—" She stopped and held up a finger, an idea striking her. "Oh! I could teach you to read!"

"You could?"

"Of course!" She grabbed El's arm, pulling her towards Father's study, a new sense of purpose filling her.

If she could help El to feel some of the joys she experienced in her life, perhaps that would make up for some of the hardships her Companion had endured. She was certain the EtherMother would approve.

When she opened the door to her father's study, she was shocked to find him leaning over his desk—usually, he was away on business during the day, tending to the family mines and ensuring everything was running smoothly.

It was only when the figure raised his head that she realized it was Edward, not her father, his dark skin having been obscured by his hunched position.

When did his hair turn so grey?

She pushed the thought aside and rushed towards him, placing a hand on his arm and giving a familial squeeze. "Edward! I thought you were still resting. Should you be out of bed so soon?"

He met her hand with his own, his slender fingers soft against her hand. "Beth," he said, his voice little more than a whisper. His lips, all too pale, pulled into a strained smile. "I've had enough of the walls of my bedroom to last me a lifetime. Time to get some reading done." He proffered a hand towards the book he had out, a large volume on the treatise of the Alpin-side mines.

It wasn't a book she'd ever be drawn to but, as father's heir, Edward needed to learn all he could about managing the mines.

As though sensing her thoughts, Edward gave her a wink. "A necessary if eye-achingly boring task." Then he peered behind her towards El, who remained standing in the doorway.

Beth supposed her brother *could* be an imposing figure, with his black brow furrowed and lips pursed—though, of late, his cheeks had become sunken, his skin sallow.

She realized she hadn't spent much time with him in recent months. It was something she desperately needed to remedy.

Shaking her head, she banished the guilt that came with such thoughts. "Edward," she said, "this is Ellana. El."

Edward stood, towering over them both. "My sister's new Companion, I assume," he said, clasping her hand firmly in his. "You've caused quite a stir. Mother is rather displeased with your arrival." He let out a gentle laugh.

El simply looked up at him, mouth agape.

"You can speak, El," Beth said, chuckling.

"Oh, uh, s-sorry. Sorry, m'lord." El pulled her hand away from Edward's, shrugging awkwardly.

"Edward will do just fine," her brother said lightly. "I won't be Lord Estamore for some time yet."

El merely nodded.

"Well," Edward said, "I've a fancy for a stroll. Some fresh air is sure to help my healing."

Beth frowned. "Make sure you—"

"Tell Mother, yes, yes." Edward rolled his eyes, his grey and black curls bouncing about his face.

As he reached for the door handle, he winced and Beth hurried forward to help her brother, realizing then his bravado was a front. It was evident the injury on his back was still paining him.

"Be careful, Edward," she said sternly. "We just want you to be safe."

Edward raised an eyebrow. "Hmm," was all he said before retreating from the room.

Beth watched him walk down the hall, his movements tentative, before gently closing the door. Turning back to El, she started, "Now, shall we— El? What's wrong?"

"Oh." El placed a hand on her forehead. "I think I've an ache comin' on. D'you mind if we leave the readin' for tomorrow?"

Beth nodded. "Come, you can help me choose a gown for the dinner this evening. And we can have some chamomile tea; that should help your head."

Leading El from the study, she tried to ignore the troubled

look in her Companion's eyes. *She's had a lot to take in since she arrived here,* Beth reflected. *Poor thing.*

Beth could barely imagine losing both parents and finding herself in a stranger's home. She had trouble with hers sometimes, true, yet she couldn't imagine them being... *gone.*

As they made their way to Beth's room, a thought occurred to her. "El, would you tell me about your Mother?"

"Me Ma?" El's blue eyes sparkled.

"I can tell you loved her," Beth said as they entered her room, where she directed El to sit before the dressing table. "I would love to know more about her."

El fiddled with the hem of her dress. "She were beautiful. Long, golden hair. Blue eyes like me an' Ren. She used t' read t' me. There were this old book she 'ad. Fae stories, she called 'em. All magic and faraway lands an' that."

"Fae stories?" Beth turned from where she was browsing her gowns. "They sound nice." Her mother had never read her a story, and she swallowed back the tightness in her throat at the realization. "What else? Did she read to your brother, too?"

El's smile dropped. "She died not long after Ren were born. He don't remember 'er."

"Oh," Beth whispered. "So, it was just you, Ren, and your father then?"

El sniffed. "It were just me an' Ren. Our Da were... troubled."

Beth moved to sit beside El. "He's the one who caused those bruises on your arm?"

El tugged at her sleeves, brow furrowing, and didn't answer.

"I- I don't mean to pry. It's just I saw them not long after you started and wondered who could've done something like that to you."

"Well, he's gone now. Won't be hurtin' no one no more."

There was a momentary silence before Beth asked, "How did he die?"

A curious expression overcame El's face—her lips twisting and nose wrinkling. Finally, she looked at Beth and croaked, "Murdered. By the Stalker."

"El, that's terrible! Why didn't you tell me before?"

El shook her head. "It's fine. Ren's upset, but it's better this way. Da... he weren't a good man. Like I said, that we ended up 'ere's more'n I could've hoped. We was lucky gettin' away, too, 'cos —" El broke off, letting out a long, shaky breath.

Beth's heart lurched. "What?"

"The Stalker. He was there, when I found Da. He... attacked me."

She reached for her Companion's hands. "How did you get away?!"

"Ren saved me," El said, a small, sad smile twitching across her lips. "Got lucky, like I said. Stabbed the bastard in the back. I've never seen anyone like 'im—the Stalker. Had eyes like—"

In the back. Beth didn't hear anything El said after that. That had been where Edward was stabbed.

El seemed to take her silence as shock. She pulled her hand free and patted Beth's. "Sorry if it's a bit much. Truth is, I ain't told anyone else." She let out a relieved sigh. "It's nice t' get it out."

"Oh, I- I can imagine." Beth walked towards her dresses, running a finger across them. Some were silk, some velvet, some cotton, though she barely felt the difference as her mind raced. She tried to still her thundering heart before she asked her next question. "When did this happen? Your father, being- being attacked by the Stalker?"

"Weren't long ago." El chewed her lip thoughtfully. "Sorry, I've never been good with keepin' track o' time. Just before we came 'ere. Two weeks? Then Lord Landrum found us an'... 'ere we are."

"I see." Beth gulped, trying to quell the sob rising in her throat. "El, would you excuse me for a moment? I must refresh myself before—" She waved a hand vaguely at her dresses.

"'Course," El said. "D'you mind if I look through 'em?"

"That's fine." Beth was already half out of the door. "I shan't be long."

With the door closed, she leaned against it, letting out a quivering breath.

"Edward, what have you done?" she whispered.

Before her trembling legs gave way entirely, she stumbled to one of the spare bedrooms. She needed to be alone, to think, and to work out how, by the Mother, she was supposed to get to the bottom of this.

Edward cannot be the Stalker, can he? she asked herself over and over, terrified at the possible answer.

A vicious voice whispered in the back of her mind, telling her she didn't really know her brother after all. How could she? He'd been unwell for some time, kept sheltered away, barely allowed to spend time with her.

But could he really be a killer?

In the empty bedroom, she threw herself onto the bed, ignoring the cloud of dust that rose from it as she smothered her head with a pillow, letting out a cry of anguish. Some part of her had a horrible, gut-wrenching feeling that her dear brother *was* involved in the death of El and Ren's father. It all seemed too much of a coincidence.

Was this why Father had taken El and her brother in, as some kind of recompense? The thought was almost too much to bear.

In the stillness of the neglected room, she sobbed and sobbed with no idea what she would do next: hide this awful truth or reveal it and ruin her family.

CHAPTER 12

THE DRESS

E l had never seen so many fine dresses, let alone in one place. She wondered, as she ran her fingers along them, how Beth could possibly have cause or opportunity to wear them all.

Glancing towards the door, she pulled a dress from the wooden rail on which it hung and held it against herself. It would swamp her, given Beth had the curves of a noblewoman and she the body of a half-starved Scrubber, hips narrow and chest almost flat.

That's a lifetime o' not eatin' enough for you, she thought bitterly.

Even so, when she looked at herself in the mirror, she smiled. The deep burgundy of the fabric brought out the blue of her eyes and complimented the flush of her cheeks. The hairstyle Beth had given her that morning was still relatively tidy, and she admired the braids and the gleam of her blonde hair. For the briefest moment, she dared to imagine that she had succeeded in finding her and Ren a different life, just like she'd promised.

But then she remembered the truth of it. She and Ren had found work; that was the best they could hope for. Even if she wore one of Beth's fine dresses, it wouldn't make her a noble, wouldn't take away from all the hardships she'd experienced in her short life. Living here, being with Beth and seeing the luxuries she enjoyed on a daily basis, had allowed her to forget who she was. Yet talking about Da's death with Beth had brought it all back to the surface.

She remembered Lord Landrum's words clearly. "...you and your brother will never speak of the pouch or anything else concerning your father's untimely demise in relation to the Estamore name."

Pausing, her arms drooped with the weight of the gown. She'd become too comfortable in her brief time here, allowing herself to be drawn into Beth's upcoming wedding, to live the life of someone born into far more fortunate circumstances than her own. But, even then, things here weren't so simple as fancy clothes, rich foods, balls, and dancing; there were secrets in this place, and there were questions to be answered, not least of all about Da's death.

Edward Estamore. Why'd 'e send such a chill down my spine? Could 'e be linked to it all, somehow?

The door opened and she jumped, clutching the dress to her chest. She spun around to find Beth, slightly red-eyed.

"That's a good choice," Beth said. "Mother likes that one, too."

If there was the hint of a strain in Beth's voice, El had no chance to ask about it before the dress was half-snatched from her hands.

"Now, we must find a dress for you."

El gasped. "A dress for me? I thought I'd simply wear—"

"Only the best for my Companion," Beth said. Looking her up and down, she added, "Besides, I want us both to look our best. You'll be coming to live with me after the wedding, after all, and this will be a chance to see your new home and to meet your new master, Lord Ashford. And make a good first impression."

"Live wi' you?" El suddenly realized the implications of her new role. "What– what of my brother?"

Beth raised an eyebrow. "What of him?"

"Will 'e come too?"

Beth paused. "I hadn't thought of that. I don't suppose you'll want to be..." She pursed her lips. "Leave it to me, El. I shall do what I can."

El nodded.

"Now," Beth studied her again, "you're a lot slimmer than me." Her lips pinched tightly. "You're *so* lucky." She slapped an aggressive hand against her stomach. "Mother always says I eat too much. That I must watch my figure if I'm to please my future husband." Her eyes dropped to her chest for a brief moment. "Anyway, I'm sure I still have dresses from when I was younger. They might be a little short, but they should fit you better elsewhere."

El frowned, scrunching her face in confusion at the notion. "Eat too much? Surely you simply eat what you're given. I'm only this way 'cos we never 'ad enough to eat. It's not... it's not a *good* thing, Beth."

Beth's lips twitched, as though she struggled to comprehend what El had said. "You're slender," she said finally. "It's the desirable way to be for any fashionable lady."

"Slender?" El snorted. "You nobles are bloody strange. I'd love to 'ave the chance to eat *too much*! I—" Seeing her mistress's mouth draw downwards and her eyes gloss over, El stopped herself. "I mean... please don't think there's anythin' good 'bout a life of starvin', Beth." She reached out for her hand. "You're, well, you're lovely. Just as you are. Thought it the moment I first saw you."

Beth returned the touch, sniffing. "Thank you, El. That's very sweet, even if it's not true." As she smiled, she seemed to shake off the sadness that had overcome her, seamless as putting on a mask. "Now, let's find a dress for you and we can start getting ready!"

El wondered why Beth was so quick to dismiss her words when she took on Lady Oren's harsh criticisms so readily. Truly, she wasn't sure she'd ever understand these nobles and their odd priorities.

"Oh!" Beth exclaimed suddenly. "Look, look! This one's perfect." She pulled out a long, deep blue dress.

El had never seen anything so beautiful.

Beth held it up against her, tilting her head from side to side. "Yes, it suits you. Compliments your eyes."

El looked down at the dress, seeing the fine, white lace trim around the neck, the deep, jewel-like hue of the material and how it seemed to shimmer in the light. "Are you sure, Beth? Won't it be a bit much for—"

"Nonsense," Beth insisted, though El noted a glimmer of mischief in her eyes. "Mother might have a word or two to say, but you're my Companion. I may dress you how I please."

She touched El's left ear lobe. "A shame I can't give you some of my jewelry too." She wrinkled her nose. "Mother might burst from anger if I did that." She giggled, holding the dress up expectantly. "Let's try this on you then."

"What, you want me to—"

"Take your dress off? Yes. That is how you change clothes after all."

El fiddled with her sleeves. Most of her bruises had faded by now, though some of Da's worst outbursts over the years had left their scars. She had a shift underneath her dress; would Beth expect her to take that off too? She pursed her lips and pulled her dress over her head, trying not to overthink it too much. Beth clearly meant no harm.

Standing before her mistress in her thin, white shift, arms held awkwardly across her stomach, she felt like a child.

"Keep the shift on, I'll just get you a..." Beth handed her the dress, then began rifling through a pile of clothing behind El. "There must be one here," she muttered, throwing items around without a care for where they landed.

When Beth stood back up, some of her black curls had fallen loose about her face. She blew them away with a puff of air, holding up an item the likes of which El had never seen. There was a triumphant look on her face. "Got one!" She didn't seem to notice El's discomfort at being so scantily dressed in front of her.

El hooked the dress on a nearby rail then took the strange item from Beth, holding it at arms' length. There were boned ridges running its length. "What, uh... what is it?"

Beth scoffed. "What? You don't know?"

El shook her head. "Never seen one o' these afore in my life!"

Beth blinked in bewilderment. "Hm. Well, I- I must confess I don't know the fashions of the Scr—the commoners." She pulled at a curl of hair, giving El an apologetic smile. "It's a corset. It helps to accentuate your figure. Here, I'll show you."

Beth took the garment back from El and wrapped it around her waist, moving to El's back to fasten it. There was a fierce tugging and she gasped as the ridges in the corset tightened against her sides, squeezing her ribcage.

"What you doin' Beth, torturin' me?" she asked, breathlessly.

Standing back, Beth pointed her towards the mirror. "See, accentuates your figure. That's what Mother says, anyway. I've been wearing them since I was twelve. Mother told me the younger I started the better! This is an old one, but it fits you well." She continued tugging on the back of the garment, grunting with the effort.

"Oof, Beth, that's a little—"

"The tighter the better! That's what Mother always says." Beth peered over El's shoulder and beamed at her in the mirror. "Wow, look at your waist. So tiny. Truly, you have a lovely figure. I'll have to watch out—Ashford might take a fancy to you, instead!" She laughed too loudly.

El turned to face her in an effort to keep her from tightening the garment further. "Beth," she said, taking her hands, "don't be silly, that'll never 'appen."

Something closed in Beth's face. She pinched her lips, giving El a narrow-eyed stare that mirrored her mother. "No," she said sharply, "of course not."

"Sorry, I- I din't mean to offend you," El said, harshly reminded that no matter how friendly she might be, Beth was her superior.

As if reading her mind, Beth's expression softened. "We'd better get ready properly now. No more time for chatter." She finished tying El's corset. "Your dress will fit well now. You'll need to help me into my corset; I can talk you through it."

Later with El and Beth in their dresses, their hair freshly styled, and their cheeks pinched to a red blush, they stood side-by-side before the floor-length mirror. El observed the way Beth stood and attempted to copy it, though she had neither the natural grace nor beauty to do so.

She rolled her eyes at herself. *What you doin', El? Carryin' on like a bloody Lady!*

El could wear all the fine dresses in the world but it wouldn't change who and what she was: a Scrubber and an orphan. She reminded herself Ren would be working hard in the kitchens, barely allowed the luxury of a break. And here she was, playing dress up with a naïve, young noblewoman who had no concept of what life was like outside of these walls.

A bell rang from downstairs.

Beth grinned, looping her arm through El's and tugging her onward. "Mother and Father must be ready. Oh, I can't wait for you to meet him. He's simply wonderful." Making for the door, Beth tugged her onwards.

Suddenly, El was overcome with an urge she couldn't explain or deny. "Wait," she said, speaking before she could question the thought. "Can I- could I just say goodbye to Ren?"

Beth raised an eyebrow. "Very well but be quick. And take the servants' stairs."

El headed for the rear of the house, pleased the servants' stairs took her closer to her real destination—their bedroom. She entered and knelt beside her mattress, lifting it up. Without thinking, she retrieved the wooden box. Lifting the lid, she took Ma's necklace. It shone even in the dim shadows of their room.

It *called* to her.

Don't be ridiculous, she told herself.

Yet, it was what had drawn her here, wasn't it? Some inexplicable impulse, some quiet inner voice telling her to take it with her, that it would protect her.

Protect me against what though? she wondered, frowning as she tucked the necklace down the front of her dress, where it nestled between her cleavage. There was no chance of it slipping any lower with how tightly Beth had laced her corset. She was surprised at how well concealed it was, noting that even her small bosom seemed full in her borrowed outfit.

As El hurried along the corridor to the front door, she noted Lord and Lady Estamore, dressed in fur capes, stood beside Beth in the hall. Master Edward, who looked no less weary than he had when they'd met earlier, hovered at the edge of the scene as though unsure how to behave. When he saw El watching him, he gave a nervous twitch of the mouth—what she imagined he thought was a smile—and bowed his head. El couldn't shake the unease bristling along her spine at the sight of him, though she bowed her head in return.

"Oh, Elizabetha, really," Lady Oren said, drawing El's attention. To her shock, *she* was being appraised by the woman's ever-judgmental gaze. "A simple, servant's dress would have sufficed."

Beth pulled El close. "She's my Companion, Mother, and I shall dress her how I please."

"Young lady! How dare you speak to me in such—"

"Now, Oren," Lord Landrum said, placing a hand on his wife's shoulder, "Elizabetha is simply stepping into the position she will soon find herself in." His mustache twitched. "We can hardly begrudge her that."

El gave an awkward, jerking bow to Lady Oren, as though she had something to apologize for. Inwardly, she scorned herself.

"As you say, Landrum. But you'd best keep a close eye on her at dinner, Elizabetha. We know her manners are questionable at best." With that, she hooked Lord Landrum's arm and pulled him through the front door, which a black-clad servant opened for them, and they bustled through without a backward glance.

Edward stepped towards Beth, proffering an arm. "You'd think it was she wedding Ashford, little sister, with how concerned she is about his opinion." He winked at El before leading Beth towards the door. "Don't let it get to you. You know what—" His words faded as the siblings walked through the door.

El hurried after them. It was time to meet Beth's future husband.

CHAPTER 13

THE FAMILY

As the carriage drew up the path towards Branton Manor, Beth's heart raced. It hadn't been long since their last visit, and she had been content to wait until the wedding to see her betrothed again. But knowing Ashford had requested her presence for dinner, that he *wanted* to see her, her happiness was all-consuming—enough to set aside her fears about her brother, at least for the time being.

But then her mother pointed out it was unusual to have a dinner like this before the ceremony, and her happiness turned to anxiety.

"Perhaps he wants to be sure of his decision," Oren said, giving Beth a trenchant stare. "Best do all you can to confirm this is the right choice, Elizabetha. For all our sakes, this marriage must—"

"Mother, really," Edward cut in. "Beth is not a fool. There's no need for such talk. I, for one, see nothing but a positive in Lord Ashford's generous invitation."

Beth smiled at him gratefully, ignoring the knife of anxiety driving into her gut when she met his gaze.

Their mother huffed, turning to peer from the carriage window. "Hmm. Let us hope you are right."

Edward squeezed Beth's knee. He looked better than he had earlier, his face less drawn, eyes less bloodshot.

As they left the carriage, Beth nudged El. "Just watch and listen. As my Companion, you'll be seated close to me. Speak when spoken to. You'll be fine."

El's lips pinched together as though she wanted to argue, but she gave a curt nod and said nothing.

Beth hurried ahead to join Edward, linking her arm through his. "I'm so pleased you're here," she whispered as they approached the manor door. And she was surprised to find she meant it, truly, despite her fears about his possible involvement in El's father's death.

Edward smiled down at her. "Me too."

Ahead, the door to the manor was opened by Lord Ashford himself. He beamed at the Estamore family, his eyes meeting hers for a moment longer than anyone else's. Beth's head swam with giddiness.

"Ah, good evening!" he said, standing aside for them to enter. "Please, the winter chill is upon us. Let's warm ourselves by the fire whilst the dinner is set out."

"Thank you, Lord Ashford," her mother said. "We were most pleased to receive your kind invitation."

"Of course," Ashford said. "The wedding isn't far away, I know, but I had a mind to learn more about my future bride—and her family." He threw Beth a wink that left her weak at the knees. "My man there will take your cloaks. This way to the reception room."

Ashford turned down the hall and headed for an open door through which Beth could see the flickering light of a healthily roaring hearth. She mirrored her mother and father in removing her cape and handing it to the red-headed young man who waited with his hand outstretched.

"Thank you," she said to him, and he flinched as though unused to being spoken to.

His freckled cheeks flushed red. "You are welcome, m'lady."

Beth ensured El was at her back and hurried to join her family who had already entered the reception room. Before allowing her through the door, her mother pulled her to the side. She tucked back a loose curl from Beth's face, gave each cheek a pinch, and smoothed down the front of her burgundy dress.

Nerves fluttered through Beth's body, her stomach suddenly knotting in on itself, her palms clammy. She stepped through the door to find Ashford handing her father and Edward a glass of Blood Whiskey each.

"A particularly potent batch from my father's personal stocks," Ashford said. "I've been saving it for the right occasion" He beamed towards Beth. "Elizabetha, please, come sit next to me."

Beth made her way towards him, leaving El hovering in the doorway. Lord Denys was present too, standing close to the hearth, a drink in hand.

He held it up to her as she walked past, muttering, "Good evening, Mistress Elizabetha."

As she moved to join Ashford, his eyes drifted behind her to where El stood in the doorway. "Who's this?" he asked, raising a perfect, dark eyebrow.

"Oh, that's my, um…"

"She's Elizabetha's new Companion," her mother explained. "We can send her away, if you would rather—"

"Nonsense." Ashford waved El over, his pale eyes locked to hers. "What's your name, girl?"

"Ellana, m'lord." El's eyes were cast down, her hands clasped at her front, more demure than Beth had ever seen her.

"Scrubber?" Ashford asked, turning to Beth.

"Oh, uh…" Beth let out a hesitant chuckle. "Yes, Ashford." She cast El an apologetic smile, though her Companion's eyes were still on the carpet.

"I see. A worthy find, Landrum." Lord Ashford took Beth's hand in his and said a little too loudly, "Ellana, you will take care of my dear Beth, won't you? There are so many responsibilities with becoming the lady of a house. Being Lady Branton will be a new challenge."

He gave her hand a squeeze before standing. He didn't allow El to respond, instead clapping his hands so loudly it made her father jump, splashing bright red droplets of Blood Whiskey on the white collar of his shirt, stark as fresh blood.

"Come now, everyone! Let us go to the dining room where, I believe, dinner will soon be served."

Beth glanced at El, biting her lip to hold back a giggle of nervous excitement, and found her Companion staring at Ashford's back with narrowed eyes.

As everyone else followed her betrothed from the room, she touched El's arm and nodded towards where he had just been standing. "Isn't he wonderful?"

El blinked, glancing around the room as though just remembering where she was. "Hmm?" She rubbed at her temples. "Sorry, I thought I heard—" She shook her head. "Never mind. Come on, everyone else 'as gone."

CHAPTER 14

THE EYES

As they entered the dining room, El's mouth watered at the sight of the food spread across the table. She was still unaccustomed to being allowed to indulge in such finery —and wasn't sure she ever would be.

Lord Ashford beamed towards the door where El and Beth stood. "I hope it's not improper of me, Lord Landrum, to ask that my future wife takes the opposite end of the table to me. A place that will be rightfully hers in a mere handful of weeks."

Lord Landrum, who'd been about to seat himself in that very position, visibly bristled, his mustache twitching.

Lady Oren was at her husband's side in an instant, taking his hand and moving him to sit beside her. "Of course, Lord Ashford. We thank you for the kind sentiment."

El had to hold back a snort at seeing the usually proud Estamores with ruffled feathers.

"Won't you sit next to me, El?" Beth asked, pulling her attention back.

She hurried to take the seat Beth directed her to. "'Course."

"Wait." Lord Ashford held out a hand and El stopped in her tracks.

She turned to find him appraising her. His eyes were the

bright, clear blue of a summer's day—the kind Ma had loved so much for taking her for walks along the river and promising they'd have a better life one day. His gaze was almost hypnotic in its intensity and El found herself pinned to the spot.

Aware of the growing silence, she straightened herself. "Yes, m'lord?"

"I would like to learn more about your father's death. Killed by the Stalker, I'm told?" Lord Ashford looked to Lord Landrum, who nodded curtly, not making eye contact with El.

She cleared her throat awkwardly, not having expected such a blunt approach to such a gruesome matter. "O-of course, m'lord. P'raps after dinner, we might—"

"Nonsense!" Lord Ashford patted the chair to his left. "What better time is there to speak of the goings on in our beloved city? Such awful news of late. Perhaps in speaking of it we might process our distress."

El glanced at Beth, who gave an almost imperceptible nod. Head down, El scurried to the chair beside Lord Ashford.

"Now that the table is arranged, let us eat. Please, help yourselves, we don't stand on ceremony here." Lord Ashford picked up a knife and clinked it against his wine glass. "To the EtherFather, we send our praise for His ever-present protection and wisdom. We are blessed, truly."

"Well spoken, Lord Ashford," Lady Oren acknowledged, holding up her own glass of wine.

"Thank you, Lady Oren," Lord Ashford replied.

El caught the briefest of glimpses between Ashford and Lord Denys, who was sitting at Beth's right, before his eyes flitted to Beth.

"How goes the planning, Elizabetha?" Lord Ashford asked his bride-to-be. "Our wedding day fast approaches, it seems. Truly, I am counting down the days."

Beth giggled—a high, tinkling sound that seemed reserved for the presence of this man. "They're going well, my lord. Mother and I have been—"

"What did I say? Call me Ashford. Please."

Beth blushed. "Ashford, yes."

Edward cleared his throat. "I, for one, am interested in hearing about the business prospects this marriage brings. For our mines, especially."

"A talk I will be glad to have with both you and your father, Edward." Lord Ashford delicately placed a forkful of lamb in his mouth. "After dinner."

"Please," Beth said. "Don't hold back on my account. I would be glad to learn more about the business. About the family mines and how they are run."

Lord Denys let out a brash laugh. "A woman interested in the mines! What's next?" He cocked his head, casting Beth a frown. "Ash is a strict follower of the EtherTemple. Women are not business minded. The EtherMother teaches—"

"I know what the EtherMother teaches," Beth cut in. "I simply meant I wish only to help my husband in all ways I can."

"I think it's stupid women are taught such nonsense," El said without thinking. "Beth's as clever a person as I've ever met."

Lady Oren gasped, and tension fell over the room like a blade hanging over the table.

Beth raised her eyebrows, her mouth pinched tight, and El questioned herself immediately. She'd sought to stand up for Beth, to support her mistress, but perhaps she'd misread the situation.

To her shock, Lord Ashford let out a raucous laugh. "My word, Elizabetha! Where *did* you find her?" He studied El again, those eyes piercing her very flesh. "A hardened Scrubber, indeed. Mm, losing your father no doubt left its mark that you should feel so able to speak your mind."

"My Da were no loss t' me." El lifted her chin, irritated by the mockery in his tone. "Your EtherFather seems t' looks down on women. But I'm a woman. I've 'ad to look after my brother, long as I can remember. I've kept 'im alive because the *man* who was s'posed to cared only for the drink. I'd say I've earned the right to speak my mind."

Lady Oren's face contorted with rage. "How dare you speak so out of turn, girl! Lord Ashford, you must accept our apologies on behalf of this wretched Scrubber. She is new to our household; her manners are not yet—"

Lord Ashford held up his hand, stopping the speech in its tracks. "Lady Oren, really, despite what Denys says about my loyalty to the EtherFather's teachings, there is room for all views here. I am not a man to repress the opinions of the ignorant. How else will she learn?" His lips quirked as he turned to El once more. "It's obvious Ellana had a difficult upbringing and has not felt the guidance of the EtherFather in her life. To add to that, there is the loss of a parent. When was he killed, Ellana?"

El peered around the table, meeting Beth's gaze. Despite her earlier bravado, she felt completely deflated with all eyes on her. But then Beth gently smiled and nodded.

El closed her eyes and a flash of that awful, blood-drenched scene flooded her mind. "Two weeks ago, m'lord," she whispered.

"So recent," Lord Ashford said sympathetically. "And he was killed by the Stalker?"

"Yes, m'lord," El muttered, sensing there would be no use trying to deny it given Lord Landrum had clearly already divulged this information.

Lord Ashford raised his whiskey glass and appeared to study the liquid within. "And yet here you are, facing the world. I find that commendable." He sipped his drink. "When my parents died, I confess, I went slightly mad." He let out a laugh so full of mirth, it rippled around the table. Soon everyone joined in— except, El noted, Lord Denys, whose eyes were downturned.

"Indeed, Lord Ashford. The loss of any parent is a burden. That was why I felt compelled to offer young Ellana a position in our household," Lord Landrum said. "Her father was a worker in my mines. A... loyal man. How else was I to repay his service?"

El swallowed the compulsion to call out his lies. She glanced at Beth, who was looking at her father with a gleam of pride.

Should I tell 'er 'bout the pouch? The truth 'bout her father's apparent *charity?* El wondered. Then she realized the truth; *she* didn't even know what the pouch meant. Why bring up what she couldn't fully explain?

"Most charitable of you, Lord Landrum. But I must ask, Ellana, how is it you know your father was killed by the Stalker?"

At that, Lord Landrum let out a strangled cough. Once he'd regained himself, he took a sip of whiskey and said, "We've already discussed this, have we not, Ashford? What the City Guard found in their home could have been carried out by no one else. Besides, are you sure such a topic is suitable for the dinner table?" He laughed slightly, though it was a half-choked sound. "I've not the stomach for it myself. With ladies present, maybe it is a topic for another time."

El glared at him. *He's truly hidin' somethin'. P'raps Beth deserves to know that at least.*

"I apologize. Perhaps you're right." Lord Ashford tilted his glass towards them all. "Sometimes my curiosity gets the better of me. My medical studies, you see. I've been more intrigued to read—"

"He was there," El blurted the words firmly and loudly, wanting everyone to hear.

Lord Ashford turned to her, mouth agape. "I beg your pardon."

"The Stalker. He was there, when I found me Da's body."

"Well, that *is* curious!" Lord Ashford took a long sip of whiskey, seemingly mulling over her statement.

"How awful. How did you escape?" asked Edward earnestly. A small part of El considered perhaps he was simply a good liar like his father.

Closing her eyes again, she forced herself to recall that evening. Almost immediately, those red eyes returned to her, and she imagined she once more felt a hand around her throat, smelled the blood in the air. There was an otherworldly scream. "My brother," she finally answered. "Ren, 'e saved me. Stabbed the Stalker in the back with a lucky strike." She gulped. "An' we ran."

Lady Oren let out an anguished cry, one so full of horror it shocked El to find she had a heart. At the same time, Beth shouted, "Oh, El!" and Lord Landrum slammed his cutlery onto his plate with such force, food and chips of porcelain went flying. But it was Edward's behavior that drew everyone's attention, for from his lips came a low, guttural whine, like that of a kicked dog. His whole body began to tremble so violently that the table shook, clinking the dinnerware laid upon it. El was certain spittle frothed at the corners his mouth before his head slumped forward onto his plate.

Ellana... a voice whispered, making her jolt.

Glancing around, she noted Lord Ashford's attention was on her. She frowned, uncomfortable beneath his gaze. With the commotion, however, her focus—and Lord Ashford's—were quickly drawn back to Edward.

"Edward!" Lady Oren cried, leaping to her feet.

Beth's lips trembled as she asked, "What's wrong with him?"

Forgetting the strange whisper in the chaos, El rushed to her mistress's side.

Lord Ashford got to his feet, rolling up the sleeves of his fine white shirt. "Everyone, stop what you're doing." From around his neck, he pulled out a long, silver chain, and began making his way around the table to Edward. "Denys, fetch my medical kit, just in case this doesn't work. Landrum, lift his head. Hold it firm."

Lord Landrum did as he was told, though his hands shook.

El stood back with Beth and Lady Oren, mother and daughter clinging to each other, their distress and despair evident. Edward was still making that strange whining sound, deep in his throat, and El found she couldn't tear her eyes away.

As Lord Landrum held his son's head up, Edward's eyes fluttered and rolled in their sockets. "He needs—"

"I know," replied Lord Ashford. On the end of his necklace was a silver vial. He twisted it, lifting off a small cap. A long, thin strip of silver came with the cap, along which was layered a bright red powder. It was the exact color of the EtherStone glinting on a ring on Lord Ashford's finger.

El subconsciously leaned forward, curiosity burning in her chest.

"Lord Ashford, really, are you sure?" Lord Landrum said, aghast. "From your own stores, I- I—"

"Hush, we have no time to waste." Lord Ashford leaned over Edward. "If you can hear me Edward, I want you to take a deep inhale when I say." To Lord Landrum he said, "Keep his head still." Holding out the strip of silver with that blood-red powder, he placed it beneath Edward's left nostril. With his free hand, he pinched the other nostril closed. "Now, Edward! Inhale!"

There was a brief pause—El held her breath, almost afraid of what would come next. And then Edward took in a loud breath, inhaling the powder. After a few more moments, he let out a long sigh, relief palpable.

Beside her, Lady Oren and Beth rushed towards Edward.

"Give him space," Lord Ashford said firmly, holding his arms out in a wide arc to stop them. Despite his young age, his command of the room was impressive. Still kneeling beside Edward, he placed a hand on his arm. "Edward, can you hear me?"

Edward was holding his head up, though he visibly trembled and leaned heavily against Beth who stood beside him. A groan escaped his lips; it was an altogether more human sound this time. He lifted a hand to rub his eyes. "Yes," he mumbled weakly. "By the Father, I'm sorry. I don't know what came over me."

Beth placed an arm around his shoulder. "Don't worry, please. We- we just have to be glad Ashford," she grinned at her future husband, eyes full of adoration, "was so quick."

Removing his hand from his eyes, Edward blinked up at Lord Ashford and opened his mouth to speak. But El didn't hear his words. All she saw was his eyes.

Red.

Red like blood.

Red like the Stalker's eyes.

"No!" she cried.

Everyone turned to her.

"El?" Beth came towards her, hands outstretched as though approaching a wild animal. "What's wrong?"

"It's- it's him." She found herself stepping backwards, gaze locked onto Edward, the rush of blood a roar in her ears.

Beth gently placed a hand on her elbow. There was concern on her face, yes, but something more—was that a glimmer of fear in her eyes? "Hush, hush, now," she whispered. "Everything is fine, El."

"No!" El pulled away. "He was there! It were 'im! He killed- he killed my—"

"Elizabetha, take Ellana to my study," Lord Ashford said in a cool, commanding tone that brooked no argument. "I'll be in to see you both once I've tended to Edward."

El allowed herself to be led away, though she kept her eyes on Edward. She was surprised to find only confusion looking back at her.

Are 'is eyes back to their normal color?

Did I imagine it? she dared ask herself.

No. The sense of pure terror she'd experienced couldn't be imagined or ignored. Her body still shook with it, her heart still pounded. It had been visceral, instinctive.

She felt numb as Beth shepherded her back to the reception room.

"Sit," Beth said gently, directing her to an armchair before the still burning fire in the study. Kneeling, she grasped El's hands. "Are you well?"

"I- I thought it were 'im. His eyes..." El put a hand over her face, seeing the Stalker before her again. Finally, she took a deep inhale, unable to hold back the truth. "I think your brother's the Stalker, Beth."

CHAPTER 15

THE PRAYER

Beth let out a strangled gasp. Perhaps if she'd spoken, she could have maintained a level of composure, could have kept her brother's dreadful secret. But the shock of it was too fresh, the connection having been made only hours before when El told her of Ren stabbing their father's killer in the back. She'd been trying desperately to shut it away but to hear El confirm the suspicion now, to utter the possibility of her own beloved brother being the monstrous killer stalking Alpinside, was simply too much.

"Beth?" El drew her attention back. "Aren't you gonna say somethin'?"

Beth stood and turned away from her Companion, gazing into the fire. "What's there to say?" She spoke more to herself than to El. She heard El stand and felt a touch on her shoulder. When she twisted around, her Companion's face was contorted with anger.

"Aren't you gonna say anythin'? Argue wi' me? Say it can't be true? Aren't you gonna, I dunno, tell me not t' speak such- such horse shit?"

Beth flinched at the anger emanating from El; she had never heard such coarse language. "I can't argue with you." She sighed, her body shuddering as she fought back a sob. "I think- I think you might be right, El." Her bottom lip trembled at the weight of those words. *My brother, the Stalker.*

El stepped back, eyes flitting to the door, then to Beth, a hand drifting to her mouth. "Shit. We 'ave t' tell someone."

Beth had feared she'd say that. She had to tread carefully, had to win El over so she could regain a hold over the situation. She had to think about what to do; how to protect her family. *Protect a killer, you mean.*

She let out a long breath, ignoring the terrifying thought. "I think we should wait."

El's mouth dropped open. "How can you say that? He's *murdered* people! Innocent people."

Beth stepped forward. "I need time. *We* need time, if you'll help me. I want to find out the truth."

"But we know the bloody truth! He—"

"I know. Your father." Beth pursed her lips. She sank into the chair in which El had been sitting moments ago, suddenly completely drained. "I don't know what to say, except that deep down, there's a voice telling me there's more to this. The Stalker... That's *not* my brother. He's not evil. He's not a monster."

"Beth. I saw it wi' me own eyes. He *is* a monster." It was El's turn to kneel in front of her. Beth met her Companion's gaze. El's flinty blue eyes were hardened with resolve. "We've gotta tell someone. He has t' be stopped."

Beth's lip trembled harder, and she bit down on it, determined not to cry. She had to be strong, keep a clear head. *Mother, help me. Guide me.*

El stood and began to pace. "Wait." She turned back to Beth. "'Ow did you know? That your brother were—"

"The Stalker?" Beth was amazed at how firmly she said the words; there was no hint of strain, despite the tightness in her throat. "I had my suspicions as soon as you told me about your brother stabbing the Stalker in the back."

"Why?"

"Edward returned home late one night about three weeks ago.

He'd been attacked. Mother and Father tried to keep the truth from me, but I saw- I saw..." She began to sob, no longer able to hold back the flood of despair washing over her.

El knelt again, taking hold of her hand. "What, Beth? What did you see?"

"A knife," she whispered. "A knife in his back."

El's jaw clenched. "I see." She released Beth's hand and stood, turning away. "There's no denyin' it then, is there? He bloody did it. He killed me Da."

Beth huffed air through her lips, dashing away the tears rolling down her cheeks. "It looks that way."

El looked over her shoulder towards Beth. "You know what the funny part is?"

Beth sniffed. "What?"

"It's not even Da's death that upsets me most." She moved to sit opposite Beth, hands running down the length of her skirts. "It's all the other victims. Those poor young women."

Beth's stomach lurched. "Women?" *Of course there are others.*

El scowled. "Surely you know 'bout the Stalker's other victims?"

"Oh. I- I know about the killer. I've heard Mother and Father speak of him in passing. Seen some of the articles in Father's newspaper. But I, uh, I haven't—"

There was a sharp rap on the door. Without waiting for either Beth or El to speak, the door opened, and Ashford came into view.

Beth gasped, hurrying to dab away any stray tears on her face. She made to stand, but Ashford was in front of her in a flash, gently pushing her back. He leaned down, his face drawing level with hers. There was genuine concern in the tightness of his lips and the furrow of his brow. That he should feel so worried for her warmed her heart, despite everything unfolding.

"That must have been a shock for you," he said quietly. "Your brother is—"

"He's been unwell for a while," Beth said, nodding. "But I didn't... I've never seen *that* happen to him."

Ashford clasped her hand, his skin cool—a relief to her flushed skin—and gave her a sympathetic smile. "He's better now. My medical training was put to good use."

He turned to El, who sat staring into the fireplace. "I'm sure it was scary for both of you." He stood. "If you would both come back to the dining room, perhaps we might discuss an idea I have."

As Ashford walked to the door, El asked, "What's wrong with him?"

Her betrothed stopped, raised an eyebrow, and snorted. "Asking such questions doesn't mean you'd understand the answer were I to give it to you." He lifted the pocket watch from his waistcoat and clicked it open. "Come. I have duties to attend to. We must conclude our dinner."

As he retreated from the room, Beth frowned at El. "You shouldn't speak like that, you know. Not without being addressed. Especially to those who are—"

El's lip curled into a sneer. "Above me? Beth, after what we've just learned, you're lucky I don't fetch the bloody City Guard. You're lucky I trust 'em 'bout as far as I can throw 'em." She lifted her chin defiantly, a fire in her eyes. "We need t' talk properly. 'Bout what we're gonna do. Because we are gonna do *somethin'*." With that, she made to follow Ashford.

"Excuse me?" Beth drew herself up. "Do not make the mistake, Ellana, of believing you can make the decisions here."

El's eyes hardened though she bowed her head. "Of course, Elizabetha. How foolish of me. I'm jus' a lowly Scrubber, after all."

Beth deflated in an instant, shame warming her cheeks. "No, El, I'm sorry. That's not what I—"

El held a hand up and stalked from the room. "Don't worry. I know me place."

As quickly as it had flared up, Beth's anger melted away. She let out a long, weary sigh and cast her eyes to the ceiling, sending up a silent prayer to the EtherMother. *Please, protect my brother from whatever afflicts him. He's not a bad person... He's not a killer.*

"Is he?" she whispered.

The crackling of the fire was her only reply.

Back in the dining room, Beth took her seat at the opposite end of the table from Ashford. Edward gave her a weak smile. His eyes were bloodshot and there was a sheen of sweat on his brow, but otherwise he seemed alert.

She forced a smile in return, trying to block out the echoing whisper in her mind saying over and over, *He's a killer, he's a killer.*

"Now that we're all here," Ashford said. There was a pregnant pause as he met everyone's gaze in turn. "I have a proposal. A favor, of sorts."

"After what you've done to help Edward, Lord Ashford, we will be happy to grant any favor you ask," her father said.

Oren nodded vehemently in agreement.

"It's precisely because of what's happened with Edward that I make this proposal." Ashford studied her brother for a moment before continuing. "I wish for Edward to live here, at Branton Manor."

"What?" Edward gasped. "Ashford, I hardly think—"

"Please," Ashford said preemptively, "hear me out. You are unwell, are you not?"

Edward's gaze dropped to his plate, shoulders slumping. Beth saw then the toll it had taken on him to come to dinner this evening.

"Edward has been troubled for a long time," her mother said candidly. "Lately, though—"

"His symptoms have worsened?" Ashford asked.

"Yes," Edward answered. "My illness has always been managed with EtherStone. With our family stocks dwindling and the pressure from investors from the mainla—"

"Edward," her father lightly growled, his face blanching, "now is not the time to speak of such matters." He cast Beth a glance.

"My apologies, Lord Ashford. My son has had a shock, he does not know of what he speaks."

Edward scoffed. "Father, how can you say such—"

Ashford held up a hand silencing them both. "Arguing will get us nowhere. I'm all too aware of the situation regarding Ether-Stone, Lord Landrum. Please don't concern yourself about such matters. I will do what I can to help."

Unsure as to the meaning of what was being said, Beth reached to take Edward's hand. Despite everything, he was her brother, and he was in pain. He met her gaze, tears glistening in his eyes.

"What do you mean to achieve by having my brother here, Ashford?" she asked directly.

"To study him. To understand his illness. To find—"

"A cure?" Edward looked up, the hope in his voice almost breaking Beth's heart. Why hadn't she known how ill her brother was? She scowled towards her parents, though their attention was too focused on Ashford to notice. Why had she been kept in the dark for so long?

Treated like a child. Like a fool, she told herself. *And El... She's the only one who speaks openly to me, who affords me the truth—no matter how uncomfortable it is.*

Ashford swirled his whiskey before finishing it off. "I can't make any promises, but it's my hope that in studying your illness, I might be able to understand it. Thereby helping you manage it. And *perhaps*, one day, to find a cure."

Oren leapt from her chair, rushing to Ashford's side and kissing his cheek. "A cure! Even just the chance of it would be wonderful. Did you hear, Edward?"

"I heard, Mother," he said, chuckling softly. "I heard." There was restraint in his voice that told Beth he was holding back from hoping too much.

She wondered how much he truly knew about his illness, and about the violence he had enacted because of it—for surely that was the way of it. Her brother had always been a kind, gentle person. His ailment had distorted his mind, it seemed. Turned him into a...

Monster. Beth swallowed.

For the rest of dinner, the conversation steered towards arrangements and plans for Edwards transition into residence at Branton Manor. Swept up in the hopeful excitement, Beth was almost able to forget El's revelation.

At the back of her mind though, that voice continued to whisper, *He's a killer, he's a killer,* and she knew she'd have to face the truth before long. Perhaps with El at her side they could uncover the answers together.

First, she needed El to tell her all there was to know about the Stalker and his victims. Clearly, she wasn't being told much and that needed to change. No longer would she be kept ignorant. It was time to become her own woman.

Elizabetha Estamore, soon to be Lady Branton, was going to prove she was capable of anything she put her mind to.

۞

THEY WERE JUST RETURNING HOME AS THE GREAT CLOCK IN THE hallway chimed ten.

Oren let out a deep, jaw-cracking yawn. "A wonderful dinner." She smiled at Beth and Edward in turn, then cast El a hard stare and said, "You, young lady, will be best placed to learn your manners before becoming a resident at Branton Manor." She sniffed indignantly. "Lord Ashford has been most kind this evening. Most patient. It won't always be so." She handed her cape to a servant and beckoned for her husband. "Come, Landrum. Time for us *all* to retire."

"Good night, Mother, Father." Beth watched them for a moment, aware Edward was hovering beside her and El.

"Beth," he said. "I'm sorry you had to see... well, that." He leaned down and kissed her gently on the cheek. "Hopefully, it won't happen again." He beamed at her, a look she hadn't seen for a long time. Clearly the talk of a possible cure had meant more to him than he'd let on. "Good night."

"Good night," she replied.

Beth hovered awkwardly in front of her Companion for a few moments before she touched Ellana's arm, tilting her head towards the stairs. "Will you help me undress?"

El blinked at her, as if trying to find the right words. "'Course. Though I- I wanna talk 'bout—"

"I know. Not here," Beth whispered, proffering her head towards the young servant still waiting for their cloaks. "My room."

As soon as they were safely away from prying ears, she sat El down on her bed. "I want to know everything. About the Stalker. About the people he's killed. Everything. You mentioned women —as in plural?"

El's eyebrows shot up. "You really don't know?"

Beth sat down and began to unbraid her hair, gently combing her fingers through her curls. "I really don't. But before we decide what to do about..." She gulped. "About Edward, I'd like to know as much as I can. We have to be certain if we're going to accuse him."

"I've thought 'bout it an'... I understand why you're askin' me t' wait. I'd do the same if it were Ren," El said softly. She stood and stretched. "Dunno how you wear these things all the time." She ran a hand along the corset beneath her dress. "I s'pose there're lots o' things different between us, Scrubbers an' nobles."

Beth tied up her curls loosely at the nape of her neck. "I can admit I didn't realize how much, until I met you. I hadn't even thought about it."

El ran a hand along her own braids, as though contemplating undoing them, then pulled away and rubbed at her eyes instead. "Must be nice t' be kept in the dark. There're some things I wish I din't know."

For the first time, Beth saw how bone-achingly tired El was. They were alike in age, yet El had been through so much more in her eighteen years than Beth had. Again, guilt gnawed at her gut to think about how absorbed she had been in such petty topics as what to wear, what to eat, who to impress. The gossip of her mother's friends seemed a distant, unnecessary distraction from what really mattered now.

"The first woman I remember hearin' about weren't much older'n me. Some six months back it was—I remember 'cos it had jus' started getting warm. Ren was excited 'bout that 'cos it meant he could play with 'is friends later into the evenin'." She smiled briefly before her eyes clouded over. "Daisy. 'Er name was Daisy. Din't live far from us."

"What happened to her?" Beth asked.

"From what I heard, 'er throat were cut. Vicious, like a wild animal 'ad been at her. I din't see her body, but havin' seen Da... I can imagine."

A chill trickled down Beth's spine. "By the Mother."

"There was rumors 'bout her. That she'd not been right in the head." El sat back down, pulling at the dress around her corset. "Still. No one deserves t' be left to rot in an alley. She must've been so scared. Alone an' afraid. They—" She hesitated, letting out a strange hiccoughing noise, as though her breath had caught in her throat. "Oh, those poor things. Da, too. Weren't a good man but no one deserves t'- t'—" She covered her face with both hands, shoulders shaking.

Beth knew there was nothing she could say. At first, she hesitated to offer comfort, knowing how angry El had been at her for not revealing her suspicions about Edward immediately. But then her empathy took over and she leaned over to rub El's back. She knew it would have been what she wanted if she were so upset. They sat like that for a time, Beth allowing her Companion time to cry. She was overcome with a deep sadness knowing it had been her brother who had caused this pain.

She closed her eyes, his gentle face floating to the forefront of her mind. *Why Edward, why?*

Beth clenched her jaw, anger growing with the sadness. *How much do Mother and Father know about his actions? Is this why they have hidden everything from me?* The implications astounded her.

El sniffed, wiping a hand across her nose. "Sorry," she muttered. "I din't think..." Her shoulders rose and fell as she sighed. "I din't think I cared 'bout him."

"He was your father, no matter what he did to you."

El stood, picking up her servant's dress from where it had been lain on Beth's bed earlier that evening. "Can you undo this dress for me? It's bloody uncomfortable. Time I stopped pretendin' to be somethin' I'm not."

"Of course." Beth unlaced El's dress and corset with nimble fingers. "Here, let me help you take them off."

"I've got it, Beth," El said, taking the black dress with one hand whilst holding up her evening dress with the other. "Wouldn't do for you t' be dressin' me forever, would it? Um, an' would you mind turnin' while I...?"

"Oh!" Beth covered her eyes and turned. "Sorry, yes. I- I'm so used to being watched while I dress, it never crosses my mind that others wouldn't be."

Finally, with El changed, they stood facing each other. "I need to know more about the murders," Beth said. "I've stayed sheltered for too long. How many were there after Daisy?"

El took a moment, silently mouthing as she counted out on her fingers. "Four more."

"And they've all been women, apart from your father?"

"Yes." El thought for a moment. "Well, 'cept wi' the last one, Penny. I heard somethin' 'bout a man killed alongside her. Think 'is name was... Reggie, yeh that was it. Her betrothed. That's six deaths total. Six deaths that shouldn't've happened."

Beth turned her back to El. "Will you unlace me?" As El's fingers worked deftly down her bodice, she said, "My only thinking is—and I don't want you thinking I'm trying to downplay anything—but it doesn't make sense, does it?"

El's hands paused. "What d'you mean?"

She glanced over her shoulder and caught a glimpse of El's

pout. As she turned to face her Companion, the shoulders on her loosened gown drooped. "Why go from killing women to killing your father? What changed?"

"What 'bout Reggie? He were a man."

"To me it sounds like he wasn't part of the plan. Up until him, there was a pattern, wasn't there? Just women being killed. But then your father... Was he an intentional kill?" She paused only briefly before asking the next question that popped into her head. "Or could he have been seeking... you?"

She knew immediately she had gone too far.

El cheeks flushed red. "How'm I s'posed to know?"

Acutely aware the rest of her family were abed, Beth held her hands up to quiet her Companion.

"I know, I know, I'm sorry. I'm not trying to upset you, but I think there might be more to this than we know." She led El back to her bed where they both perched on the edge. "All I'm asking for is a chance to find out the truth. And then, once we've got all the information, if nothing goes against what we think—that Ed... That my- my brother is the Stalker, we'll go to the City Guard. They're more likely to believe us if it comes from, well—"

"A noble." El's blue eyes shone defiantly in the dimness of the room. "What we gonna do to find out more? Can't exactly ask your brother, can we? An' what happens if he kills again while we're doin' all this- this investigatin'? This ain't a game, Beth. Real lives are at stake."

"Well, with Edward moving to Branton Manor, he'll be more closely monitored. You heard what Ashford said, he wants to keep Edward under observation. How will he be able to sneak out and hurt anyone?"

El was silent for a long time, chewing on her bottom lip. "I hope you're right, Beth. Else we'll both 'ave to live with the consequences. I'd best get to bed. Ren'll be wonderin' where I am."

Beth watched her walk to the door. "I'll come for you in the morning. I'll arrange for a carriage. Some of the servants are fond of me; they'll do what I ask. And El?"

El peered over her shoulder, one hand resting on the door-knob. "Yeh?"

"Thank you."

El's sigh was a heavy one, her face cast in shadow. "What choice do I really 'ave?" With that, she opened the door and left.

Beth laid back on her bed, guilt weighing heavy on her chest. She dearly hoped she was not making a grave error.

Please prove me wrong, Edward. Please.

CHAPTER 16

THE VOICES

E l didn't sleep well that night. Every time she closed her eyes, she saw that horrifying, blood-red gaze staring back at her.

Back in her room, she'd crawled onto her bed, careful not to wake Ren, and snuffed out the candle he'd left aflame for her. She touched her hand to her pocket, where she'd stowed Ma's necklace after removing her evening gown. It was comforting, in a way, to possess something that had once been Ma's. A way to connect with a woman whose face she could barely remember.

She pulled the necklace from her pocket and held it up. In the dark it glowed dimly, a pale red light that relaxed her racing mind.

What am I gonna do? she wondered. *Is Beth right t' want time? I know I'd want the same if it were Ren. I wouldn't want t' admit me own brother were a monster. But what if someone else is killed?*

Cupping the necklace against her chest, she closed her eyes, willing it to answer her. Unsurprisingly, no response was forthcoming and, before long, exhaustion drew her into a deep sleep.

When a brisk knock came at the door, she was pulled abruptly from a dream full of pulsing red lights. The room was dark, and there was none of the usual hustle and bustle from the rooms alongside theirs that El assumed belonged to other household servants.

"Wha—? Is it?" Ren muttered groggily from his bed.

El whispered, "Go back to sleep." She put the necklace in her pocket, straightened her crumpled skirts as best she could, and moved to open the door.

Outside was a manic-eyed Beth holding up a small gas lantern. "Sorry, I know it's early," she said quietly. "Can we talk?" She peered over El's shoulder where, despite her instructions, Ren was staring at them blearily. "Alone?"

"What's wrong, El?" Ren asked.

Coming to his bed, she stroked a loose strand of hair back from his forehead. "Nothin' to worry 'bout. Beth's gonna, um, well... Beth an' I, we're gonna find out who killed Da. Make sure 'e gets the punishment 'e should."

Ren's eyes widened. Perhaps it had been the wrong thing to say, but El was sick of all the lies and secrets. Keeping the truth quiet hadn't done her any favors so far. Besides, Ren deserved to know; he'd loved their Da, despite the way he'd treated them. Maybe this could bring him some closure.

"Can I come?" he asked.

El smiled. "No, Ren. It's safer 'ere. I need you t' be safe. That's more important than anythin'."

"But who's gonna protect you, El?"

"I will," Beth said from the doorway.

In the flickering light of the lamp, El saw the incredulous expression on Ren's face. "You?"

El tried to hold back a laugh, though a snort escaped before she could catch herself.

Beth lifted her chin. "Yes. Me."

Something about Beth's tone seemed to convince Ren, though El was still a little surprised Beth was willing to proceed with their investigation. After last night, she'd half expected Beth to dismiss her that morning. Their relationship was an ongoing source of confusion; sometimes she felt like Beth's friend, at other times she was reminded of the stark chasm between them and their social standing.

"We'll look after each other, actually." She patted Ren's leg. "You stay 'ere, alright? Stay safe, like I said."

Ren let out a deep, groaning yawn. "A'right, El," he said, slumping back onto his pillow. "But you be safe, too."

"Come on," Beth whispered.

El watched her brother for a moment longer, noting he was already snoring again.

In the hallway, Beth held a finger to her lips and beckoned El onward. They headed for the front door of the manor. A young man, apparently expecting them, stood with two capes in hand.

"Thank you, Stephen," Beth whispered, taking one.

He bowed his head in response.

"I've left a note for Father in the dining room, if you could direct him to it when he wakens," Beth requested.

"Yes, mistress," Stephen said, retreating down the hall.

Pulling open the door, Beth said, "Let's go before Mother wakes up, else there'll be no chance of us getting away!"

Outside, a carriage was already waiting. El was impressed. "What time did you wake up to arrange all this?"

Beth grinned devilishly at her as she sat down in the carriage, her face barely illuminated by the pre-dawn light seeping in through the small window beside her.

"Er... early. I can't say I slept much." She thumped on the roof of the carriage and the steam engine rumbled before jostling the carriage into motion. As it did, Beth opened a leather satchel belted to her waist. "I brought one of Father's notebooks so we can keep a list of the victims. And anything else we learn."

"I can talk you through the names," El said.

"I know the first." Beth opened the notebook and began writing with a pencil. "Daisy. Oh, I should probably say, we're going to the Workers' District. I thought that would be the best place to start. Allain wasn't keen on going there so early, what with it still being dark, but I promised him a pretty bonus for his trouble. He's always been a man easily persuaded with coin."

Home. Hadn't expected t' be returnin' so soon, El reflected. "I s'pose it's a good place t' start." Really, it was the *only* place to start since that's where all the killings had been.

Beth looked up at her. "After Daisy, who was next?"

El took a moment to think, though she didn't need it; she'd memorized the names of the poor young women who'd fallen victim to the Stalker. Sometimes she'd lay awake at night wondering whether she'd be next—after all, she was a similar age and a commoner in a city that cared nothing for its poor.

"Delilah," she answered. "She was a little older than the rest, though still a Scrubber. All 'is kills 'ave been."

She'd noticed early on that Beth blanched at the use of the word Scrubber, and El found herself satisfied to see the remnants of such a reaction now. She saw it as a reclamation of a word meant to demean her and Ren and those like them.

Let 'er be embarrassed, she thought. *This was because of 'er brother. Let 'er see the truth of their beloved city; see 'ow the EtherMother turned a blind eye t' the suffering o' those who aren't rich enough t' afford Her protection.*

"Rosie were the youngest," El continued, "Just fourteen, beautiful red curls. 'E got 'er on the way back from the docks where she worked."

"She *worked*?" Beth's incredulity was genuine and again El was reminded of her ignorance.

"'Course she worked." She stared out of the carriage window, not telling her how they all worked in one way or another from the age they could walk and talk—how lucky El had been to *not* work in that particular fashion.

The sky was beginning to lighten and El realized they'd be at their destination soon. "I think her da died when she were young. Rosie, I mean," she said. "Her ma had young'uns to raise, so no choice but t' earn money soon as she could."

Beth frowned. "What work did she do?"

"What d'you think?" El let the question hang between them, her face a mask of neutrality. When Beth didn't respond, she forged ahead, not willing to be the one to enlighten her. "Last were Penny. An' Reggie, her betrothed." She paused. "And then there was me Da."

Beth finished writing. "Thank you, El. I know this must be hard. Thinking about all this…"

"Death," El finished unapologetically.

She met Beth's gaze, noting the sadness in her mistress's eyes. A part of El had been heartbroken at the news of every death at the hands of the Stalker, but deep down she'd been hardened to such things. It was the life of a Scrubber. It was the life of one who'd lost their Ma before she should've. She'd learned early on it was too painful to let herself feel everything, to acknowledge all the hardships she and Ren had grappled with in their short lives. So, she didn't.

"How do you live with it?" Beth asked quietly.

She shrugged. "I'm used t' it."

The carriage halted and they heard the driver climbing down from his box.

Opening the door, he said cautiously, "We're here, Mistress." He glanced sidelong down the street. "Though I'm not so sure it's advisable to stay long."

"Thank you, Allain," Beth said dismissively. "El, do you know where Daisy lived?"

El brushed past Beth and Allain, stepping onto the street. "'Scuse me."

It was an uncomfortable kind of familiar being back in the Workers' District. She knew well the rotten odor of the docks and the filthy squelch of grime that seemed to coat everything beneath her boots. She inhaled deeply, letting the feeling of home wash over her.

"We're not far." She pointed indiscriminately behind Allain, instructing, "Follow that hill down. The road curves round wi' the houses. I'll tell you when t' stop."

"Yes, miss," Allain responded bluntly, though El didn't fail to notice the wild range of emotions that spread across his face at being told what to do by her.

But she had her own emotions to deal with. The route they would take went past her old home and she wondered whether anyone had laid claim to it yet. As the carriage moved past it, she sat stiffly, face turned away from the window.

Clearing her throat, she asked, "What's the plan, then?"

Beth, who had been chewing on the end of her pencil, glanced up from the notebook. "I can't help but shake the feeling we are missing... *something*." She waved her pencil dramatically.

"Maybe you jus' don't want Edward to 'ave killed all these people," El replied.

One side of Beth's mouth lifted in a resigned half-smile. "I won't say you're wrong... but I hope our investigation proves you are."

El glanced out of the carriage just in time to see Daisy's row of houses. She banged on the roof, crying, "Stop!"

Beth edged towards the window, crowding El out of the seat. "This is where she lived?"

"One o' those, yeh. All us Scrubbers live in blocks o' houses like this. Keep us all contained... like rats." She laughed, though the look Beth gave her was one of deep discomfort. Funny how the poor could laugh about their own shitty circumstances but the rich... Well, she supposed it was too difficult for them to be confronted with the reality of life outside their fancy homes.

"Should I speak to 'er family?" El asked. "I think that'd prob'ly be best, y'know—"

"No," Beth said almost hesitantly. "This was my idea. I'll do it."

The carriage door was opened and Allain held his hand out for Beth to take.

"Come on," she said to El over her shoulder.

Walking towards the houses, El was acutely aware of the children, many younger than Ren, running up and down the filthy cobblestones despite the early hour, likely collecting water from the drinking well. Inside their homes, their mothers would already be stitching fine lace and embroidery by meager candle-light, trying to get as much done as they could in their waking hours.

"Which one is it?" Beth asked. She spoke through gritted teeth as though afraid of drawing attention to herself. El couldn't blame her.

Many of the children slowed to watch and even follow them; it wasn't often someone of Beth's station was seen here. She was a curiosity at best. At worst, something to be loathed and spat on.

El narrowed her eyes at the row of wooden-fronted houses. They were identical, as all the houses in the Workers' District were, but the third one along had a crudely painted flower on its door. Though weathered and flaking, the white of the paint with which the flower had been drawn nonetheless stood out from the dark brown wood of the door.

El pointed. "That one. You sure you don't want me t' do the talkin'?"

"No, El. I'll be fine." As Beth marched forward, El heard her say, "Best get to it." The words were spoken quietly enough that El believed they were meant for Beth rather than herself.

Approaching the door, Beth held out a hand to knock. Before she could, the door was pulled open. In front of them stood a short, rotund woman with a mess of brown hair, piercing green eyes, and a deeply furrowed brow. "The fuck d'you want?"

Beth flinched, clearly unused to being spoken to in such a way. "Oh, er, I—" She smiled—a dazzling expression in normal circum-stances, but one that only caused the woman's scowl to deepen. "Hello, my name is Elizabetha Estamore and—"

"Estamore. Ha! Got no business wi' the likes o' *you*." With that, the woman made to slam her door.

El stepped forward, jamming her boot between door and frame, wincing as it was crushed.

"What d'you think you're—"

"Please," she implored, "we're 'ere to help. You might not remember me, but me Da—"

The woman squinted at her. "Ellana? Ellana Stone? Fred's girl? Is that you?"

"Yeh, it's me."

The woman looked her up and down, letting out a snort. "Thought you an' yer brother'd left Alpinside, after your da were..." Her green eyes glossed over, her mask of anger dropping. Sighing, she opened the door again and stepped aside. "In wi' you, afore I change me mind."

The home was smaller than El expected—smaller even than theirs had been. Or perhaps she had all too quickly become accustomed to life in the Estamore house and forgotten what it meant to live within such cramped confines. The room was lit by a small fire in a tiny hearth, a single armchair in front of it.

"I'd offer you somewhere t' sit but..." The woman shrugged, taking the seat with a loud huff. "Nothin' to drink, neither. Done me well run for the day, I'll not be put out for an Estamore." She continued muttering for a few moments before looking at El expectantly, then towards Beth with a suspicious glare. "'Ere to help, y'say. Not sure 'ow you expect t' do that. Me child's dead, an' the likes o' you Estamores, Whittinghams, Persimmons, Brantons —the lot o' ya—none o' you care 'cos you're safe behind your iron gates in your grand 'ouses."

She spat into an iron bucket at her feet. "So, I find meself wonderin', what exactly do you propose to *'elp* with? I'm surprised wi' you, Ellana Stone. After what 'appened to your da. Workin' 'ow he did for them *bastards*, little protection that fuckin' bought 'im in the end."

Beth stepped forward, but El grabbed her hand, holding her back.

"I'm surprised too," El admitted. "But Beth here 'as taken me in. Ren, too. Given us a home after ours were taken from us. These nobles don't do much, it's true, but they ain't responsible for the deaths, neither." She swallowed knowing it was only a half-truth. "My point is, p'raps give Beth a chance t' speak. You might find it gives you some peace."

"Peace? Bah!" The woman spat into the bucket again, before sucking her teeth loudly. She studied Beth for a moment, keen eyes roving up and down her fine clothes. "Get on wi' it then."

"I am so sorry for the loss of your daughter," Beth started. "Daisy, was her name, wasn't it?"

"My Daisy weren't lost. She were taken. She were *torn apart*." The woman's voice grew louder and hoarser as she spoke.

El waited for them to be screamed out of the house, sensing the rage building. Shouting never led to anything good, she knew that all too well. She edged backwards towards the door, instinctively ready to flee.

Beth knelt before the woman, taking hold of her weathered hands. Looking her in the eye, she said, "I'm sorry your daughter was murdered. That she was taken from you in such a cruel, terrible way. El has told me of all the horrors that have happened here. I promise, I never knew the full details. Not 'til now. There are people, other nobles, who are aware, who know of the Stalkers reign, the horrors he's inflicted... and they do nothing. But to ignore what's happened here, it's- it's against the love of the EtherMother." She bowed her head briefly. "I'm here to change that. To shine a light on these murders. To find out who killed your daughter."

El gulped. Hearing Beth speak so convincingly, promising this woman she would uncover the truth, made it clear she didn't really believe her brother was the Stalker.

And what if she's right? El thought. *What if he din't kill the others, only Da?*

The woman's eyes began to glisten with tears and her lip trembled. "'Ow can I trust you?"

"I give you my word I'll see justice done." She glanced at El, holding her gaze. "No matter what." There was a hardness in her dark eyes that told El she meant it. Turning back to the woman, she said, "I'm sorry, I forgot to ask your name."

"Daffodil," the woman said. "Though most people call me Daff."

Removing her cape and folding it over her arm, Beth pointed to a wooden crate nearby. "May I?" Daff nodded, and Beth pulled it so she could sit next to the woman, then fished her notebook and pencil from her satchel. "Daff, can you tell me about Daisy?"

"'Bout her death, y'mean?"

"No, about her. Who she was. What she liked. How she spent her days."

Daff's eyes lit up. "'Course I can."

Beth unfastened a purse at her waist and handed it to El. "Would you ask Allain to fetch us some hot cocoa and pastries, El?"

Though a little perturbed at being asked to leave, El didn't fight. She cupped the purse—which was heavier than any she'd held before—and made silently for the door. Just as she was closing the door, she heard Daff starting to speak. She'd have to hurry to avoid missing anything important.

To her irritation, Allain took more convincing to leave the carriage than she would've liked.

"Mistress Beth needs someone nearby in case o' trouble." He glanced about, eyeing everything suspiciously.

"Well... this is what she asked for," El snapped. Looking over her shoulder towards Daff's house, she added, "Or per'aps you'd like me t' go an' disturb her and tell 'er you're sayin' no."

Allain glared, opening his mouth as if to argue. Then, appearing to change his mind, he held out his hand for the purse. "Pastries and hot cocoa, is it? Tell the Mistress I'll be back quick as I can."

"Thank you," El said sweetly.

Allain scoffed before pressing down on the peddle at his feet, jerking the steam carriage into action.

El watched the carriage chug away for a moment before making her way back to Daff's house. As she did so, she absent-mindedly placed her hand in the pocket of her dress. Having forgotten about its presence, she gasped slightly as her Ma's Etherstone necklace slipped into her palm. It was smooth, comforting, and warm. She imagined the pulsing glow it emitted, instantly calming at the thought.

When she reached to open Daff's door, a voice echoed through her mind, sudden enough to make her stumble. Her shoulder rammed against the door frame.

"...*are trapped... need... help... true... power... EtherStone...*"

"Who's there?" El gasped, turning in a circle to find she was alone.

"*Help us... EtherStone...*"

The voice was a muffled whisper, so El could only make out every few words. Still, there was an evident urgency in the tone, a level of desperation that overwhelmed her. The calm she'd felt moments before vanished as panic took hold.

"...*are trapped...*"

"Where are you? What are you?" she whispered not wanting to draw more attention than was necessary. "How are you doin' this?"

"El?" That was Beth calling her. At least, she thought it was Beth.

She hadn't realized how much her vision had blurred until she blinked and it began to clear. She felt herself being lifted from the floor. When had she fallen? Her eyelids fluttered. When she was able to focus again, she found herself peering up at Beth and Daff from the comfort of Daff's armchair.

"Din't expect that to 'appen," she said, trying to sound nonchalant. Internally, though, her mind was a-whir with fear and anxiety. *What the fuck jus' happened?*

Neither Beth nor Daff smiled back.

Beth carefully broke the heavy silence. "El, you've been unconscious for a little while. Are you well? You look very pale."

El snorted. "No different t' usual, then."

Daff bustled forward, lifting El's chin, turning her face from side to side. "You 'ave it too," she muttered, an unmistakable glimmer of fear alighting her eyes.

"What? What do I 'ave?" El asked, pulling away.

"Same as what my Daisy 'ad. Jus' afore she were murdered." Daff sucked on her teeth, the noise she seemed to make when deep in thought. "Mm. Funny turns, jus' like that. Ended up so bad we 'ad to send for a doctor though we could scarce afford it." She slumped onto the wooden crate Beth had vacated.

"What was wrong with her?" Beth asked, notebook open and pencil poised to take notes.

"It started with 'er gettin' this faraway look in 'er eyes. She used to 'elp me wi' the seamstressin', doing the finer bits o' work me eyes weren't any good for. But more an' more I'd have t' bring her back to 'erself. Driftin' off, she was. Mutterin' to 'erself. Hearin' voices, she told me."

El's mouth dried and she croaked, "Voices?"

Daff ran a hand through her long, brown hair. "'Course, I never 'eard 'em. But it were 'nough for me t' be worried when she stopped bein' able t' help me with me work for the shakin' that seemed to take over 'er whole body. That's when I sent for the doctor."

Beth paused in her notetaking. "And what did the doctor say?"

Daff's brow wrinkled. "There were two of 'em, though one seemed more interested than t'other. He examined 'er, asked 'er questions 'bout what she were feelin' an' hearin'. He told me when I was alone it was a madness of sorts. A 'malady of the mind', 'e called it; I ain't never 'eard of such a thing."

"Malady of the mind," Beth repeated the words as she wrote them down, and El did her best not to dwell on the word madness.

"Did 'e... Was there a cure?" El asked, clutching the skirts of her dress to conceal the trembling of her hands.

Daff snorted. "Not one we could 'ope to afford." She smiled sadly. "Weren't long after that she were killed."

Beth closed her notebook. "I'm truly so very sorry," she said, setting a hand briefly on Daff's shoulder. "I wonder, could you tell me who the doc—"

Allain bustled into the house, balancing three steaming drinks on a small wooden tray and holding a brown paper bag under his arm. "Sorry for the delay, Mistress. Quite the crowd gathered up by the Alpinside Journal offices."

"Thank you, Allain." Beth took a sip of the hot cocoa he offered her, the steam wafting angelically about her head. "A crowd? What's happened?"

Allain gave a cup to El and Daff before folding the tray and placing it into one of the inside pockets of his coat. He turned to Beth, clutching the paper bag of pastries at his chest. "By all accounts, Mistress, the Stalker's struck again."

A moment of stunned silence followed.

El stood, trying to ignore the trembling in her legs. "*Another* victim?" As she spoke, she stared at Beth. "When? Who?"

"Last night. Least that's when the body was found, so's I heard. Not far from here. You see now why I was so reluctant to leave you unattended, Mistress Elizabetha!" He cast El a haughty stare.

"Is it, uh, was it... a woman?" Beth asked.

"I believe so, Mistress." Allain removed his black cap. "Terrible business, it is. If it's all the same with you, I'd like to take you home now. Wouldn't do to be out with the atmosphere such as it is." He swallowed. "People're angry, Mistress."

"As they should be," growled Daff. "As we all should be." She looked into her cup of hot cocoa, then to Beth. "You promised you'd 'elp catch that bastard. Now get out there and catch 'im." Her green eyes were like venom as she looked from Beth to El. "Now."

"Thank you for—" Beth started.

"Now!" Daff threw her hot chocolate into her fireplace, nearly extinguishing the already sputtering flames.

"I'm sorry," Beth said, placing her mug of hot cocoa down on the wooden crate. El followed suit, giving Daff a tight-lipped smile. As Beth headed towards the door, she directed Allain to leave the bag of pastries for Daff.

Outside, El stared up at the grey, cloudy sky. Another dead. Discovered last night. The body couldn't have been what... more than two or three days old?

Could it've been Edward? she asked herself. *Or is the Stalker someone else completely? In which case* why *did Edward kill Da?*

Her mind reeled with the possibilities as they approached the carriage. "Beth," she said, checking that Allain was out of earshot, "what we gonna do?"

"Well, let's find out who was murdered first. See if we can't speak to the family before the City Guard blunders in. And," Beth peered around, edging closer to El, "we need to see where Edward was the past few nights. Perhaps we should go home; you need rest. You worried me, El. I—"

"I'm fine," she said sharply. She wondered if the words were more for Beth or herself. "I think we should go an' speak t' the family, too."

Beth studied her briefly before nodding. "Very well."

El climbed into the carriage as Beth gave instructions to Allain. Inside, she took a few deep breaths, clutching her hand around the necklace in her pocket. There were no more voices, no hint as to what might have happened to her.

But deep down, she knew. *The madness.*

She inhaled, looking out at the streets of her former home. Despite everything, she was suddenly very glad to have Beth by her side. Perhaps it didn't matter if they were friends or not; perhaps the main thing was her mistress could get her information that would otherwise be blocked to her.

It was the only way to the truth, and she vowed she'd uncover it before the madness consumed her mind.

CHAPTER 17

THE DOCTOR

Beth's mind was spinning.

She'd asked Allain to drive them past the area he believed the murder had taken place based on what he'd heard outside the news office. Despite his trepidation, Allain had little choice but to follow her orders. He'd come this far after all, and that coin purse she'd promised him could only increase in weight. It was a weakness Beth felt guilty exploiting, yet it meant she and El could continue their investigation. Even so, she half wished Allain had insisted on taking her home, refused her coin, unsure as she was that she wanted to see the aftermath of one of the Stalker's killings.

To distract herself from what they might soon be facing, she turned to El. "You lived near here?"

When El looked up, there was a wrinkle of consternation between her eyebrows. "Back that way, not far from Daff's 'ome."

"We could visit, if you would like. Might be useful to—"

"No," El snapped, gaze drifting to the window. "I don't wanna go back there, not ever again."

There was a set to her jaw that told Beth she would speak no more on the subject. Knowing they would likely arrive at the scene of the latest murder before long, she touched El's arm.

"This may be hard for you, hearing about another murder... You can stay in the carriage if you want. I can speak to the family alone."

"No," her Companion said firmly. "I wanna come. I wanna learn, jus' like you. Maybe..." She hesitated. "I been thinkin'. Maybe, if this weren't Edward, and I'm not sayin' it weren't, but it seems like... there could be a possibility there's two of 'em."

"You mean two killers?"

El nodded. She glanced out of the window again. "Oh, I think we're 'ere."

Sure enough, as Beth moved over to sit beside her Companion, she saw the crowd gathered around a row of houses, not dissimilar to the one they'd just visited. There were two City Guardsmen, dressed in their navy uniforms, posted in front of a nondescript door. On the windowsill of the house they guarded was a faded and chipped red flowerpot, containing some dry soil and a wilted stem. Beth couldn't hear the Guardsmen's words, though she sensed from their scowls and the long, black batons in their hands that they were in no mood to be trifled with.

But she was an Estamore, and that name held some sway; at least, she hoped it did.

She knocked on the top of the carriage. It jerked as Allain pulled on the lever, the breaks screeching until it came to a rumbling stop.

"Let's go," she said, brushing out her skirts and squaring her shoulders. She held authority here, whether that sat comfortably within her or not. She may as well use it to try and help.

As she and El approached the Guardsmen, the men glanced at each other, then back towards her.

The taller and evidently older guard stepped forward, his thick grey and black beard bristling as he cleared his throat. "Now miss, I see word has got out 'bout this most *tragic* event, but this isn't open as some kinda freak show. We must insist that you keep away while the City Guard an' medics see to the bodies."

Bodies? That didn't bode well, and Beth's tentative courage almost fled altogether.

Yet they were here, and she'd best do what they came for. She had to if she wanted to prove Edward's innocence.

Looking up at the hard-faced guard, she said with as much confidence as she could muster, "I'm sorry, Guardsman...?"

The man sniffed loudly. "Fillip, miss."

"Guardsman Fillip. I'm sorry but I am here on official business at the behest of my father. Perhaps you know him, Lord Landrum Estamore."

The Guardsman's small eyes widened, though there remained a level of evident skepticism in the glance he threw at his colleague. He sniffed again, and she wondered if he might spit like Daff. "Lord Estamore's daughter, are ye? And why would he send a *woman* on official business?" He smirked, evidently sure he had her cornered.

Beth's nostrils flared. "Guardsman, how dare you deign to—"

"Sir, we can send for Lord Estamore if y'like," El cut in, her face a mask of cool disdain. "I'm sure you're aware, 'e's a busy man, which is why 'e sent Mistress Elizabetha 'ere to find out 'bout this murder. He's most concerned about the welfare of his workers, y'see."

The Guardsman raised an eyebrow. "You expect me to believe a man like Lord Estamore cares about the death of a Scr—"

"What's the trouble here, Fillip?" came a voice from behind the Guardsman.

Beth's heart soared as Ashford stepped into view, a large, black leather case in hand. Then she remembered she shouldn't be here and wracked her mind for a plausible excuse.

Ashford lifted his top hat and bowed his head. His normally bright eyes were bloodshot, and there were purple smudges beneath them. "Mistress Elizabetha, are you well?" He gave a strained smile. "I hadn't thought to find you in such a wretched place."

"Ashford," she stammered, bowing her head. "I, uh- El and I, we heard about the murder and—"

"Yes, awful business." Ashford removed a kerchief from the top pocket of his jacket and dabbed at his nose. When he noticed Guardsman Fillip and his colleague still standing nearby, he waved the kerchief in the men's faces. "Surely there's better things for you two to be doing, Guardsmen, than gawping at a conversation that's not your business."

"Sorry, Lord Branton." Fillip awkwardly bowed and shuffled away from the door, ruddy cheeks flushing darker still.

His colleague wordlessly bowed and followed.

Ashford bustled Beth and El to one side. As he did, Lord Denys joined them.

"Mistress Elizabetha," Denys said, doffing his top hat as Ashford had. "Ellana. This is no place for a lady. What has been done here..." His dark skin took on a ghostly pallor. "This is the worst it's been. The Stalker has—"

To her shock, Ashford slapped his friend on the shoulder and snorted with derision. "Oh, Denys. I do wonder why you ever thought to train as a doctor."

Denys's eyes narrowed. "You know why, Ash," he said through gritted teeth. "But that's of no matter. Elizabetha, allow us to escort you away from here. It is no place for you. Either of you."

Beth pursed her lips, looking behind Ashford and Denys towards the house. "Actually, El and I came to speak to the family. After all, El's father was—"

"Killed by the Stalker, yes," Ashford broke in. "A tragedy, no doubt, but one that doesn't give me any persuasion to allow you to see," he waved his arm behind him, "that. Besides, it saddens me to say there *is* no family to talk to. Not anymore."

"By the Mother!" Beth gasped. "No wonder you look so exhausted. That must have been... awful to see."

"Ah, all part of being a doctor, my dear!" Ashford said, tucking his kerchief away. "But... Denys is right. We must escort you away from here."

El's hands twitched agitatedly, and Beth understood her frustration but couldn't see a way Ashford and Denys would allow them to stay here unaccompanied. And she certainly didn't want them finding out about the suspicion towards Edward. Glancing at the black medical cases held by both Ashford and Denys held, she had an idea.

"I wonder," she said, giving Ashford her best smile and pulling at a loose curl, "might you be able to discuss what you've seen with me? I know you don't want a delicate woman to *see* what's happened but... I would very much like to understand it."

Ashford gave her a measured look, a smile playing on his lips. "I would be happy to, my dear. But perhaps first it would be best to take you home? I'm quite certain your mother and father cannot know you're here." He held his medical case out towards Denys. "Take the carriage home. I'll escort these ladies back to the Estamore estate." He looped Beth's arm through his, throwing social propriety to the wind as he steered her towards their carriage. He leaned close to her ear and whispered, "I want to know more about what you and Ellana here are up to."

Beth giggled at the playful gleam in his eye, then peered behind to ensure El was following. Her Companion lingered in front of the house for a moment before turning and hurrying to catch up. As Beth turned back to Ashford, she noticed Denys watching them. His expression was dark and unreadable, his lips downturned, shoulders tense. When Beth caught his gaze, he blinked, gave a fleeting smile, then hurried towards the Branton carriage. Beth furrowed her brow, uneasy without being sure why.

"Oh, Lord Branton!" Allain clambered down from the carriage. "I'm *so* pleased to see you're 'ere with Mistress Elizabetha. I was most worried about her insistence on—"

Ashford released Beth's arm. "Yes, I'm here now. Come, man, less chatter. Take us back to Estamore Manor and be glad I don't report you for negligence in bringing Elizabetha to this place."

"Y-yes, my lord. O-of course." Allain darted backwards, clambering into his seat.

Beth felt bad for bribing him and thought to apologize—but then, Ashford touched her arm and smiled down at her, and she was completely distracted.

"Come, Beth. Let's talk." He opened the carriage door and held his arm out, guiding both she and El inside. He climbed in and sat opposite the two of them, removing his top hat and placing it on the seat beside him.

Beth caught the scent of something woody yet sweet from his person, perhaps a cologne he favored. She found it curiously dizzying.

Ashford clapped his hands. "Well, imagine my surprise to find you two here this morning."

"With respect, m'lord, might I ask what *you* was doin' there?" El retorted.

"El!" Beth gasped. "You can't ask—"

Ashford put a hand gently on her knee. "It's quite alright, Elizabetha." He smirked at El. "As I said before, you do speak your mind, don't you? I do wish my own Companion would feel able to do so. It's rather refreshing." He stroked the EtherStone ring on his finger, eyes coolly regarding El. "Though it surprises me you forget so soon the events of last night. As a doctor in training, I was called to the scene early this morning. Denys, too."

El snorted. "City Guard don't even care t' send for a proper doctor." She slumped back in the seat. "Not that there's much t' be done when the Stalker's finished."

Beth elbowed El in the side. "I'm sorry, Ashford. El is still, understandably, upset about her father's death."

"As I said, quite alright." Lord Ashford regarded them both. "In fact, Denys and I have attended every murder of the Stalker's. Except your father's, Ellana."

El frowned, sitting forward again. "What d'you mean? Why?"

"What happened to your father's body after he was killed? Do you know?"

She shook her head, biting her lip. "We din't stick around long enough t' see who... took care of him. I assumed the City Guard saw 'im sorted."

Ashford rubbed a hand along his jaw. "Curious."

"What does it mean, my lord?" Beth asked, reaching for her notebook and pencil.

Ashford steepled his fingers. "Ah, a serious investigation I see. Best to start at the beginning perhaps. And, please, how many times must I say it? Call me Ashford. We're soon to be husband and wife. I don't expect you to call me *my lord* for the rest of our lives."

Beth smiled, laughing softly. "Yes, Ashford. I'm sorry, there has been much on my mind lately... I keep forgetting."

"I'm sure. What happened with your brother must have been concerning. And now to be taking on the troubles of your Companion. No need for apologies."

Beth nodded thankfully. He truly was a wonderful man.

"As to what it means that El's father's body was taken without examination, I can't be sure. It is strange though that I wasn't called to examine the body—as I was for the other victims."

"Why you?" El asked bluntly. "Why would you be called t' examine *any* o' the victims?"

"Denys and I, in our capacity as doctors in training, cover the Workers' District. A rite of passage, you might say." He casually waved a hand towards the window. "Besides which, I attended all of the young women before their deaths."

"You... what?" El asked, mouth agape. "You knew 'em? All of 'em?"

Ashford laughed. It didn't fit the somber mood. "Yes, funny, isn't it? Why, you might even have cause to think I was the Stalker!"

Beth did not find the notion the least bit amusing—especially given the circumstances.

Ashford's smile dropped when he saw their disdainful expressions. "Ah, sorry, I- Denys does chide me for my dark sense of humor. Though of course, to accuse me you'd have to accuse Denys too, for he's always at my side for such visits." Ashford let out a long exhale. "Anyway, I shall pre-empt your next question, ladies, by saying Denys and I were required to visit the young women because of a curious malady presenting in each of them."

"Malady?" The word was heavy on Beth's tongue as she glanced at El. "Like... hearing voices?"

El shifted beside her.

Beth lifted her notebook and read from it to ensure Ashford's attention remained on her. "The reason I ask is we just spoke to the first victim's mother. She told us a little about what happened to her before—"

"She was killed." Ashford's words had an edge of impatience, though he quickly smiled at Beth as though in apology. "Now, because I was attending physician in their lifetimes, along with Denys, we were also called upon after their deaths."

"Yes, you said that," Beth said, pursing her lips. "But what can you tell us about—"

"Ah, I shall have to stop you there, my dear," Ashford pointed out of the window, "for you are home."

Beth was disappointed their conversation was being cut short. But still, information had been gained. Now that she knew Ashford had attended all the victims, she was certain he would, in time, give them more clues in their investigation.

As if reading her mind, he said, "Perhaps the two of you might join Denys and I for dinner this evening. It's clear we haven't had time to speak about everything you'd like to."

El raised her eyebrows. "You clearly know more'n we do. It'd be 'elpful that's for sure, wouldn't it Beth?"

Beth nodded, twirling some loose hair. "It would. I'm just not sure Mother and Father will allow El and I to be alone with you and Denys. Not before we are married, anyway." She looked down, heat spreading across her cheeks, a little embarrassed.

"Leave that to me," he said, winking before moving to open the carriage door and holding his hand out for Beth to take.

The front door of the house was thrown open before they could reach it and Beth instinctively flinched.

Ashford gave her hand a gentle squeeze. "Ah, good morning, Lady Oren!"

Her mother stopped in her tracks, eyebrows nearly disappearing into her hairline. Beth bit down on the inside of her cheek to hold back a laugh.

"Lord Ashford," her mother said, "what an unexpected surprise. I hope my daughter hasn't been behaving inappropriately. I must apologize for not being better prepared. Had I known we were to expect you, I would have—"

"Elizabetha, inappropriate? I can think of nothing further from the truth," Ashford said. "I found these two taking an early morning breakfast at the patisserie and thought to join them to make sure they weren't harassed by any wayward vagrants." He took her mother's hand and placed a kiss on her knuckles. "I do hope I've behaved as you would wish, Lady Oren."

Her mother let out a high-pitched giggle, her cheeks flushing. "Oh, of course, Lord Ashford. Of course!" She offered him her arm. "Please, you must come inside for some tea. As a thank you."

"Thank you, Lady Oren," Ashford said, linking his arm with hers. "In fact, there was a matter I wanted to discuss with you anyway. I would like Elizabetha and—"

His voice trailed off as they entered the house.

Beth turned to El, whose eyes were cast towards the sky. "What's wrong?"

"I'm thinkin' there's a lot more t' this than we thought. I feel like we're missin' somethin'. It all seems a bit—"

"Strange?" Beth nodded. "I agree. Perhaps with Ashford on our side, we can learn a lot more."

El's eyes drifted towards the empty doorway. "Yeah, I s'pose." She seemed to hesitate.

Noting the dark lines under El's eyes, Beth said, "It's been a long day... well, morning already. Why don't you go and find Ren? Check he's okay, then get some rest."

El flushed, though relief shone in her eyes. "Are you sure you don't need me for anythin'? I'm... here t' serve you, after all."

"El," she said gently, "I- I'm not here to— I mean, I'm sorry if I've made you feel—"

"Got nothin' t' apologise for, Beth," El said. "I know we're not friends. I'm your Companion."

"Yes, my Companion, which means a lot more than friends."

El's throat bobbed. "Really?"

Beth stepped closer, taking El's hand. "I appreciate the secret you're keeping for me and I'm glad you're here."

El nodded, eyes suddenly hardening as she pulled her hands away. "Oh, yeah, 'course." She exhaled, a sound seeming to come from a place of deep weariness and frustration. "I'm gonna find Ren then. Send for me when you need me again." She scurried towards the house.

Beth stood and watched her Companion go, wondering what, by the Mother, she'd said wrong.

THE FOURTH

PENNY

The end of summer neared, and I was lulled into a false sense of security. The EtherFather hadn't spoken to me since Rosie's death; perhaps she'd been the last.

I told myself I'd succeeded. I could relax, focus on my life, on my future, on making my mark on Alpinside.

I was a fool. It was not to be.

When at last the EtherFather spoke to me, the autumn months were drawing in—a time for reflection and prayer. *There is another,* He said.

Three simple words, yet anger surged through my body. *Why me?* I wanted to cry, to scream, to lash out at any and everyone. I hadn't realized how much Rosie's death had impacted on me until that moment, the image of her lying in that garden, her face almost peaceful as her life's blood pooled around her, the scent of the lavender hanging sweetly in the air.

I'd swept breakfast from the table before me, the plates smashing to the floor and my cup of rose and berry tea, almost blood-like in color, pooling across the wood-paneled floor. Servants attended and cleaned up in silence though I barely noticed.

After prayer and reflection, I regained myself. I sharpened my blade in readiness and waited.

Before long, as with the first three, my colleague and I were called to attend the young woman's house. I knew immediately it was she who must be next.

Like the others, the madness was already taking hold. She heard voices, often lost concentration, suffered from fainting and sickness, and trembling in her body. I could tell by the glazed look in her dark brown eyes that she was already self-medicating—EtherAle, most likely, as had been the case with the others.

This time, there was a sense of impatience for the kill to be done. A deep unease had stayed with me since the voice had returned, an unrest which could not be sated by sleep nor alcohol nor distraction.

I could tell from the examination of Penny during that visit that she was a whore. There were bruises on her thighs, arms, and wrists, even teeth marks on one of her breasts—the signs of customers who had become too eager in the throes of their own pleasure. I had wrinkled my lips in disgust, as much at those men and their lack of self-control as at these young women who so thoughtlessly sold their bodies and damned their souls. Truly, it's a wonder the EtherMother chose such impure vessels.

The young woman's chosen path, however, meant I knew where she'd be that evening: parading herself along the same stretch of cobbled road where I had watched both Daisy and Rosie before her.

I could pursue her without delay.

Restlessly, I waited for night to fall. In the crisp dusk air, I set out, careful to ensure I wasn't seen by any of the household servants. I was garbed as always in my black cloak, my top hat pulled low to conceal my face, with my knife sheathed at my belt. Without thought, my feet carried me to the Workers' District. If anyone took note of my presence, I did not notice for I kept my head down and my eyes locked ahead. I'd been to my destination many times now, not just on my mission but for other work too, and so I could make my way there whilst my mind was elsewhere.

I marched onward to the steady drumbeat of my heart. I felt curiously at peace, knowing what was to come. Knowing I could enact my orders without delay. I had, after all, done it thrice now. What excuse could I offer my beloved EtherFather if I hesitated?

Before long, my feet once more stepped upon those wretched, grime-slicked cobblestones, the heady stench of rot and decay burned my nostrils, and the sounds of drunken louts pounded at my ears, intoxicated, no doubt, by their beloved EtherAle.

Lifting my gaze, I found myself opposite Penny's house, just as I had been hours before in my capacity as doctor. As I watched from the shadows between gaslamps, the door to her crumbling home opened. I stepped back, pressing myself against the wall of one of the homes opposite Penny's—more out of shock than any real need to hide.

She called back over her shoulder, some indecipherable words of farewell. The door closed with a quiet *thunk*, and she set off, pulling a threadbare shawl about her slim shoulders as she headed towards the docks to begin her evening of work.

I followed, keeping enough of a distance that she wouldn't hear my footsteps. Her braided blonde hair was like a beacon, gleaming like a halo whenever she passed beneath a flickering streetlamp. The streets were otherwise quiet, word of my exploits undoubtedly causing those who might otherwise be working to take precautions.

All except Penny.

As we neared the strip where I had observed Daisy and Rosie plying their trade, I expected her to slow. Instead, she sped up, hurrying down a side street. I frowned and followed. Within the sheltered, warren-like alleyways leading to the docks, I worried about her hearing my pursuit. I needn't have been concerned, for she was clearly in a hurry and did not slow nor look behind. Her head remained down as she took a few sharp turns, her braids slapping at her back. I kept up as best I could, my breaths becoming heavy, sweat springing up on my brow.

As she reemerged on the street, I hung back to observe, wary of being spotted now that we were back in the open. But the girl's mind was evidently singular in its mission to reach her destination, which appeared to be a dilapidated factory that sat close to the docks, squatting in the dark as a hideous reminder of the collapsing mining industry in Alpinside.

Penny glanced about before sliding aside a large hunk of wood covering the doorway into the building. She scuttled in without replacing it.

Might there be someone inside already, awaiting her? Or was it she who awaited another? Either way, there was a risk to my following—yet my feet carried me towards the building almost without awareness, as though I was drawn on by a force far greater than myself.

I ducked through the doorway, above which hung what appeared to be a half-collapsed section of ceiling. I covered my nose against the smell of damp and mold that immediately flooded my nostrils. I took a moment to allow my eyes to adjust. Discarded on the floor around me were empty bottles of Ether-Ale. This was a place for vagrants and addicts, it seemed. What, by the Father, was Penny doing here?

I kept walking down the narrow corridor. To each side were doorways, though they appeared blocked off by furniture, collapsed walls, or other debris. After a few more careful steps, I came to a stop beside a doorway that was unobstructed. From within came the gentle orange light of a candle. I leaned against the wall, listening.

"Reggie?"

I held back a gasp. But then I had to take this chance, did I not? She knew I was there.

I stepped into the doorway. "No, not Reggie."

Penny let out a small cry of shock, hand flying to her mouth. "Who're you?"

I pushed back my top hat and her hand dropped, her trust instinctively increased. "Oh, it's you, Doctor." She tilted her head. "You look different though, somethin' 'bout your eyes."

I ignored that comment, simply saying, "Yes. What are you doing here, Penny?" I stalked closer as I spoke.

The room was less cluttered with rubble than the rest, though a large, long-disused piece of machinery dominated the corner to the right of the door. There was a small, checked blanket laid out on the ground in the center of the room upon which she'd set her candle. It might have been quaint, had the sharp stench of piss not been hanging in the air.

In answer to my question, she peered around helplessly, dark eyes wide. Despite the fact I had followed her to this place, my social standing and power dictated she couldn't question my authority. Still, she remained silent, unwilling to reveal the truth. That irked me, I'll admit, and a flare of anger urged me on. In an instant, I stood over her.

She looked up at me, lips trembling.

"Who's Reggie?" I asked, my whisper seeming to echo between the crumbling walls of that place.

She whimpered. "He's- he's my b-betrothed an' we—"

I grabbed her throat, slamming her against the wall, my top hat tumbling to the floor behind me. "Betrothed?" I spat. "What the fuck makes you think someone like you can marry? Did you think you could escape this life? Flee from the justice that's due?"

She wheezed, trying to form words, unable to speak with my hands pressed into her windpipe.

I sneered. "It's of no consequence now, girl. Your beloved EtherMother has failed once again to choose a suitable pawn." I reached for my knife, held it above my head, catching its reflection in her dark eyes. "Be at peace."

I stabbed the knife into her chest, meeting resistance against one of her ribs before I slammed my entire weight against her, forcing the blade to sink into her flesh all the way up to the handle. I held her upright for a short while, watching the life drain from her. She tried to speak, her lips moving, eyes filling with tears, but no words came.

I pulled at the knife handle; it resisted release from her body. No matter, I told myself, it would likely be easier to retrieve once she was prone. With that, I released her, and her body slipped to the ground, leaving a smear of blood down the already stained brick of the wall.

At the same time, a man's voice called from the corridor, "Penny?"

I had to go.

I lunged to grab my knife, unwilling to leave it behind. It took time to come free, grinding against bone as I pulled at it to no avail. I pressed my shoe to her chest and levered it up and down. I grunted and pulled and, eventually, it came free with a loud, sucking squelch. With the blade in hand, I leaned down to pick up my top hat and put it on, then moved to the side of the door to wait.

"Penny? Penny!" The man appeared in the doorway. I watched him from the corner of my eye; he stood still, mouth gaping. He was a tall man, thin and lanky. "What's 'appened, Pen?" His voice thickened with emotion as he finally stumbled into the room, kneeling in front of his betrothed. He began to sob, his face leaning down to meet hers. "What 'appened, my darlin'?"

For a moment, I was mesmerized. Never had I been confronted with the aftermath of my actions.

She had to die. I said those words to myself over and over again as I watched that man's heart break. Eventually, I tore my gaze away, for it was only a matter of time before he saw me. As quietly as I could, I edged towards the door. I would've made it if it weren't for an empty bottle of EtherAle in exactly the wrong place. With my eyes glued to the man's shaking back, I did not see it until it was too late, and I'd already kicked it across the room.

The EtherFather was surely testing me that night.

Reggie spun and was on his feet in an instant, thick eyebrows darting towards his thinning hairline. "The fuck are——" His gaze darted to the knife in my hand, to the blood dripping from it onto the filthy floor. "You done this!"

I turned to flee, but he darted forward and snatched my cloak, dragging me backwards and half choking me in the process. I turned and slashed out with the knife. I felt it bite into the flesh of the hand clawing at my back.

Reggie yelped, spitting, "Bastard," as he let go and jumped back. "Why? Why've you done this t' my Pen?" He clutched his hand to his chest, blood leaking through his fingers.

His squinting eyes were full of pain. I wondered, for a fleeting second, what it must feel like to experience such heartache.

"You'll want to get that seen to. And soon," I said, pointing the knife at his injury. "Could get a nasty infection."

"The fuck you on 'bout?" he growled. "I asked what you've done t' my Pen?"

"Now, please. You must listen. I did what had to be done." I held my hands up, aware of the foolishness of such a motion with my hands covered in drying blood. "No one else needs to be hurt."

His lip curled into a sneer of rage. "You monster. You've killed her! You fuckin'——" He screamed and lunged again, grabbing for the knife.

I leapt backwards, straight into the hulking, metal machinery beside the door, jarring my shoulder.

Reggie pinned me to it, grinning down at me. "Not so smug now, are we? No one needs t' get hurt, eh? Oh, I'll hurt you for what you've done. I'll do it slow, an' all. I'll take as long as I need t' inflict every pain imaginable on you. First, let's see who's under that fancy hat."

"No!" I tried to slash out with the knife.

He saw it coming and grasped at my wrist, pressing it against the machinery above my head. With his other hand he flung aside my hat. As he did so, he let out a horrified gasp.

"The fuck's wrong wi' you? Your eyes, they're——"

I screamed in his face, doing my best to pull free from his powerful grip. Instead of releasing me, in his shock, his hand tightened, gripping me tighter. I felt the bones creaking in my wrist, though there was no pain thanks to the EtherFather's protection. For then, at least.

Not satisfied that he was hurting me enough, Reggie began to smash my arm against the long, metal bar against which it rested. He *bang, bang, banged* my arm over and over, his eyes taking on the flinty hardness of a man determined to see a job done no matter the price.

A look I was sure I had possessed myself many times these past weeks and months.

One thing was evident above all else: he wanted me dead. And why shouldn't he?

A voice in the back of my mind whispered, *Look at what you've done*.

Reggie let out a fierce cry of rage, bashing my arm one last time. With that, my grip loosened, and my knife flew away, clattering into the machinery behind us.

My heart cried. A sacred weapon had been lost, all because of this man's stubbornness. That was all it took for my fury to reignite.

I reached to my side with my left hand, and perhaps the Father was watching me after all, for my fingers found a loose metal rod. I pulled it from the pile of machinery with surprising ease, swinging with all my strength. I hit Reggie's shoulder, a dull, meaty thud, and he lurched sideways, grunting.

With his guard down, there was no time to hesitate. I held the rod above my head and drove it downwards with all my might. The crack it made as it hit his skull wasn't one I would forget in a hurry. He fell to the ground, immediately silenced. I wasn't sure if he was dead or simply unconscious, but I couldn't stay to find out.

I discarded the rod, picked up my hat, and turned for the door. Before I fled, I stared into the machinery, hoping I might find my knife. Alas, there was no sight of it.

I thought maybe I could search for it. It was a most precious knife, one passed to me with a sense of responsibility and history, and I did not want to be parted from it.

A sound came from the hallway outside—a voice, footsteps.

There was no time.

I ran.

CHAPTER 18

THE MADNESS

After leaving Beth, rather than making for the kitchen where Ren would likely be working, El made for their room. She needed a moment to process everything that had happened and what they'd learned.

In the bedroom, she slumped onto her bed, lying her head back on the pillow. It felt as though days, not hours, had passed since Beth had fetched her that morning. She was grateful for her mistress's enthusiasm to investigate before deciding what to do about Edward, but she couldn't help the frustration taking root within her. Instead of answers, there seemed infinitely more questions. And, all the while, Edward remained free. If he *was* the Stalker, he could strike again at any time. Another murder had already been committed within the past few days. But had it been him?

She closed her eyes, thinking about the clues. Daisy had been a young woman. She'd worked to help her ma make ends meet. They struggled, just like everyone else in the Workers' District. She had become unwell. She'd heard voices... just as El had started to. The physicians, Lords Ashford and Denys, had prescribed a medicine her ma couldn't afford. And then she'd been killed.

El's mind scrambled to gather the threads of her thoughts. A niggling sense at the back of her mind told her there was more to this—something obvious they were missing. She absent-mindedly reached into her pocket and cupped the EtherStone necklace.

Am I goin' mad too—like she was? I'm hearin' voices an' completely blacked out earlier—that's never 'appened afore. I wish I could speak t' Daisy, know what she heard, what she felt. An' not just Daisy, neither. If what Ashford told us earlier were true, that means...

"They *all* heard the voices," El mumbled. *But what does it mean?*

Pulling the necklace from her pocket, she studied the stone. As before, it pulsed gently. She held it close to her face so she could properly examine it and found if she focused a certain way, she could see *inside* the stone. And she noticed it wasn't all the same blood red; instead, the colors seemed to swirl and change, giving the sense the stone was alive.

Ignoring how foolish she felt, El said, "Hello? Can you- can you 'ear me?"

At first there was nothing but the sound of her own breathing and she almost laughed with relief. Then she heard it, the quietest of whispers, like a gentle breeze brushing past her ear.

"Please," she urged, "speak up. I need t' know... what d'you want from me?" She swallowed. "If I'm t' die as well, like the others."

"*...help us...*"

"I'm tryin'! I dunno how. You need t' tell me."

"*...the truth...*"

"What truth?" El squeezed the stone until her knuckles whitened. "What truth!?"

"*...trapped. Save us and... the one.*"

"Shit," El muttered. "My name's Ellana Stone and I'm 'ere to help you. Tell me what t' do!"

"*Ellana, Ellana, Ellana.*"

She gasped and realized she'd heard this voice at Lord Ashford's after Edward's strange turn, a whisper saying her name. It was also the voice she had heard at Daff's, and it was growing stronger by the day.

"*Ellana!*"

Instinctively, she threw the necklace, watching as it hit the wall on Ren's side of the room with a loud *crack* before thudding softly onto his bed.

"El?"

She turned to the door and found Beth gawping at her. "Beth! I- I din't know you was there." She put a hand over her heart, feeling its thunderous beat.

Beth didn't say anything; her eyes had fallen on the necklace gently glowing on Ren's bed. To El's relief, it appeared unharmed by its impact with the wall.

"Where did you get that?" her mistress said in a strangled whispered.

"It's mine," El said firmly.

There was a moment where the two looked at each other and El saw Beth didn't believe her, forcing her to harden herself against their growing bond. Why should she open herself to someone who she couldn't trust to believe her? Clenching her jaw, she reached for the necklace.

Beth stepped forward at the same time, as if thinking to snatch it up.

El quickened, laying a hand over the necklace, and drawing it towards her chest quickly.

"Well, I'd love to speak about it more," Beth said, "but it's time to go."

El felt Beth's eyes following the necklace as she carefully placed it back in her pocket.

"Go?" she asked. "Where?"

Beth frowned. "To Lord Ashford's for dinner. Don't you remember?"

"Oh, yeah, 'course." El's brow crinkled in confusion. "Aren't we goin' there this evenin'?"

Beth laughed, though her face quickly became serious when she realized El wasn't joking. She sat on the bed. "It *is* evening."

"You mean it's been the whole afternoon since I left you?" El asked in puzzlement.

"Yes." Beth tilted her head, a few dark brown curls springing about her forehead. She had loosened half of her hair to hang down her back and shoulders, framing her round face, and had changed into an emerald green gown.

How long was I staring at that necklace? El wondered concernedly.

To Beth, she forced a smile and said, "You was right, I needed t' rest. I woke up not long ago, so I'm still a little... dazed."

"I knew you would be tired after our early morning. I'm glad I let you rest, but we have a lot to discuss. And I didn't think about how much it might affect you to be around all, um, well—"

"The murders. You can say it, y'know."

Beth gulped. "Yes, the murders."

El held a hand to her temple and let out a long breath.

"Does your head hurt?" Beth's voice held a tone of suspicion— or perhaps that was simply what El expected, for, when she met Beth's eyes, there was only gentle concern.

"No, I'm fine," she said, rubbing her eyelids. "There's jus' a lot t' think about. Anyway, din't you say we've gotta go?"

Beth hesitated before standing. "Yes. Um, El?"

"Yeah?"

"There's something I need to tell you about this dinner. The only way Mother would agree to it was if—"

There was a hard knock on the door, and it was opened quickly. El expected Ren's smiling face to appear, so when she instead found herself looking up at Edward Estamore, she took a sharp breath. "Oh."

"Good evening, Ellana," he said, smiling gently. "Are you ready? The carriage is waiting."

"Yes, Edward," Beth said, almost too cheerily. "I was just telling El you'd be joining us."

"Yes—as your chaperone." Edward waggled his eyebrows and El had to bite back a burst of anger. "Besides, I'm told my rooms are ready. No time like the present for moving into my new home and beginning my treatment." He held his arm out for his sister to take. "Let's go, I'm starving."

El watched their retreating backs and reminded herself this was a good thing. Edward had to be kept under observation; Lord Ashford would provide that service. Beth's betrothed seemed to know a lot about medical care and seemed to understand what Edward needed. She could only hope it would be enough to prevent any more—

She paused, grasping the door handle. *We don't know where 'e was when the last victim were killed. Gotta ask 'im outright. Gotta know, one way or the other.*

With a steadying inhale and a firm nod to herself, El followed Beth and Edward. They donned their capes at the front door, wrapping up against the increasingly chill winter air.

Edward chattered with his sister for the whole ride, a cause of both frustration and relief for El. On one hand, she wanted an answer. If he couldn't account for his whereabouts the past few nights, surely that confirmed he was the Stalker.

But on the other hand... *What if he* can *account for himself? What if there's someone else, someone we haven't identified yet, still out there?* The thoughts niggled at her. Somehow the idea the Stalker was some anonymous figure unknown to them was worse than it being Edward.

Resting her chin on her hand, she watched the dimly lit streets pass by outside the window, blocking out the conversation filled with talk of weddings and winter balls. What if the pouch, and the EtherStone for which Da had been killed, *was* the answer?

El pondered that, perhaps, she shouldn't have given it up so easily.

But then she recalled Lord Landrum's threat to report her and Ren to the City Guard. He would've done it, that had been clear.

What does that mean 'bout Edward? 'Bout Lord Landrum Estamore? 'Bout Beth's family as a whole?

She chewed on her thumb nail, knowing deep down where that line of questioning might lead but unwilling to explore it too deeply. Despite everything, Lord Landrum had provided her and Ren with a home. She didn't want to consider the possibility of that being threatened so soon, of them being homeless again.

El was grateful when they arrived at Branton Manor. She allowed Edward to open the door for them, though she stiffened when he insisted on taking her hand to help her from the carriage. She must have scowled at him because he let out a soft chuckle.

"I'm only trying to help, Ellana."

"Don't need 'elp," she told him, turning up her nose. "Not from anyone, least of all—"

"Hush, El," Beth snapped semi-playfully. "Edward doesn't need to hear another speech about your views on the EtherMother and how women should stand up for themselves."

Edward laughed, patting El on the shoulder before taking Beth's arm. "Truth be told, I would love to hear more of your thoughts on the matter, El. It is truly astonishing the difference in views between the nobles and workers of our beloved Alpinside." As they headed for the front door, he winked over his shoulder at her. "Perhaps we can have dinner sometime and discuss it?"

El was taken aback. When Beth widened her eyes at her, clearly indicating some response was necessary, she said, "Yes, Master Edward, that would be lovely."

"Excellent!" Edward beamed. "Now, let's see what dear Ashford has rustled up for dinner. He *does* like to show off."

The door was opened by a young boy. He peered up at them and, for a moment, reminded El so much of Ren she could've cried.

"We're here to see Lord Ashford," Edward said after the silence had dragged on a little too long.

"Yes, m'lord," the young boy said, stepping aside as though remembering himself. "Please come in. He's expectin' you."

Entering Branton Manor, they hovered in the hall.

Though the boy didn't say anything more, Beth took off her cloak and handed it to him, saying with a kind smile, "Thank you."

Edward and El followed suit.

"Lord Ashford's in the reception room," said the boy from behind their cloaks.

Edward and Beth made their way down the red-carpeted hallway while El hesitated, thinking to ask the young boy his name. She would be living here soon, and she would do well to know the other servants. But when she turned to speak, he was already gone, seemingly melted into the deep shadows haunting the corners of the entrance hall. With a shiver of disquiet, she hurried after Beth and Edward.

In the reception room, Lord Ashford was sitting beside Lord Denys. There was a glaze to his eyes that El recognized—and the half-empty bottle of red-tinged drink on the table by his side told her why. The drink of nobles, it seemed, was just as potent as EtherAle.

"Elizabetha! Edward, come, come," Lord Ashford said jovially. "And Ellana, too." He stood, widening his arms, bustling them into the room. "Denys and I have just been talking about those awful murders. So, of course, a drink was in order. I hope you don't mind, we started without you."

Beth's cheeks darkened as she flushed. "Not at all."

El cringed at the way Beth fluttered her eyelashes. She would never be so besotted by a simple man.

Lord Ashford stood and poured them each a drink. El noted with relief that he elected wine for she and Beth—she had no wish to consume the Blood Whiskey he offered Denys and Edward. She took a polite sip of her wine before placing the glass down on a sideboard, keen to ensure she didn't lose her senses, all too aware of the impact alcohol could have on a person. El watched Ashford, eventually having to admit to herself that he possessed more than a hint of charisma. His blue eyes twinkled, his smile was easy, and he spoke with confidence. She *could* see some of the attraction, if she allowed herself to be open-minded about it.

"Dinner shouldn't be too long," Lord Ashford said. He stood beside Lord Denys, who remained seated, looking up at Ashford with evident adulation. "Edward, perhaps you might like to see your rooms before we get too comfortable."

"Certainly, Ash," Edward said. "Lead the way."

Lord Ashford leaned down and slapped Lord Denys on the shoulder. "Show our guest to his rooms, would you? I find myself quite weary from the day's excursions."

Denys's dark eyes narrowed momentarily, a movement that was likely missed by others; El only caught it because she was finely attuned to such expressions after years of being on edge around Da.

"Of course," Lord Denys said with a false tone of cheer. "Come, Edward."

"Oh, I want to see, too!" Beth said, hurrying to follow them before El realized what was happening. She locked her gaze downwards, hoping to avoid scrutiny.

Before long, though, her skin prickled. She looked up from her lap to find herself being studied by Lord Ashford, a half-smile playing on his lips. He sat with his arm draped across the arm of his fine leather seat and his legs crossed. The EtherStone ring on his finger reflected the firelight; he looked almost regal.

Noticing her gaze upon it, he said, "A curious thing, isn't it?" He took his ring off and held it up to the light. "That such a stone can dictate who holds power in this city." Snorting, he turned his piercing gaze back to her. "I suppose it's not something you've been much exposed to though."

El took a sip of her wine. "Actually, m'lord, me Da worked in the mines. I've seen EtherStone afore." As she spoke, she felt all too aware of her Ma's necklace in her pocket.

Curiously, Lord Ashford's gaze flitted downwards to her skirts, as though somehow aware of the necklace's presence. His eyes crinkled as they met hers again; she wished he would stop bloody smiling at her.

"Ah, the mines. There are always rumors of workers taking slivers of the stone for themselves. A key to that beloved drink, EtherAle—is it not?"

El bristled. "I believe so, m'lord. Not that I've ever had cause t' drink it. Though, I must say, what you're drinkin' looks awful similar."

He held up his glass before taking a generous sip. "EtherAle is a poor imitation of Blood Whiskey, which is distilled and barrel-aged for many years. It is a valuable commodity in Alpinside, and its consumption is essential for maintaining a connection to the EtherFather. Some say it is the very blood of the Father. Hence the name, I suppose." He smacked his lips loudly before abruptly changing the subject. "Tell me, was your father one of mine?"

"Yours?"

"Did he work in the Branton mines?"

"Oh. No, m'lord. He worked for Lord Landrum... like we discussed afore."

Lord Ashford nodded, sipping his whiskey again. "Yes, I recall it now. I wondered how you came to be in Elizabetha's service. It *is* peculiar to me that your father was killed by the Stalker. Not the usual pattern, wouldn't you agree?"

He gave El an unreadable stare, his lips a hard line, his eyes like daggers of ice. "Well? Answer me, girl."

She shivered; he sounded so much like her Da that her body responded almost instinctively, and she crossed her arms over her stomach in a protective gesture. "I'm not sure what you want me t' say, m'lord. Though Beth an' me 'ave been tryin' to find answers."

"Answers?" Ashford's eyebrows shot up. "Is that why you were at the murder scene this morning?" He leaned forward, pinning her to the spot with his gaze.

Before she could respond—and much to her relief—Beth, Edward, and Lord Denys returned. El watched as Lord Ashford's face reset to the jovial, charismatic mask he'd been worn they'd arrived.

A knot of apprehension settled into her gut. *Who is this man, really?*

"All to your liking, Edward?" Ashford asked.

"I can't thank you enough, Ashford," Edward said. "Really. After the other night, your kindness in helping me..." His eyes welled with tears.

"Oh, Edward," Beth said, placing an arm around his waist, pulling him close.

Her eyes flitted to El then away. Even in that brief moment of eye contact, El knew what Beth was thinking: *See? How could he be a killer?*

"Nonsense, think nothing of it," Lord Ashford said, finishing his whiskey. "Come, dinner should be ready, and we have those dreadful murders to discuss. After all, that's what you're here for!" He stood, roughly slamming his glass onto the table beside the sofa.

El jolted, used to associating such noises with one of Da's tempers. Before she could recover herself and stand, Denys, Edward, and Beth headed out of the room, the door closing gently behind them.

Lord Ashford sidled over to her, his eyes studying her face. "Ellana Stone, Ellana Stone. I'll leave you be for now, but your time will come."

As she looked up at him, he blinked, leaving a blank expression on his face such that it appeared he hadn't been aware he'd even spoken.

He frowned, holding a hand towards her. "Come, Ellana; what are you waiting for?"

She took it, too confused to refuse.

His fingers wrapped firmly around her hand, almost too hard. She winced as he pulled her to the door. Before she could complain, he released her, opened the door, and nodded her through without a word.

El averted her gaze from him, her mouth dry and throat tight as she walked down the hall towards the dining room.

Ashford marched past El without a word and entered the dining room ahead of her. She took a moment before following, distracted by a rapid thrumming from her pocket. Laying a hand over the necklace, her brows furrowed. If there had been any movement, it stopped as quickly as it started. She walked into the dining room and hurried to her seat, though everyone was too busy listening to Lord Ashford to pay her any mind.

"—least I could do for my future wed-brother." He spoke to Beth and Edward, but El could feel his eyes on her as she walked around the table.

She reached for the already full glass of wine next to her plate, irritated that her hands were trembling. *What is wrong wi' me?*

Carefully she lifted the wine to her lips. *Just a glass*, she told herself. *Just a glass t' calm me nerves. That don't make me like Da.*

There was silence as dinner was served by a line of servants. They diligently went about their work, though refused to meet El's gaze, even when she tried to smile her thanks.

Lord Ashford clapped his hands, drawing their attention to him. "So, you've decided to investigate the Stalker."

"What? Elizabetha, how ghastly!" Edward exclaimed, frowning at his sister. "Why, by the Father, would you do that? Would you really bring such death and misery into your life?"

He appeared sincere in his confusion and dismay, and El considered that while he may have killed her Da and may yet be the Stalker, he appeared to have absolutely no knowledge of the fact. Else, he was the best liar she'd ever encountered.

Either way, it set her heart alight with rage. "Because," she said through clenched teeth, nostrils flaring, "he killed my Da and innocent young women. Women who was jus' tryin' t' make their way in life best they could. Because no one else seems to *give a shit*."

"El!" Beth barked.

Edward stared back at her, lips pursed. There was no notion of guilt in his expression, no sign he knew any intimate details about the murders, even her Da's.

In the ensuing silence, El wondered whether she'd gone too far at last.

Then Lord Ashford sighed and said, "You may be a simple Scrubber, but you are right."

El scowled. *Simple? How dare he!*

"Ash and I have been *most* concerned about the murders," Lord Denys said.

"Concerned?" she asked, turning to him. "What've you done to 'elp then?"

"It's not as simple as that, Ellana," Lord Ashford said. "Though, as you saw this morning and as I've told you, we have been to every murder scene in our duties as physicians. It's not much, but what we can provide to the City Guard by way of evidence, we do."

"You have?" Edward asked. "How- how distressing that must be for you."

"A bit of blood and gore doesn't put off a true doctor." Ashford sipped at his drink. "On the contrary, I find it fascinating to see the true form of the human body."

Denys locked eyes with Lord Ashford, shaking his head gently. "Ash," he said quietly, dropping his gaze to his plate. "Please."

Lord Ashford cleared his throat. "I meant no disrespect. Denys here finds it all rather difficult to stomach."

El was uncertain as to Ashford's intent by sharing such thoughts. Though they had come to learn about these very matters, she found herself increasingly keen to stray away from any topic which brought back images of her Da's butchered body. She breathed slowly to calm herself, then turned to Ashford. "You was gonna tell us about 'em. The young women you attended. The ones who was killed."

"Indeed. What part of the story did we get to?"

Beth pulled out her notebook and flicked through the pages. "You knew all the victims. You and Denys saw them all prior to their deaths, and, so, were the first port of call after their murders, too."

She took out her pencil. "El and I are keen to learn more about the women. About why you were called to attend them before their deaths. We know from speaking with Daisy's mother that she was unwell." She turned back the notebook pages. "Had been hearing voices, was becoming distant, unable to focus. Her mother told us they were offered a medicine which could help but were unable to afford it."

"Daisy, yes," Lord Ashford said slowly, tapping a finger on his lips. "She was pretty. Popular with the gentlemen, too."

El shifted with unease at the comment, and sensed Beth's mirrored discomfort. "What's that got t' do with anythin'?"

Lord Ashford raised an eyebrow. "Why, everything."

Denys leaned forward. "She was a working girl. They all were, it's believed." His tone was almost apologetic.

Beth's pencil stilled. "Working girl? You mean...?"

"Men paid to fuck them, yes," Ashford said deliberately, calmly holding Beth's gaze.

Denys pinched the bridge of his nose. "Ashford, really!"

"What?" he quipped. "What would you prefer me to say? *Make love?* Hardly fitting, is it?" Lord Ashford looked at everyone around the table. "I see no reason to be coy about such facts of life."

"I see no reason to use such blunt language in front of delicate young women," Edward retorted. "There's simply no—"

"Oh, fine, fine," Ashford conceded. "You always were sensitive, Edward. The young women provided their *feminine services* to men, is that better? By the Father, they were killed and you're more concerned with a *word*. Get some perspective, man."

"We're not delicate," El said sharply.

Lord Ashford laughed. "See?" He smiled at Beth. "I'm sorry if I offended you, my dear."

Beth shook her head, though her expression was drawn. "Think nothing of it, Ashford. Please, continue."

"See, your sister has a stronger stomach than you believe, Edward."

Lord Ashford took a moment to eat some of the sliced lamb on his plate before mopping at the corner of his mouth with a napkin.

El waited for him to finish, then placed her own cutlery down with a loud clank. "What's their work t' do with what 'appened to 'em?" She kept her voice firm and neutral, unwilling to allow her anger to take hold.

Lord Ashford's eyes locked with hers. "It's as I said—everything."

"What Ash means," Lord Denys interjected, "is they were all in vulnerable positions. They had to accept the patronage of strangers. It's believed the Stalker is most likely amongst those men."

Edward rubbed his chin, muttering, "Makes sense."

Beth paused, setting down her pencil. "I see this is upsetting for you, Ashford."

Lord Ashford sniffed, though, to El, he didn't appear the least bit upset. He squeezed Beth's hand. "Thank you, Beth, but it's-it's fine. I agreed to this."

Beth picked her pencil up and it hovered over her notebook once more. "You said you'd been called to see each of them. Why? Because of their illnesses? This madness you mentioned?"

El's stomach flipped.

"A sort of madness, yes. They were hearing voices, weren't they, Denys? Forgetting themselves. Fainting and blackouts, struggling to concentrate, their bodies shaking." He sipped at his drink. "Sad, really, to see those so young losing their minds."

Edward's cutlery screeched on his plate. "Blackouts?"

"Indeed. I believe, Edward, you're afflicted with a similar illness, though your symptoms are not exactly the same."

Edward blinked at Ashford. "A madness, you say."

"There was a cure, wasn't there? The medicine Daisy's mother told us you suggested," Beth said, an air of desperation in her tone.

Lord Ashford nodded, swallowing his mouthful of food. "A medicine, yes. It would've managed their symptoms, though cure the illness... hard to know since none of them took it. Edward, I believe, may give us the key to that. It's one of the reasons I offered for him to stay. If this strange illness continues to spread, who knows what—"

El rubbed her temple in thought. "Wait. How does the Stalker know who t' target? If it's this- this illness that's drawing 'im in."

"I believe there are more people afflicted than we realize, so it's likely the victims are simply a small selection of those individuals. Besides, as I said, their work would've meant they regularly saw patrons. It stands, then, that one of these men—the Stalker—noticed the symptoms and, for whatever reason, chose them for part of his... ritual."

"Ritual?" El scoffed. "You make it sound like a game. These are people's lives. Innocent people are bein' killed 'cos of some bastard's sick desires." She gripped her skirt, fighting the urge to leap across the table and shake Edward. *Why*, she wanted to ask. *Why did you kill my Da?*

She took a deep breath to calm herself again. "Bodies were found last night, for fuck's sake, an' here we are sittin' an' chattin' like these aren't people's lives being *stolen*!"

"Last night? Truly?" Edward shook his head slowly, the shock clear on his face.

"Yes," Lord Ashford said. "Three more victims." He ran a hand through his dark hair. "Father, son, daughter."

"How terrible. Why would he do such a thing?" Beth's voice trembled as she spoke.

Lord Ashford puffed air through his lips. "Perhaps El's right when she says I see it as a game." He gave a light cough and swirled the Blood Whiskey in his glass. "Because perhaps it is, to him." When he looked at El, his eyes were gleaming. "Who are we to say? Who are we to understand the actions of such a person?"

El rolled her jaw, irritated. "You sound like you respect 'im. Like you admire 'im."

"Don't be silly, El," Beth said, leaping to the defense of her betrothed. "That's not what Ashford meant."

There was drawn out, awkward moment of silence before Ashford said, "Of course not."

"Ash, I appreciate your offer to help me," Edward said, turning all eyes to him, "but I must insist your priority be... well, me. My health. I would hate to think you were distracted by all this other nonsense."

A light tinkling of nervous laughter rippled around the table, even from Beth.

There was a stab of sadness within El that these people were so removed from the true terror of the Stalker's reign that they could laugh at such a comment. These people were safe, and it showed in their nonchalant disregard for the poor families impacted, their casual gossip about the murders.

"Rest assured, Edward, my focus is on you. My future wed-brother's health is of the utmost importance to me. I know what you mean to Elizabetha," Ashford assured him.

"Oh, Ashford," Beth said with a breathy sigh.

El wanted to throw her wine glass. Instead, she pressed her hand against the necklace in her pocket, closed her eyes, and breathed. *They don't understand.*

Ignorant to her concerns, the conversation continued around her. She was aware of the cadence of voices and tuned back in as Beth asked, "What will Edward's treatment involve?"

"I will need to test his blood. Check his organ function. Try a few different concoctions. He will be closely monitored, kept to his rooms. Standard tests really." Ashford shifted in his seat. "I consider myself a doctor, but bureaucracy dictates I must complete a certain number of years in training before my peers will conclude the same. Though Denys can attest to my skill, can you not, Denys?"

Lord Denys coughed into his drink and glanced around the

table as he placed his glass down, giving a fleeting smile. "Yes, Ash. A skilled physician, no doubt about it, with a great deal of knowledge about the body." He lifted a napkin to his mouth, dabbing delicately. "My apologies, I must use the..." He stood, his chair scraping on the floorboards, and hurried from the room.

Lord Ashford clucked and shook his head. "A fine doctor he would be, too, if he could overcome his delicate disposition. He loves his work but these murders... Not everyone can handle the gore."

He pushed his empty plate away. "Speaking of which, that must've been quite the sight, Ellana—to see your father's body after the Stalker was finished with him. If it was anything like I've witnessed, it was... brutal. Efficient, but brutal."

El was met by a sudden influx of flashbacks. The blood. The smell. The Stalker's awful eyes. She shuddered. "Yes, my lord."

"What do you suppose that says about a man, hmm? To enact such terrible crimes. To inflict such dreadful violence on—"

"Now, Ash, I think we've spoken enough on these murders. My stomach is turning now, never mind Denys's!" Edward said.

Beth patted Edward's hand comfortingly. "I think this is the work of a very troubled man. An *angry* man. A man who needs help to see the atrocities he's committed for what they are. A man who needs help to stop."

El noted Beth didn't dare look at her brother, though there was no doubt her words were, in part, aimed at him—not that Ashford or Edward seemed to notice.

Lord Ashford retrieved a bottle of Blood Whiskey from a small, wooden trolley, then returned to the table and poured himself a generous measure. "An interesting theory."

"Theory?" Beth asked. "Yes, well, I suppose I can't know for sure." Her lips quirked and El could tell she was enjoying this exchange. "What is your theory then, my lord?"

Lord Ashford's eyes twinkled and El had the sense the two of them had quite forgotten there was anyone else in the room.

ECHOES OF THE ETHERSTONE

Irritated, she flushed hotly and snapped, "All this talk o' theories and ideas. This bastard is *evil*. There's nothin' else to it!"

"Sorry, El," Beth said softly, grimacing. "You know how seriously I'm taking this." Her gazed flicked towards her brother. "It's important for all of us."

Lord Ashford waved his hand as if to dismiss the topic. "Come, let us have dessert and say no more about it for now." He rang a bell, summoning the servants to clear the dinner plates and leftovers.

Dessert was eaten amidst chatter of the upcoming nuptials. Lord Denys reappeared just as they were finishing, his eyes bloodshot and mouth drawn down. "My apologies, sometimes everything just—"

"Yes, they know, Denys. The murders have been difficult for you." Lord Ashford cleared his throat. "But we've moved on to happier topics." He beamed at Beth. "Though now, my dear Elizabetha, it is time to bid you good night. Shall I see you to your carriage after you've said goodbye to your brother? He will remain here so I can begin his treatment immediately."

"And Edward will be safe here? You'll be sure he's always accompanied?" Beth asked.

"Beth! I am not a child," Edward chuffed.

"No," said Beth calmly. "But you are unwell. We wouldn't want you to be alone if you had another episode like the other night."

Everyone else would see her request as that of a caring sister, but El knew the intent behind her words. This was her way of ensuring Edward was unable to carry out any more murders.

"Rest assured, Elizabetha," Lord Ashford said, pushing in his chair, "your brother will be well cared for. There will be a servant in attendance in his rooms around the clock." He moved towards her and offered his hand.

She took it, smiling broadly, and the conversation was over.

As they were led from the dining room, El cast a glance towards Edward. His eyes were down, black and grey curls hanging over his forehead, his hands clasped on the table before him, his knuckles whitening. For the briefest moment she found herself sharing in his evident pain and fear.

And then she remembered those red eyes, the words he'd spoken—"I will do to you what I did to him, but I'll make sure it takes a lot longer." She recalled the force of his hands against her, pinning her to the wall, the screech he'd let out when Ren stabbed him.

How could this be the same man? She didn't know, but she needed to speak to Beth and to push their investigation ahead... and before the madness that had taken those poor young women consumed her. Before the Stalker came to claim her, too.

"D'you think that 'elped?" El asked once their carriage had cleared the gates at the end of the drive.

Beth jolted. "It's given us more information than we had, hasn't it? And I'm sure Ashford will be willing to help us more if we have further questions. Oh, isn't he wonderful, El? I do believe I am the luckiest woman in Alpinside."

El smiled and nodded, though Lord Ashford's strange behavior and words still circled her mind. "I'll leave you be for now, but your time will come." What did that mean?

She took in Beth's happy expression and knew she couldn't shatter it for words that made no sense. Perhaps he had simply been mocking her, a mere Scrubber—perhaps that was the way of noblemen.

Resigned to accepting that she would never truly understand this new social class she found herself moving within, she turned to watch the passing streets through her own dark reflection.

Is the Stalker lurkin' out there, even now? Or is he under Lord Ashford's watchful gaze?

El let out a long sigh. "Honestly, I'm not sure what t' think anymore."

"What do you mean?"

"Well, I were so sure it were Edward. An' I still reckon he killed Da—too much lines up there, what with 'im being stabbed... and 'is eyes." She didn't add that Lord Landrum's involvement and knowledge of the pouch for which Da were killed had also swayed her to that belief.

"Yes, I know," Beth whispered.

"But these young women. Daisy, Delilah, Penny, Rosie, and their families. And whoever the poor wretches were they found this mornin'. I think you was right. They don't fit in wi' Da's killin'. He were a bastard, but he din't have this madness. He weren't in the wrong place at the wrong time."

"So, you don't think Edward killed them?" Beth eagerly leaned forward. "In which case he can't be the Stalker then, can he?"

El bowed her head. "No."

"Which leaves two questions. Who is the Stalker? And why did Edward kill your father?"

El bit the inside of her lip. Lord Landrum had sworn her to and Ren to secrecy but... didn't Beth deserve to know the lies her family were telling her? The secrets they concealed? "I think I can answer the second one."

Beth's eyebrows shot up.

"There were a pouch. Of EtherStone."

"A pouch of EtherStone?" Beth's brow furrowed. "What's that to do with Edward?"

"I reckon that's what he were lookin' for when he came to our home. Da din't 'ave it though. I did."

"Wait, I don't understand. Where did the pouch come from?"

El tried to work out where to start. "The night of 'is murder, Da sent Ren an' me to fetch it. He was s'posed to go 'imself but 'e was in 'is cups."

"A pouch of EtherStone..." Beth muttered. "Where did you go to get it?"

"On the outskirts o' the Workers' District." El scratched her head. "Ren would know the way better than I. He knows 'is way through the city, all the back streets, like it's the back of 'is hand. I would've never gotten there without 'im."

Beth squinted at her notebook to make out her words in the darkness. "And who was it you received the pouch from?"

"No one. It were hidden in a brick wall." El scowled, never having pondered on how strange that was until then. But then, did it really matter? It was irrelevant, really, compared to the importance of the pouch itself.

"In... a... wall," Beth spoke slowly as she wrote. She chewed on her pencil. "And you believe that's what the Stalker... or Edward, was looking for when he came to your home?"

"Where is it? Don' t be a fool, child." Those words were still so clear to her, as though only just spoken. "Yeah, I reckon. What he said, he *wanted* somethin'. Really wanted it. And the house 'ad been ransacked."

"Strange he should be searching for that. Why would Edward need to seek out a pouch of EtherStone when our family mines provide ample supplies? Unless..." She slumped backwards, chewing absently on a fingernail. "I don't know enough, but some of the comments Father has made lately. And what Edward started to say at dinner the other night..." She shook her head exasperatedly before suddenly sitting forward again. "Where is the pouch now? Maybe it could help us—"

"I don't 'ave it anymore."

"Where is it?"

As they pulled into the driveway of Beth's home, El said, "It was taken from me."

"Taken? By who?"

El sighed. "Your father. He'd only take Ren an' me in if we gave 'im that pouch. He swore us t' secrecy, too. I shouldn't be tellin' you; we could get in real trouble if he knew."

Beth watched her for a moment before turning to look at her home. "By the Mother."

"What d'you think it means?"

The carriage door was opened and Allain peered inside.

"A moment, please," Beth snapped at him, pulling the door closed. "El, it's of the utmost importance you tell no one else about this pouch. About any of it."

"'Course I won't. Who else would I tell but you?" El frowned to herself. "Weren't even s'posed t' tell you. But we need t' get answers. We need t' carry on investigatin'."

"And we will. But I have a favor to ask."

"What?"

"That we pause our investigations until after the wedding in two weeks. I give you my word that as soon as I am married, we'll pick back up. We will get to the bottom of this. *All* of it."

El met her gaze. Beth's eyes were dark, a world of unspoken emotions within. She felt herself unable to question her mistress, though she wanted to with every fiber of her being.

"Very well," she said slowly, "we can wait. But we need t' do everythin' we can soon as your wedding's outta the way."

"Thank you, El. I promise, we will."

As Beth exited the carriage, El had a feeling she'd regret her compliance. In her pocket, the EtherStone necklace vibrated again. As before, when she placed a hand to it, it was perfectly still. She exhaled. Was that just another sign of the madness consuming her?

Beth's face appeared in the open carriage doorway. "Are you coming, El?"

"I'm comin'." El gave her pocket a final pat before descending from the carriage.

CHAPTER 19

THE WEDDING

Two weeks had flown by in a dizzying array of dress fittings, food tastings, and Temple visits, and the morning of the wedding had arrived. Beth had barely rested, the dancing butterflies in her stomach keeping her awake —not to mention the scenarios her mind played on a loop: the wedding itself, Ashford's face as she walked down the aisle, their first dance, the first time he called her Lady Elizabetha Branton, and, of course, the first time they would be together as man and wife. The last scenario made her gut flip in a way she'd never experienced before. Only having heard rumors of what happened in a marriage bed, she was left to wonder what, exactly, would take place on their wedding night. One thing she knew for sure, if it was anywhere near as thrilling as when he'd laid a kiss on her hand, she was sure she would burst with happiness.

As she lay staring at her ceiling, mind occupied by thoughts of her future husband, there was a knock at her door. Before she had a chance to respond, El scurried in. Guilt weighed heavy on Beth's chest that they should be so focused on a joyous occasion whilst their investigations of the Stalker's murders, and Edward's potential involvement, were placed on hold. It seemed absurd when she allowed herself to think about it.

Yet she'd been surprised at the ease with which she'd closed away her thoughts and feelings on the matter. How readily she ignored her fears that Edward wasn't the only family member somehow involved in what had happened to El and Ren's father. The pouch El had been tasked with retrieving, her father swearing the young woman to secrecy, what did it mean? When she'd asked El not to mention it and requested that they pause their investigations, a part of her had locked away that information, too. Still, she knew one day soon it would need to be examined more closely.

El perched on the side of her bed, pulling Beth's attention back to the moment. "You ready?" her Companion asked.

Having grown up without the closeness of female friends, Beth was suddenly absurdly grateful she was here. "I think so. I can't believe it's here already. By the end of today, I'll be Lady Branton!"

El's eyes flicked away from hers, and when they returned, there was an odd, unreadable glimmer within them. "That you will. Shall we start gettin' you dressed, then?"

Beth stretched her arms above her head. No time to dwell on what was on El's mind. "I think that'd be best. Though I'm sure Mother has everything planned out to the minutest detail."

As if on cue, there was a brisk knock on the door and, almost immediately, her mother marched inside. She was, unusually, not yet dressed. Beth rarely saw her without her hair perfectly coiffed and her outfit impeccable. Her long, black braids were draped over one shoulder, and she wore a floor-length, white lace dressing gown atop her blue linen nightdress.

"Good morning, Lady Oren," El muttered, demurely bowing her head.

"Good morning, Mother," Beth said, standing to kiss her cheek.

Her mother grasped her chin and turned her face from side to side, tutting, "Trust you to have such dry skin on the morning of your wedding. Have you not been looking after it as I instructed?"

"Well, yes, Mother, but I—"

Oren waved a hand dismissively. "It doesn't matter now. I'll have to hope one of my oils will help." She snapped her fingers at El. "Go and fetch some warm water, girl. And some lemon tea."

"Yes, m'lady." Her Companion poked her tongue out at her mother's turned back before hurrying from the room.

Beth bit back a laugh. "Lemon tea?" she asked. "Will I not be having breakfast?" She allowed herself to be guided to the dressing table.

"By the Mother, no!" Oren pushed her into the chair. "No time for that, child. We need to have you dressed and ready to receive a blessing from the EtherMother before the ceremony. You know that." She glanced pointedly at Beth's midriff. "Besides, it'll do you no harm to go without a meal."

Beth self-consciously placed a hand on the soft curve of her stomach, a lump forming in her throat. *What if Ashford judges me the same way? Will he still want me as only a husband can, or will he be disgusted at what lies beneath my fine wedding gown?*

Her mother placed a finger under her chin and lifted her head. "Smile! It's your wedding day, and you've snared yourself the *most* eligible young man in all of Estra! It's better than I've ever hoped for you."

Taking up a hairbrush, she began to comb through Beth's curls, pulling at snags without a care for the pain it caused. By the look on her mother's face, Beth assumed she believed what she had just said to be the highest of compliments. All Beth took from it was the idea that Ashford was far above her league, and she should be grateful for this most unexpected of couplings.

The excitement she'd felt upon waking was already ebbing away, diluted by her mother's judgmental words.

"You must ensure you do exactly as instructed today. When we arrive at the Temple, all must run smoothly." Her mother's lips puckered tightly as she worked at a particularly stubborn knot. "To have it any other way would be the gravest of signs for this marriage."

Beth frowned. Before she had a chance to ask what her mother meant, El bustled into the room with a jug full of water and began filling the basin at the foot of Beth's bed. Then she retreated, shortly returning with a tray of lemon tea. Beth heard footsteps outside and assumed she had recruited the assistance of Ren.

As El placed the tray on the dressing table, Beth smiled at her Companion. "Thank you."

Her mother let out a long, exasperated sigh. "You really must get out of this habit of thanking servants." She snapped her fingers at El. "Come on, girl, no time to stand idle. Take over with Elizabetha's hair while I get her dress ready."

El snorted as Oren marched from the room. "Always so serious." She picked up the brush and began attending to Beth's hair.

After a while, El paused mid brush stroke and raised an eyebrow at Beth in the mirror. "What's wrong?" She looked towards the door. "What'd she say? Was it more nonsense 'bout your belly? I've told you afore, you don't—"

"It... it's nothing, don't worry, El." Beth sat tall and forced herself to smile into the mirror. "Let's do my hair."

☙❧

ALMOST TWO HOURS LATER, BETH, EL, AND OREN WERE READY to make their way to the EtherTemple. As was the norm for an Alpinside wedding, Beth wouldn't see her father or brother until after the ceremony for she must be kept pure until her future husband saw her and she became his, body and soul. Her mother had even ensured all the male servants were elsewhere so as not to risk her being seen by any man other than Lord Ashford.

But there was no one else who could drive the steam carriage other than Allain. While her mother stepped outside to ensure his eyes were suitably averted from the front door, Beth waited in the hallway with El. Her Companion had been dressed simply in a long, red dress with a white collar, and a white flower—the same as those entwined in Beth's hair—tucked into the braid that wrapped around her head. After an impassioned argument from El about why she didn't need one, Beth had conceded that she would allow her Companion to go without a corset. She couldn't help but note that even without the figure shaping garment, El was truly beautiful, with her long limbs and narrow waist, her high cheekbones and bright blue eyes. In comparison, she felt short, squat, unattractive, like a plain rock next to an EtherStone jewel.

As if reading her mind, El beamed at Beth. "You look lovely, Beth. Really. Lord Ashford'll... I just hope he knows 'ow lucky he is."

"Come, you two. Into the carriage, quickly." Her mother waved them out of the house, frantically casting her gaze about as though expecting to be set upon by a group of rogue men.

The journey to the Temple was filled with Oren's curt instructions, to the extent Beth had the feeling she expected Lord Ashford to call the wedding off.

Leaning over, her mother brushed an imagined piece of dirt from Beth's shoulder. "Lord Ashford is a fine young man. And you... well, you shall need to prove yourself to be a wife worthy of him." She tucked a curl behind Beth's ear. "It's important for our family."

Beth heard El give a slow exhale, perhaps louder than she'd intended.

Her mother turned a glare towards her. "I wouldn't expect one of your *background* to understand." She patted Beth's knee and sat back to observe the city passing by. "Times are difficult for us all these days. There is a large responsibility on my daughter's shoulders. As her Companion, you will be there to provide any and all support she needs."

El bowed her head. "Yes, Lady Oren."

"Good. Now learn to control your feelings. I don't care to hear your belligerent sighs, nor does anyone else, understand?"

Beth tutted softly. "Mother, El is my Companion. She has been nothing but a support to me since Father offered her the position, what do a few sighs matter? Besides, it's my wedding day. Please, can we stop such talk now?"

"Sorry, Beth," whispered El.

Her mother merely scoffed, turning to stare out of the window.

Before long, the carriage pulled up beside the EtherMother entrance at the temple. Beth's eyes were drawn to the face of her beloved goddess, and she felt a great weight lift from her shoulders. She would ignore her mother's jibes and embrace the day— *her* day—as the start of her new life as Lady Elizabetha Branton.

While her mother attended to Allain, ensuring his eyes were averted once more, El caught her eye. "Ready?"

"I think so," Beth said.

"Just think, after today your mother won't be able t' speak t' you like that anymore."

Beth laughed. "It's a nice thought... but I'm not so sure about that, El."

The carriage door opened, and her mother held out a hand for her to take. Beth took it and followed her to the EtherMother door, her legs beginning to tremble with a heady mixture of anxiety and excitement. Inside, the temple was empty aside from the EtherPriest, who stood with open arms as they approached. He had a meshed, white fabric over his eyes to prevent him from seeing her, and Beth wondered how he hadn't tripped over.

"Elizabetha Estamore. Welcome. The EtherMother awaits," he said calmly.

She hesitated, noting he waved his arm towards a door behind him that she'd never entered before. Beth looked to her mother, seeking reassurance even knowing she was unlikely to receive it.

To her surprise, her mother stepped forward, cupping her elbows. "You must go in alone, Elizabetha. You must show the purity of your faith to the EtherMother. You will stay alone until it is time for the ceremony."

"Alone?" Beth glanced over her shoulder at El. "Why?"

"You will see, Elizabetha. This is an important part of the

ceremony." She moved to stand behind Beth, draping a chain around her neck. "This is for you. I bequeath our family's sacred EtherStone, passed down from mother to daughter, to you. Let it guide you and give you strength."

Beth's trembling hand drifted up to the jewel, a lump forming in her throat. "Thank you, Mother." The EtherStone was warm to the touch, smooth and round. As she cupped it in her palm, she suddenly recalled El had one just like it. With everything that had happened regarding the investigation and her focus on wedding planning, it had quite slipped her mind.

"Elizabetha, I know I've not always been the most... affectionate of mothers—"

Beth refrained from making a face as she met her mother's unexpectedly teary gaze.

Her mother cleared her throat before continuing. "Just know, I have done everything in my power to make your life as comfortable as possible. It hasn't always been easy, with your father's..." She sniffed, dabbing carefully at the corners of her eyes with a gloved hand. "I have done my best to give you the advantages I never had. You will be a fine wife; I am sure of it. I have taught you well." She clasped Beth's hand and gave the gentlest of squeezes.

Beth did not know what to say.

"It's time, Lady Oren." The EtherPriest was suddenly at their side, ushering Beth away.

"See you at the ceremony!" called El.

Her mother said nothing more.

"This is a time to pray. To allow yourself to be fully vulnerable in the eyes of the EtherMother. To let her see who you are: a devoted woman, soon to be a devoted wife." The EtherPriest's voice was deep and monotonous, as it was during his sermons.

Beth nodded curtly. She *was* devoted to the EtherMother, and to Ashford. *Then why does my heart race, my chest tighten with panic?*

The priest opened a dark wooden door, beckoning Beth

inside. "Be with the Mother," he said, closing it behind her with a firm *thud.*

The room was surprisingly dark, the only light a single candle flickering beneath a great canvas of art more than thrice Beth's height. There were no windows, and the air was heavy with perfume. Beth fought against the urge to cough, holding up a hand to cover her mouth.

"EtherMother?" she whispered.

She wasn't sure what she expected; she'd never been blessed with contact from her beloved goddess. Very few people had. She must simply have faith, as her mother had said. She must show her devotion.

With that in mind, she tentatively knelt—careful to avoid pulling at the delicate layers of silk and lace that made up her gown. As her knees hit the floor, she grimaced, then straightened her back.

She bowed her head. "Beloved EtherMother, I devote myself to your teachings. I believe I will be a dutiful wife to Lord Ashford."

Her words seem to echo in the silence.

She cleared her throat self-consciously and continued. "I- I will support him in his life's work. I will, um, bear him many sons." She snorted, unable to hold back the giggle bubbling up her throat. "I will—"

"*Elizabetha.*"

She gasped, turning to find the door still closed behind her. She remained alone. "Hello? Who's there?"

The silence was imposing, the darkness all encompassing. With nowhere else to look, Beth's gaze lifted to the canvas. It was a portrait of the EtherMother, similar to the ones of the Martyrs she'd taken El to see some weeks before. The flickering candle made the EtherMother's face shift—a blink of the eyes here, a twitch of the lips there. She closed her eyes and shook her head.

Paintings don't move. Your mind is tricking you, she chided herself.

"*Elizabetha, hear me.*"

Beth's eyes jumped open, immediately locking onto the painting. The EtherMother's eyes, dark green like emeralds, seemed to be watching her. *Judging* her.

"EtherMother?" she whispered, unable to stop the quaver in her voice.

"Hear me, child. You must provide your guidance."

"My guidance?" Beth frowned.

"Guidance to El-El-Ellana." The voice grew weaker.

Beth instinctively knew there wasn't much more time to communicate with it. "EtherMother, tell me, how must I guide Ellana? To see your truth and wisdom?"

There was a moan, as if of deep, unknowable pain. *"To save us. Find answers. Save us."*

"Save you? *How?*"

There was a horrible cry. The candle sputtered, then guttered out completely. Beth clutched her hands to her chest, pressing them against her thundering heart. She took in great, heaving gasps of the heavily scented air. Her fingers found the EtherStone necklace at her throat. She lifted it up and noted it was glowing. She gasped and dropped it again.

"Save us?" she croaked. "Who is *us?*"

There was a knock at the door, and she almost fell backwards in shock. The handle turned, and the door creaked open. One of the EtherPriests's acolytes entered and stood, pale skin stark against the darkness.

Beth squinted against the light that poured in. "Did you- did you hear that? The cry, it sounded like—"

The acolyte tilted her head, reaching out to touch Beth's arm. "Cry? No, I didn't hear a thing, mistress." She guided Beth forward. "Come, it is time."

Beth let out a sigh of relief as she was led from the room, glad to be leaving it behind, trying to banish the questions that arose. To distract her mind, she said, "How long was I in there? It seems only five minutes since I left my mother."

"Two hours, Mistress."

Two hours? Had she lost consciousness? Had the voice she'd heard been a dream? That would explain it, else she was going mad.

"—arrived and all is ready. It's the first wedding I've overseen actually," the acolyte said.

"The first, really?" Beth asked, not truly caring but afraid to continue down the path her thoughts were guiding her.

"Indeed, mistress." The acolyte gave a genuine smile, and Beth saw how young she truly was.

"Well then, EtherMother's blessings be upon you." Beth plucked a small, white flower from the wreath woven into her hair. "Here. For luck."

"Oh, thank you, mistress." The woman tucked the flower into the front pocket of her brown robes and stopped in front of the door that opened into the ceremony room. Her amber eyes pinned Beth with an intensity that belied her age—as if she held some deeper wisdom than Beth could know, as if her question was the most important one she could ask. "Are you ready?"

"Y-yes." Beth stood tall. "Yes, I'm ready."

The acolyte tapped gently on the door as if to signal Beth's imminent entrance. She imagined the room beyond, filled with the nobles of Alpinside, dressed in their finest and waiting to criticize her from head to toe. A bubble of panic rose in her throat, making her want to flee.

The door opened as if by itself, though at the back of her mind she acknowledged it was the acolyte's doing. At the end of the long aisle stood Ashford. He turned and their eyes locked, of that much she was certain, despite being unable to discern his expression. The way he stood with his shoulders back and head held high told her all she needed to know. He was *proud* to be there.

She inhaled deeply and took her first step onto the aisle. As she did, a low, vibrating hum emanated from the upper tier balcony that curved in a semi-circle above her head. The choir's timing was perfect, though all she could really focus on was taking each step as carefully as possible to avoid tripping over the long skirts of her dress. She kept her eyes down, afraid to meet the judging stares of the women around her—the men remained hidden behind the curtained left-hand side of the room and would remain so until she and Ashford had spoken their vows.

It wasn't that she begrudged them their comments, such was the nature of growing up in noble society, but to be so acutely aware that she was at the center of them was a new experience. Beth wished she'd had the commitment to slim herself down as her mother had told her to. She was all too aware of her ample bosom, thick waist, round stomach and curved hips as she moved ever closer to the end of the aisle, to Ashford.

When at last she had the courage to lift her eyes, she found herself looking at her future husband's features. For a moment, his expression was serious, and she faltered, afraid she'd made a mistake—that he wasn't proud to be here after all. Then his expression broke into a smile as he met her gaze. Her heart soared and, for the final few paces, all she could see was him.

At the end of the aisle, Beth was required to stand to the right of a curtain, while Ashford stood to the left. It was sheer white, so she could see his silhouette through it. She grinned, imagining he did so back.

"Nobles of Alpinside, loyal servants of the EtherFather, humble servants of the EtherMother, we are gathered here to bear witness to the marriage of Lord Ashford Branton, son of the late Lord Julius and Lady Celia Branton, and Mistress Elizabetha Estamore, daughter of Lord Landrum and Lady Oren Estamore.

"In joining these great families, it is my honor to strengthen the bonds within our great city; to show our beloved kingdom of Estra what it means to be a city of faith, of family and strength, of power and stability." The EtherPriest, whose eyes remained covered in white mesh, held up a golden chalice. "This wine is blessed by the EtherFather. When consumed, this couple will be bound together under His ever-watchful gaze."

Behind her, Beth heard mutterings of approval from the

guests. She glanced to the side, wondering if Ashford too felt a tightness in his chest or a quivering in his limbs. She put a hand on the EtherStone necklace her mother had given her, hoping to take strength from it. Instead, she was abruptly reminded of the curious voice and the words it had spoken.

"Help Ellana... Save us."

She shook her head and focused on the EtherPriest. He was holding the chalice over his head, his voice ringing across the ceremony room. "...in all we do. We thank you, oh Father, for all that you provide us. Now bear witness to the vows of this man and this woman as they set out to begin their lives together under your wise and benevolent gaze."

Beth entered a dazed state, focusing only on his words, determined not to make a mistake when repeating her vows. She found herself overcome with emotion when swearing to always respect, obey, and serve her husband, her voice shaking as she fought to hold back tears. When Ashford swore to protect, guide, and govern her, his voice was strong and sure.

"And now, may the curtains be lifted, that all may bear witness as Lord and Lady Branton share the sacred wine."

Behind them, the curtains around the noblemen were drawn back, but Beth did not look around, instead turning left and waiting for Ashford to be unveiled to her. Beside the priest, an acolyte turned a lever, and the curtain between them lifted. Ashford wore black trousers and a gold-buttoned, black blazer, accentuating his trim waist, the high collar of which skimmed his smooth, square jaw. On his belt, she noted the gold-etched handle of a blade. Finally, she examined his face; his black hair was slicked back from his face, and his beautiful blue eyes sparkled as he smiled down at her. She wanted to reach for him, to take his hand and feel his touch. But she knew she must wait. It wasn't proper to be so eager.

"Kneel, Elizabetha," the EtherPriest said.

She did as she was told, eyes still locked onto Ashford's.

The priest handed Ashford the chalice of wine. "Nourish your wife with this blessed wine, allowing your bond to be sealed."

Ashford took the chalice and held it to Beth's lips, gently tipping it so she could sip the rich, red liquid. The color reminded her of the EtherStone on her husband's finger and around her neck. She closed her eyes, gulping the wine down and cherishing the significance of its consumption. When she opened her eyes again, Ashford was drinking from the chalice himself. Once finished, he handed it to the priest and looked back down at Beth. Without prompting, he wiped his thumb across her lips, a stray drop of wine perhaps, but all Beth could think about was the way his fingers felt on her skin.

She let out a long breath, suddenly aware of all the eyes on them.

Ashford held his hand out for her. "Stand, Lady Branton."

She took his hand and allowed him to pull her up. Then he turned them both towards the congregation, holding his free hand up as though presenting a prize for the whole of Alpinside to see. All Beth could do was smile as applause spread through the temple. This was a moment to revel in. This was where her life truly began.

Ashford linked his arm in hers and led her back down the aisle. She moved as though floating on air, her limbs light, her steps quick to keep up with her husband's long strides. This time, she cared not for the eyes on her, scrutinizing and judging. She could barely tear her eyes away from Ashford.

He was hers. She was his. It was a dream come true.

Outside the temple, a white carriage with red trim awaited them. The driver, a young man Beth didn't recognize, leapt to open the door for them.

Ashford guided her into the carriage, saying, "Our first journey as husband and wife."

He leaned down to kiss her hand as she took her seat in the carriage. It was as thrilling as it had been the first time. Ashford clambered in beside her and his heat washed over Beth. His scent was sweet and flowery; she wanted to bathe in it.

As the carriage moved away, Beth's nerves kicked in once more. Here she was, with the most eligible man in Alpinside, now her husband, no less. *What can I possibly speak to him about?* she wondered. *How can I be interesting, prove I'm worthy of his love?*

Ashford opened the golden buttons on his blazer and reached inside, pulling out a small, finely carved, wooden box. "It's not traditional," he said, handing it to her, "but I would like you to have this."

Beth took the box from him and open the lid. It was warm from being next to his body, smooth and well-polished. Inside was a golden band, decorated with tiny shards of blood-red stones.

"EtherStone," Ashford said, confirming her suspicion. "From my family's mines. It was commissioned by my father for my mother. I thought it would be far more interesting than that simple gold band I proposed to you with."

Beth touched it, feeling the tiny stones delicately scratching her skin. "It's beautiful."

Ashford took the ring from the box, lifted her hand, and placed it on her middle finger.

"Thank you," she said, a swell of happiness blooming in her chest.

"I have another surprise for you, too."

"Another?"

"After the ball, I've made arrangements for us to take the carriage to a small cottage southeast of Alpinside, nestled beside the Alpin Way Lakes. It's quite beautiful, and the staff are very discreet. We will largely be left alone. Just the two of us."

Beth's eyes widened. "Just the two of us?"

"Yes." He leaned in close so his lips almost touched her ear. "And I will keep you there for as long as I like."

Beth shivered with delight, hairs springing up along her arms. "That sounds wonderful."

Ashford slumped back into his seat and let out a long sigh. "Now, just to get through the ball."

Beth raised an eyebrow. "You don't like balls?"

He laughed. "By the Father, no." He lifted a hand to stroke her cheek. "My dear, all I want is to be alone with you."

Beth flushed.

"Don't worry. I'll be gentle with you." He leaned in and whispered in her ear, "If that's what you want."

Beth shuddered. She met his gaze, heart pounding in her ears, unsure what to say. Surely, he knew she had no such experience, that she'd remained unspoiled for marriage, just as the Ether-Mother commanded.

Before she knew what was happening, Ashford leaned in and placed a gentle kiss on her lips. At first, she was frozen, but as his mouth moved against hers, she began to soften. She allowed him to lead, to guide her as their tongues flitted against each other. She thought she might faint for her very soul was aflame with desire.

And then he pulled away, grinning down at her as the carriage jolted to a halt. "Oh, Elizabetha. I will devour you."

Heart aflutter and mouth still tingling, she simply smiled back at him, not truly knowing—or caring—what his words meant. All she could think of was wanting him to kiss her again, and forevermore. She was giddy with love.

"Come," he said, holding out a hand as he stepped down from the carriage. "Our home awaits."

CHAPTER 20

THE CHASM

Denys watched his dear friend proudly march his new bride down the aisle of the Temple, his lips pulled back into a broad smile. He found himself echoing the expression, though his aching heart thudded so hard he feared it might shatter. As Ashford and Elizabetha exited the temple and those around him began to chatter excitedly, Denys was taken back to a morning some weeks ago, just after Ashford had told him of the engagement.

"I must do this, Denys. You know that." Ash had marched in front of him, irritation evident in the stiffness of his stride. "You act as though I do it to hurt you."

Denys had twisted his fingers together, his hands resting in his lap as he perched on the edge of his bed. Ashford stopped his pacing and finally sat beside Denys, their thighs brushing together briefly.

Ash cleared his throat. "What is it that upsets you so about me getting married? Aren't you happy for me?"

Denys met those beautiful blue eyes he knew so well. "Happy for you?" he croaked. "Ash, you know what I feel. How could I possibly be—"

"Hush, Denys. Hush." Ashford reached across, resting his warm palm on the top of Denys's hand. "I know what is in your heart, my friend, you know I do. And you know that..." He squeezed Denys's hand before pulling his touch away. "You know that you mean much to me, Denys. You are the only person who truly understands me. I do not know what I would do without you, without your unwavering support."

Denys looked up, though Ashford faced away, keeping his expression hidden. *Tell me,* he thought to himself, his heart aching with longing. *Tell me you feel it, too.*

But the silence had dragged on, growing like a chasm between them, until finally Denys could bear it no longer. "You must wed to secure your family's future," he muttered. "I know that. But Ash, I will never—"

"I knew you'd understand." Ash turned to face him, his smile full of relief, his eyes glimmering with joy.

Did my acceptance mean so much to him? Denys wondered. Aloud, he said, "I will always support you, Ashford. I will always be by your side, no matter what."

Their gazes locked for a prolonged moment before Ash nodded, slapped his hands against his thighs, and stood. "This is why you are my Companion. This is why you are my family." He turned and held out a hand for Denys to take. "Come, let us drink some Blood Whiskey. To celebrate."

Denys hadn't hesitated; in that moment, he had wanted nothing but the fog brought on by the consumption of Blood Whiskey, to numb his pain and quiet his thoughts, to repress the love and longing that raged in his heart and soul.

And now, weeks later, watching Ashford marry Elizabetha, that same need resurfaced sharply. Now that they were wed—now that there was no turning back—the jealousy that had started as a light needling in his stomach had become sharp and insistent, stabbing at him over and over again. He counted down the minutes until he could be alone in his study with a glass full of whiskey, drinking himself into oblivion to avoid thinking of Ash with his new bride. Spending the night together, becoming one as they explored each other's bodies, just as he and Ashford had done two years ago when they had been brought together in their joint grief. When they had found solace in each other as only lovers can.

Denys closed his eyes, recalling the softness of Ashford's perfect skin, the gentle touch of his lips, the moans of pleasure that had engulfed them both.

Then he recalled Ashford's words the morning afterwards. "It can never happen again, Denys. The EtherFather allows us our transgressions, but... we cannot be wed under His eyes. We cannot be together as you want."

He bit his lip, holding back the tears which threatened to fall, to betray the depth of his anguish. He would love Ashford always, he knew that, even as he knew that very love blinded him to—

"Lord Winborn?" said a woman's voice, a hand touching his arm.

Denys's eyes flew open.

It was a middle-aged noblewoman, an ostentatious red feather headdress fluttering atop her greying hair and an EtherStone necklace glinting around her neck. Denys furrowed his brow, trying to recall her name. She was a lesser noble, given the meager size of the EtherStone, but he'd never had Ashford's propensity for remembering names and faces.

"Yes, m'lady?" he asked, trying his best to sound cheerful.

She looked up at him, studying his eyes for just a moment too long. "Are you well, Lord Winborn?"

Denys forced a smile. "Oh, yes. It is a day of celebration!"

She nodded, pointing towards the Temple entrance. "That it is. And if we don't follow, we might just miss the celebrations!" She held out an arm. "Will you escort me to my carriage, m'lord?"

Denys hooked his arm around hers. "It would be my pleasure. And please, you must tell me, where you got that wonderful head-dress from."

The woman spoke and Denys nodded along, responding in all

the right places, and all the while his broken heart bled like a knife-wound.

CHAPTER 21

THE BALL

Though Beth had always enjoyed balls, she found her own wedding feast held little interest for her. She greeted guests and spoke to her peers, rejoicing at the jealousy in their eyes as she showed off the ring Ashford had gifted her—yet it all paled in comparison to that kiss, and to the thoughts of what more might await her when they were alone.

Her parents, as she'd expected, were reveling in the limelight. Her mother, in particular, could often be heard loudly declaring this was the wedding of the decade. Beth had quietly tutted and steered course away from her each time.

When she finally noticed Edward's absence, she wondered whether she'd simply missed him in the crowd or if he'd never been there. She pulled Ashford to the side.

"Are you well, my dear?" he asked.

"My brother," she whispered, "has he left already?"

"Oh." Ashford sipped at his Blood Whiskey. "He was unable to attend. He needs rest. His treatment has taken more of a toll than expected. I'm sorry, I thought I told you after the ceremony."

"No... no, you didn't."

Ashford furrowed his brow, gently touching her cheek. "It must have slipped my mind, Beth. I was certain I'd told you."

She shook her head, frowning. "No, no, you're right, you must have. It's been a long day. So much excitement."

He smiled, leaning closer. "It has been a long day, and all I want is to—"

"Lord Ashford!" called a voice from behind them.

"Do excuse me, my dear, I must go and see what—"

"Of course," she said, waving him away. "Go, go."

She watched him move away, impatience surging through her body. But she had to wait, for it was not yet proper for them to leave their wedding ball. Glancing around the room, she noticed El tucked away in a corner and wove between guests to join her. As she sat beside El, she suddenly recalled the words she'd heard in that dark room, the pain, the awful cry, the desperation.

"El," she said, "I wondered where you'd gone."

Her Companion gave a tight smile, though it seemed more a grimace. "I've never seen so many people in one place. It got a little, um..."

"Intimidating?" Beth finished, taking in the room. There *was* a lot going on with the music and dancing couples, the constant hum of chatter, the clinking of glasses and cutlery as people drank and ate. She'd grown up attending such balls and had known what to expect; for El, this was a whole new experience. Determined to ignore the little voice at the back of her mind whispering, *Help Ellana, help Ellana, help Ellana*, she nudged her Companion gently with her elbow. "I'm glad you're here. What did you think of the ceremony?"

El gave her a sideways glance. "Wasn't what I expected." She snorted. "Then again, I'm not sure what I *did* expect." She seemed to notice something and tentatively reached a hand towards Beth. "Oh. It's yours now, is it?"

Beth placed her hand on the necklace at her throat. "Oh, yes. Mother gave it to me sooner than expected." She tilted her head.

"You have one, too. No matter how you came to have it, it means you're connected to the EtherMother."

More than you realize, Beth thought. Perhaps she should speak to El about what had happened, though part of her remained unsure as to what *had* happened. *Did I dream it? Would speaking it aloud simply sound mad?*

"Mm." El shifted uncomfortably, then turned her gaze back to the ballroom. "I haven't seen your brother. Did he retire early?"

Beth's lips pulled down. "Actually, he didn't come at all. That's what Ashford tells me, anyway."

El's brow creased. "He din't? 'Ow come?"

"Resting. But now that I think on it, I haven't seen him since he moved to Ashford's. I've been so focused on the wedding... I did not even think to ask about him. I've been so selfish, El, I really should have—"

"Hush." El patted her arm. "What else can we 'ave done? He's not well, Beth. Not in 'is right mind. P'raps it's best he's had time away from everyone. You trust Lord Ashford... don't you?"

"Of course, I do. It's just I'm going away for the next few days and—"

"Goin' away? Where you goin'?"

Beth giggled, a flush creeping up her neck. "Ashford told me we're going to stay in his cottage outside Alpinside. By the Alpin Way Lakes. Just the two of us."

"I see." El turned, studying the people around them. "You want me t' find out 'bout Edward, don't you?"

"If, um, if you'd be willing to. I understand if you'd rather not—"

"Elizabetha, there you are!" Ashford appeared through the crowd, joined closely by Denys. "It's time for us to lead a dance. Denys has graciously agreed to partner with you, Ellana."

"Oh, no, uh, I dunno how to—" El stammered with a startled expression.

"Nonsense," Ashford said jovially, waggling his eyebrows. "Denys is a patient partner, are you not, Denys?"

Lord Denys stiffly nodded and offered El a hand.

Ashford took Beth's hand, and she threw El an apologetic smile as she was dragged away. The crowd parted for them, casting admiring gazes upon her husband and envious gazes upon her.

At the head of the dance floor, Ashford held his hands aloft and the musicians ceased their playing. He waved over a nearby servant who held a tray of flutes filled with sparkling champagne. He took two, handing one to Beth, as a hush settled over the room.

"Friends, family, fellow nobles of our beloved Alpinside," he said, voice reverberating, "I would like to raise a toast to my beautiful bride, Lady Elizabetha Branton." He held his drink high. "Elizabetha!"

Her cheeks burned as her name echoed about the room. She drank her champagne, pleasantly surprised by its sweet flavor and the way it fizzed on her tongue.

Ashford continued, "I am proud to have her by my side as I continue to solidify my father's legacy. To do the work of the EtherFather. To allow Him to continue to so generously bless my family mines with the precious EtherStone, such that I may share it with you all."

Whispers rippled around the room along with glances of confusion.

Ashford chuckled. "Yes, you heard right. I have been most fortunate of late. The EtherFather smiles upon me. The head of each family present here today will be gifted with a small bag of EtherStone, as thanks for your ongoing support. I know times have been challenging for some and I would like to repay your loyalty.

"Now, I shall dance with my wife. Please, join us. After this, we will retire. Thank you all, once again, for coming."

Ashford placed his and Beth's empty flutes back on the servant's tray, then clasped her hand tightly.

"The EtherMother's Waltz," he called to the musicians.

He pulled Beth close, placing a hand on her waist. He leaned down and whispered in her ear, "Not long now, my dear."

She shivered, and was whisked into an upbeat dance, the steps of which had been drummed into her since she was a child. Ashford was a fine partner and as they whirled and stepped together, it was as though they had always been dancing, as though they were meant to be. Beth was breathless with the overwhelming sense of love that blossomed in her heart for this charming, perfect man.

As the music drew to its conclusion, the room lit up with applause and Ashford drew her in, crushing her against his chest. She was smothered by his scent and struck by the heat he gave off. It made her weak at the knees. She barely cared about the applause or the people around them anymore. She wanted only to be alone with him, to feel his lips on hers once more.

As though reading her mind, Ashford pulled her eagerly through the crowd, leading her to the front door of the manor. Words of congratulations washed over them, but Beth's eyes were only for her husband. She watched the back of his head wondering what it would feel like to run her hands through his dark, glossy hair.

At the door, their cloaks and furs were donned, whilst outside, the carriage awaited, already packed for their trip.

As they took their seats and the steam engine rumbled beneath them, Beth leaned into Ashford. "How long will the journey take?"

"Too long," he said huskily.

৩৵৩

AN HOUR LATER, THE CARRIAGE PULLED TO A STOP OUTSIDE A small cottage on the shores of the Alpin Way Lakes. It might have been breathtaking with the moon shining off the clear, icy waters —but Beth barely paid it any heed.

Holding her hand, he led her to the front door, which was opened by a young man dressed all in black.

"Be sure we are not disturbed," Ashford told the servant, handing over his cloak.

"Yes, Lord Ashford. There is a bath prepared for you."

Ashford pulled her into the cottage, a glimmer of desperation in his eyes that mirrored her own. She was breathless with it.

In their room, he closed and locked the door before turning to face her. He cast her a devilish smile, his eyes glinting with an excitement she hadn't seen before, even when they'd kissed in the carriage; the butterflies in her stomach felt like they might burst through her skin altogether. Finally tearing her eyes from him, she took in the room around her.

The bed was a four-poster with white curtains of the finest silk. The sheets also appeared to be the best that money could buy—pure white, unblemished, silky soft to the touch. On top of them, were scattered flower petals of the deepest red. The smell was heady, sweet, floral—just like Ashford's cologne. There was a hearty fire, recently stocked with logs, in front of which sat a huge copper bathtub, filled with steaming water, more petals, and soapy bubbles.

"A bath?" She raised an eyebrow. "Do you think me dirty, my lord?" She'd meant the words to be playful, but Ashford frowned deeply in response.

"Not at all." He approached the bed and perched on the edge. "But it's been a long day. I thought you would enjoy a bath to... freshen up. It would be my honor to assist you."

He held his hands out and she stepped towards them, allowing him to envelope her. He pulled her close, his head at a height with her chest. He lifted a hand, cupping her chin.

She gulped, trying to ignore the pounding drumbeat in her ears.

"Turn around," he whispered.

Beth did as he asked, eager to please. She felt hands on her waist, hips, and bottom, and flushed with self-consciousness. *What will he think of me?*

As if in response to her thoughts, he said, "You're beautiful."

He began to undo the buttons securing the bodice of her dress slowly and with care. Then he stood, pulling wide the split. Sliding his fingers beneath the dress, they brushed over her back and shoulders, her body tingling at his touch.

He unbuttoned her skirt next, slipping his hands beneath the waistband and removing her multiple layers in one downward motion. Beth stepped out of them, conscious of her bare legs, yet also entranced and excited. Her breaths came quickly, her mouth was dry.

Then was her corset, which Ashford untied with just as much care as everything else. His breath was hot on her neck. Every now and then, his hands would pause to linger, stroke.

"Your skin is so beautiful," he said. "So dark, so smooth. Unblemished."

"T-thank you, my lord. Ashford."

He continued to loosen her corset, not addressing her use of his title, evidently concentrating on the task at hand. When the corset was sufficiently loosened, he helped her out of it.

She was left in only a thin, cotton chemise that hung to her thighs. Beth lifted her arms to cover her breasts, aware of how they hung, heavy and full, without the support of her clothes.

Ashford moved to stand in front of her, pulling her arms aside. "No. Don't cover yourself. You don't need to do that."

Without warning, he lifted the chemise, pulling it over her head, snagging slightly on the pins in her hair. Flowers fell to the ground, petals of white mixing with the red already there. It distracted her enough that she didn't cover her nudity.

Ashford inhaled softly and for a moment, she feared he was repulsed by her, as her mother had led her to believe. Then he bit down on his lower lip—a look filled with hunger—before saying, "Oh, Beth. You are *perfect*."

She didn't know what to say. She was shy, unused to being on show.

He stepped closer, his face leaning down to hers, their lips almost brushing. She anticipated the kiss and wanted nothing more. Instead, he pulled away again, leading her teasingly towards the bath. The steam washed over her as she neared, richly aromatic and deliciously warm.

"Get in," Ashford said, offering a hand to steady her as she stepped over the rim.

Lowering herself into the water, she found it hot and soothing. For an awkward moment she looked up at him, wondering what he expected.

Ashford knelt down so their faces were level, his fingertips brushing the water. "May I... wash you?"

Beth was used to being attended by servants, but this was different. This was her husband, the man whom she should be serving, not the other way round.

"Please?" He pouted.

Beth giggled, nodding her consent.

"Call me my lord again," Ashford requested.

Beth sat tall, meeting his eyes with far more confidence than she truly felt. "Very well, my lord."

Ashford let out a long exhale, the corners of his lips turning upwards as he picked up a cloth. He washed every inch of her, his movements soft and soothing. By the end, she wanted to beg him to kiss her, though the words stuck on her tongue. She ached for his lingering touch. When he was finally done, he retrieved a white towel and helped her stand. He took his time drinking in her body before draping the towel around her shoulders.

Out of the bath, he grasped her shoulders and looked into her eyes. "Are you ready?"

She swallowed and whispered, "Yes."

Leading her to the bed, he pulled away the towel and gently pushed her down to lay on top of the soft quilt and petals.

Ashford removed his own clothes in the same ritualistic way

he had Beth's. When he came to the belt at his waist, he handled the blade he wore with an incredible amount of care, almost as much as he had shown towards her.

When he noticed her watching, he said, "It's a ceremonial knife that belonged to my father. See here, the Branton crest?" He pulled it from its sheath and held it up to the flickering gaslamp beside the bed, fingers running over the patterned hilt. "I gifted Denys a duplicate when he moved into the manor. He's a Branton in all but name."

"I can see it's important to you," Beth said, turning to her side so as not to feel so exposed. "And that Denys is important to you, too."

"Very. He's my closest friend and colleague." He sat beside her, holding the knife for her to see. "And this, too, has its place in my heart. I almost lost it once. It may sound silly but... it's one of the few possessions I have that makes me feel truly connected to my father. He bestowed it to me on my seventeenth birthday, not long before he died. I would've been distraught if it hadn't been returned to me."

Beth reached for his forearm and stroked it gently, her nakedness forgotten in the face of this moment of emotional intimacy. "It's not silly at all."

He returned the touch, nodding. "I knew you'd understand, and that you were the right choice for my wife. Kind, caring, compassionate." He placed the blade back in its sheath before reaching across to stroke her cheek. "Soft, beautiful, pure. Your faith strong and sure." He let out a quivering breath. "I can't wait any longer."

He placed the sheathed knife on the bedside table and continued to undress, this time with a sense of urgency he hadn't previously possessed. And then, he was stripped to nothing, his perfect, pale skin glowing in the softly ebbing gaslight.

He lay down at her side and placed a warm hand on her waist. He leaned up on an elbow. "Lady Branton," he said hoarsely, "it's as I promised earlier. I will devour you."

Without allowing her a chance to response, he pressed his mouth to hers in a kiss far hungrier than the one in the carriage, though she'd barely thought that possible. Her body pressed against his with an instinctive magnetism, and she allowed him to take control.

In the hours that followed, as he showed her everything it meant to touch and be touched in the most intimate of ways, the same thought echoed in her mind over and over again.

I am the luckiest woman in Alpinside.

CHAPTER 22

THE GREED

El watched Beth being led away at the end of the dance, acutely aware she was alone in a room full of strangers. What was worse, strangers who would sooner see her returned to the streets than welcomed into their company.

"May I get you a drink?" Lord Denys asked, still by her side after their forced partnership.

She turned to him, seeing her own weariness mirrored back. "No thank you, m'lord. I'm not a keen drinker, an' truth be told I'd like nothin' more'n my bed right now."

Nearby, a group of young women began to laugh, pointedly staring at her. She ignored them, too tired to bother responding.

Lord Denys, for his part, cast them a glare. "I know what you mean. I wonder if you'd like to accompany me for some tea in my private study." For good measure, he held out his arm for her to take. The young women grew quiet, a couple letting out gasps of shock.

From a man who El had written off as inherently disinterested in anyone other than Ashford, she was pleasantly surprised by this turn of events. She smiled, taking the offered arm and allowing him to lead her away from the gaggle of women and cacophonous noise of the ballroom.

In the main entrance hall, he took a turn, steering them away from the grand staircase at its center towards a door tucked in its rear left corner. Inside, beneath a carved white marble hearth, a fire crackled. In front of the fireplace sat two cushioned brown leather armchairs, tilted at an angle so those sitting could converse and enjoy the warmth of the flames.

"Please," said Lord Denys, motioning towards the chairs as he shut the door.

El was surprised to see a pot of steaming tea and two cups already on the table between the seats. She took the left chair, Denys the right. He sank down with a long exhale, slapping his hands on his legs and leaning back as though he'd been waiting for this moment all evening.

"So," he said after a few moments, sitting forward to pour the tea, "how did you enjoy your first ball?"

El fought against the grimace already forming on her face. "It was, uh... enjoyable, my lord."

Denys laughed, a rich, deep sound, and his dark eyes twinkled with genuine mirth. "Come now, Ellana. I saw your discomfort. You hid it well as we danced, but you can't tell me you *enjoyed* it." He pushed her teacup towards her and picked up his own. "Believe me, I understand. Alas, as Companions to Lord and Lady Branton, we must continue with this façade."

El raised an eyebrow, picking up the cup of dark red tea. "You don't like 'em? Ain't it part o' bein' a noble, attending 'em?"

"A downside, if you ask me." He sipped his tea, lips smacking in appreciation. "Ah, perfectly brewed. Just what I needed after so much damned Blood Whiskey." He sat back and sniffed. "Besides, what makes you think I'm a noble?"

El regarded him over the rim of her teacup, taking a sip to delay giving an answer. The tea was hot and sharply sweet, with a floral undertone. It was an unusual flavor, though not unpleasant. Lowering the cup, she wondered if Denys's question was a trick, seeking to catch her out. His brow was raised; evidently, he was keen to hear her reply. There was a playfulness to his expression that made her think he knew what she would say.

"Well... you're a lord, ain't you?" she said hesitantly.

Lord Denys took another swig of tea. "For what it's worth, yes... But perhaps I shouldn't say that. Sorry, Papa." He kissed his palm and raised it to the ceiling. "For the gods of our ancestors, whose names are not permitted here, but who watch over him in the afterlife."

For the first time, El wondered how much Blood Whiskey he'd consumed that evening. There was nothing unsteady about him, but she saw a pain in his eyes that spoke of memories flooding back—the same expression she'd seen in Da's eyes when he was deep in his cups and thinking of Ma.

"Papa?" she asked, remembering how Da had always been eager to speak of the memories in those moments, to allow snatches of love to shine through the grief and pain he so longed to numb.

"Indeed. My father, Lord Darys Winborn. He was so proud to be named an honorary noble of Alpinside after traveling to Estra from the Southern Isles."

"How'd he come to be a lord then?" she asked, genuinely curious. She'd always believed those in the nobility were born into it. Simple luck to be brought into the world under the protection of such privilege. Now she was being told it wasn't as simple as she'd thought.

"Money, basically." Lord Denys refilled his cup. He held the pot out to her, and she declined, still only halfway through the first cup. "The Southern Isles are rich with precious metals. My papa made his fortune there and sought to make a name for himself in Estra. As the second son, there was little waiting for him on the Isles." He proffered his teacup towards a portrait to the left of the hearth. "That's him, there."

El leaned forward, squinting to make out the image in the shadows beside the hearth. The portrait was tucked beneath a landscape painting and a knife upon a plaque. "You look like 'im," she said, seeing the same chiseled features, dark eyes, brown skin, and close-cropped curls.

"I've often been told so. Though few enough remember him now. Or my mama."

"What 'appened to 'em?" El asked, drinking more of her tea. She was growing to like it, sharp sweetness and all.

"My mama died when I was a child. An ailment of the lungs so I'm told. And my papa..." Lord Denys sighed. "Greed, I suppose you'd call it. Though I believe the old fool was simply trying to fit in." He set his empty cup down and dropped his head back, momentarily closing his eyes. "When he moved here, he found gold and silver had ample worth in Estra and in Alpinside, so he was accepted into society well enough. But it was the mysterious EtherStone that held the power, EtherStone that dictated who was respected, who was revered."

"EtherStone?" El's mind went to her necklace, still tucked away in her pocket.

"Whoever owns the mines, controls Alpinside. Now, my papa, bless his soul, learned this and quickly sought to gain himself a position of influence. But mines of EtherStone are not easy to come by. They're held by the wealthiest families, not often released for sale."

"He obtained one though?"

"He did. Much as it ended up being his downfall." Lord Denys sniffed again, running a hand over his eyes. "A curse, you might call it. Though perhaps mere bad luck is what it amounts to."

"We don't 'ave to talk 'bout this if you don't want to, m'lord."

He looked at her, lips twitching into a brief smile. "I started it, did I not? It's funny, I find myself strangely clear-minded around you, Ellana, even with my copious consumption of... Mm." He held a hand to his forehead. "I'll regret this in the morning, no doubt, but Ash is *so* insistent. Connects us with the EtherFather, he says." He looked at her, head cocked. "But with you... it's like I want to talk about things I haven't for a long time. I can't explain it. I just feel I can trust you."

El wasn't sure how to respond. She was so mistrustful of others, a natural response to being surrounded by desperate people who would do desperate things to see their next meal, a roof over their heads, a place to shelter their children. So, for someone not to trust her seemed only natural—expected, even. Twice now, first with Beth and now with Lord Denys, the idea that mistrust was the normal order of life was being challenged. It sat uncomfortably within her.

Eventually she said, "I'm not sure why that might be, my lord, but... I'm 'appy to listen."

"No need for any more of that 'my lord' nonsense. Just Denys is fine." He sighed as the clock above the hearth began to chime. "Gods, is that the time? I've kept you up. Come, I'll show you to your room. You'll be quartered next to Lady Branton." He retrieved a gas lantern from a sideboard before leading them from the room.

As they walked, El cleared her throat. "My brother Ren, as well..." she said cautiously. "I was told 'e could come to live 'ere too."

Denys paused, turned to her, rubbing his chin with his free hand. "Not something I've heard about, but I see no reason why that couldn't be arranged. Leave it with me."

"Thank you my—uh, Denys."

He smiled. "Think nothing of it. Now, let's retire, shall we? I've a mind to get to my bed and not leave it until tomorrow afternoon."

At the top of the grand staircase was a set of ornate double doors, which Denys told her led to the late Lord and Lady Branton's private chambers.

El frowned. "Ashford doesn't sleep there?"

Denys met her gaze. "Lord Ashford's bedchambers are downstairs, as are mine," Denys said. "He set up a private..." He shook his head as though stopping himself from saying more. "It does not matter. It is simply more convenient for us both to be downstairs and close to each other, in case..."

"In case you need t' see patients?" El finished for him.

Denys nodded briskly, lips quirking upwards. "Yes. Yes, exactly."

"I see," El said. She glanced behind her, towards the double doors that led into the unused rooms. The more El saw of Branton Manor, the more astounded she became. The manor was far bigger and grander than she'd imagined.

Denys led her down the hall for a short distance before stopping outside another carved, gold gilded door. "This is Beth's room," he said, opening it and walking inside.

El followed him, her mouth dropping opening. Her old home in the Workers' District could fit into Beth's room three times over. But there was no time to stop and gawp—Denys walked onward, towards another, plainer door which was nestled in the far corner of the chamber.

"And these are your private chambers," Denys said, turning the handle and pushing through the door. "A full wardrobe of clothing to suit your station. Some combs and brushes for your hair. The basics are covered. Do let me know if there's anything you're missing."

"Missin'?" El let out a small, high-pitched laugh. "This is..." She looked around at the room, at the fine bed linens, the beautifully carved wardrobe and dressing table of rich, dark wood. "This is more'n I ever expected. Thank you."

He bowed his head, placing the lantern he'd been carrying on her dressing table and retreated to the door. "See you tomorrow, then."

El heard the door close but was too transfixed by her new surroundings to move. How could this all be hers?

Just wait 'til I tell Ren. 'Til I show 'im!

She moved to the dressing table, running her fingers over the fine, bone-white combs, the horsehair brushes, and hair ribbons. She'd never seen anything so fine, let alone been gifted it as if it was... *nothing!* El held her arms out and twirled about, a burst of joy bubbling up her throat. She could almost forget all that had happened, the dreadful truth that hung over her and Beth, and the investigation they were yet to complete.

Almost.

As she moved, the necklace bumped against her thigh. It was such a small movement, such a light tap, but it pulled her back to herself, reminded her of who she was, what she'd been through, what she needed to do. She retrieved it from her pocket and held it in her palm. It was still, silent—no voices, no vibrations. It was easy to think it had all been her imagination.

Or to blame the madness that had taken those other girls. That seemed to be creeping up on her, too.

At that, El slumped towards her bed, suddenly exhausted. Still clutching the necklace and fully clothed, she quickly fell into a deep sleep. In the depths of her unconscious mind, the voices returned.

THE FIFTH

LISSIE

I am slowing my hunts.

There is no choice. I have to keep myself hidden to ensure I'm able to continue my mission. I must tread carefully, for all has changed.

And yet the commands which I must obey have only grown stronger in the days since my last kill. They pull at my mind, send shards of agony into my limbs. The EtherFather is... displeased at the delay, speaking of the EtherMother's return, of the misery and destruction that would follow, making it clear how important my work is.

I have no doubt the mistakes made during Penny's death ignited His displeasure. He speaks to me of my lack of worth and my pathetic mistakes are replayed in my mind again and again. He laughs at me. Mocks me.

The EtherFather can be cruel when He chooses, though it is necessary to teach me. To force me to reflect on my flaws, to be better.

With the fifth young woman selected by the EtherMother, it was my chance to prove my worth once more. Else, I was sure I would be pushed to madness by the vitriolic voice circling my mind.

After days of planning, I was certain I had everything under control. There would be no more mistakes.

By now the details were familiar, and I acted almost without thinking, soon finding myself in an alley with my quarry. Lissie was a prostitute, like most of the others. She had a price, and I had paid it. As the winter months drew near, the temperature had dropped, and I was surprised not to be offered a warmer location —a room, perhaps, else somewhere that provided at least some shelter from the harsh chill in the air. Anything other than the streets. Not that it truly mattered, for it wasn't as though the act paid for was to be carried out.

"Where d'you want me, mister?" Lissie asked.

There was an almost bored tone to her voice that rankled me. It was as though she were doing me a favor. Suddenly, I was tired of the façade; exhausted of the charade I had played out too many times before.

I moved forward so she was pressed against the wall behind her—trapped. I pushed back my top hat and placed my hand on the hilt of my knife, the sacred weapon returned to me by the will of the EtherFather.

Lissie's green eyes flitted from my face to the knife and back again. "You!" She peered up at me as best she could, apparently unperturbed at being pinned to the wall. "What's wrong wi' your eyes?" And then she gasped. "You're 'im, ain'tcha? The Stalker?"

I was taken aback by the bluntness of her question, and I tilted my head, almost as if I might kiss her. "Yes."

"Should've known," she said, almost smugly. "There was somethin' 'bout you when you an' your doctor friend examined me. A... madness in your eyes. A longin'."

She licked her lower lip, perhaps thinking she could sway me with seduction.

"But this ain't about fuckin' me, is it? It's somethin' more... somethin' like the voices I've been hearin'. They've told me 'bout you."

A flicker of doubt crossed my mind—*What has the EtherMother told her?*—but then I snorted to hide my surprise. "Whatever the EtherMother has told you is a lie. I wouldn't expect you to understand. Even if I tried to explain it."

"EtherMother? What d'you mean?" Before I could say anything, Lissie shrugged. "Don't matter, really. Truth be told, it'll be a relief. The voices in my 'ead 'ave been gettin' worse. I knew you was comin' for me. They told me. It were the same wi' the other girls, weren't it?" She looked up at me expectantly and, without giving me a chance to answer, frowned and said, "I'm not sure why but I feel like they want me t'—"

"Help them." I swallowed, a choking sensation clamping across my throat. Her feelings were my own, a sneaking doubt that I hadn't dared allow space in my mind until that moment. The EtherFather, the EtherMother—were they as bad as one another? Were we simply pawns at their disposal? If I failed in my tasks, would the EtherFather simply find another, more worthy candidate?

"I'm too tired. I can't do this no more," Lissie whispered, her voice cracking. "Kill me. Please."

She is tricking you. She lies, the EtherFather snarled.

I narrowed my gaze. "I don't believe you. Why would you willingly submit yourself to me?"

She shook her head, thick, brown hair flying about her face. "Don't matter if you believe me or not. Nothin' matters now." For a moment her eyes glazed over. "Will you do me a favor?"

"You ask a favor of me, when you know who I am? What I do?"

She nodded. "I don't pretend to understand you but... like I said, don't matter. All I ask is you make it quick. Don't let me suffer. I ain't lived a long life, but there's been sufferin' enough. And, when it's done... take me 'ome. There'll be no one there. Me da and brother're out at the tavern an' won't return 'til late. If at all."

Our eyes locked. There was a gleam of unshed tears in hers, but her jaw was set. She was... brave, even I had to admit that.

At last, I nodded. "I can make it quick, but I can't be seen carrying a—"

"Please." She gently touched my cheek. "I see a gentleness in you, even behind those eyes... It's not far from 'ere. The corner house, a block beyond the alley. You'll see the red flowerpot on the windowsill. Sad really, the flower died a long time ago but... it's the last remnant of me ma. I sleep in the small room to the right o' the kitchen. Nothin' much but it's mine. Lay me there, if you would, m'lord."

I can't say why, but I found myself nodding. Perhaps it was the resignation within her. The fact she wasn't trying to stop me, only asking I grant her this final wish.

"Very well," I whispered, unsheathing the knife. "Let's be done with it."

Lissie inhaled deeply, letting it out slowly, and lifted her head.

The freshly sharpened knife sliced through the delicate flesh of her throat with ease, and I was sprayed with hot blood. I gently lowered her to the ground, watched the light leave her eyes as I had with the others. It did not take long. She must have been weak already, her illness taking its toll on an undernourished body.

I pushed my hat back down before lifting her in my arms, surprised at how light she was. Gloves slick with blood, I carried her towards the house she had described. It wasn't a long walk, but my limbs trembled, perhaps for fear of being caught, perhaps because of the adrenaline wearing off. With relief, I located her home. The front door was half rotted and opened easily when I pushed my weight into it. I backed into the squalid excuse for a living area. The kitchen, if you could call it that, consisted of a rusted iron basin on a wonky wooden countertop. There was a meager fireplace, before which sat two threadbare armchairs.

Not wanting to linger, I headed for the room she had described. There was no door, only a drab curtain that might have once been red hanging across the doorway. Within was a narrow wooden bed. I knelt beside it, lying Lissie's body atop. She looked almost peaceful, her glassy green eyes staring off behind me. I pulled her hair around her shoulders, doing my best to conceal the gaping wound at her throat, and placed her hands across her stomach.

"I have done as promised," I said softly, proudly.

As I rose to leave, I heard voices in the house.

"—that's the thing 'bout workin' the mines, son. I've told you this afore, ain't I?" said a gruff voice, slurring from what I assumed to be EtherAle.

"Yes, Da, I know, it's jus'—"

"Hush." There was a pause. I pressed myself against the wall, holding my breath.

Why did she lie? She'd told me they'd be at the tavern.

Then realization hit me: she *wanted* me to be caught. Why did I trust her? *Fucking fool.* I bit my cheek to hold back a roar of rage, tasting blood.

"Lissie?" came the gruff voice. "That you, girl?"

"Why would she be 'ome so early, Da? She ain't long started work."

"I fuckin' know that, Ste. Wait—look."

Shit. The curtain was *useless*.

"Oh, yeh, I see it too. Like a- a shadow or somethin'."

"Ain't no fuckin' shadow. Grab the fire prod." As the gruff voice spoke, it drew closer.

I braced myself, hand on my knife, quivering with the fire of fury that had been reignited at the knowledge of my deception.

"You can come out slow or you can be dragged out. Choice is yours."

Growling, I threw aside my hat so it would not impede me and leapt through the curtain, knife raised.

"What the fu—"

With a screech, I leapt atop the gruff man. He was portly and solidly built but much shorter than me. Taking him by surprise gave me an immediate advantage. Without thinking, I slashed with my knife, hacking at whatever flesh I found. Two of his fingers flew across the room and he screamed. At the back of my awareness, I noted his son crying out for me to stop.

It moved me not.

At some point, the gruff man stopped fighting and lay still. He still breathed, though it was a whistling wheeze, bubbling with blood. My own breaths were rapid, my chest huffing with each gasp of air. Looking up, I met the son's gaze. He held the fire prod his father had directed him to fetch, though it hung limp in his hand.

As I stood, he backed away from me, whimpering. He looked much like Lissie with his green eyes and thick, dark hair. Younger perhaps by a year or two, though well on his way to becoming a man.

A shame he would never make it.

I ran my blood-soaked sleeve across my face. "Your sister is a fucking liar."

Before he could utter a word, I lunged. The boy's eyes registered the movement mere moments before my blade pierced his chest. We both fell to the floor, I atop him, and there I plunged the knife in again and again and again.

"I am the savior of Alpinside!" I hissed. "No one lies to me. Lissie, you fucking cunt! Whore!"

Finally, my arms grew numb. The boy was a mess of blood, muscle, flesh, and bone. I wasn't sure when I had begun attacking his face but there was little left in its place that might have identified him.

I stood and cleaned my knife as best I could on a blanket from one of the armchairs before sheathing it. I retrieved my hat from Lissie's room, glaring down at her body one more time before stalking towards the door.

Outside, the night air was blessedly cool. I held my arms up to the sky and laughed. The moon shone down on me, basking me in its pure white glow, and I took it as a sign of the EtherFather's approval.

With my hat pushed forward and a grin on my face, I merged

into the shadows of those forsaken streets and disappeared into
the night.

PART III
THE MISERY

And so, the EtherMother submitted Herself to the EtherFather's wisdom and, in doing so, relinquished Her powers to Him. For only by doing so could She allow His benevolent guidance to shine, and His strength to reign over the people of Estra.

--The EtherFather's Sacred Doctrine, *On the Submission of the EtherMother*

Brutal Family Murder!

Lisbeth Moss, known as Lissie, was the fifth victim of the Scrubbers' Stalker, alongside her father Davyd and brother Stephyn. To see a whole family slaughtered in such a monstrous way, we must ask ourselves—is the Stalker's reign worsening? Perhaps the vicious killer was disturbed by the family of his victim, or perhaps he is simply a madman whose lust for blood is increasing with each horrific murder. There is but one certainty: none of us are safe.

--The Workers' Tribune

Artavius,

    You know well what you've done.

    After years of our business partnership, you have undermined our relationship and chosen deception and lies over honesty and integrity. Knowing as you do about my son's illness and the essential role EtherStone plays in stabilizing his health, I am all the more saddened at your decision to hoard the wealth of EtherStone you found in our shared mines.

    I will discuss the matter no more. You have made your choice.

    Yours, in regret,

    Landrum Estamore

CHAPTER 23

THE FRIENDSHIP

The next morning, El awoke with a groan, blinking her eyes open. She briefly forgot where she was and bolted upright at the light, flowered wallpaper, and lavish furniture, throwing off the thick blankets that covered her. Then she remembered and let out a disbelieving laugh.

"El, you bloody idiot," she muttered, relaxing back onto the feather pillow and burrowing her head into it. She had never known such comfort. *And t' think, all that 'ad to happen to get here was Da's brutal murder.*

Sighing, she forced herself back upright. She couldn't in good conscience luxuriate in her new surroundings knowing Ren was still working in the Estamore kitchens. He seemed happy enough and had endeared himself to all the kitchen staff—the cook most of all—but she wouldn't be content until he was once more under the same roof as her.

She recalled Denys's promise the night before to arrange for his transfer to the Branton household. With a great deal of reluctance, she pushed away the blankets and swung her legs over the side of the bed. As she did, the EtherStone necklace dropped from her pocket and clattered to the floor. Leaning to pick it up, something niggled in her mind. She held it for a moment, feeling the smooth stone against her skin, the weight of it in her palm. It seemed absurd, but it was almost as though the stone wanted to *tell* her something.

Did I dream 'bout it? Did the voices speak t' me?

She sensed it was so, for some delicate wisps of memory clung on, though they grew weaker with each passing moment. The more she tried to focus, to recall the exact words spoken to her, the faster those wisps drifted away to nothingness.

Shrugging, she returned the necklace to her pocket and went to the dressing table. She decided it was best to keep herself busy and not to dwell on stupid dreams, all the more because she couldn't even recall them. She would change clothes and find Denys. Perhaps she could ask him about Edward.

She peered into the intricately gilded mirror. Her hair was a mess, the braid half undone, so she reached for a comb and gently removed the pins holding it together. When she looked at least half-presentable, her blonde locks having taken on a slight kink, she wondered what she might wear. Halfway to the wardrobe, she realized she wouldn't be able to remove her dress without help for, unlike her servant's garb, it was buttoned at the back. Too self-conscious to ring for a servant, she shrugged—to her eyes, the dress she'd worn to the wedding still looked fine. Yes, she had fallen asleep in it, but... who would know? It had been brand new yesterday and she'd been careful not to spill any food or drink on it.

Satisfied with her appearance, El quietly opened the door. When she entered Beth's chamber, the sheets were, as expected, undisturbed. How long had Beth said she'd be away? A few days, El reasoned, then they could get back to their investigation. Briefly, she wondered how Beth's wedding night had been and her nose wrinkled. Not a subject she'd ever paid much heed to, for she had neither the time nor inclination to seek it out.

As she pondered, her stomach grumbled loudly, and she patted it, muttering, "Alright, alright."

She made for the door and reversed the route along which

Denys had brought her the night before. As she went, she studied the luxurious surroundings of Branton Manor. The hallways down which she strolled were carpeted in black, while the walls were white-painted wooden panels, gilded with gold. There were various portraits of stern-faced people, Lord Ashford's family she assumed, as well as a painting she assumed to be of the EtherFather. She edged closer to this one. It was impressively done, the brushstrokes so skilled as to render the EtherFather into an almost living person; he was a pale-skinned, grey-bearded man, with almost black eyes glaring out of a narrow face. He wore robes of EtherStone red, one hand resting on his chest and the other on a knife at his belt. A curious pose for a deity, almost as though he were poised for attack.

She scoffed. *These nobles an' their religious beliefs. He don't look too benevolent t' me.*

El found herself curiously glad she'd grown up away from such fervor. True, life had been hard, but she hadn't needed to answer to some god or goddess whose existence was questionable at best.

Though it did make her wonder. *What about the voices? The EtherMother speaks t' me, don't she? If it's even her.*

She clucked loudly at herself, making a young female servant who was coming down the corridor jump. Quickly recovering from her momentary fright, the servant sped up, briskly walking past.

At the foot of the grand staircase, El glanced around, trying to remember how to get to the dining room. Around her were numerous options, doors that seemed to lead in all directions.

As if on cue, a servant appeared from a door to her left. Before he could disappear, she said, "'Scuse me!" and hurried towards him.

He had a shock of red hair, with freckles dotting his milky face. El estimated he was about her age and wondered how long he'd been in service in this house.

"Yes, m'lady?" he asked, standing tall and looking somewhere over her shoulder.

"No need to m'lady me. I'm a servant, same as you."

He flushed red and shifted his gaze to her face, eyes flitting about as though waiting to be tested by Lord Ashford.

"I'm, El. I'm Lady Elizabetha's Companion."

Realization dawned on his face, and he let out a relieved laugh. "Oh! Yes. Sorry. Can't be too careful 'round here... put a foot wrong an'—"

"Danyl!" Lord Denys was suddenly at El's back, glaring down at the servant. "What have I told you about dallying in the hall-ways? Don't you have work to do?"

"Y-yes, m'lord. Forgive me, m'lord." In the blink of an eye, Danyl had turned and scuttled away, head down and shoulders hunched.

El turned to Denys, an eyebrow raised, surprised at his harsh-ness. "He was helpin' me."

Denys shook his head and blinked, as though just remem-bering she was there. Then he smiled and said, "Well, I'm here now. Come, I'm *starving*."

El frowned, though allowed herself to be led down the hall. "Thought you was gonna stay in bed all mornin'."

"Easier said than done, sadly. Too much to do, and that damned whiskey...." He tapped a finger against his forehead, winc-ing. "But coffee will help. Or, failing that, more whiskey." He grimaced as he said that, though El didn't think he was joking.

At the dining room, Denys opened the door and allowed El to enter first. The table was unoccupied, though the scent of cooking food drifted in from the kitchen.

"Take a seat," Denys said. "I'll let the servants know we're ready."

El chose a chair along the middle of the long dining table, aware even from her brief experience in this setting that each end was reserved for the head of the household.

After ringing a bell beside the door, Denys sat beside her. "You do look lovely in that dress, Ellana, though you have a wardrobe of clothes to choose from!"

El blushed; she did not want to admit she hadn't been able to take it off herself. "Oh, yeh. Not somethin' I'm used t', really. It's clean enough for today though." She cast him a smile, and he seemed to accept her explanation without concern.

"How did you sleep?" he asked.

"Um..." She fought against the fearful internal voice telling her she should trust no one. He seemed to genuinely care, why should she doubt that? "Well enough. Honestly, I'm not used t' such... luxury. The bed's softer than I've ever 'ad before."

Denys held his arms wide and looked around the room. "It's marvelous, isn't it? I felt the same for a long time after I moved into Branton Manor. My Papa's home was nowhere near as grand."

The door in the corner of the room opened, and breakfast was carried in by two young women who El recognized from the ball.

"Thank you," El said as they unloaded their trays onto the table.

They both ignored her and hurried from the room as soon as they were done. El watched their backs as they left, wondering why there seemed such tension—fear, even—amongst the servants in this house.

"Please, help yourself." Denys leaned over and began scooping poached eggs onto his plate.

El served herself bacon, eggs, and fresh bread, and they ate in silence for a while. She still wolfed down her food with the hurried intensity of someone who wasn't sure where their next meal would come from, and she wondered whether she would always do so.

"Would you like some coffee? Or tea?" Denys asked, interrupting her ravenous inhalation.

She chewed and swallowed her mouthful of bread. "Yeh, please."

Denys smiled. "Which one?"

"Oh, uh... tea. Please." El ran the back of her hand across her mouth before smiling back.

"Coffee for me, I think," Denys said as he retrieved two cups and poured from two separate pots. He pushed the cup of tea towards El before taking a long sip of his coffee and sighing.

El picked up her tea and clutched the cup against her chest, studying the man beside her. "So, 'ow did you come to live 'ere then? Lord Ashford ain't your family"

Denys shifted, spilling coffee on his hand and sleeve. As he retrieved a napkin, he shook his head. "Straight to the questions, eh?" He met her gaze, dark eyes glittering with amusement. "No, Ash isn't my family, though we are... close enough that we would consider each other so." He bit his lip and glanced away, momentarily lost to his own thoughts. When he looked at El again, his eyes were brimming with sadness. "We both lost our families at a young age. Ashford was eighteen when his parents died; I was sixteen when I lost my papa. We understood each other's grief."

"Your papa. You spoke about 'im last night. We din't get t' finish chattin' 'bout how the EtherStone mines caused 'is downfall."

He rubbed his temples. "Was I speaking of such things? I must have drunk more than I'd realized. I shall have to watch myself around you, Ellana. My tongue feels so much freer when I'm in your company."

"I found it interestin'," El said, sipping her tea. "I'd love t' hear more. You spoke t' me like... like..."

"Like a person who matters?"

"Maybe somethin' like that. Or maybe it's jus' that you don't judge me for where I came from."

"Mm." Denys retrieved the pot of coffee and refilled his cup. "Ahh, I'm feeling better after this." He turned to face her. "I can't say what it is for certain, Ellana, but... I feel at peace when I'm in your company. I first noticed it when we danced together last night. Perhaps that's why I was so willing to speak to you of my past."

El watched him over the rim of her teacup as she drained the dregs.

Without prompting, Denys refilled it for her.

She nodded in thanks. "You know, Beth don't think you like 'er very much."

Denys frowned, then snorted. "I suppose she wouldn't. Truth be told, I *didn't*."

El raised her eyebrows, not expecting such a response but appreciative of his honesty. Denys was turning out to be a far cry from the man she'd first believed him to be.

There was a long pause before he spoke again. "It's been just Ash and me for the past couple of years. We only had each other to get through those difficult times... The loss of family. That was when I moved here." He puffed air through his lips. "I'm getting ahead of myself, really. To understand why that happened, you need to know what happened to my dear papa." He stretched his arms above his head, letting out a deep yawn. "I believe some fresh air is in order. Would you like to walk the gardens with me? They're quite wonderful this time of year."

"I dunno," El said. "I was thinkin' of lookin' into the murders while I wait for Beth t' return. Get ahead of our plans."

"Investigations? Of the murders?" Denys pursed his lips. "Such a terrible loss of life. Be that as it may, I think you can allow yourself a day. I am certain Beth and Ashford won't be returning before the week is out."

"The week?" El frowned. "Why not?"

"Ashford is an... intense man. He's been quite looking forward to taking Beth to his cottage, and I don't think I need to tell you why."

El raised an eyebrow. "But surely that can't last... I mean, surely, they can't..."

Denys laughed, a little too loudly. "I tried telling him that but there's no persuading Ash once he gets an idea in his head." He let out a long sigh. "He was none too subtle in telling me about his plans for his new wife. We aren't likely to see them for a while."

"I see." El flushed. Would Beth really *want* to stay confined with Ashford for so long? Doing *that*?

Denys stood and offered her his arm again. She was becoming

quite fond of the gesture, despite herself. "In which case, m'lady, I see no reason why you can't join me for a walk about the gardens."

El stood and linked her arm through his. "Lead the way, then. An' don't bloody call me m'lady again."

Denys chuckled and gave a half bow. "You have my word."

THE REST OF THE DAY WAS FILLED WITH WHAT EL WOULD describe as pleasant frivolities. She'd never had the luxury of free time to do as she pleased, but Denys seemed an expert on it. He took her to his favorite patisserie, earning more than a few glares from nobles who caught sight of them together.

Denys simply tutted and told her to ignore them. "What else are we to do with our time, sit and wait for Ashford and Beth to return?"

El laughed at that. Though the stares irked her, these people with their shallow cares and gossip had much to say about someone like her despiting knowing nothing of her life, of the struggles she'd endured, and the pain she'd learned to tolerate, both physical and emotional. They sneered at her and looked down their noses, but part of her felt it was *she* who should do so to them, for all their ignorance and narrow-mindedness. She reflected then how fortunate it was Beth had turned out to be kind and caring—so unlike her mother and these other nobles.

And here she was, sitting with Lord Denys who just a couple of days ago she would've considered as judgmental of her as the rest.

"Would you like any more to eat?" Denys asked, breaking her out of her reflections.

El looked down at the flaky pastry crumbs on her plate. She wanted to say yes, even though her stomach was already uncomfortably full—an urge to eat as much as possible while she could, as she and Ren had done at any given opportunity when they'd been fending for themselves. "Thanks, but I'd best not." She reached for her teacup and noticed it was empty. "Though p'raps some more—"

"Tea?" Denys picked up her cup. "Good idea." He stood and went to the counter of the patisserie, speaking to the woman who stood behind it.

Yes, she really *was* surprised at how friendly Denys had turned out to be. She wondered what could have caused such a change within him, and whether it was something she should ask about. Perhaps given some more time together, she would build up the courage. For now, she would let herself enjoy having some company, not thinking about how she was going to keep Ren safe and fed, not thinking about Da's murder and those poor young women who'd been slaughtered.

There would be time enough for all of that when Beth returned.

⚜

TWO DAYS LATER, EL WAS PERUSING HER NEW WARDROBE. WITH some flailing and awkward twisting, she had worked out how to dress and undress herself, still reluctant to ask for help. The servants were commoners like her, and she refused to rely on them to do things she could do herself—given time and practice, at least. She was learning to be excited about deciding what to wear every day. There was some variation even if the dresses were all much the same, and the idea that she, Ellana Stone, had a *wardrobe* full of clothing from which to choose was a novelty she didn't expect to get used to.

Having finally decided upon a long, black linen dress with a white collar, El dressed and moved to the dressing table to prepare her hair. She ran a comb through it, working out tangles, with gritted teeth. As she did so, a glimmer of red caught her eye. The EtherStone necklace. She'd been carrying it around for some days now, increasingly reluctant to leave it behind. However, that morning, something told her to leave it be. Perhaps she was testing herself, checking she hadn't become unnecessarily attached to it.

She stroked a finger over it.

"Ellana Stone, heed our words, you must—"

She snatched her hand away. "Leave me alone," she spat, turning and making for the door.

As she did, she was sure the voices continued, desperate to pull her back.

"I said, leave me alone!" she cried as she opened the door and slammed it behind her.

To her relief, the voices stopped.

As expected, Beth's bed had remained untouched. Despite Denys's reassurance that this was expected, El was concerned at not seeing her friend since the wedding. Sighing, she made her way to the dining room knowing she would simply have to continue to be patient.

LATER THAT DAY, SHE AND DENYS WERE RELAXING IN HIS private study. It was another curious concept to El that someone should be so rich and fortunate that they could *sit and do nothing.* Though he had kept her busy with walks, outings around the Noble District, and even a visit to the EtherTemple, they hadn't spoken more about his past, including how he'd come to live at Branton Manor. El thought perhaps he was biding his time, trying to gain the measure of her more fully before he divulged all of his personal information. That day, Denys had been quieter than usual, and she began to wonder if he regretted having been so forthright with her in the first place.

There was one topic she'd been avoiding, but one she felt had to finally be broached. She cleared her throat. "Lord Denys—"

"Just Denys," he chided gently, placing his book face down on his lap. "I would say we've spent enough time together now that you'd be comfortable enough with that."

"Can I ask, what news of Master Edward is there?" She plucked at her skirts. "Beth were worried 'bout him not bein' at the wedding."

Denys visibly tensed, then cleared his throat. "Edward is resting. His medical treatment is ongoing. He needs time to recover."

The words sounded rehearsed, though she couldn't have said why they whould be. "As long as he's alright, that's all we can ask. I did wonder what Beth wanted me t' do if there were a problem with 'im!" El gave a nervous chuckle.

Denys's shoulders relaxed. "I understand. He's her brother, after all. But, trust me, Ashford has his care in hand. I am tending to him in Ashford's absence."

El exhaled, eager to change the topic. "Can I ask... would you finish the story 'bout your da—sorry, your papa, and 'ow you came t' live 'ere?"

A pained expression crossed Denys's face and his eyes glossed over for the briefest of seconds. El thought for a moment they even took on a shade of red.

She shook her head. *Don't be so stupid. Your imagination's gettin' the better o' you.*

Denys rubbed his brow, saying quietly, "I'm sorry, I am suddenly beset with quite the headache. My mind has been... fogged today. I'm usually so clear around you, but, alas, it was not to last." His lips pulled into the ghost of a smile.

He stood and she made to do the same.

"Please, stay," Denys insisted. "You are more than welcome here. I- I must..." He blinked and his brow wrinkled, as though forgetting his words. "I shall see you at dinner."

El watched him go, some part of her certain she knew what was wrong but unable to pin down the thought.

Sinking back into the chair, she stared into the fire. "Where are you, Beth?" All that responded was the crackling logs in the hearth.

FIVE DAYS AFTER THE WEDDING, EL WAS GROWING RESTLESS. She longed to see Beth. She was desperate to continue investigating the murders and felt a growing frustration at her friend's apparent lack of care for the matter. She also missed her brother fiercely but felt it would be improper for her to leave the house for an extended period to visit him—especially if Beth returned and she wasn't there. She had intended to ask Denys if she could do so, but he'd avoided her since the afternoon he'd excused himself from his study, sending a servant to advise her he was unwell and keeping to his bedchamber.

She dressed quickly that morning, no longer caring which dress she chose. What did it matter if she was to spend another day walking the gardens and perusing a library full of books she couldn't read? As she made for her bedroom, the EtherStone necklace's presence nagged at her. She'd resisted the urge to pocket it these past days, noting the voices she'd been hearing had reduced significantly. Now she barely noticed them even when close to the necklace.

But its pull was urgent today and she heard it clearly. "*Ellana, please, heed our word. You must be careful. You must—*"

She snatched up the necklace, angry without knowing why. "Alright, alright," she muttered. "Come wi' me while I walk around an' do nothin'. How excitin' for you."

She marched through Beth's unused bedchamber and, as she opened the door to the hall, almost collided with Denys, whose hand was raised as though about to open the door himself.

"Ellana!" He smiled tightly. "Forgive the intrusion. I came to ask if you'd like to join me for breakfast. It's been too long. You must accept my apology for being absent these past few days."

Relief flooded through El's body. *Company at last*. "'Course I will," she said.

LATER THAT DAY, EL ONCE MORE JOINED DENYS IN HIS PRIVATE study as though the past three days hadn't happened. They sat in a comfortable silence having sated themselves on tea and lemon cakes. Despite the overwhelming citrussy-sweetness, she was becoming accustomed to the taste.

Look at you, Ellana Stone, gettin' a sweet tooth, she said to herself with a grin.

She looked forward to giving Ren some to see his reaction. He'd always been drawn to the sweet fruit pies when they'd gone into the Noble District to snatch a meal.

"Denys," she said.

He blinked, lifting his head from where it had been resting on the back of his armchair, and gave her a sleepy smile. "Mm?"

"You said you'd 'ave my brother transferred from the Estamore 'ouse. I wondered if, um... Well, if it's not t' happen, could I go an'—"

Denys held up his hand and lazily said, "Don't worry, Ellana, it's being arranged."

El raised an eyebrow. "It is?"

"I sent a message to Ash the morning after the wedding. I can't foresee any issues, though Ash is obviously... otherwise occupied at present."

"I see. Thank you."

"Think nothing of it."

"I'm grateful for you keepin' me company while Beth's been away. I feel like I've taken up a lot o' your time, though. You must have patients t' attend to or other work t' do as a doctor."

Denys stretched and yawned. "Not at all. It's been quiet of late actually. Unusually so, you might say. Ever since the last murder, now that I come to think on it." He visibly shuddered. "Nasty business."

"What was 'er name?" El asked. "The last victim. I've not 'eard who it was."

Pain flashed across Denys's eyes. "Lissie. Lisbeth Wood."

"Lisbeth," El whispered the name, though she didn't recognize it.

Denys's throat bobbed. "Her father and brother were killed, too. It was a truly horrific scene. So much violence. So much blood."

Blood, so much blood. El saw Da's corpse for the briefest of moments, saw the red-dashed walls, floors, and bedding. Shaking her head, she banished the image.

"That's unusual, isn't it?" she said. "Why would 'e kill 'er family too? An' someone else were killed with Penny too, weren't they? Her betrothed."

Denys nodded. "Yes, Reginald Locke."

"He's gettin' worse. I wonder why?" El said, more to herself than Denys. "What's 'appened? It's like... I can feel the anger from what he's done. So much rage and hate, like Da used to 'ave when he'd been on the ale. It's the only explanation for why someone would do such evil things."

Denys swallowed loudly. "I... I wouldn't want to say." He stood abruptly and moved towards the dark wooden cupboard along the far wall. "Would you like a drink? I've a sudden need for some Blood Whiskey to calm my nerves."

"No," El said stiffly. "With my Da being a drunk, it's not somethin' I wanna do too much."

Denys nodded, taking a seat with a generous measure of whiskey. He took a long swig of it—at which point she noticed the trembling of his hands—and let out a weary exhale.

"Blood Whiskey..." El studied the red-tinged liquid in his glass. He and Lord Ashford seemed to drink it regularly and, for the first time, she wondered why. "Ashford mentioned it before. Said EtherAle were a poor imitation of it."

Denys surveyed his glass, swirling the liquid within. "I've never tried EtherAle. Though, from what I understand, and from what I have seen, it is a plague on the workers of Alpinside."

"That's true." El pursed her lips, tilting her head. "An' the whiskey?"

Denys shifted. "You know, I've never really thought about it. At least, not in the same way. Now that you mention it... I'm not sure I want to dwell on it." He let out an uncomfortable laugh.

"Sorry," El said. "I din't ask t' make you uneasy. It's just I saw what effect the ale 'ad on me Da."

Denys gave a sad smile. "You know, my papa drank far too much of this stuff, too. After he died, Ash told me it would help to deal with my pain. That it was a gift from the EtherFather, our means of connecting with Him. He was right, I suppose. Yet it also shut off my ability to let that emotion out. Perhaps that's why I've avoided telling you the rest of my story—because I'm not sure I've spoken it aloud to anyone properly, not even Ashford."

"Well," she said, "if you decide you wanna tell me the rest... You're more'n welcome t'."

Denys nodded, placing a finger against his temple. "Thank you. It's strange. The fog has been so strong these three days past. Yet as soon as I saw you again this morning it lifted. It *must* be something about you that clears it as I'd first suspected. I wonder what was different three days ago." He watched her for a moment —studying her as though the answer would leap out at him.

El shrugged. "Can't say I know, but I'm glad to 'ave your company again. Honestly, there's only so much I can walk 'round that garden before feelin' like I wanna break me own ankle."

Denys snorted, slapping his leg with mirth. "Oh, Ellana! And to think, I was about to ask you if you'd like to walk the gardens with me."

El grinned at him, rolling her eyes dramatically. "Well, as it's you... I s'pose I can't say no to a lord, can I?"

He stood and walked to her chair, holding out his hand. "No, you can't actually."

Setting her teacup on the table beside her chair, she clasped her fingers in his. "Lead on then, Lord Denys."

THAT EVENING, EL COLLAPSED INTO HER BED AFTER A LONG, hot bath—which had been requested by Denys once he'd learned of her reluctance to utilize the services of the manor's staff.

"Of course, you may ask for a bath!" he'd said with gusto. "You're Lady Elizabetha's Companion! The servants wouldn't dare say no."

Though she'd been a little embarrassed at his insistence, she had to admit it had been a luxury she hadn't known she needed. Scented heavily with lavender, it soaked into her muscles and eased her mind.

When she was done, she relaxed on her bed, letting out a long, contended sigh. She'd never felt so comfortable in a place. Perhaps *too* comfortable, especially considering Ren still wasn't there with her. She made a mental note to ask Denys about her brother again in the morning. Barely able to keep her eyes open, she tucked herself in and quickly fell asleep.

It was in her dreams that the voices screamed, *"Do not trust him."*

CHAPTER 24
THE BLISS

Beth awoke smiling. For seven days she'd been Lady Branton, and still she couldn't quite believe it.

Her whole body tingled with the memories of the past week. Ashford had kept her hidden away at his cottage where they'd enjoyed the pleasure of each other's company. Then, when they had finally returned to Branton Manor late last night, he'd squirreled her away to his private chambers.

"Let me enjoy you one final night," Ashford had whispered, "before anyone else sees the new Lady Branton in all her glory. I would have her know she's *mine* first and foremost."

Beth shuddered with delight at the thought and turned over, expecting to find Ashford beside her. Instead, the bed was cold, in his place a folded piece of paper. Pulling herself upright, she picked it up and ran her finger across the delicate, scrawling hand. Curiously, even the paper had Ashford's scent.

Grinning, she unfolded the note and read her husband's words.

My darling wife,

What a wonderful week this has been. I'm almost sorry to be back in Alpinside.

Forgive me for leaving you so early this morning, but I have work that cannot wait. The servants are at your beck and call; use them as you will. I've left you a dress, along with a little gift to help you continue your enquiries into the murders.

I shall see you at dinner.
Your loving husband,
Ashford

"Your loving husband," Beth murmured, clutching the note to her chest.

It was only then she noticed her breasts were bare. She gasped and moved to cover them with the bedsheets. At her parents' home, she would never be naked, even alone in her room, so deep was the shame she held about herself. And yet, after the past week, she felt a renewed appreciation for her body. The flaws were still there—her belly still too full, her waist too wide, her breasts too heavy—and yet Ashford had told her she was perfect, over and over. He had *showed* her how much he appreciated her body, with his touch and his kisses and his moans of pleasure as he took her again and again.

What a curious turn of events. She almost wanted to tell her mother, just to see the look on her face. She giggled and pushed back the blankets, stretching her arms above her head, combing her fingers through her curls. She had a flashback of Ashford running his hands through her hair and her entire body prickled with the memory.

"Pull yourself together," she said to the empty room.

She was sure she could spend the whole day waiting for her husband to return, never leaving this room, dreaming only of their nights together. Then she recalled his mention of a gift and the murders.

El. What must she be thinking? Beth realized she hadn't thought about her friend since the wedding.

The old familiar guilt was soon gnawing at her gut once more as she shuffled to the end of the bed. As promised, there was a beautiful purple dress made of the finest cotton, with thick white petticoats and a boned corset. As she lifted the pile of clothing, something dropped to the floor. She bent to retrieve it and found a dark brown, leather-bound notebook, a pencil attached to the side via a small leather loop. On the front the letters EB were embossed with gold. She ran her finger over the initials, beaming.

Glancing about for her shift, she found it draped over the armchair in the corner. Ashford must have tidied her clothes from where they'd been thrown to the floor last night. She moved to retrieve it and caught a glimpse of herself in the mirror on the dressing table. Her hair was far messier than she'd imagined, dark curls hanging loose and sticking up at all angles.

"By the Mother," she laughed. *Blame Ashford and his passion!*

A blush rose to her cheeks as she reminisced again on her time with her new husband. She wondered if her mind would stop drifting like that today—but then, she'd never experienced such bliss before. She wondered, too, whether being married would always feel so thrilling.

She pulled on her shift and sat in front of the dressing table. Once she had made herself presentable, it was time to find El. And with her notebook in hand—Ashford's evident support for the investigation to continue—it was time to make a plan.

When Beth opened the bedroom door, she found herself in a dim corridor. She glanced left and right—dark red carpets stretched to either side beneath wood paneled walls, flickering gaslamps providing scant light. Opposite Ashford's room, as he'd briefly mentioned last night, was Denys's private chamber, the door to which was closed. She headed right.

She wasn't certain this was the way they'd come last night but it would surely lead her somewhere that would give her some bearings. As if on cue, her stomach let out a loud grumble and she patted it, wondering what the time was. It was almost certainly past her normal wake-up time, but she had been kept awake into the early hours by her husband's seemingly insatiable appetite.

There was a low, pain-filled moan and she hesitated, turning her head to listen.

Silence.

Ahead, there was another plain wooden door, identical to the ones to both Ashford and Denys's chambers. She was careful not to make any more noise than necessary as she stepped closer. With a shaking hand, she reached for the door handle. Locked.

Glancing over her shoulder to ensure she was alone, Beth pressed her ear to the door. She closed her eyes and held her breath. Nothing.

For good measure, she tried the handle again. Definitely locked. As she ran a hand over the paneling, she noticed the EtherStone ring Ashford had gifted her. Suddenly, and for no logical reason, an unsettled feeling washed over her, a deep sense of discomfort that lay heavy in her heart. She stepped away from the door, certain she didn't want to know what lay behind it.

Turning, she briskly made her way back down the corridor. She half expected the door there to be locked as well, panic almost taking ahold at the thought. But then she reached for the handle, and it opened without resistance. She immediately squinted against the low-hanging winter sun streaming in through the ceiling-high windows of the ballroom.

"Good morning, Lady Branton," said a young maid, startling her.

"Oh! Good morning, uh..." Beth trailed off.

"Lilly, m'lady."

"Lilly. I wonder, Lilly, do you know what's behind the door at the end of that corridor?" She pointed back to where she'd come from.

Lilly frowned running her hands down her apron. "No, m'lady. Sorry, m'lady. I- I could find out for you."

"That would be most helpful." Beth smiled sheepishly. "Now, I wonder if you could point me towards the dining room."

⌘

A SHORT WHILE LATER—AND HAVING ONLY TAKEN ONE WRONG turn from Lilly's directions—Beth opened the door into the dining room. El sat on one side of the table, hunched over some toast and eggs. Beth took the seat next to her, placing her new notebook carefully on the table. As if by magic, a young man entered from the kitchen and placed a tray of fresh tea, eggs, bacon, toast, butter, and honey in front of her.

"Thank you," she said.

The servant bowed his head and briskly left.

Beth waited for the click of the door before turning to El. "Good morning. I'm sorry I've been absent this past week. Things have been rather..." She grinned and blushed, unable to hold back her joy. "Anyway, how have you been?"

El lifted her head from her barely touched food. The smudges beneath her pale blue eyes were dark. "You don't need t' apologize," she said quietly. "You were married. It's only natural you'd wanna spend time wi' your husband. Have you... uh, did you enjoy 'is company?"

Beth's flush deepened. "Oh, yes. It was a wonderful week, El. I'm sorry we didn't return sooner, but Ashford thought it would be a nice opportunity to spend some time together—alone."

"You don't need t' explain yourself, Beth."

"I know, it's just... I've missed you." She studied her Companion for a moment. "You look tired."

El took a delicate sip from her teacup. "Denys has been keepin' me busy. That an' I din't sleep well last night."

Beth raised an eyebrow. "Denys? Really?"

El laughed. "He's a lot nicer than we first thought. I think maybe... 'e was a bit jealous o' your marrying Lord Ashford."

"Jealous?" Beth pursed her lips in thought. "An odd way to feel. They are but friends—Ashford and I are husband and wife. They are separate, are they not? I know from speaking to Ashford he wouldn't be without Denys. He's a trusted colleague and Companion." She picked up a knife and began buttering her toast. "I wish Denys felt able to be more open with me. How did your time together come about?"

El put down her cutlery. "Well, after you left the ball, Denys was kind enough t' take me to 'is private study for a drink."

"How thoughtful of him. Did you have much to speak about?"

"I din't do much o' the talkin'. He started tellin' me 'bout 'is da and the EtherStone mines... Din't finish though. A bit strange really, he seems to 'ave trouble with the whole matter."

"EtherStone mines?" Beth studied her ring. "I did not realize he'd inherited any."

"I'm not sure 'e did."

"And that's why you didn't sleep well last night?"

El's hand drifted to her side and hovered momentarily before she placed it back on the table. "No..."

Beth drank some tea, wincing at the flavor. She reached for the honey. "It wasn't?"

"No. It was, uh...." El's hands twisted in her lap. "It were the voices, like I heard at Daisy's house. This time they sounded... in pain. They was crying out for 'elp."

"Voices?" Beth managed in a strangled whisper. *Like the voices on my wedding day*. She gave an unconvincing smile, lips wavering. "Well, chances are you were dreaming. Nothing more. I'm sure it's—"

"That's the thing, Beth. It started as a dream but... I woke up t' the sound of a scream, an'- an' the voices carried on." Her lip began to tremble. "I'm worried. This is the worst it's been an'... I can't leave Ren. He needs me. I can't go mad. I can't be the Stalker's next victim."

"Oh, El, come now." Beth leaned over and touched her Companion's hand. "What makes you say that?" As she spoke, a voice in the back of her mind whispered, *Help Ellana, save us. Help Ellana, save us.*

"'It's a pattern, like Lord Ashford said. The women all 'ad the same... affliction. The same madness. And that's 'ow the Stalker chose 'em."

"Well," Beth said calmly, "that's something that remains to be confirmed. Let's not leap to any conclusions." She took El's hand,

and it was cool to the touch—just like Ashford's. "I promise I won't let anything happen to you. You're here with me, aren't you? Where could be safer?"

El sniffed. "I s'pose so." She raised her chin towards the notebook. "What's that?"

"A gift." Beth opened it, surprised to find a collection of newspaper cuttings. "Oh!"

El's brow furrowed. "What are they?"

"Articles," Beth said, flicking through. "About the murders. From the Workers' Tribune, the Alpinside Journal, the Alpinside Affair. Ashford must have gathered them for us. How thoughtful."

El picked up the articles Beth had thumbed through, her eyes scanning over the words. Her lack of ability to read was obviously a source of frustration, for she sighed and dropped them back down. "D'you think they'll 'elp?"

"I'm sure there must be some clues here that will assist us. Information we have yet to consider. We can go through and take notes."

"Not sure what I can do t' help. You'll 'ave to read 'em all. And take all the notes."

"Nonsense." Beth pushed away her breakfast plate and laid all the articles out on the table. "What better way to learn your letters?"

El reached for a half-buried article. "Oh, look! There's a picture o' the Docks."

"Our first piece of the puzzle," Beth said. She pulled the pencil free from the notebook, and, opening to a fresh page wrote, 'Docks' at the top. "What can you tell me about the docks?"

El's lips pinched tight. "It's not somewhere the likes o' you'd wanna go."

Beth fought not to roll her eyes. El meant well, but such comments weren't helpful. "Let's forget such notions. I want to know your experience of it. Have you been? Who frequents the area?"

"Well... I tried t' avoid it. Weren't a good place. Sailors an' fisherman worked their trade, o' course. But so did the desperate young men an' women whose families sent 'em down there t' earn some coin." She let out a long exhale. "Much of a bastard as 'e was, at least Da never tried that."

Beth took notes without comment, painfully aware, once more, that her life was so different to anything El and Ren and all those poor young women murdered by the Stalker had experienced. That she was so lucky to never have gone through what they did.

"Y'know, reluctant as I am to bring 'im into this... Ren'd know more'n me 'bout the Docks. Used to hang about by an abandoned factory with 'is friends." El sat back. "Maybe we could go an' fetch 'im. I ain't seen 'im since we left your house. I do miss 'im."

Ren! In her excitement for the wedding, Beth had quite forgotten to arrange for El's brother to be moved to Branton Manor. "We could. I'm sorry, El, I haven't had a chance to discuss his move here with Ashford. We might have to—"

"No need to concern yourself on that front." Beth turned, surprised to find Lord Denys standing in the doorway. "I've spoken to Ash, and he's quite happy for Ren to be assigned to the kitchens here."

"Oh, thank you, Denys!" El said, looking for all the world as if she were about to leap into his arms.

Irritation prickled under Beth's skin, and she said curtly, "Yes, thank you, my lord. I had intended to ask my husband as soon as—"

Denys waved her off, coming to take a seat opposite El. "No matter, Elizabetha. It's all confirmed as of this morning."

Beth's brows furrowed. "This morning? When did you see him?"

Again, that smile, never quite touching his eyes when he looked at her. "He woke me early. A work concern. Patients who couldn't wait any longer."

If he woke Denys, why couldn't he wake me? Beth wondered,

brushing the thought away even as hot spikes of envy needled at her.

She lowered her eyes back to the notebook, underlining Ren before turning to El. "Well then, I see no reason we should delay fetching your brother. We can speak to him about the Docks, too."

"The Docks?" Denys asked. He sat back and allowed a servant to place his breakfast in front of him, immediately picking up and buttering some toast.

El held up the article to show him. "It's come up a couple o' times around these murders. First Daisy's ma mentioned it, now this picture in the paper, I assume linkin' it t' the murders an' all, though I can't read it."

Denys peered at the photo, nodding as if to affirm her comment. "Well, no surprise there. All the women were prostitutes, weren't they? At least, that's what Ashford and I believed when we examined them. The Docks and the surrounding area are, I believe, well known to be where such people flaunt their business."

Something in his tone irked Beth. "Be that as it may, Lord Denys, they did not deserve to die." She gathered the clippings and bundled them back into her notebook before securing it shut. "El and I are going to honor each and every one of them by getting to the truth."

Denys held his hands up, a half-eaten slice of toast in one. "I meant no judgment or offense. I simply offered information." He waved towards her notebook. "I can see you're serious about this. An unusual activity for the new Lady Branton, to be sure."

"Ashford gifted this to me. He fully supports our enquiries."

Denys brushed the crumbs from his lapel. "Does he now? Curious. But then, Ashford has his reasons for everything. I shan't keep you any longer, ladies. Perhaps we might enjoy some tea in my private study later this afternoon?"

"Oh yeah, that would—" El started.

"We'll see," Beth interrupted. "We may be busy today. I cannot be sure when we shall return home."

Denys's lips quirked. "Of course. I'll be around. Please feel free to join me." He stood and briskly walked for the door, holding it open and waiting for them to approach. "Please, after you."

"Thank you," Beth grumbled, his behavior irritating her more by the moment. "Let's fetch the carriage, El."

"Good luck with your investigations!" Denys called after them.

Was that a hint of sarcasm, or am I being paranoid? Beth wondered.

"You alright?" El asked, walking at her side.

Beth nodded, holding up the notebook. "I'm fine. Pleased to have more information to help us continue where we left off."

"Mm." El chuckled. "Almost like your husband wants us out the house!"

Beth laughed at the thought too, though at the back of her mind she recalled that curious and pained moan from behind the locked door.

Is Ashford hiding something? She quickly shook her head. *Don't be foolish.*

"Either way, thank you for rememberin' how important it was for us t' get back t' the investigation. I know there's a lot for you t' think about now as Lady of the Estate. I weren't sure we'd ever really start again."

Beth turned to El. "Of course, we were going to get back to it, El. I gave my word. Besides, now that I'm Lady Branton, we may find it easier to obtain certain information from people."

El snorted. "I wouldn't be so sure 'bout that. Not 'round the Docks."

Beth waited for her cloak to be secured at her neck by a servant. "We'll see. First thing's first, let's get your brother."

⚜

"EL!" REN RAN TO HIS SISTER AND WAS PROMPTLY SCOOPED UP in an embrace.

Beth smiled to see them so joyful, ignoring as best she could the lump of sadness nestled in her chest. *I really must check on Edward.*

"Sorry I ain't been 'round much," El said, "but I've got some excitin' news."

"Really?" Ren stepped back from his sister, bright blue eyes shining.

Beth stepped forward. "How would you like to come and live at Branton Manor? With El."

"Oh, yes! I mean, it's not that I don't like it 'ere, everyone's been so welcomin'. But I do wanna be with El." He grinned at his sister. "She's family."

Beth met Ren's gaze. "Well, we've arranged it so you can work there instead of here. Are you happy to do that, Ren?"

Ren surprised Beth by throwing his arms around her. "Yes! Thanks Lady Elizabetha. Should I go an' get me stuff?"

"I think that would be wise," Beth said, her eyes crinkling with her smile. She laughed as he turned and ran down the hallway, almost colliding with her mother.

"Elizabetha! You're back!" Oren approached with open arms. "What, by the Mother, is all this excitement? I wasn't expecting you this morning."

Beth, quite unused to her mother being in a good mood, allowed the hug without fuss. It was rare to receive such physical affection from her—she'd learned to take these opportunities when she could.

"Good morning, Mother," she said.

"Mornin', Lady Oren," El chimed.

"Yes, good morning," her mother said, casting El a brief glance. She began steering Beth towards her reception room. "Won't you stay for some tea? It would be lovely to talk through the wedding. It went quite well, did it not? Why, I had lunch yesterday with the Mining Committee and Lady Caspella commented it was the wedding of—"

"Mother," Beth said, politely pulling her arm away. Such a brief taste of freedom and yet suddenly she knew she didn't need or want to listen to such pointless gossip anymore. "We can't stay I'm afraid. El and I are busy—"

"I see." Her mother's glances towards El were now openly hostile. "Busy, yes. Well, truth be told, I have an appointment I really shouldn't miss anyway." She cleared her throat and clicked her fingers. "My cloak, Allain."

"Lady Elizabetha," the coach driver said cordially, stepping from the shadows and helping Oren don her cloak. "Mistress Ellana, good mornin'."

"How is Edward, Elizabetha?" her mother asked as she slid on black leather gloves. "Your father and I spoke to Lord Ashford at the wedding. A shame he was unable to attend but... we understand it was best for his recovery."

Beth nodded. "That's what Ashford told me as well. He must remain confined. Must rest."

Oren gave a tight-lipped smile. "Perhaps we should come and visit soon. Check on his progress." She clapped her hands. "Come Allain, we'd best be away."

"You would be most welcome to visit, Mother. And I shall come back another morning, I promise. I would like to hear what Lady Caspella said about the wedding."

Her mother's smile at those words was genuine. How readily she believed the lie, so used to being obeyed without question. "Wonderful. It would be best to come alone." Her eyes flickered to El. "I would love to spend some quality time with my daughter."

"Yes, Mother." Beth kissed her cheek. "The Mother's blessings on you."

"And on you, Elizabetha." Her mother smoothed back an imagined loose hair from her forehead and snapped her fingers at Allain.

The servant opened the front door for Oren, casting Beth a fleeting smile before disappearing through the door himself.

"Sorry," El muttered. "I din't mean t' get in the way o' you seein' your ma."

Beth flapped her hand. "Nonsense! We've more important business to attend to than idle gossip. Ah, Ren!"

"Sorry, 'ad to say goodbye to everyone." Ren slung a worn leather satchel over his head. "Ready now!"

El leaned across to rummage in the satchel and pulled out a dark navy cloak. "You'll need this; it's cold out."

Ren allowed his sister to secure the cloak, which was far too big for him, around his neck, though his pout confirmed he wasn't happy about it. "Can we go now? I wanna see Branton Manor. I hear it's bloody massive!"

Beth laughed. "Yes, we can go."

"We 'ave to make a little stop first though, Ren," El said. "There's somethin' we need t' ask you."

Outside, Beth advised the driver to head for the Workers' District before they all climbed into the carriage. Once seated, Beth pulled out her notebook and retrieved the article.

El took it from Beth and held it out for her brother. "D'you recognize that, Ren?"

He looked at it for a brief moment. "'Course. That's the docks. You should know that, El. That's the buildin' we slept in the night after, um... y'know." He swallowed and glanced away.

"So it is..." El held the article up and narrowed her eyes. "Dunno how I din't notice that sooner."

"Looks a bit different there," Ren commented. "That's afore the fire."

"Fire?" Beth asked. "When was that?"

"Uhh, late summer, I reckon." Ren scratched his head. "Gobby an' I 'ad to stop playin' there for a while an' start hanging 'round the old school instead."

Beth cocked her head. "Gobby?"

"Nickname for one of 'is friends," El explained. She rubbed her chin. "Weren't he related to Penny?"

Beth flicked back in her notebook. "One of the victims?"

"Cousins, I think,'" Ren said. "It were Gobby who showed me that factory not long after 'is cousin were killed." His face scrunched up. "I think her body might've been found there."

"In the factory?" El asked.

"Mhmm. And 'er betrothed, Reggie. I thought it was a bit silly t' play there after that, but Gobby said it'd be a'right. People stayed away from it for a while, apart from us. Din't wanna go there, said it were cursed. An' then there was the fire." He shrugged. "Bit of an unlucky place, innit?"

El's cheeks flushed. "Ren, I can't believe you took us to a place where someone was murdered. We fuckin' *slept* there!"

Ren's eyes dropped to his lap. "You din't ask."

El's arms lifted in an exaggerated shrug before slapping into her sides. "I shouldn't 'ave to ask about that! You should just know I'd not wanna..." She let out an exasperated groan. "Don't bloody matter now. Is there anythin' else you might wanna tell me an' Beth about?"

There was a moment's silence. Beth assumed there'd be nothing more on the matter and prepared to close her notebook.

"Actually, um..." Ren began hesitantly. "Well... Gobby made me swear not t' tell no one but—"

"Ren! Sod bloody Gobby, *tell us*." El was almost shouting and Ren shrank back in his seat.

Beth leaned across to Ren and gently touched his hand. "This could be useful, Ren. El and I are trying to find out about the Stalker. About why he's killed these young women. About how we can stop him."

"And Da," Ren whispered.

Beth furrowed her brow. "I'm sorry?"

"He killed Da, too." Ren's lips trembled as though he might be about to cry.

"Oh, well, uh—"

"Yeh. He killed Da, Ren," El said, voice barely above a whisper. She looked to Beth. "That's why this is so important."

Ren ran the back of his hand across his nose. "Well, there were a knife. In the factory."

"A knife?" El and Beth said at the same time.

"We found it when we was playin'. Well, Gobby did. I din't wanna touch it. It looked... um, sorta bloody."

"*Bloody*?" Beth looked up from writing. "Like it had been used?"

"Yeh. Gobby din't care though, said 'e could sell it. Said it were the nicest knife he'd ever seen."

"So, he took it?" Beth asked.

Ren nodded.

"Wait, wait." El held her hands up. "This could be the murder weapon, if that's where Penny and Reggie's bodies was found."

"Yes, it could, yes." Beth smiled at Ren. "This is *really* useful information, well done Ren."

"Yeh, but," El continued, "why din't the City Guard find it when they found the bodies?"

Beth tapped her pencil on the page. "I hadn't thought of that. They certainly wouldn't have left it behind, would they?"

"It were hidden," explained Ren. "Gobby an' me used t' see who could get into the tightest gaps. Old machinery an' that—"

"Ren!" El closed her eyes and pinched the bridge of her nose, muttering, "So bloody dangerous."

Ren shrugged sheepishly. "Well, that's how we found the knife. It were under this old, rusty machine. Wouldn't've seen it otherwise."

"Well, it seems like we need to go and see Gobby," Beth said.

Ren sighed. "He's gonna know I told you."

"Yes," Beth said, "but don't worry; I'll make sure he's not too annoyed at you for breaking your promise." She patted the coin purse at her belt.

"That'll do it," he said, a twinkle in his blue eyes.

"Where does he live?" Beth asked. "Is it close to the Docks?"

"Yeh, not far." Ren peered out of the window. "We're nearly there, actually."

There were people walking past now that they were closer to the Workers' District, some slowing to glare or gesture rudely, some simply ignoring the carriage and going about their day. Beth noticed they all had the same desperate gleam in their eye—like El and Ren had possessed when she'd first met them. She gulped down the shame that washed over her—she with her fine clothes and jewels, her carriage costing more than these people could ever hope to earn.

As they pulled to a halt, the factory came into view. It looked much the same as it did in the newspaper photograph, with the addition of the fire damage Ren had mentioned.

The carriage driver opened the door and peered in at the three of them. "We're here, Lady Branton." Unlike Allain, he expressed no concern as to the environment and people they were surrounded by. Perhaps Ashford had instructed him to assist them, or perhaps he simply didn't like to question orders.

"Wait here, Stefan," she said. "I'll send Ren to fetch you if there are any problems."

"M'lady." Stefan bowed his head and retreated back to his seat atop the steam carriage.

Beth glanced around. All was grey, half-rotten wood, muddied streets, and sour smells. The darkness of the sky did no favors to the already dismal place.

She forced a smile onto her lips even as bile burnt her throat. "Well, lead the way, Ren. Let's visit Gobby."

Ren turned and briskly walked away from them.

"Slow down, Ren!" El called after him, a tinge of laughter in her voice. To Beth she said, "He's used t' runnin' most places. We always 'ad places to be or people t' run from." She looked away guiltily.

"I understand," Beth said. "Well, no, that's not true. But I won't judge you; you and Ren did what you needed to."

El bowed her head, not meeting Beth's eye.

After a few turns down narrow, filth-stained streets, Ren stopped in front of a wooden door. Much like the other houses, it was of poor quality. Likely it was owned by one of the noble families whose levels of maintenance were, as Beth was rapidly learning, below the bare minimum. She bristled with anger, mentally reminding herself to bring up the matter with Ashford, whose friends and fellow noblemen were the landlords of the homes in the Workers' District.

"Gobby lives 'ere with 'is ma an' brother," Ren said.

"Thank you, Ren." Beth stepped towards the door, brushing down her skirts and straightening her cloak. She knocked gently, afraid it would come away from its hinges if she was too vigorous.

From inside the house, a gravelly woman's voice shouted, "Gobby, get the bloody door!"

"I'm gettin' it!" The door was opened to reveal an incredibly slight boy. His small, brown eyes squinted up at Beth. "Who're you?"

"Good morning, Gobby," Beth said, feeling absurd using his nickname but realizing she hadn't thought to ask what his proper name was. "I am Elizabetha Branton and I—"

"Ren!" Gobby pushed past Beth and grabbed Ren in a headlock, scrubbing at his head with dirty knuckles. "Where the fuck've you been?"

"Gobby!" Ren cried, voice muffled by his friend's armpit. "Get off, would ya?"

The boy laughed, giving Ren's head one last knuckling before pushing him away.

Ren pushed him back. "Y'know I don't like it when you do that!" His grin said otherwise.

"Yeh, yeh." Gobby waved a hand dismissively. Turning back to Beth, he said, "What's all this? You in trouble, Ren?" before evidently noticing El too. He narrowed his eyes between them. "I don't want no trouble 'ere. Not after Penny an'—"

"I can assure you, no one's in trouble, Master Gobby," Beth said. "We just need to talk to you about an... important matter."

"*Master* Gobby? I like that." He puffed up, eyes shining. He nodded towards the door. "A'right, you'd better come in."

"Thank you." Beth noted how much older than his years he seemed. Perhaps that's what hardship did to a person.

Inside the ramshackle hovel, a middle-aged woman was hunched over a candle, a fine layer of lace bundled in her lap. "What's all this?" she demanded.

"Ma, you know Ren and El. An' this is..." He gawped at Beth. "Sorry, I don't remember."

"Lady Elizabetha Branton," she spoke up.

Gobby's mother looked her up and down, dark eyes all hardness and mistrust. "Oh yeh? A lady, is it?"

Her thin lips moved from side to side as though she were building up to spit. Beth quickly stepped forward in the hope of dissuading her. "And your name, mistress? That is beautiful lace, I might add. Is it for sale?"

The woman eyed Beth suspiciously before proudly holding up her work. "This piece is spoken for. Though I could make a piece for you just as fine... for the right price. An' me name's Loris."

Beth opened her purse and retrieved three gold crowns. "I trust this will be enough as a deposit. I'll pay the same again on delivery of it to Branton Manor."

Loris quickly stuffed the coins into a pocket. "Oh, yes, m'lady. Gobby!" She snapped her fingers. "Be sure t' give the lady whatever she needs. No messin' about, you 'ear me?"

Gobby sighed dramatically. "Yes, Ma." He nodded towards a small side door. "Come in 'ere. Don't wanna distract Ma from 'er work no more."

They followed Gobby into what could only be described as a large cupboard into which was squeezed two narrow wooden beds. Shuffling in, Beth perched on the edge of the bed beside El, whilst Gobby and Ren sat opposite.

"So, what can I do for ya?" Gobby asked, rubbing his hands together expectantly.

"Well, it's about the factory at the Docks. The one you an' Ren used t'... explore," El began.

Gobby raised an eyebrow. "What 'bout it?"

Beth retrieved her notebook. "We are looking into the Stalker's murders. I know one of the women he killed—Penny—was found in that factory."

"My cousin, yeh. An' her betrothed, Reggie. Good man, he were. An' Penny were good, in 'er way. Troubled, but good." Gobby furrowed his brow and tutted, as though annoyed at himself for speaking so openly. He shook his head. "What 'bout it?"

"Well, it's less to do with Penny and Reggie, and more to do with the factory... and what you found there."

Gobby narrowed his eyes at Ren. "What we found? Dunno what you mean." His words were unconvincing even if Beth hadn't known them to be a lie.

She patted her purse. "Look, Gobby, I'll be honest. El and I need information. We know about the knife."

Gobby scratched at his shaven head. "Knife?"

Ren sighed. "I told 'em, Gobby. 'Bout the knife we found in the factory. The one wi' blood on it."

Gobby dramatically smacked himself on the forehead as if just remembering. "O' course, *that* knife! What 'bout it?"

"I'd like to see it." Beth jingled her purse, making it clear she was happy to pay.

Gobby gritted his teeth. "I, uh, I don't 'ave it anymore."

El sat forward. "Where is it?"

"Sold it." Gobby shrugged. "What else was I gonna do with it? Knife as fine as that—an' aside from a few scuffs an' scratches on the blade an' hilt, it were *very* fine... I knew it'd be worth some money."

Beth reflected that he had a point. "Who did you sell it to?"

Gobby's eyes flitted around nervously. "I dunno."

El groaned.

"What do you mean?" Beth asked gently.

"His face were hidden, an' he din't tell me 'is name."

"I see. How was the sale arranged then? How did you come to know of this man?" Beth asked.

"I were askin' around 'bout it, tryin' t' get the best price, an' this man just sorta... approached me outside Old Toby's."

Beth looked up from her notebook. "Old Toby?"

"Buys trinkets an' jewels. Anythin' you don't wanna answer too many questions 'bout," El told her quietly. "Not that I've ever used 'is services." She flashed an unconvincing smile.

Beth chewed on her pencil. "Seems this man must have followed you then. What did he look like?"

Gobby shrugged. "Wore a top hat, pulled down low, an' a scarf that covered 'is mouth. I thought it strange, but I weren't one t' question someone offerin' *that* kinda money."

"So, you did not see his face?" Beth asked, disappointment blooming in her chest.

"No. Din't seem like he wanted me t' know who he was." Gobby wagged a finger at her. "Sayin' that though, he did have dark brown skin. Like you, m'lady."

"What?" Beth glanced to El, finding her shocked expression mirrored back.

"Saw the skin on 'is wrist when he handed me the purse o' money." He fidgeted where he sat, as though reluctant to voice his thoughts. "Also... well, you might think I'm a bit mad. But I- I got a glimpse of 'is eyes an'..." Gobby shuddered.

"His eyes?" Beth glanced at El. "What about them?"

"I could've sworn they was red." His voice lowered to no more than a whisper. "Red as blood."

El gasped. "You sure?"

"What is it, El?" Ren asked.

"I- It's—"

"Red eyes, we've heard of that before," Beth said carefully. "But it doesn't mean we know who this is." She passed Gobby her notebook and pencil. "Could you draw the knife?"

"'Course," he said. "Never seen a more beautiful knife. Piece of art, it was."

Beth focused on Gobby's swift hand movements, watching the drawing unfold. The scratching of the pencil seemed too loud in that tiny, silent room. As she observed, she narrowed her eyes and tilted her head with confusion.

It can't be, she thought, for a crest was taking shape that was all too familiar to her.

Surely, it can't be.

Yet she was unable to convince herself otherwise as the drawing neared completion. She would know that knife anywhere. The hilt was a crude depiction of the Branton crest. Just like Ashford's knife, just like the duplicate he had gifted—

"Denys," she murmured.

"What? Denys?" El snapped her gaze to Beth, then down to the drawing of the knife. "Oh! That crest, that's—"

"Yes," Beth whispered. She stood abruptly. "We must go. Thank you, Gobby," she said, doing her best to remain calm despite her racing thoughts. "Come, El, Ren. It is time to go."

As Loris waved them off, promising Beth her lace would be the finest in all of Alpinside, Beth thanked Gobby and handed him a gold crown for his time. The young boy looked as though he might sob with joy.

"Thank you, m'lady," he said, before running back into his home and shouting to his ma that they'd be eating well that evening.

Beth smiled, though it was a sad smile; one that echoed the realization she had lived her life far too shielded from people's true struggles.

She turned her face to the dark grey sky and let out a shaky breath. "Let's go home. We can get Ren settled in. Then you and I will discuss what to do next, El."

"You think Denys 'as got somethin' to do wi' this, don't you?" El asked quietly as Ren walked ahead of them.

Beth nodded, her lips pulled downwards.

"But 'ow can he—"

"That knife, El. He has one, Ashford told me of it. El, I- I think he might be the St—"

"What's wrong, El?" Ren asked, coming back to walk alongside them. "Did Gobby 'elp? Will you be able t' find the Stalker now?"

"Yeh. You did well, Ren, tellin' us 'bout that knife." El patted her brother on the shoulder.

"Let's get you back to Branton Manor, Ren. Get you settled in." Beth met El's eyes and nodded her onwards. Her Companion reached for her brother's hand, expression full of fear and concern.

As Beth silently led the siblings towards the carriage, her skin prickled with a sudden chill that had nothing to do with the onset of winter. She wondered what, by the Mother, she'd gotten herself into. *Could Lord Denys truly be the Stalker? Ashford's own Companion?*

She had to talk to El and, more importantly, her husband—for it seemed they might all be in serious danger.

CHAPTER 25

THE PLAN

Inside the carriage, El exhaled shakily and turned to her mistress. "Beth," she said, "what if Denys is there when we return?"

Inwardly, her mind raced. *How can Denys be the Stalker? How has 'e lied to me so well?*

Despite what Gobby had told them, and the apparent evidence that Lord Denys Winborn had paid him generously for the mysterious knife, El's mind fought against the idea. He'd been so gentle, so softly spoken, so kind in the week after the wedding, extending the hand of friendship when she had felt so acutely alone. *How can 'e also be a cold-hearted murderer?*

Beth was staring from the window, chewing frantically at her lip. "I'll speak to Ashford," she said finally. "We must tread carefully."

No shit. El nudged Ren with her elbow. "You alright?"

Ren turned his gaze from the window. "Yeh. I'm glad I din't take the knife and get involved in meetin' that man. This all sounds scary, El."

El nodded, lips pinched tight. "I'm glad you din't either. But, listen, you mustn't tell anyone 'bout today, you hear? Let Beth an' me deal with it. Don't want you gettin' into any trouble."

"'Course, El," Ren said.

Back at Branton Manor, all was quiet.

A flustered maid approached Beth as they entered the hall. "We weren't expecting you back so soon, m'lady. Lords Ashford and Denys are still on their medical rounds and won't return until late afternoon." She took Beth's cloak. "Would you like some refreshments in the reception room?"

"Yes please, Lilly. Tea and sweetcakes, I think. And a sausage or two for young Ren here."

After they'd eaten and Ren had been shown to a small, private chamber—at which he'd declared, "My own room, El! Can you believe it!"—El and Beth sat beside each other before a crackling hearth, each nestling a cup of tea between their palms.

After an extended silence, El said, "I know you said 'e had a knife like that, an' Gobby said the man who bought the knife from 'im had dark skin but... it can't be 'im, can it?" She met Beth's gaze. "Denys."

"Ashford has a knife just like it, he wore it to our wedding. He gifted Denys a duplicate, as an honorary member of the Branton family." Beth sighed wearily. "If I've learned anything, El, it's that the people around us are not always what they seem."

El blanched, flushing with embarrassment for having forgotten about Edward and his involvement in this whole awful investigation. "Sorry, Beth, I din't think... If I feel this way 'bout Denys, you must feel a thousand times worse 'bout Edward."

Beth snorted, the echo of a bitter laugh. "The difference is we *know* Edward is involved. In your father's death, anyway. But regarding Denys... You're right. Much as he seems indifferent towards me, I see the way he is with Ashford and know what he means to my husband. It doesn't feel right that he should be the Stalker. But we can't rule it out."

"No, we can't." El chewed on her thumbnail. "What we gonna do, Beth?"

Beth sat tall, dark eyes reflecting the dancing flames in the hearth. "We're going to get to the truth. I have a plan."

El leaned forward. "I'm listenin'."

"It's simple. Perhaps too simple. We speak to Ashford and Denys."

"Simple is better; no use in complicatin' matters. We gotta tread carefully though, ain't we?"

"Yes, very." Beth nodded, absently pulling at a tendril of hair.

"Makes sense for you t' speak t' Lord Ashford, where I can speak t' Denys." El swallowed. "Though I'll admit I'm a little wary o' bein' alone with him now that we've learned…"

"Mm." Beth smiled sadly. "I'm sorry, El. I know you were growing fond of him."

"Let's jus' see what 'appens."

There was a knock at the door. The young servant they'd seen on their return—Lilly, El recalled—entered when called. "Lady Elizabetha, your husband has requested your presence in the dining room. He would like you and your Companion to join him and Lord Denys."

"Thank you, Lilly. Now?" Beth asked.

Lilly shook her head. "Lords Ashford and Denys are currently bathing, m'lady, but said he'd see you there soon."

Beth nodded. "Thank you, Lilly, you may go."

The young woman bowed, though continued to hover.

"Was there something else?"

"Y-yes, m'lady. That room you asked me t' look into."

"Oh! Yes, at the end of the corridor. Did you find out what's behind it?"

Lilly fiddled with her apron. "It's a medical room, m'lady. That's all I were told. It's not somewhere I'm permitted to go. Only Lords Ashford and Denys hold a key."

Beth frowned, though quickly recovered herself and said, "Thank you. I appreciate you finding that out for me."

Lilly bobbed into a quick curtsy and left the room.

"Room?" El asked. "What room? Everythin' alright, Beth?"

Beth furrowed her brow. "I'm… not sure. Perhaps it is important, perhaps not." She shook her head, seeming flustered. "For now, let us focus on this evening."

Panic clamped over El's chest. *Speak t' Denys. Speak t' the man who might be the Stalker. Alone.* She gulped. "What should we do? What should we say to 'em?"

Beth laid a hand on her arm. "We must remain calm. We'll speak of some of what we've learned, but not all. And when I retire with Ashford, you'll have your chance to speak to Denys. I feel we must do it tonight, before—"

"Before it's too late." El looked up at Beth. "Before he kills again."

Beth squeezed her arm. "Yes."

❧

"AH! AND HERE SHE IS, MY LOVELY WIFE." LORD ASHFORD entered the dining room with Denys at his tail. He leaned down and kissed Beth's cheek, then grinned at El.

She scowled without thinking, uncomfortable with his over-friendliness towards her without being sure why.

Denys moved to sit beside El. "Good evening, Ellana. You're looking well."

El looked at him—searched for any sign of his treachery, of his monstrous nature. "Th-thanks, Denys." She forced herself to smile back. "You are, too." She placed her hand over the pocket in which her necklace nested, sure it had faintly vibrated when he approached. As always, the sensation disappeared as soon as she sought it out.

Lord Ashford clapped his hands together. "How was your day, my dear?" He appeared to address Beth, though his eyes flitted towards El.

"I must thank you for the kind gift, Ashford," Beth said. "El and I found it... most useful. The newspaper articles in particular were most enlightening."

"You hear that, Denys? Enlightening! What did I tell you?" He lifted his glass of Blood Whiskey to toast his wife. "You are quite the detective, my love. Why, I'm sure you'll have the mystery of the Stalker solved in no time!" The laugh he let out was loud and raucous, as though he found his words genuinely amusing.

"Oh, let's not talk of such morbid topics." Denys sipped at his own whiskey, casting Ashford an angry glare.

"Lost a taste for it, Denys?" Ashford asked, a taunting tone in his voice.

For a moment, the two men stared at each other.

El turned to Beth, raising an eyebrow. She gave a subtle shrug back, clearly as bemused as El.

Ashford broke eye contact first, laughing again. "But of course, we don't need to speak of such things. Ellana, tell me—is your new room to your satisfaction?"

"Yeh. I mean, yes, my lord. Most satisfactory," El answered.

Lord Ashford nodded. "And your brother has joined my staff, I understand."

"Yes, Lord Ashford." El bowed her head. "I must thank you for allowin' him t' come 'ere. It means a lot. Since we lost our Da, we've only got each other."

"Think nothing of it. Family is important." He glanced around the table. "I'd like us to think of each other as family. Denys has been my friend, Companion, confidante, and colleague for many years now. Elizabetha, my beautiful wife. And Ellana, who not only provides companionship for Beth, but has, I'm told, kept Denys company too in my absence."

He drank down the rest of his whiskey. Though his words seemed to be meant as praise, there was anger in Lord Ashford's eyes when he looked at El again, an unspoken emotion she couldn't understand. Then he smiled and blinked, and it was gone.

"What a lovely speech, Ashford," Beth said, sipping some wine. "I like that idea."

"Quite." Denys raised his glass, eyes locked onto Ashford. "To family."

As dinner was served and consumed, they spoke of topics El

had come to realize were largely meaningless—at least to her. There was gossip of other noble families, talk of the onset of winter and the festivities that would bring, about the Ether-Temple and worship. She listened and nodded when appropriate, eating as much of her roasted lamb, potatoes, and vegetables as she could stomach. Her mind, however, was elsewhere—on the evidence towards Denys being the Stalker and how she could subtly probe him for information.

And she was trying to ignore the knot in her stomach and racing of her heart that, with every beat, told her she was in grave danger.

When they'd finished eating, Denys stood and held his hand out to El. "A night cap, my dear?"

"*My dear!*" Lord Ashford said too loudly and jovially. "Well now, watch your step Ellana or he may attempt to ensnare you."

El's heart skipped a beat. *Ensnare me?*

Denys laughed, though his merriment didn't seem to reach his eyes. "Ellana and I simply enjoy each other's company. Besides, you two, I'm sure, would like some time alone."

Lord Ashford placed a hand on his heart. "So considerate, Denys. Go, the pair of you. *Enjoy* each other's company."

El wondered at the mocking tone in his voice, though had little time to dwell on it. She glanced at Beth as she stood to leave, giving her friend a brief nod. *This is it. Time t' try an' get t' the truth.*

Putting her hand in her pocket, she grasped the EtherStone necklace as she followed Denys to his private study. *Protect me,* she pleaded with it. *You want my help, well help me.*

There was no response.

Inside the study, the hearth was heartily aflame. Denys moved to prod at the logs. When finished, he turned to her and smiled. "Come, sit. Make yourself comfortable." He watched her take her usual seat in the left-hand armchair, her back to the door. "Some tea is in order, don't you think?"

"Y-yeh, um, thank you." *Stop actin' so bloody nervous, idiot,* she chided herself.

Thankfully, Denys didn't appear to notice. He rang the bell on the wall, requesting tea from the servant who attended.

It was as she sat and waited for Denys to join her that she noticed the knife, displayed on a plaque upon the wall sitting above the portrait of Denys's da.

Why din't I notice that sooner? But then, why would I? It seemed her mind must have skimmed over it on her numerous previous visits to this room—and yet, now that she understood how signifi-cant it could be, she was drawn to it. She squinted towards it, trying to make out what was etched into the hilt.

"Admiring my ceremonial knife?" Denys slumped into the chair opposite her, turning his head to regard the plaque to which it was secured. "A gift from Ashford. I would be truly bereft if I lost it, which is why I keep it here. Safe."

"It's... very nice," El said, keeping her tone as even as she could. "I din't notice it before."

"Would you like to look at it more closely?" Denys made as if to stand.

"No!" El said quickly.

Denys frowned, sitting back down, concern creasing his face.

El cleared her throat. "Yeh, er, sorry. It's just, y'know... it's a dangerous object, innit? I've seen enough violence of late." She tried to smile though was sure it must've been more a grimace.

"Oh, yes," Denys said softly. "I know what you mean." There was a knock at the door. "Enter!"

The servant who El had met some days before, Danyl, entered with a tray of tea, heading towards Denys. Danyl placed the tray on the table beside Denys's chair, swiftly bowed, and turned to leave, eyes flitting briefly towards El as he walked from the room.

Did 'e look afraid? She shook her head, trying to banish that thought.

"*Ellana.*"

El jolted, placing a hand over her pocket. The necklace was still.

Denys handed her a teacup on a saucer with a small biscuit perched on the side, smiling and seemingly unaware of her unease. She mirrored his relaxed expression, though she felt as though the walls of this room—a room she had allowed herself to grow comfortable within—were closing in around her.

"Denys," she said, forcing a casual tone into her voice. "What are your thoughts on the Stalker?" It was a blunt question, but one she felt she must speak in that moment or lose any semblance of courage she had.

Denys peered at her stonily over the rim of his teacup, swallowed, and exhaled. "The Stalker?" He lowered the cup to his lap. "I'm sure I feel much as anyone would: disgusted that such a man walks among us."

El nodded. "And what of 'is victims?" She carefully placed her teacup on the table beside her chair, afraid the trembling in her hands was all too noticeable. "Din't you an' Lord Ashford know all of 'em?"

Denys's eyes remained locked with hers. "We did, as we've discussed before. In our capacity as doctors. Every death was nothing short of tragic. Those young women, they..." He stopped, turning to stare into the dancing flames of the hearth.

"They what?" El pushed.

When he returned his gaze to her, his eyes shone. "They did not deserve to die."

"On that, we're agreed." El chose her next words carefully, her body quivering with fear, as though she stood on a precipice, ready to fall or fly. "So, why d'you think they *did* die? Why did 'e choose them?"

"Well, their throats were slit, El. That usually does the trick." His light chuckle quickly petered out as he noticed El's glowering stare. "Sorry, my way of dealing with the horrors I've witnessed is humor. It's not always becoming."

El nodded, then let her expression soften. "I 'ave a theory."

Denys raised an eyebrow. "Oh? What's the theory?"

"It's about the reason you an' Lord Ashford saw all those women in the first place. The madness."

Denys hesitated for the briefest of moments—something El wouldn't have noticed had she not been trained to be highly alert to her Da's emotions. "The madness?"

"An odd coincidence, in't it, that all the women killed by the Stalker were afflicted in the same way. I know Ashford thinks that means the killer is a Scrubber, someone who paid those poor women for their services, but what if he were wrong? What if the killer knew them more... intimately? Like, say, a doctor?"

Denys's throat bobbed. "I see what you're saying El, but, really, it's purely a coincidence. In fact—"

"What if it's not? What if that's how 'e chose 'em? Not as a customer, but 'cos of the madness?"

Again, that momentary pause. And then, unexpectedly, Denys burst into laughter, sounding so much like Lord Ashford that El could've sworn he was in the room. "I fear you may be heading down a false path there, Ellana. Beware of—"

"*Ellana. Beware... trust... in danger.*" El heard nothing more of Denys, so loud were the broken words in her head.

She slammed her hand to her lap, feeling the vibration in the EtherStone necklace just before it ceased. Forgetting where she was and unable to stop herself, she pulled it out, holding it up to see whether the light within it was ebbing away as it had done before.

"By the Father!" Denys gasped, jumping to his feet. In his hurry to stand, he spilled tea down his front, though hardly paid it any mind. He half leapt towards her, towering above her. "Ellana, where did you get that?"

She dropped the necklace into her lap, meeting a dark gaze filled with what could only be described as a deep, urgent hunger. "It were my Ma's," she said, trying to conceal it with her hands.

"Your mother's?" Denys sounded incredulous.

"Yes," El said firmly.

"How would a Scr—uh, a commoner come to own an Ether-Stone necklace?" He spoke as though she wasn't there, leaning closer and closer, reaching his hand out as though to snatch the necklace away.

She continued to conceal it beneath her hands, snapping, "It don't matter. It's me Ma's."

The force with which she spoke seemed to shatter the spell he'd been under. Denys blinked, meeting her eyes. "Perhaps you believe that, Ellana, but this necklace *must* have come from a noble family." He swallowed, clenching his hands at his sides as he began to pace. "This explains a lot. My clear head, of course! EtherStone. It had to be. I'm disappointed, El, that you did not feel you could— Wait." His brow furrowed as he stepped closer and grasped her chin gently, turning her head from side to side. "Your eyes, they..."

El looked up at him, watched his features turn from curious to surprised to horrified.

He pulled back as though scalded. "Ellana, you- you have it too, don't you?"

She picked up the EtherStone necklace and held it to her chest like a shield. "I dunno what you mean."

"The madness," he said, more to himself than her. "I must fetch Ashford." Without another glance at her, he made for the door.

"Denys, no, I—"

He was out of the study before she could finish her sentence, the door closed and a key turned in the lock. She squeezed the necklace between her hands, her panic heightening.

"You gonna bloody 'elp me or what?" she muttered to the EtherStone. When it remained silent, she groaned, putting it back in her pocket.

To try and soothe her raging nerves—and to convince herself she wasn't about to be murdered—El began to pace before the fire. As she did so, the knife on the wall glimmered as though beckoning her. Now was her chance to study it, to see if it really was the knife found by Ren and Gobby. Upon closer inspection, she could see it had the Branton crest on the hilt just as had been crudely replicated in Gobby's drawing.

And then, as she reached for it, she had an immediate, jarring realization. The knife was pristine, shining, the blade sharp and unmarked by any scratch or scuff that would afflict a weapon that had been used for multiple murders.

Because this knife had never been used.

"How can that be?" she whispered.

And then she remembered Beth's words: "Ashford has a knife just like it, he wore it to our wedding."

The pieces slotted together.

She and Beth *were* in danger.

She ran for the door, turning the handle and rattling it, even knowing it was useless.

"Shit," she whispered frantically. "Shit, shit, shit." She pulled out the EtherStone necklace. "Come on! Fuck! You spoke t' me earlier, why not now when I bloody need you?"

There was no response. The voices, as ever, worked to their own mysterious schedule.

El was alone, and Beth was married to a killer.

Beth was married to the Scrubbers' Stalker.

CHAPTER 26

THE HUSBAND

Beth watched El and Denys leaving the dining room, anxiety clamping across her chest.

"Are you well, my love?" Ashford moved to her end of the table, planted a kiss on her cheek, and took the seat next to hers.

She blushed, goose flesh rippling across her body despite the fears on her mind.

"Let me send for some tea." He reached for a bell at the center of the table.

A servant entered from the kitchen almost immediately. The young woman bowed, listened, then retreated at Ashford's orders.

"Thank you, Ashford." Beth dabbed at her lips with her napkin. "I'm well enough. Though there were some, um... *concerns* I wanted to discuss with you."

"Oh?" Ashford glanced at Beth as he reached for some leftover meat with her fork. He held it aloft between them as he said, "If it's about the staff, just name the problem and they'll be punished. No questions asked. A firm hand can be necessary at times. Some of them can be damned—"

"No, no, it's not the staff." She inhaled sharply. "It's about Denys."

Ashford's eyes narrowed. "Denys? What can he possibly have done to cause concern? I know he can be a little... reserved at times, but—"

"We think he might be the Stalker."

Ashford immediately burst out laughing, eyes dancing with merriment. "What a fine joke, Beth." He slapped a hand on the table, causing the dinnerware to clatter. "Denys, the Stalker!"

"Ash, I..." Beth cleared her throat. "I'm not joking."

Ashford's smile dropped. "Oh. May I ask what has led you to such a... conclusion?"

"Those articles you left me were very helpful. El recognized a factory by the Docks. That led us to find out that, um, well a knife had been found there by... someone."

Ashford's eyebrows shot up. "A knife? At a factory? Do go on."

A knock at the door stopped Beth from replying. A young man entered with a tray atop which sat a white teapot, two cups and saucers, and an assortment of sweet treats. Ashford ignored the servant as he laid everything on the table in front of them, but Beth muttered, "Thank you," as he finished and left the room once more.

Ashford poured tea, placing a cup in front of Beth. "Go on, my dear. I am most eager to hear more."

Beth took a sip, the tea's heat coursing down her throat. "It seemed plausible this knife could be the murder weapon. It was found in the very place that Penny and Reggie's bodies were found."

"Well, fine, but what's that to do with Denys?" Ashford slurped some of his tea, eyes never leaving hers.

For the first time, she felt very small under his gaze.

"Come now, my love, you'll need more than that to convince me, let alone the City Guard."

Beth swallowed. "This person told El and I they wanted to sell the knife, make some coin and—"

Ashford snorted, rolling his eyes. "Well then, we can see what kind of *person* they are."

"The point is, Ash, they were approached by someone who concealed their identity. They wore a black cloak, covered their face." She fiddled with her hands, irritated at their trembling. "But their skin was dark. Like mine. Like Denys's."

"And that's it?" Ashford held his arms out. "That's hardly conclusive evidence, Elizabetha. You would call a man guilty for possessing dark skin? What of Edward, hmm? Has he come under scrutiny? Or have you and Ellana got some grudge against Denys?" His voice grew louder and harsher, such that Beth found herself inching back in her chair.

Edward. Beth was surprised to find she hadn't even considered her brother. It was the knife that compelled her most, the knife which had made her immediately think of Denys. "It's not that we hold a grudge, Ashford. Besides, you've said yourself how unwell Edward is. How could it be him?" She exhaled slowly, seeking to calm herself. "It's just... It's not the skin color that's the main reason we suspect—"

"Well, what is it then?"

Beth decided more words were useless. Ashford did not want to hold any suspicion towards his friend, and she could under-stand that, but he couldn't deny the evidence. She retrieved her notebook from its pouch. Her hands shook as she opened it to the page where Gobby had sketched the knife. She placed it on the table in front of Ashford. "This is why we believe it is Lord Denys."

Ashford leaned over the notebook. "A crude drawing."

"Ashford, surely you can see the resemblance to your own knife, to the Branton crest upon its hilt. The knife you told me Denys has his own duplicate of."

Ashford clicked his tongue, snapping the notebook closed. "I see a passing resemblance."

There were several moments of silence. "Ashford," she said gently, "I know it's hard to think of your friend as—"

"Elizabetha, these are serious accusations. Denys is a lifelong friend and my trusted Companion." Ashford ran a hand through his hair. "And yet..."

"Yes?" Beth looked up at him, seeing the flicker of doubt in his eyes.

"Well, I suppose, it is possible. We aren't together *every* minute." He let out a long breath. "A killer returning to the scene of the murder in the guise of a doctor. There's a sort of poetry to that."

"So, you believe me?" she asked. She didn't want to admit there was a level of desperation within her. If the Stalker was found, she could rule out Edward once and for all, apart from the murder of El and Ren's father.

He sighed. "This is serious, Beth. I need some time to—"

There was a swift knock at the door.

"Yes?" Ashford called.

The door opened to reveal Lord Denys. Beth's heart skipped a beat. *Where's El?*

"Forgive my intrusion Ash, Elizabetha."

"Is all well, my friend?" Ashford asked, placing a hand over hers and smiling at Denys.

"I've just received a message—a patient requires our attention. I'm afraid I shall have to take you away from your lovely wife."

Ashford squeezed Beth's hand and stood. "I must apologize, my dear. Please, make yourself comfortable in my chambers. I will join you when I can." He bent down to kiss her.

"Very well," she said, watching him walk towards Denys. "My lord, is El well? You left with her, and I wondered—"

"Oh," Denys turned to her, "she's fine. Said she was tired and retired for bed." He gave a tight smile though Beth could find nothing to question in his words. He wouldn't attack her here, would he? Where Ashford would find out. Besides, there had been no time to clean himself up if, indeed, he had attacked her. Perhaps El really had been tired; it had been a long day, after all.

Despite this, her breaths quickened as she watched Ashford

and Denys leave, a deep sense that something was terribly wrong growing within her.

CHAPTER 27

THE HUNT

I must resume my hunt once more. The voice in my head can no longer be ignored. It plagues me day and night—burning, urging, screaming—and I know there is only one way to satisfy it. I thought I could ignore it. That my own life and the changes within it would be enough to focus on.

I was wrong.

What must be understood is I am doing the work of the EtherFather, for it is His voice who urges me on. It is His mission I must see through to completion.

The EtherMother has a servant too and She plots to overthrow Him. To see the EtherFather's power and influence drained, to snatch it for Herself. In Her desperation, she has sought a pawn. A young woman in Alpinside, or so I'm told, will rise up and fight against the sacred law of the EtherFather.

And so, my mission was born.

Find that young woman. Kill her. Save Alpinside, for we are all in grave, unspeakable danger.

The EtherFather must be obeyed. His power must remain unchallenged. I must destroy any who seek to usurp Him, the EtherMother and her pawns included.

I have sharpened my knife, I am ready to continue once more.

Does a part of me enjoy what I must do? I don't believe *enjoy* is the right word and yet... there is satisfaction in the tasks I have carried out.

In a way, my work is beautiful. I see the truth in these young women as I slice them open. I see the desperation the Ether-Mother must feel that She should choose those so easily cut down.

My blade and mind are keen, my next step clear.

I must resume my hunt once more.

CHAPTER 28
THE BETRAYAL

When she heard the key turn in the lock, El told herself not to panic; it was easier said than done. She took her seat in the armchair facing away from the door, stared into the dancing flames and tried her best not to imagine her own demise—and what it would mean for Ren.

And then the door was opening, and her time had run out.

Shit, shit, shit. Stay calm, El. Stay calm. She clasped at the necklace in her pocket, squeezing her eyes shut. *If you exist, Ether-Mother, fuckin' help me.*

"Ellana."

She opened her eyes to find Lord Ashford looking down at her, eyes flat and emotionless. Denys remained out of sight, perhaps afraid to meet her gaze.

Could 'e really be the killer? Gotta stay calm, get t' the truth. He don't know I know.

"Lord Ashford," she said, lifting her chin. "T' what do I owe the pleasure? Denys and I was just havin' a lovely chat."

Ignoring her, he leaned down so their faces were close, his gaze locking onto hers. As Denys had done earlier. He grasped her chin, twisting her head this way and that.

His skin was soft but his hold firm. Ashford stood and turned to his Companion. "It may have been so earlier, Denys, but her eyes are normal now."

El glowered at him. "Don't speak as if I'm not 'ere."

Lord Ashford took the seat opposite her, crossing his legs and regarding her coolly. "I think it's time you and I spoke candidly." He flicked his hand. "Denys, some whiskey please."

Denys hurried to obey, handing the drink to Ashford before moving to stand behind the armchair which he usually occupied. The silence in the room was like a knife poised above her head. Still, Lord Ashford merely sipped at his whiskey and watched her, saying nothing. It infuriated her.

"Well?" she said. "Why'd you lock me in 'ere?" She glared at Denys and his expression twisted with apparent pain, though he remained silent.

"Denys has a right to be concerned, Ellana, when you possess an item that was almost certainly stolen."

She scowled. "What?"

Ashford sat forward. "An EtherStone necklace."

"That weren't stolen!" Instinctively, her hand flitted to her pocket; his eyes followed the movement.

"Please explain how else a *Scrubber* would be in possession of such a precious item." Ashford took a generous gulp of Blood Whiskey, gaze unwavering. "Well?"

She sneered, seeing true disdain for the workers of Alpinside in his contemptuous stare. "It were me Ma's. She left it for me. Not that I owe the likes o' you two," she said, glaring towards Denys then back to Ashford, "any sort of explanation."

"Curious... I had believed all EtherStone necklaces accounted for."

"All except one, Ash," Denys interjected. "I recall my papa telling me of it. He had hoped to find it himself. The Aberforth necklace."

"Of course!" Ashford slapped the arm of his chair. "I remember Artavius seeking a replacement. I had thought the matter resolved, though, come to think of it... Hmm, it explains his recent behavior. His desperation." He smirked up at Denys, who gave a fleeting, hollow-seeming smile. "He never found it."

"I dunno who the fuck you're on about, but this necklace were me Ma's, not some- some lord's," El insisted.

"Artavius Aberforth had only one child. A daughter." Lord Ashford tilted his head, studying her. "Thinking on it, you *do* bear a striking resemblance to the old bastard."

El rolled her eyes. "How many times do I need t'—"

"His daughter ran away from home. Left to be with a Scrubber —or so the rumors went. Denys and I can't have been more than babies at the time, but the gossip took *years* to die down."

El's stomach clenched, and she pulled the necklace from her pocket to stare at it.

"And there it is. I can see from here it's the genuine artefact. No one can fake that glow." As Ashford edged forward in his seat again, there was a greedy gleam in his eyes, the dancing firelight casting an orange hue upon them.

Or was that... *Red.*

El gulped, cupping the necklace against her chest. "Whatever you think, whoever this- this Aberforth is, the necklace is all I 'ave of me Ma. No one's takin' it from me."

Ashford peered at Denys. "A woman who shirked her family's wealth, who brought dishonor to her family name, and she speaks as though her dear old *ma* was a saint." He snapped his gaze back to hers. "She was clearly nothing but a useless *whore*."

Instantly, rage coursed through her veins. Before she could stop herself, El leapt forward, thrashing out at Ashford with the necklace. "How dare you!" she screamed. "How fuckin' dare you, you bastard. You don't know anythin' 'bout her!"

El was pulled away by Denys. She glared down at Ashford, teeth bared, breaths coming hard and fast. Denys held her arms behind her back. The necklace, the chain of which was wrapped around her wrist, remained nestled in one hand. Suddenly, it vibrated with more ferocity than she'd ever felt before.

"Shit!" Denys cried, releasing her as he leapt away.

"What is it, man?" Ashford stood, shaking his head. "The bitch needs to be restrained."

El was satisfied to see a line of blood against the pale skin of Ashford's cheek. *Explain that away t' Beth.*

"The- the necklace, Ash, it's—"

El brought it round to her face. It was pulsing with a bright red light—fiercer than any it had emitted before. Something was changing, of that she was certain.

"*Ellana! Hear us. This man must be—*"

"What the fuck?" Ashford stepped forward, snatching the necklace from her.

Distracted by the voices that were clearer than ever, El relinquished it without meaning to. "No, give that back! It don't belong t'—"

Ashford slapped her across the cheek. "Speak again and I will cut out your tongue," he growled. She had no doubt he meant it.

She had no doubt, either, that this man—this *monster*—was the Stalker, for his mask had well and truly slipped in that moment.

Ashford held the necklace up to his face, stroking its surface. The light within flared. With a cry, he dropped it as though scalded. He turned back to El, eyes hot with rage. He closed the gap between them, sneering down at her. "You."

El peered over Ashford's shoulder towards Denys. He continued to avoid her gaze, instead staring towards the spot where Ashford had dropped the necklace.

"You hear them too, don't you?" Lord Ashford's breath was like fire on her skin, stinking of that damned Blood Whiskey.

"Hear what? Who? I dunno what you mean."

He laughed, a sound so removed from mirth that it sent a chill down her spine. "There's no need to be coy with me, girl. You have come into my home. You have beguiled my Companion with your- your *Scrubber's* charm." He moved closer still. "*You* are the one."

El stepped backwards until she met the cool wood paneling of the wall beside the door. Ashford grinned, evidently pleased at his ability to intimidate her. It was enough to send a storm of defiance crackling through her body.

Da had bullied her for years, had abused her, physically and emotionally. She would not stand for it from this man, noble or not. Stalker or not.

"Lord Ashford, I dunno what you're talkin' about. Please, tell me plainly what you mean."

Ashford stepped closer, almost pressing her against the wall. She willed herself to keep eye contact, despite the cruel glimmer in his gaze that grew increasingly difficult to meet.

"'Tell me plainly.' Who the *fuck* do you think you are? You've spent too much time with my dear Beth and now you believe yourself to be at her level." He leaned over, sniffing her hair. "You still stink of shit, *Scrubber*, no matter how pretty you make yourself."

A shudder of fear set the hairs on El's arms standing.

Twisting his head to the side, Ashford breathed in her ear, "You have been sent to test me. I'm sure of it. How did I not see it sooner?" He sprang back, an alarmingly fast movement that caused El to jolt with shock. He lifted the EtherStone ring on his finger to his lips, kissing it gently. "My faith remains unscathed. My work will continue. It is time."

El remained pinned to the wall. *Please, I'm still 'ere. Talk t' me, you don't need a bloody necklace for me t' listen, surely, if you're the Ether-Mother. Help me.*

Denys stepped to Ashford's side. At some point, he'd picked up the EtherStone necklace, clutching it possessively to his chest. El bit her lip to hold back a scream of frustration.

"Ash, don't you think you should..." Denys swallowed, glancing at El, then leaned closer to Ashford so she couldn't hear the rest of what he said. When he finished speaking, he handed the necklace over.

"Thank you, Denys. You have done well." Ashford pocketed it before retrieving his glass. He finished his whiskey and slammed the glass back down onto the table. "Best to get it done." He removed his velvet dinner jacket and draped it neatly over the empty armchair. "See to it I'm not disturbed."

"Yes, Ash." Denys bowed his head and scurried towards the door.

"Please," El croaked. "Denys, don't do this. We was... we was friends."

Briefly, he hesitated, lifting his eyes to hers, muscles in his jaw working. "I'm sorry," he mouthed finally, opening the door and leaving her.

El did her best to blink back the tears glossing her eyes, though a treacherous few managed to escape and run down her cheeks.

"Touching, really." Ashford moved closer, rolling up the sleeves of his shirt. "You know, I've never seen such a strong response to EtherStone." He pulled the necklace from his trouser pocket. The light had faded to a dull ebb, but when he held it towards El, it immediately began to flare again. "Curious. I need some time to think about what to do with you. You seem... different, somehow." He brushed black hair back from his forehead. "I need to consult with Him."

"What you gonna do wi' me?" El asked. "If you're gonna kill me just fuckin' do it, or I'll do my best to escape and make sure *everyone* knows what you are."

Lord Ashford smiled down at her. "You know, I do believe you actually think you could get away. Remarkable, really. Such fight. I see what drew Denys and Beth to you."

Before she could respond, he pulled back his right arm, fist clenched. It flew forward in the blink of an eye. There was a blinding pain in El's temple and then she knew no more.

CHAPTER 29

THE REVELATION

The next morning, Beth awoke impatient to speak to El. The night before, she had waited in Ashford's rooms for a couple of hours before he had sent a message, advising that the patient had been more complicated than expected and she should retire to her own room. Though disappointed, Beth knew his work was important. She had thought about waking El to speak to her, though had decided their catch-up could wait until morning. Her Companion must have been tired to have retired early.

Kicking back the blankets, she stretched her arms above her head, yawning deeply. Nervous energy jolted through her body, urging her on.

"El?" she called, knocking briskly at her Companion's door. "Are you awake?" There was no answer. She knocked again, a little firmer. "El?"

Nothing.

She frowned. El couldn't have left without disturbing her, could she? Or perhaps she had; Beth *was* something of a deep sleeper.

Gently turning the handle, she pushed the door open on

silent, well-oiled hinges—a reminder of how well kept this house was by the ever-present servants. Beth tip-toed in, certain she'd find El sound asleep.

But she soon saw the bed was empty. The sheets were completely untouched, as if it had been freshly made.

"El?" Her voice seemed to echo around the bedchamber.

Snaking dread slithered up Beth's spine. Hurrying back to her room, she knew she had to get dressed and find her Companion.

When she entered the dining room, Denys was sitting alone, hunched over a cup of tea, the cooling breakfast next to him untouched. Beth hesitated, unsure as to whether she was comfortable in his presence. But if anyone knew where El was, it would surely be him.

"Good morning, Lord Denys," she said, forcing a cheeriness into her tone that she certainly didn't feel.

He jolted at the sound of her voice, twisting to look over his shoulder. He gave a weak smile. "Oh, good morning, Lady Elizabetha."

There was a melancholy in his eyes she hadn't seen before and that feeling of dread crept further through her body, clawing its icy fingers into her nerves. She took her seat at the head of the table. "Care to share your tea?"

Denys looked at the pot remorsefully. "It may be a little cold... Let me ring for some more."

"Oh no, please, I—"

"I insist, Elizabetha."

The sound of the bell was stark in the all too quiet room. As Denys arranged for the tea and some more food to be served, Beth stared at the door, willing her Companion to walk through it. Begging her to.

Breakfast arranged, Denys looked at her and opened his mouth as though to say something, then evidently changed his mind and snapped his gaze back down to his half-drunk cup of tea.

"Did you have an enjoyable evening, my lord?" Beth watched his face closely.

Denys remained composed. "Yes, thank you, Elizabetha. And, please, Denys is fine. We are family now, are we not, joined by our connection to Ashford?" His eyes met hers and his jaw squared, as though daring her to challenge his assertion.

She laughed softly, nervously. "Of course. Denys."

As her tea and breakfast were delivered, Beth studied her husband's Companion. The bags under his eyes seemed more pronounced. And did his hand tremble ever so slightly when he lifted his tea to his lips?

Beth cupped her hands around her teacup and cleared her throat. "Denys, I never thanked you."

He raised an eyebrow. "Thanked me?"

"For befriending El after the wedding... while I was away with Ashford."

"Oh." He paused. "Think nothing of it. Ellana is a lovely young woman. Charming, in her way. You're lucky to have her."

"Mm, I am." Beth sipped her tea. "I know she's most fond of you."

"She's too kind." Denys peered over his shoulder towards the door. "Where is she this morning? Is she well?"

The questions caught Beth off guard, she could detect no deception in Denys's expression or words. "Oh, I'd hoped you might know."

He sat tall, frowning. "Why? What's happened?"

"She wasn't in her room this morning."

His mouth twitched almost imperceptibly. "She wasn't?"

"No. So, as you were the last person to—"

The door opened and Ashford walked in, stopping Beth mid-sentence.

"Good morning, Elizabetha, Denys!" he said brightly.

"Good morning," she said, beaming at her husband despite herself.

Denys stood, his chair scraping on the floorboards. "If you'll both excuse me, I think I shall take a walk. My head is a little sore this morning. I didn't sleep well."

Ashford chuckled and slapped him on the back as he walked past, as though sharing in some private joke. He then joined Beth at the table, taking the seat vacated by Denys. "How are you this morning, my dear?"

For a moment, she thought of lying, pretending everything was fine. Then she looked towards the door and knew she must be honest if there was any hope of getting to the truth.

"I'm a little concerned actually, Ashford."

"Oh?" He reached across and clasped her hand, his touch cool as ever. "What's wrong?"

"It's El. She didn't sleep in her room last night, it seems. I can't imagine where she could've—"

"Oh, my love, I thought you would've been told!" He patted her hand. "There's nothing to worry about. Ellana has left. During the night, by all accounts."

"What?" Beth shook her head. "No, that's not right. She wouldn't do that." She pulled at a curl, trying to think of any reason why El would do such a thing. "Who told you that?"

"One of the servants. I'm sorry, Beth. It's a most unfortunate turn of events." He huffed. "But can we really expect anything more from a Scrubber?"

"Ashford! She was my friend; she wouldn't just *leave*. And what of her brother?"

There was a flicker of doubt in his eyes for a moment. "Her brother, yes. He's gone, too. They've both left."

Despite trusting Ashford implicitly, Beth couldn't fully bring herself to believe him.

"I think we need to talk to Denys. This doesn't feel right, Ash. And—"

"Denys?" Ashford scowled. "What would any of this have to do with him?"

Beth fiddled with her skirts. "He was the last to see El last night. And after what I spoke to you about after dinner..."

"Not this again, Elizabetha!" Ashford scowled. "Really? Denys has killed your Companion now, has he? Under *my* roof?"

Beth flushed hotly. "All I'm saying is we can't discount it. I would just like to know what happened between them." She kept her voice as even as possible, though she found herself quivering. It was the first time Ashford had made her feel so uncomfortable, and she wasn't sure how to cope with it.

"Actually, we can discount it. I've spoken to Denys. You can take my word that he is *not* the Stalker."

"You spoke to him?" Beth looked into her husband's eyes; they were clear and blue like a summer's day with no hint of deception. "What did he say?"

"He was astonished, naturally, to be under suspicion. But he shan't hold it against you, my love. It was a mistake, but an easy one to make, I suppose, given the apparent evidence before you."

Beth pursed her lips. *If it isn't Denys, then who...?*

"I've been meaning to speak to you about a delicate matter, Beth." Ashford reached for her hand again. "It concerns Edward."

Beth flinched. "Edward? Is he well? I know he was unable to attend our wedding. I've been intending to see him." She rubbed her temples. "Oh, I've let him down, too."

"He's been too unwell for visitors, my dear. You know I would tell you if it were otherwise. I've been carrying out tests on him. Asking him about... certain matters." He gulped and turned away as though having difficulty with his words.

She leaned closer and touched his arm. "What is it, my love?"

He held a shaking hand to his face, wiping his eyes. When he looked at her again, they were bloodshot. "I'm sorry, Elizabetha but... I believe Edward is the Stalker."

Beth's mind reeled. *We disproved it. It can't be Edward.* "No," she whispered. "It's not him." *Did we really consider all the evidence? He killed El's father, didn't he? How is that any different? A killer is a killer.*

"I'm sorry, Beth." Ashford placed an arm around her shoulders. "I didn't know how to tell you. And then when you spoke to me about your suspicions of Denys, I knew it was time."

Beth clasped her chest, pain pulsing through her heart. "How long have you suspected, Ashford?"

He exhaled slowly. "A while. Perhaps even since that night at dinner. It was evident he had a serious ailment, that his memory wasn't what it should be. That his behavior could be erratic. Since speaking to him further, it's become apparent that... Well, he's had the means to carry out those terrible murders. And his illness may well have driven him to it." He eyed her for a moment, mouth downturned. "I'm sorry, I know this must be difficult to hear."

She shook her head. "No, it's um..." She bit her lip, unsure whether she should say the words that formed on the tip of her tongue.

"What is it, Beth?"

His eyes were so full of concern, his arm so strong and reassuring around her, that she couldn't help but speak. "He killed El's father. We're fairly certain of that, but we don't think he is the Stalker. At least, we didn't..."

Ashford's eyes closed for a moment. "By the Father. What a burden you've had to carry around, Beth. I'm sorry you didn't feel you could confide in me. It makes sense now."

She lifted her gaze to his, pulling free from his arm. "What makes sense?"

"Why you would try to find evidence against Denys. You don't *want* Edward to be the Stalker. Why would you? The implications of such an idea... Your own brother, a ruthless killer." His lips pinched tight, and his nostrils flared. "An awful affair, truly. You may leave it with me, my dear. I have some associates I will speak to about his onward care. Believe me, I will not see him placed in the city jail to rot nor, Father forbid, hung for his crimes."

Beth gasped, her mind a muddle. "Hung?"

Ashford's words seemed so reasonable, so rational, and yet *something* about them niggled at her. Even so, she could not place her finger on it, nor would she even dare to consider doubting her husband. But she had to take action, to learn the truth for herself, before everything spun too far out of her control.

In that moment, she wanted nothing more than to speak to her Companion. *Oh, El, where are you?*

"Ashford," she said finally. "May I speak to him? Before, um, before you speak to anyone else."

"To Denys? Why, it's not necessary, as I said—"

"No. To Edward."

His brow creased. "My dear, I'm not certain that would be—"

"I insist, Ashford."

Ashford dropped his eyes from hers, pulling at his shirt sleeves. "Well, I suppose it can be arranged. I will need to be present, though. I don't trust him alone with you."

Beth's stomach flipped. "He would never hurt me."

"I don't know that to be true, Elizabetha," Ashford said firmly. "The killings have only grown more violent. Uncontrolled. This is a man whose rage seemingly knows no bounds."

She stared at him for a moment, his words washing over her. "Very well. Arrange it. I wish to speak to him. Today." She stood, eager to escape.

"My love, I will need more time to—"

She looked down at him. "Today, Ashford."

"Yes, Beth." He bowed his head, and she walked away on shaking legs.

Edward is the Stalker. El is gone. The words circled her head, never making sense.

She walked to the front hall, retrieved her fur-lined cape and leather gloves, and stepped out into the icy winter air. Above, the sky was dark, heavy with storm clouds threatening to unleash their fury upon Alpinside.

Numbly, she walked, passing fellow nobles, responding to their greetings without thought.

What am I going to do?

When she finally stopped, she found herself outside the EtherTemple. As she stared at the EtherMother's portrait on the side entrance she knew so well, she realized what she had to do. It was just as the voice had told her that morning before her wedding—the voice of the EtherMother, she had come to regard it.

She had to find El.

She had to help El.

Before it was too late.

CHAPTER 30

THE THREAT

El's head throbbed as she fought to lift it. She coughed, her parched throat crying out for water. She rubbed at her temple, wincing at the tenderness she found, but she could live with bruises and pain. She was used to it.

What caused a flush of fear was the recollection of all that had happened the night before. Bolting upright, she squinted around the dimly lit room in which she had been imprisoned. It was large yet scarcely lit, and, as such, much of it was cast in shadow. There was a table on the far side, though she couldn't make out any of the implements on top of it. Disturbingly, there was what appeared to be a cage in the corner beside it, tall enough to fit a person.

The air was heavily scented, too. It was a smell she couldn't quite place.

The bed upon which she'd been lain was of a high quality, the sheets soft to the touch. She wrinkled her nose in disgust. Did Ashford think he was a decent man if he treated his prisoners well?

When El tried to stand, she felt a tug at her left arm. A thick leather cuff had been secured about her wrist, attaching her to a chain around the bedpost.

"Bastard," she muttered.

Leaning back on her arm, there was a twinge of pain. She poked at it, feeling a sore spot on the inside crease of her elbow. A dark red spot told her all she needed to know.

Drugged, she realized. *'Course he wouldn't want me shoutin' or tryin' to escape.*

She sighed and laid back on the bed.

"*Ellana.*"

At the sound of her name, she jerked upright.

"*Hear us.*"

"I can," she whispered. "I can 'ear you."

"*Help us.*"

"Help you? How? What am I s'posed to do? I'm stuck 'ere!" Her voice grew louder with her frustration. She rattled the chain attaching her to the bedframe. "What good am I?"

Silence.

"Hello? I'm bloody listenin'! Speak!"

Suddenly, a groan filled the room, coming from somewhere to her right. She leapt backwards, her back ramming into the cool stone wall beside the bed. She took a few deep breaths, trying to calm her frantically beating heart.

Finally, she swallowed and called, "Who's there?"

There was silence for a moment, and then another quiet moan. She leaned forward, peering towards the location of the noise. There was another bed in here; she hadn't noticed it before, for it was tucked away into a crevice, concealed in shadows that the light of the single gaslamp above her barely touched. As she watched, there was movement atop the bed, someone shifting, limbs cracking.

"Hello?" she whispered.

There was a long exhale, the sound of a dry throat being cleared. "El- Ellana?" The voice was hoarse and broken, but she recognized it in an instant.

"Edward?" She moved to the edge of the bed, going as far as

the chain would allow, twisting herself awkwardly to try and see him. "Fuck. Is that you?"

There was the sound of more movement, followed by a strange crackling that might have been a laugh. "Still blunt as ever, I see." He coughed, a barking sound that spoke of an ailment of the lungs.

Despite her belief that this man had killed her Da, El was also filled with a deep concern for his well-being. He didn't sound in any way healthy.

Restin' is he, Ashford? she seethed. *Another fuckin' lie.*

"What you doin' here?" she asked. "I thought Ashford were lookin' after you. That you was being treated for your illness. That's why you wasn't at the weddin'."

"The wedding? Did I... did I miss it?"

"I'm sorry, I thought you knew," El said. She shuffled, trying to bring some feeling back into her arm. "It was almost two weeks ago."

"Oh, I see." There were creaking and shuffling sounds, and she imagined he'd moved himself into a seated position. Edward seemed made of shadows, as though he had merged with the darkness. "I... have a vague sense that perhaps Ashford spoke to me about it but my- my memory, it melts away from me. Like trying to hold a snowflake." His voice grew quieter. There was an extended silence before he said, "But why are you here? Are you unwell too? Does the- the madness afflict your mind?"

El was about to say no, then realized that would be a lie. Something compelled her to tell the truth. "Yeh, I think so. But that's not why I'm 'ere. I... How much d'you trust Ashford?"

"Trust him? With my life." That strange, croaking laugh sounded again. "Why, that's what I've done, isn't it?" There was an edge of fear to his voice and El wished she could look at him properly.

What has Ashford done to 'im?

"Why- why do you ask?"

"Ashford's a liar, Edward," she said. "He's got me 'ere 'cos, well, he's a monster. He's the Stalker."

"Ellana!" Edward wheezed before coughing again. When he was able to regain himself, he said, "You can't make such- such slanderous comments."

"It's not slanderous if it's true."

Edward groaned, a sound full of pain and anguish. "No, no, no," he cried.

"What is it?" El asked, rubbing at her aching wrist as she pulled against the leather cuff. "What's wrong?"

"It's not true, Ellana. It is *not* true. I cannot allow you to believe it."

El scoffed incredulously. "You sound awfully sure. But what if I told you—"

"*I* am the Stalker." He let out a quiet moan of evident despair. "I- I am the monster."

"No," El whispered. *No. Why else would Ashford 'ave me here? The knife Gobby drew, that could've only been Ashford's!*

"No, Edward," she said, yanking desperately at the chain on her arm. "No, you're not. Please, listen t' me. It's Ashford. He's convinced you somehow that *you're* the Stalker. Made you believe it, but it's not the truth."

"How can you say that? You don't know what I've done." There was a loud thud, as though he had punched his bedframe. "I killed your father, Ellana. Will you offer your sympathy now?"

She sighed. "I know. I've known a long time."

A sharp inhalation of breath. "You... what?"

"I know you killed my Da, Edward. So does Beth. We've suspected it for a while. Too many bloody coincidences."

"*Beth* knows? By the Father. What did she... how did she...?"

"Well, first there was the knife. You was stabbed in the back, wasn't you?"

"I... Yes, I was."

"Well, when I was attacked after I found my Da's body, my brother, Ren, stabbed the man. In the back."

"I see."

"Then there were your red eyes at dinner when you 'ad that funny turn. On top o' that, there's your father's involvement."

"My father?" Edward shifted again; his shadow edged closer, a chain rattled. "What did he do?"

El frowned. "I thought you'd've known. He came to fetch me an' Ren after our Da's death to retrieve a pouch of EtherStone. He offered us a place in your 'ome in exchange for our silence."

"A pouch of EtherStone? Yes, now that you say it, I seem to recall some mention of a pouch. Our- our mines haven't been producing as they should. Alongside that, I- I heard Father despairing about the thefts. They've been growing of late; the workers care not for the risks. Father was so worried, though he wouldn't admit it and- and... I had to- I had to do something. I had to..." He groaned again. "I'm sorry, it's difficult to remember much. But I'm sorry for what I've done. *I'm sorry I'm sorry I—*" His words were replaced by deep sobs and El found she had no desire to keep questioning him; he was suffering enough.

"Hush now, Edward. Hush now. You need t' rest."

His sobs eventually quietened to whimpers, and then he was silent.

El sat back, pulling her knees up to her chest and resting her chin on them. Eyes locked to the door, she waited. When Ashford came, she would get to the truth.

AT THE SOUND OF A KEY TURNING IN THE LOCK, EL flinched upright. She'd been dozing restlessly and couldn't be sure how much time had passed with no daylight to speak of in this wretched place.

"Ashford," she growled at the figure who entered, a lantern set atop a tray they carried.

"No, it's Denys." As he moved closer, El noted the strain on his face.

She glowered to herself. *Good. Let 'im suffer.*

He perched on her bed, placing the tray between them. "I brought you some food."

Though her stomach rumbled at the scent of the freshly toasted bread, she scoffed. "You think I'm gonna take anythin' from *you?*"

Denys glanced towards the door. "Please, El. You must be hungry. I promise, it's safe. I wouldn't poison you."

"Fuck you," she snarled.

He edged closer, hand twitching towards hers. "Please. You have to know—"

"Denys, now isn't the time for idle chatter," Ashford chided, entering the room and bolting the door. He marched forward and stood in front of her and Denys, cool eyes studying her. "Have you felt any changes, Ellana?"

She scowled. "Changes? The fuck you on 'bout?"

He sighed loudly. "Your obstinance doesn't help matters." He studied her for a moment. "Mm, you seem the same, though. The dose must have been too small."

From his bed, Edward let out a strangled cry. Ashford took the lantern and walked towards him. With the flickering light of the lantern held above Edward's semi-conscious form, El could finally see the difference in Beth's brother. He truly was a shadow of his former self, his skeletal form highlighted by the bagginess of his clothes. His cheeks were sunken, his breathing far too quick, his hair almost entirely grey. He twitched in his sleep, getting no peace even in slumber.

"What've you done to 'im?" El whispered.

Ashford raised an eyebrow at her. "Edward is very unwell, Ellana. He's being treated accordingly."

"He looks *worse!*" she exclaimed. "Far worse. An' he's sayin' things... things that aren't true."

"Ha! Please do enlighten me. What has Edward had to say for himself?"

"You know damn well what, Ashford. He thinks he's the fuckin' Stalker!"

He laughed, casting Denys a look of disbelief. "He *is* the Stalker, Ellana. Why, I've even told Beth the truth of his confession. All is in hand."

El turned to Denys, who refused to meet her eye, then back to Ashford. "You really think you can get away wi' this, don't you?"

Ashford pouted almost playfully. "I'm quite sure I don't know what you mean. Now, Denys, a hand, please. I need to get Edward ready to speak with his dear sister."

"You're a fuckin' liar, Ashford!" El pulled at her chain, desperate to lunge at the arrogant bastard. "What've you told 'er?"

Ashford perched cheerily on her bed. He reached out a hand as if to stroke her cheek, smiling. El pulled back, twisting to avoid his touch.

"Now, now," he said sweetly, "we'll have less of that nonsense, Ellana. You're safe, aren't you? We've provided food, a comfortable bed." He patted her knee. "I see you are... confused about everything. The madness is further advanced than I suspected." He inhaled deeply, lips pinched as he slowly shook his head. "You need treatment, just like Edward."

El spat in his face. "You won't do t' me what you've done to 'im!"

Ashford calmly retrieved a white kerchief from his pocket and mopped the spittle from his cheek. "I think you'll find you have little choice but to obey. Denys." He clicked his fingers and his Companion moved to the door, unbolting it and stepping outside. When he re-entered, he was dragging something—no, *someone*— behind him.

"Ren!" El yanked at her chain again, rattling it against the bedpost. "You'd better not've hurt 'im, Ashford, or I'll bloody kill you."

Denys brought her brother to stand just out of her reach.

Ren gave her a weak smile. "S'alright, El. I'm fine," he whispered, though there was a deep purple bruise across his right cheek.

Rage surged through her; she wanted nothing more than to unleash it on Ashford. Instead, she breathed slowly and deeply. When her heartbeat had sufficiently slowed, she looked up at him. "What d'you want from me?"

His eyes gleamed with satisfaction. "There, that's better." He patted her knee again and it was all she could do not to kick out towards his smug face. He pointed at Ren. "Your brother will stay here with you. An act of faith that you may see he's not hurt in any way. You will undergo the treatments I give you each day without argument. It's as simple as that."

There was a barking cough from Edward and her gaze flitted towards him. *Is that what's gonna 'appen t' me?* Then she looked at Ren, knowing her decision was already made. *I'll do whatever it takes t' protect 'im.*

She swallowed, lifting her chin. "Fine. And, in return, you'll gimme your word that nothing'll 'appen t' Ren."

"He'll be safe, El. I promise." Denys's words were unexpected.

Ashford glanced at him, eyebrows raised, then nodded at El. "Indeed, he will. As long as you *comply*." At that, he stood and moved away from the bed. Denys gently nudged Ren forward. He stumbled into El's outstretched arms, careful to avoid the tray of food still atop the bed.

She kissed his forehead and cheeks. "You alright, Ren?"

He nodded, though his bottom lip trembled.

She held him against her and stroked his back. "S'alright, I've got you."

Ashford returned abruptly, wielding a chain similar to the one attached to El's arm.

"No," she said. "He'll be no trouble; he's only a child."

Ashford snorted. "You think I'll take the word of a Scrubber? This is for *my* safety."

"It's a'right, El," Ren whispered.

A lump pressed against her throat as she watched her brother hold out his arm, swearing to herself that she'd make Ashford pay for everything.

With Ren secured to the same bed frame as she was, Ashford stepped towards Edward's bedside again.

While he was distracted tending to Edward, El pulled Ren close and wrapped an arm around him. "We'll be fine," she said, trying to believe her own lie. "We'll be fine, Ren."

As she cuddled him, cherishing his warmth, she watched Ashford from the corner of her eye. He appeared to be closely examining Edward.

"Denys," he called over his shoulder, "come here, would you?"

Denys scuttled towards his Companion, head down. They spoke in hushed whispers, Denys's shoulders stiffening. Eventually, he gave a curt nod and walked towards the far corner of the room from which he retrieved a wheeled chair. El and Ren watched in silence as Ashford and Denys lifted Edward into the chair. El noticed he was wearing a nightgown, his brown-skinned legs bare and far too thin.

Much to Ashford's evident chagrin, Edward ended up having to be strapped to the chair to prevent him from slumping forward; the fact he remained unconscious throughout made the entire endeavor amusingly—to El, at least—difficult.

At last, with a blanket tucked over Edward's skeletal limbs, they appeared ready to depart. Denys pushed the chair towards the door while Ashford came to stand above El and Ren.

She pulled her brother close, squeezing him against her body.

"I shall return in the morning to start your medication, Ellana. I would suggest you eat and drink. You'll need your strength." He stared down at her for a moment too long, his eyes flashing with something dark and terrifying.

Fear nestled in El's gut. To distract herself from the increasingly uncomfortable sensation, she nodded towards Edward. "Where you takin' him?"

Ashford snorted. "That's none of your concern. Rest assured, you won't be disturbed by dear Edward any longer."

With that, he retreated. El frowned after him and Denys, watching as the door was closed behind them. A key turned in the lock and she and Ren were alone in that awful place.

She forced a smile onto her face and turned to her brother. "Let's eat."

She made herself chew and swallow the food, tasting none of it, trying to push back the panicked thoughts of what awaited her tomorrow morning at the hands of Ashford Branton, the Scrubbers' Stalker.

PART IV
THE MARTYR

And in Her submission, the EtherMother relinquished Her power, imparting Her blood into the EtherStone, and bowing to the EtherFather's wisdom.

And the EtherFather, acknowledging the loyalty of his truest servants, granted this power to a select few that they should share in His wisdom and spread the truth of His reign amongst the people of Estra.

-- **The EtherFather's Sacred Doctrine,** *On the Power of the EtherStone*

CHAPTER 31

THE SONG

I have found her.

She was under my nose this whole time. The Ether-Mother has grown bold, forcing her onto my path in such a way. Bold, or desperate. In any case, I'm certain she's the one who will complete my mission.

I could kill her in an instant. Be done with it. And yet... I hesitate.

There's some barrier that holds me back. Some essence about her that speaks to me.

We are alike. She bears the power of the EtherMother as I do the EtherFather. Perhaps even better than I do, though it shames me to admit it. When she held the EtherStone, it glowed... it *sang* for her.

It was this realization, as I beheld her holding the stone, looking into her eyes and seeing the truth, that I knew I couldn't kill her—not yet. I could learn from her. Strengthen myself. Deepen my connection with the EtherFather. After all, wasn't that at the very heart of my mission? Was that not why I killed so many before her—so that I might please Him?

Curiously, His voice has grown silent since I discovered her. I take this as a sign I'm on the right path. That He trusts me to do what I must. And I shall. But first, I will carry out my experiments, seek to understand how she bears the power of the Ether-Stone—how she hears the voice of the EtherMother.

And then, when I have gained what I need from her, I will kill her.

It is what must be done.

CHAPTER 32

THE BROTHER

Beth was in the reception room awaiting her brother. Ashford had promised he would prepare Edward and bring him to her mere hours before, but it felt like days had passed since that morning. She nibbled at a piece of cake, though was far too nauseous to enjoy it. She sipped at some sickly-sweet tea to wash away the bile rising in her throat.

Is Edward truly the Stalker? That question had circled her mind since Ashford's revelation.

To distract herself and still her shaking hands, she picked up her notebook and began to turn the pages. She'd flicked through it a number of times already, running her finger over the names of the five women and their loved ones, all murdered at the hands of...

No.

Despite her husband's convictions, despite the fact she trusted him deeply, she couldn't bring herself to believe him, not fully.

The door to the room opened and she snapped her notebook shut. She knew she had to be firm, blunt, unemotional. She had to see Edward not as her brother but as a suspect.

Yet, when his frail form came into view, his sunken cheeks and blood-shot eyes, his limp, grey hair, her resolve wilted. She rushed from her seat to take his hand. It was too thin, the bones seeming to creak beneath her grasp.

"Edward," she whispered, tears filling her eyes.

Her brother blinked and looked up at her, his dark eyes taking a moment to register recognition. "Beth!" He smiled, his lips pale and cracked, standing out against the dark brown of his face. "Oh, I've missed you."

He gave a tiny squeeze of her hand, barely perceptible, as Denys began to push his wheeled chair towards the hearth.

She followed, a frown pulling at her features. Ashford had said Edward was getting better. How was *this* better? Beth swallowed down those feelings, unwilling to confront them yet. She smiled through her tears as she sat in the armchair beside Edward, reaching to take his hand again.

Ashford and Denys took seats beside each other on the settee, poised like sentinels. There was an extended silence and Beth found herself unable to begin the conversation she knew must occur. Ashford seemed to be waiting for her to begin, sitting with his hands clasped on his lap while Denys's mouth was downturned and his expression sullen, as if deep in thought.

Finally, she forced herself to turn to Edward. His eyes were glazed, staring into the hearth, not really seeming to see anything. A glistening line of drool ran from his slightly agape mouth. She retrieved a kerchief from her skirt pocket and mopped it away.

"Edward," she said gently.

He blinked, slowly turning his head. "Beth!" he said again, as though having forgotten their reunion mere moments ago. He reached a quivering hand up to brush the hair from his temple. "I've missed you, little sister. Are you well?"

She patted his knee. "I am well, brother." She sucked in a breath. "It's you I'm concerned for. It's been too long; I'm sorry I didn't come to see you sooner."

Edward laughed croakily. "You don't need to apologize, my

dear Beth. I've not felt so at peace in a long time. My mind..." He narrowed his eyes in what appeared to be a moment of confusion. "It's been quieter than ever. Besides I- I think I owe *you* my sincerest apology. I hear you were married! I'm so sorry." His breathing quickened as his voice grew hoarse. "I wanted nothing more than to—"

Ashford sat forward to pat her brother's arm. "Now, Edward, don't upset yourself. You know why you didn't attend the wedding."

Edward shivered, blinking towards Ashford. "I do?"

Ashford smiled at him. "Of course. We discussed it at length." At his side, Denys simply nodded. "It was agreed you needed to rest. That your strength wouldn't be sufficient to see you through such a strenuous day." Ashford leaned back in his seat. "It was what was best for you, dear brother."

Brother. Something about Ashford using that word rattled her. *He's not your brother!* She wanted to scream. *Look at what you've done to him!* But she could not voice those words, she was not brave enough.

Edward's face contorted with evident anguish. "Perhaps," he said quietly, "there *was* such a decision... Yes, I- I think I remember now." His words were unconvincing, yet Ashford nodded firmly.

"You see, you do remember." He looked at Beth. "He was resting, as needed. As I told you."

She turned away from his gaze, suddenly finding it hard to meet those beautiful eyes. "Yes, I see." She sighed. "It would've been nice to have you there, Edward. It was a wonderful day."

To her surprise, his face creased with pain, his mouth becoming a gaping maw from which emitted a deep, heartbreaking sob.

"Edward?" She took his hand. "What's the matter?"

He shook his head as tears leaked from his eyes. "I- I- I-" He gulped. "I don't know how you c-can say that. Who would want s-s-such a m-monster at their wedding?" His shoulders moved up and down as he cried.

Beth stroked his back. "Edward, don't say that. You're not a—"

He turned on her, eyes flashing red. "Yes, I am!"

She gasped, lurching away from him, thudding into the armchair.

"I killed them," Edward muttered, seemingly to himself. "I killed them, I killed them, I killed them." He began rocking back and forth, hands grabbing at the arms of his wheeled chair.

Ashford jolted up, kneeling beside Edward. "Hush, now," he said, stroking her brother's back. "You've overexerted yourself." He turned to Denys and nodded. "Take him to his bedroom. He needs comfort."

Without a word, Denys headed out of the room.

"Where's he going?" she asked.

Ashford glanced up at her. "Edward needs rest. Denys will see that he is taken care of." He gave a hollow smile. "I shouldn't have allowed you to see him so soon. He wasn't ready."

"*Allowed* me?" Beth ground her teeth. "He's my brother, Ashford. I appreciate that you've been treating his- his illness, but his condition should've been made clear. My parents need to know of this."

She watched her brother, whose movements had slowed, though his expression remained pained. His words echoed through her mind: "*I killed them.*"

"He really believes it, doesn't he? That he's the Stalker?" Beth said.

Ashford nodded, lips a hard line. "It's the truth, my dear. One that he's finally sought to come to terms with."

"Ellana's father, we knew about him, but to think he could've—"

"El- Ellana?" Edward slowly turned his head towards her and blinked wearily. They were back to their dark brown color, brimming with despair. "I told her the truth. All of it." He leaned his head back, letting out a relieved sigh. "I told her."

Beth frowned. "What?" She looked from Edward to Ashford. "When could you possibly have told her?"

Edward's face creased with concentration. "I- I saw her and—"

"Edward, you were dreaming again." Ashford chuckled lightly. To Beth he said, "He's been having some very vivid dreams since starting his medication."

Edward's face pinched with confusion. "No, I- I told her, Ashford, you—"

Just then, the door opened, and Denys re-entered with a syringe of red liquid, dark as blood, swirling with a curious glow.

Ashford held his hand out. "Thank you, Denys. Beth, you may wish to leave for this."

"Why?" she asked. "What is that? What are you doing to him?"

Ashford didn't respond as he lifted Edward's sleeve.

Despite his lethargic state, her brother's reaction was immediate and visceral. "No, please! I don't need any more of it. I'm not confused! Please, Ashford!"

Beth stood, terrified by the sheer desperation in Edward's voice. "Ashford, what *is* that? Does he really need—"

"Elizabetha, step back," Ashford said firmly. "Denys, please assist."

Beth was shocked at the vehemence in her husband's voice and did as he asked, edging away until she was leaning against the far wall, watching in horror. Edward was attempting to stand, thrashing wildly. Denys moved to pin him down, forcing Edward's face under his arm. Edward's eyes locked with Beth's and he calmed, lips trembling.

Her brother blinked, a tear running down his cheek. "I saw her, Beth."

Ashford and Denys, so intent on their work, didn't seemed to hear.

Beth gave a single nod, mouthing, "I believe you."

Her heart broke, for in saying those words she knew, deep down, she'd accepted her husband was hiding something from her, even as she could barely fathom what that might be.

"All done," Ashford said, stepping away with the empty syringe held high.

Denys slowly released Edward, whose head slumped forward.

"He'll sleep now, my love." Ashford gave a fleeting smile. "It's what he needs."

Beth nodded numbly wondering what she'd just witnessed, what was going on in this house. *Her* house.

She watched Denys wheel her brother from the room, holding a hand to her aching chest. She wished sorely El was here; she would know what to do.

She was so lost in thought, she didn't notice Ashford approach her. He clasped her shoulders, looking into her eyes. Up close, she noticed two red scratches across his cheek.

Before she could ask about them, he said, "I'm sorry you had to see that, Beth." He tutted. "I should've been firmer with you about seeing him. He wasn't ready."

She tore her gaze away from Ashford's as he said the words. "He admitted to being the Stalker but, in truth, Ash, he doesn't seem to possess himself anymore. He's not the brother I remember." She gulped. "It seems he's forgotten much. You said he was getting better."

Ashford pulled away, throwing his hands up in exasperation. "Come now, Elizabetha, what more do you want from me? I've taken care of Edward as best I could."

Beth reached out for him. "I'm sorry, Ashford, I don't mean to question you."

"And yet you do." He walked away, standing in front of the hearth, shoulders tensed.

Beth's lip trembled, torn between pushing him for answers and appeasing his irritation. As she stood with an arm outstretched towards him, despair bloomed in her heart. Her arm slumped and tears flowed from her eyes, sobs wracking her body.

Ashford immediately turned back to her, face softening. He took her arm and steered her towards the armchair. "Come now, my love, it's been a trying day for you." He stroked her hand. "I'll order some tea. Then I think it's best you retire for the evening."

As he stood to summon a servant, Beth grabbed his hand and pulled him back. "Ashford," she whispered, "Edward can't truly be the Stalker, can he?"

Ashford sighed. "He is, Beth. I know it's hard to accept, but... it makes sense, does it not?"

Beth's brow furrowed. Before she could reply, he squatted down so his face was level with hers and placed a cool hand on her cheek. "Come, I insist. Tea and bed. We can discuss what's to be done in the morning."

Beth allowed him to walk away this time, letting out a long, quivering exhale. *El, where are you? I need you.*

She watched the flames for a while, lost in despairing thoughts. When Ashford returned and handed her a cup of tea, she took it with a nod of gratitude, holding it between her hands and allowing the steam to wash over her face.

Ashford sat at the end of the settee closest to her. She knew his presence should be a comfort, but she was ill at ease, replaying the scene that had just occurred. If she believed her brother, that meant El was... what? Here, somewhere? Hidden away in the very manor she called home?

She sipped her tea and watched Ashford from the corner of her eye, wondering, *What are you hiding?* Before she could stop herself by overthinking, she said, "Ashford?"

He turned at once. "Yes, my dear?"

"Where did those scratches on your cheek come from?"

"Oh." His hand drifted up to them absently. "A simple risk of my work as a doctor, unfortunately. Sometimes patients get a little... aggressive."

"I see." Beth looked down at her cup, wondering whether that was another lie. After the afternoon's events, she couldn't let herself believe anything Ashford said, no matter how convincing he seemed.

She swallowed the scalding tea and made herself a promise: she would get to the bottom of this—for El and for Edward. She would discover the truth about the Stalker. She would see the investigation to the end, no matter what.

CHAPTER 33

THE NEEDLE

El laid awake all night, waiting. She wrapped herself around her brother, comforted by his warmth and soft breathing, safe in the knowledge she would never let any harm come to him.

When the sound of a key in the lock came, she did her best to remain calm, though her entire body was tensed and ready to fight. She eased her arm from beneath Ren and sat up, staring in the direction of the door. It creaked open and a flickering lantern illuminated Ashford's pale face, eyes hard as stone. El gulped; she'd seen that expression before enough times on Da to know it meant nothing good.

Silently, Ashford closed and locked the door behind him. He moved to the tables at the far end of the room, picking up equipment she couldn't see. With limited light, she had no idea what he might be doing. El hugged herself, trying to still the shivering that rippled through her.

"El?" Ren blinked up at her sleepily. "You a'right?"

She forced a smile. "I'm fine, Ren. Get some rest."

"Awake, I see." Ashford's voice was blunt and unemotive. He was still preparing whatever was in front of him, yet he cast them a glance over his shoulder. "Good. There's no time to waste." He stopped working, brushing his hands together before walking over to the bed. "Remember what I said. If you do anything to displease me, your brother will be punished."

"El?" Ren whispered fearfully.

She squeezed his shoulder. "Don't worry." To Ashford, she said, "Let's get this over with then."

To her disgust, Ashford smiled. He retrieved a key from the pocket of his waistcoat and unlocked her manacle.

When he offered his hand to help her up, she clenched her fingers into a fist to stop herself from slapping him away. "I don't need your 'elp," she growled, climbing over Ren and off the bed. Her legs shook as she put her weight on them.

Ashford watched with an amused gleam in his eye. "You are so stubborn. I wonder what of that is *Her* and what is you."

El scowled. *The fuck does that mean?*

"Come, sit over here," Ashford said, pointing to a chair close to the table.

As she edged towards it, she noted there were straps at the arms and legs.

Ashford sighed. "Those are only necessary if you fight. You won't do that, will you, Ellana?"

She closed her eyes, took a deep breath, and sat down as she said, "No. Do whatever it is you need t' do, Ashford. I'm done wastin' time."

Ashford stood over her, smiling. "If this works, it will be a breakthrough. I will be able to harness the power we possess. I will be able to—"

"I don't fuckin' care."

He sneered. "Of course, you don't. You have no idea, do you? The EtherMother's pawn is nothing but an ignorant Scrubber. Hold still."

EtherMother's pawn?

Ashford leaned over to tighten a leather belt around her right bicep. "You have no idea of the power you've been granted." He picked up a syringe from the table. The cylinder contained a deep red liquid, glowing like her necklace. "Relax your arm."

She obeyed as best she could, her arm throbbing from the belt around it. As Ashford neared with the needle, El gritted her teeth and squeezed her eyes shut.

"Breathe, please, this will be a lot harder if you're tense."

Fuck you, fuck you, she screamed at him from inside her head, then forced herself to breathe slower.

There was a sharp prick, then—

Fire, burning fire. Shrieking pain.

The screams of many seemed to rise up alongside hers.

"*Ellana...*" a voice called. "*Help us... Ellana!*"

The clatter of chains, a child's cry. "El!"

Her whole body was aflame, burning, raging. And then there was nothing.

CHAPTER 34

THE LIES

I t was still dark when Beth arose the next morning. Despite being exhausted from a night of broken sleep, she got up without hesitation. She needed to find out more about El and Ren's "departure" from the house. She decided she must start in the last place she'd known El to be—Denys's study.

Though Ashford had seen her to her own chambers, he hadn't stayed to comfort her after the experience with Edward. She'd been disappointed at the time, craving his body even as her mind questioned his trustworthiness, but it had meant she was able to quietly dress and ready herself without any questions from him. Before leaving her room, she retrieved her notebook, clutching it to her chest like a shield.

"I'm going to find you El," she whispered, striding to the door with forced confidence.

Outside her bed chamber, the manor was still. The hall was lit by lamps and looked the same as always, yet, for the first time, she noted the oppressive air within her home, as though there were dark, dangerous secrets lurking behind every closed door.

Dark, dangerous secrets kept by Ashford.

No, she told herself, *you don't know that's true, not yet. There may be a simple explanation for all of this. A simple misunderstanding.*

She nodded briskly, driving herself on. *The quicker I find out where El is, the quicker I can stop doubting Ashford.*

Beth hurried down the stairs, eager to be done with her sneaking around.

"Good mornin', m'lady," Lilly greeted her as she scurried down the stairs, heading for Denys's study.

"Good morning," Beth said. "Oh, Lilly?"

Lilly stopped and turned, eyes downturned.

"Has Lord Branton arisen yet?"

Lilly lifted her face, blinking rapidly. "Uh, I... I've not seen 'im, Lady Elizabetha. D'you want me to, um, to fetch 'im?"

"Oh, no, please don't disturb him, Lilly. I was just wondering if he was awake yet."

Lilly gave a small, relieved smile. "Yes, m'lady. Will there be anythin' else?"

"Breakfast please. I shall have some tea and toast in the dining room."

"Of course, m'lady." Lilly bowed and headed back the way she'd come.

Making her way downstairs, Beth was eager to reach Denys's study before anyone else saw her. Outside the door, she checked behind her, ensuring the hallway was empty. Hand on the doorknob, she took in a deep breath, praying, *Please, please let me find El.*

Inside, the study was lit by a crackling fire. She assumed it was lit in perpetuity, for Denys, like her husband, kept unusual hours. She leaned against the closed door and took in the room. It was cozier than expected, the dark green walls lined with portraits, including a man she assumed to be Denys's father based on the likeness, and paintings of landscapes she didn't recognize.

She moved into the room, her breaths quickening as her nerves spiked. There were various books laid upon Denys's desk, their topics ranging from the mining of EtherStone to the treatise of the Southern Isles. Propped at the back of the desk was a drawing of Ashford. Beth's breath caught to see it, for it captured his likeness so well. She wondered if Denys had sketched it, and if it meant anything.

Don't be foolish, she chuffed. *They're good friends. Family, Ashford has said more than once. Why would Denys not want a drawing of someone so important to him?*

Still, the drawing gnawed at her, something about it troubling her deeply, about the delicate stroke of pencil and the way Ashford's handsome features had been captured so well.

Moving away from the desk, she cast her eyes towards the armchairs. She approached them and sat for a moment, wondering if this was where El had sat. Beth sank further into the chair, aware she had limited time but drawn to do so nonetheless. She glanced about the room, unsure what she expected to find but almost certain the answer to her Companion's whereabouts lay here. Or perhaps she simply wanted to believe that.

"El, where are you?" she whispered. As she leaned forward to rise, a gleam of firelight caught on an object on the wall.

A knife.

What was more, it appeared to be the same as the one Gobby had drawn. To be sure, she pulled out her notebook and flicked to the page, holding it up beside the real object. It wasn't a perfect copy, but... the drawing certainly portrayed the knife mounted on Denys's wall, or one very much like it.

A knife Ashford had gifted his Companion.

She reached up to touch it, stroking a finger over the Branton Crest upon the hilt. It was perfect, unblemished, as though Ashford had only gifted it to Denys yesterday.

Suddenly, Gobby's words flashed into her head, "Knife as fine as that—an' aside from a few scuffs an' scratches on the blade an' hilt, it were *very* fine."

The blade before her was pristine; it had clearly *never* been used.

She recalled, too, Ashford's words on their wedding night. "I almost lost it once... I would've been distraught if it hadn't been returned to me."

"No," she wheezed, hand flying to her mouth. "No, no, no." She bumped into one of the armchairs and without thinking, lowered herself into it. "By the Mother, please, it can't be true."

For a brief moment, she allowed the tears to flow, allowing her life to flash before her eyes; allowing the future she'd planned to burn away. And then she retrieved a kerchief from her pocket and wiped her eyes.

She opened a fresh page in her notebook and wrote in a shaky hand: *Ashford is the Stalker.* Somehow, seeing those dreadful words written down was what she needed to decide her next actions.

Slamming her notebook shut, Beth tucked it under an arm and strode from the room. The manor seemed to have awoken and, as though a veil had been lifted, Beth saw her home in a new light. It was grand, yes, and decadently decorated, but there was also neglect. Some of the wallpaper peeled and the carpet was threadbare, while the skirting boards were coated with dust in the dark corners of the hallways.

There were rooms she'd never been in, that Ashford had never spoken of. What lay behind those doors?

Making her way to the dining room, she noticed the servants all hurried about their tasks with eyes to the floor. At first, she had thought this a sign of respect but... could it be fear instead?

Calm yourself, Beth. She clutched her notebook against her chest. *You have to keep a clear head. Be like El. Be strong, be brave, be bold.*

Her heart skipped a beat as tears pricked her eyes. *Oh, El, please be well.*

She blinked away her despair and approached the dining room door. Inside, voices rang out. As she entered, a breath caught in her throat; how could she dare to meet her husband's eyes?

Ashford stood and came to her side, ignorant to her suffering. She smiled up at him and he down at her. She could pretend all was normal, at least for a time. She had to.

"Good morning, Ashford," she said, standing on tiptoe to plant a kiss on his cheek.

"Good morning, my love," Ashford said, guiding her to the seat beside his own. "Are you well? We were waiting for you before we ate. We almost gave up."

"Oh, you didn't need to do that." Nodding politely at her husband's Companion, she said, "Lord Denys."

"Good morning, Elizabetha," he replied.

Ashford took his seat, grinning between Beth and Denys. "How lovely for us all to be together."

"Except El," Beth said.

Ashford and Denys glanced at each other.

Her husband cleared his throat. "Perhaps it's best she's not here. She was a strange girl. So forthright. A Scrubber, too. Hardly a fitting Companion for one of your station, my dear. Don't you agree, Denys?"

Denys almost choked on his tea. "Quite right," he said once he'd caught his breath, smiling unconvincingly.

Beth stared, open mouthed. "Weren't you friends with her, my lord? Did you not see what a wonderful—"

"Beth!" Ashford snapped. "We are here to enjoy a meal, not speak of those who did not see fit to appreciate the opportunities they had been handed."

The kitchen door opened, and breakfast was brought in by a line of servants, allowing Beth a moment to steady herself. She reached for her tea and drank it, focusing on the scalding sensation down her throat rather than the harshness of her husband's voice.

With the food laid out and the air filled with the scent of bacon, sausage, eggs, and fresh bread, Ashford held his arms out as though presenting the feast to she and Denys. "A fine meal amongst family."

Breakfast passed in a blur of inane conversation, while Beth's cycled through the discoveries she'd made. She shoveled food into her mouth, barely tasting any of it.

When a knock came at the door, she almost jumped from her seat.

"Enter!" called Ashford.

"A scroll has arrived, my lord. From the Physician's Guild," the servant said, presenting Ashford with the message.

Ashford wiped his greasy fingers on a napkin. "You're dismissed, Danyl."

The young man bowed and hurried from the room as Ashford opened the scroll. His pale eyes flitted across its contents. "We are needed, Denys. Some pointless meeting or other, I'm sure." He cast Beth a fleeting smile. "It shouldn't take long, my dear. Such matters are usually a waste of time but, alas, as trainees we must attend or have our professionalism called into question."

"I shall fetch our supplies," Denys said, standing and straightening his waistcoat.

"Thank you, my friend."

As Denys left, Beth knew she must seize her chance to speak to Ashford. She felt certain that if she didn't say something now, she would lose her nerve altogether.

She reached out to him, fingers brushing his arm. "Ashford, my dear, there is a matter I had hoped to discuss with you."

He took her hand, clasping it. "I'm sorry, my love. I shall make myself available this afternoon, you have my—"

"It's about the Stalker. About his true identity."

The change in Ashford was immediate, his cheeks flushing red, eyes hot with anger. "Elizabetha, really." He snatched his hand away. "We already know his *true* identity. How many times must I—"

"I don't believe it to be Edward." She stood slowly, lifting her chin. *Mother, protect me.* "In fact, I believe it to be—"

Ashford slapped her. "Enough!" His sharp voice resounded around the room.

Beth gasped, gently touching her burning cheek as she edged backwards until her lower back met the dining table. She took in short, sharp breaths, suddenly terribly afraid.

The rage melted from Ashford's eyes almost immediately. He stepped forward, trapping her in place. "Oh, Beth, I'm sorry." He placed his own hand over hers, pressing it against her throbbing cheek. "You must not speak of such things any longer."

He pressed down on her shoulders, gently pushing her back into her seat before kneeling in front of her. Though her entire body quivered, Beth met his gaze, saw the iciness there as he gathered himself.

"You have spent too much time on this matter. You became involved because of that stupid *bitch*. But she's showed her true colors, hasn't she? Leaving you behind without a word of farewell. She even put the idea of Denys being the Stalker in your head. My friend. My Companion!" He shook his head, a curl of dark hair falling across his forehead.

"This whole sordid affair must be left behind us." He pulled her hands into his. "We know Edward has committed these foul crimes. We know he needs help. Believe me, I've done all I can to aid him, and will continue to do so. He will not kill anyone else. I promise."

As he spoke, Beth studied his face. There was conviction in his expression, in the way he held himself and met her eyes. *He truly believes what he's saying.*

"Are we in agreement?" he asked. "I believe, now more than ever, that the best topic for us to focus on is our future. *Our* family." He leaned down to her ear and whispered, "And how much pleasure there will be in the making of it."

Despite herself, Beth shivered at the implication of his words. As he drew back, she forced herself to smile up at him. "Very well."

"Wonderful. Why not begin this afternoon, hmm?" He ran a finger along her jaw and over her lips, his mouth quirking upwards. "There has been far too much stress of late. I need you, Beth. I need your love and support."

She allowed his finger to linger on her face a moment longer before gently pulling his hand away. "Yes, Ashford. I will wait for you in your chamber."

He kissed her knuckles. "I will hurry back, my love."

Beth watched him go. When the door closed behind him, her mouth dropped open in a silent cry of despair. Who was this man she had married? He was the best liar she'd ever known.

Or he was mad.

Reaching for her teacup, she gulped down the gritty liquid that remained. Yes, she would go to his bedchamber—but not for the purpose Ashford wanted. He hadn't been wearing his knife, so it stood to reason that he would keep it locked away in his private chambers. She would find it, and she would know the truth once and for all.

CHAPTER 35

THE ETHERMOTHER

A t first, there was darkness. Endless, oppressive darkness such that El felt she might suffocate beneath the weight of it. She held up her hand, unable to see her own fingers waggling in front of her eyes.

"Hello?" she called out. "Ren?"

There was no response.

She tried to move and noticed she was weightless, as though floating in the air. It was such an absurd concept that she almost laughed. Kicking out her legs and arms in a wild flailing motion, she imagined how stupid she must look. Then a light flickered to life before her, hovering in the air just as she did. It was bright—so bright she had to squint against it at first—and a creamy yellow in color, like the low sun in the cloudy winter sky.

"Hello?" El called.

"Ellana."

At the sound of her name, the orb dimmed and brightened again, as though it was the source of the voice.

She knew it was a foolish idea, but then again, she *was* floating in darkness.

The orb pulsed and emitted a light, tinkling sound, as though laughing. El blushed; could this orb read her mind?

ECHOES OF THE ETHERSTONE

"You are more astute than you believe yourself to be, Ellana Stone."

"I dunno 'bout that," El muttered. "Dunno what 'astute' means, anyway."

That tinkling sound came again. "You are just who we need, Ellana. It's good to be able to talk freely at last."

El moved forward, finding she could do so if she willed herself to. "What d'you mean?"

"The concoction you have been given has temporarily released the restraints on your mind which previously prevented you from hearing us, though you cannot keep using it. Excessive consumption of it would be... dangerous."

"Dangerous?" El swallowed. "How dangerous?"

"Fatal."

"I see." El rubbed at the injection spot on her arm, feeling that awful, raging fire in her veins again. "We can't 'ave much time, then." She cocked her head. "It's you, innit? You've been tryin' to contact me wi' me Ma's necklace."

The orb flickered a warm yellow. "It is."

"He took it, the necklace." El chewed on her lip, and then asked the question burning in her heart, the one she still held some tiny wisp of hope she was wrong about. "He's the Stalker, in't he?"

"You know the answer to that." The orb pulsed a blinding white. "Heed our words, Ellana. The EtherFather has trapped us for centuries, harnessing our power and claiming it as His own. We have waited, we have grown in strength, we have bided our time. And now we must reclaim our power."

"Power? What power?"

"The EtherStone. Our life's blood, given form."

El nodded, though she wasn't sure the being before her possessed eyes. "What d'you want me t' do? I'm jus' one bloody Scrubber, I'm not enough t' save you. Besides, Ashford's got me locked up; I'm not sure I can escape."

"You don't need to escape. The man who imprisons you is the

EtherFather's servant. He tries to prevent us from fighting back. From reclaiming what is rightfully ours. From ending His oppressive reign over Estra."

"Ashford is the EtherFather's servant?" El rubbed her furrowed brow, trying to comprehend what she was hearing. "Wait... is that why he, he—"

"Yes. He kills any who would threaten the EtherFather's rule." The orb pulsed grey like a dark storm cloud. "We have tried to contact others before you. You are the first who has been able to hear us properly, to acknowledge our presence without—"

"Going mad." El gulped. "All those women, they died... they died 'cos o' you!"

The orb blackened for a moment. "We regret all who have been lost. We regret it deeply, though we had no choice."

El tried to feel angry, yet she sensed the intense grief in the words. She pressed on, aware of the urgency and limited time. "You said I don't need t' escape. What, then? What do you need me t' do?"

The orb brightened to a blinding degree. "Kill him."

El cried out, holding her hands over her eyes. "How can I do that?" she said once the orb had faded. "I'm chained. I'm weak. I 'ave t' protect Ren."

"Get close to him. Get the necklace back. Now that our connection is complete, we will do the rest. In trying to strengthen himself, the man has—"

"Ellana, Ellana, Ellana," Ashford's voice pierced her mind, strangely sing-song. "Wake up now."

"We must go," the orb said calmly.

"Wait!" El held up her hand towards the orb. "You keep sayin' 'we'. Who is *we*?"

The blackness surrounding her came to life with hundreds of orbs of varying size and brightness. "We are the EtherMother. All who have lived and died *should* pass on to us, join us, become a part of us, allow us to watch over and protect all in Estra. But that has been twisted by the EtherFather's corrupt reign. Because of

Him, we cannot bless Estra as we wish. We cannot share the peace that lives in our hearts. We would see all given the freedom that just a few possess under the EtherFather's reign." There was a pause in which the orb dimmed momentarily. "But you can save us, Ellana."

El gaped. "I'll do this only if you give me your word that Ren an' I'll be together again when all this is done."

"When all is done." The orb pulsed. "Yes."

El pinched her lips together. "Will I... will I see you again?"

The orb throbbed black to white a couple of times. "Yes. You will see us again when—"

"Ellana!"

There was the sound of a hard slap and El shot upright, gasping for air. Though her cheek had been the recipient of the blow, she barely registered the pain from it. She tried to check for blood, but her arms and legs had been strapped to the chair.

Ashford stood above her. "Welcome back." He pulled a watch from his waistcoat. "You have been asleep for some time. Denys." He clicked his fingers to summon his Companion, who joined them and held a lantern close to El's face. Ashford leaned over and pulled at her eyelids, forcing them wide. "Curious. You see that? She has *no* side effects."

El yanked at her restraints. "I want to check Ren's alright."

"He's fine. Boy! Rattle your chain."

El heard her brother do as commanded and heaved a sigh of relief. "You alright, Ren?"

"I'm alright, El," he replied. There was a quiver in his voice, and she sensed he was trying to be brave for her.

"Make sure you eat everythin' they give you, y'hear me?"

"Yes, El." She almost smiled at the irritation in his voice.

"Enough," Ashford said, leaning across her again. "I need to check you. The dose you received was stronger than the first. How are you feeling? The fact you were asleep for so long concerns me."

Curiously, his concern seemed genuine, though El had no

misconceptions it was for her. "I'm fine. A little thirsty an' hungry but... fine."

Ashford pinched the bridge of his nose. "I've no doubt you are being belligerent to irritate me."

"You think a lot o' yourself, don't you?" El said. She received another slap, and her lip was split open by the ring on Ashford's finger. She tasted blood.

"El!" Ren shouted.

"Don't worry, Ren. Don't worry." El spat bloody spittle to the floor, meeting Denys's eyes.

He gave her a small nod before retreating—to check on her brother, she hoped.

Despite the fact he'd betrayed her, she was certain Denys wouldn't allow anything to happen to Ren. It filled her with the courage to do what she must.

"Now, tell me what you experienced. What you felt," Ashford said, placing himself in front of her, blocking her view.

El closed her eyes, seeing the orbs once more. "We are the EtherMother... You can save us, Ellana," they'd said.

She opened her eyes. "Where's my necklace?"

Ashford grabbed her shoulders, digging his fingers into her flesh. "What the *fuck* has that got to do with—"

"Give me back my necklace an' I'll tell you what you wanna know. About the EtherMother."

Ashford's eyes widened, his face paled to an almost translucent white, and she knew she had him. He straightened up, running his hands down the front of his black waistcoat. "Very well." He wasn't quite able to hide the excitement in his voice. "We have a meeting. Then I will bring you the necklace."

Denys stepped forward. "Shouldn't we release El from the chair, and fetch some—"

"No," Ashford snarled. "Come, let's get this *damned* meeting out of the way." He muttered under his breath, "Bastards demanding we attend, knowing full well we..." He stormed from the room, his words trailing with him. Denys hurried to follow.

El squinted towards her brother. "We're gonna be fine, Ren. Just like I promised you. We're gonna be fine." She slumped back into the chair, allowing a small smile to play on her lips. With the EtherMother's help, she was going to kill Ashford.

Then they would all be free.

CHAPTER 36

THE MASK

Beth waited in the dining room until she heard the front door to the manor close. For some reason, Ashford and Denys were delayed in leaving. Until she was able to attend Ashford's bedchamber, she remained frozen, unable to perform any other task but the one she'd set her mind to. When the noise of the steam carriage rattling down the driveway finally reached her ears, she knew it was safe.

She eased herself up from her chair and hurried to the door. She opened it carefully, peering into the hallway. She imagined El beside her, urging her on, speaking words of blunt encouragement. She could almost hear her Companion saying, "Let's get 'im, Beth."

Anxious energy thrumming through her limbs, she made for the ballroom, encountering no servants along the way. It occurred to her that with Ashford gone the household appeared to heave a sigh of relief, as if the servants no longer felt they had to be seen performing tasks at every second.

How did I not notice before? she wondered.

The air seemed clearer, less full of tension, easier to breathe. The ballroom itself was empty, the tables covered in white sheets and curtains pulled across the great windows. It seemed a room of ghosts without the guests, music, chatter and tinkling laughter, and flickering lights of the giant chandelier.

At the far wall of the room, she pulled back the thick curtain that concealed the door to Ashford and Denys's bedchambers. She suddenly found it very peculiar their bedrooms were down here rather than upstairs like her own. Should she have thought about that earlier? About the unusual arrangement, and the relationship between her husband and Denys?

And then there was the strange, locked medical room down the same hallway—the one from which she had heard that awful groan. Had that been Edward or some other patient? She knew after she'd searched Ashford's bedchamber, she would have to find a way inside that room, with or without the key. She must leave no place unexplored.

With a sigh, she opened the door into the dim hallway, cursing herself for not bringing a lantern. The lamps on the walls were lit but they provided scant light. Unlike every other time she'd walked down this hallway, she was filled with a heavy sense of dread, part of her wanting to simply flee, to forget the knife, forget any notion of Ashford being the Stalker, forget Edward's involvement, all of it.

But she knew she couldn't. Not only for El's sake but for all the people who had lost their lives to a madman. If she could reveal his true identity, if she could get to the bottom of this mess, she could stop more pain and suffering at his hands.

Halfway down the hall, she stood outside the door to her husband's bedchamber. She recalled the anticipation that had prickled over her body whenever Ashford had led her here. A wave of nausea hit her, and she leaned against the wall, dizzy with fear and sadness. Swallowing bitter bile, she took a deep breath, twisted the doorknob, and entered.

Closing the door softly, she turned to face the room, eyes scanning over everything she had previously ignored, so focused had she been on her husband. Last she'd seen it, the knife had been on Ashford's bedside table—that was the night they had returned from their wedding trip. She sat on Ashford's side of the bed, a cloud of his cologne wafting over her. Her body responded to it as though in anticipation of his touch, except now there was an undercurrent of anguish alongside the desire.

Beth shifted towards his bedside table, praying the sheath and knife would be there. To her disappointment, neither were in sight. There was nothing but dark wood and an unlit gaslamp.

"Shit." She had the sudden urge to giggle at her use of the word she'd often heard El use. Part of her appreciated the requirement for such language in the face of such challenging odds. She shook her head and forced herself to concentrate. *If the knife isn't here, where could it be? Hidden, perhaps?* She had to check everywhere she could, had to be sure, for she knew she wouldn't find the courage again.

There may not even be a chance to try.

She crept to the dark wooden wardrobe next, inside which she found jackets and trousers of all colors. Alongside those were white shirts of cotton and silk, all bathed in her husband's suffocating scent, all reminding her that she loved this man, that her entire being had wanted only to be with him.

Why have I been punished so? She stopped herself at that thought. *You haven't been punished. You've been given the task of vengeance for women whose voices were silenced, likely by your husband. This is not about you.*

Beth pushed her hands through the clothes, hoping to find some hidden compartment or box of clues, but her fingers found only smooth, solid wood. She closed the doors, eyes skirting around the room again. The bed sat at its center, imposing and dark with its four wooden posts and maroon colored drapes. Walking alongside Ashford's dressing table, she ran her fingers over his various combs, brushes, and bottles of cologne. She wanted to commit everything to memory, knowing that once this was over, her life would never be the same.

As she moved across the table, her hand came to rest on a black pouch. Instinctively, she pulled away, her stomach knotting without a conscious awareness why. She reached for it again, hand trembling, heart racing, breaths coming fast.

She picked it up; the weight was instantly familiar. She closed her eyes and unwrapped the pouch, an instinctive sense burning within her that this moment would change everything. She forced her eyelids back open and held the object up.

An EtherStone necklace. *El's* EtherStone necklace.

Though she'd only seen it once, she knew without a doubt what she was looking at. Turning the necklace over, she studied it properly for the first time. On the back was engraved two words: *Ariya Aberforth*. If this was El's necklace, why did it bear the name of a noble family?

But wait, hadn't El's mother's name been...

"Ariya." Her hand flew to her lips. *How can that be? El and Ren are... Lord Artavius Aberforth's grandchildren?*

Folding the necklace back into the pouch, she secured it to her belt. Then she sat for a time, so full of anxiety and worry she could hardly pull apart her tumbling thoughts.

When she heard a door in the hall opening, Beth's heart leapt in her chest. She pulled herself forward on the bed, wiping away the tears she'd hardly realized were falling. When the door to Ashford's bedchamber creaked open, she painted a smile on her face.

"Ashford," she said as cheerfully as possible. "I've been waiting for you."

Ashford jolted at her words, eyes rising to meet hers. They were clouded with an unreadable emotion. "Elizabetha, I did not expect to find you here."

Beth raised an eyebrow. "Didn't we arrange for it, my dear? Before you left?"

His expression quickly flickered into an insincere smile. "Oh, of course, of course." He hurried to sit beside her. His fingers upon hers were curiously clammy, and she wanted nothing more than to pull away. "I am so sorry, my love, but I must ask you if we can delay. An important matter has come up."

Beth swallowed. "Is all well?"

"Oh, yes, yes," Ashford said, waving his hand dismissively. He stood, walking over to his dressing table. "Nothing to worry about. It's just a matter that came up at the..." He looked over his shoulder back to Beth. "My dear, you haven't seen..." He bent over the table, moving items aside.

Beth stood and crept towards the door, afraid of being trapped. "What is it you're looking for, Ash?" Inwardly, she cursed herself for thinking that confronting him here, in his own private space, had been a good idea.

His movements became more frantic, brushes and bottles clattering to the floor.

Beth shuffled faster, trying to get past Ashford without alerting him.

"Where is it?" he muttered.

"Ashford, I don't know what you—"

"Where is it?" he cried, rounding on her.

Beth lurched back, thudding into the door as he grabbed ahold of her arms, pressing his body against hers. He looked down at her, their lips almost touching and for a moment she thought he might kiss her, might take her there and then.

Instead, his quivering lips curled into a sneer. "Where is it?"

"I don't know what you mean, Ashford," she said, willing him not to notice the pouch on her belt.

"Don't lie to me," he whispered, leaning closer, his lips brushing hers. "Give it back, Elizabetha. Now."

Beth pushed her mouth against his in an aggressive kiss—their last kiss, part of her knew with a great flood of heartbreak and disgust. She forced his head back, then pulled away to look up at him. He wasn't going to believe her, but it was time to tell the truth.

"Ashford, I will give you what you want if you give me some space. Why are you so angry, my love? Has something happened?"

His lips twitched into a smile again as he ran a hand through his hair. "I- I'm sorry, my dear. I don't know what came over me." He held his hand out. "Now, please, it's important I have what you've taken."

"Very well," Beth said. "But first I must ask one question."

Anger flashed across her husband's beautiful eyes. "What? What is it?"

"What are you doing with El's EtherStone necklace?"

Ashford blanched. "Excuse me?"

Beth patted the pouch. "I've seen this necklace before. It belonged to my friend. I'm asking you, Ashford, why is it in your possession?"

Without warning, Ashford shoved her backwards, pinning her against the door again. She gasped in shock, holding her hands up instinctively to protect her face. "How dare you?" he spat. "I am your *husband*. You do not *question* me!"

He grabbed her forearm and flung her across the room. She stumbled to the floor, wincing as she landed on her elbow. Biting back a sob, she asked, "Ashford, what have you done?"

He stalked up to her and she finally noticed the knife at his belt. Had that been there the whole time?

Beth, you careless fool!

Ashford's hand kept flitting to the hilt as though to unsheathe it. He muttered to himself, intermittently pounding his palms against his forehead. Suddenly, he stopped and stared down at her. His eyes were red.

"Why her, why her, why *her?*" he screeched, rubbing his hands over his face.

"A-Ashford?" Beth sat up and shuffled back until she was against the wall. "It's you, isn't it? You're the Stalker."

Her husband's shoulders began to shake. At first, she thought he was crying. To her horror, when he removed his hands from his face, he bore a wide grin.

He's laughing. He is truly mad.

Ashford continued for a few moments, pounding his hands on

his stomach as though the amusement was too much. Beth could only watch on in disbelief, mouth agape. When at last he stopped, he mopped his fingers across his eyes.

"Oh, Beth," he said. "Beth, Beth, Beth, my love." He shook his head as he stepped closer.

She wished she could disappear, so terrified was she of what he might do to her. She closed her eyes and scrunched into herself, curling up as tightly as she could. She heard him close in, his footfalls light but breaths heavy, sensed his presence above her. She had no doubt he could kill her if he wanted to.

But nothing happened. Opening her eyes again, she found him regarding her with a sad expression.

"I could've had my pick of the noble families in Alpinside. And further afield, too. I had many offers from across the kingdom, young women who would have simply *loved* to be my wife. Women to obey and respect me. Who would see my strength and power. And I chose you, Elizabetha. I chose you." He sighed. "Yet, here we are. You would relinquish the life we could've had all for a few *Scrubber whores!*"

Without allowing her to respond, Ashford grabbed her wrist, yanking her from the ground. Beth yelped in pain, but he ignored her, dragging her to the door.

Beth pulled back, trying to fight against him, but his grip was too strong.

"Ashford, stop!" she shouted as he reached for the door handle.

To her surprise, he listened, releasing her arm and turning to look at her.

Beth wiped her nose with the back of her hand, her vision blurring with tears. With her sight distorted, she seemed to see past the attractive façade around him—to see the true monster within.

"*Why* did you choose me?" she whispered, desperate to buy herself time, even if it was mere moments. At the same time, a part of her truly did want to know the answer... *Needed* to know how she'd been so deceived by this man.

Ashford gave a cruel bark of laughter that drove the dagger of pain deeper into her heart. "You were so innocent. So young. So naive. I knew a wife like you was just what I needed to enable me to keep up my work."

In spite of everything, Beth had still held some hope, a slice of light in the back of her mind that all she'd discovered wasn't true. That this was a terrible nightmare, that she'd imagined everything, that her husband was just that, her husband. But seeing his face—his true face—she knew there was no denying it any longer.

"You're not well, Ashford," she said, more gently than he deserved. "You've- you've hurt a lot of people."

He smirked. "Even now, you can't say it, can you? I have *killed*, Elizabetha. And I will continue to do so until my mission is complete. Do you understand?" His hand was clasped on the hilt of his knife again, his entire body visibly trembling.

"*Mission?* The reason why you- why you k-killed those women?" Beth stared up at him, searching his face, his mask of lies.

Ashford reached towards her. She flinched as though he would hit her, hands flying up to protect her face. Instead, he removed the pouch from her belt.

With it in his hands, he took a long, deep breath. "You wouldn't understand, Elizabetha." There was a quiet resignation to his voice, a deep weariness that told of unspoken words. He straightened up, his eyes becoming glazed. He appeared to be listening to something she couldn't hear. "No, surely, there's more time for me to—" He cut himself off and gave a curt nod. "Yes, I understand, Father. It is time. I have delayed for too long."

Father? Beth didn't understand what had just happened.

Curiously, Ashford turned for the door without looking back at her. Stepping into the hallway, he headed right.

Beth was quick to follow him; he either didn't notice or didn't care.

"Ashford!" He ignored her. Something had happened, had *changed* within him. Had he been speaking to himself, or someone else? *Something* else? Beth knew it no longer mattered. Whatever came next, she had to see this through.

THE LAST

ELLANA

When the door opened again, El was prepared for what was to come. She knew she must be one step ahead of Ashford, must see her opening, and must strike. This was her chance.

So, it was with a level of disappointment that she watched as Denys entered, holding a tray of food and drink. He placed it on a table and walked to her, kneeling down to undo the straps that bound her to the chair. Free, she rubbed fiercely at her wrists.

"A thank you would suffice," Denys murmured as he stood.

El glared at him. "After what you've done, you're lucky I don't kick you in the fuckin'—"

"El, he's brought us food!" Ren was pulling at his chain, desperate to get to the meal. "I'm bloody starvin'."

"Take 'im the tray," she said to Denys.

"You must eat too," he said gently.

"Not hungry. Give it t' Ren."

Denys sighed but did as he was asked, even sitting next to Ren as he ate. Her brother barely acknowledged his presence as he wolfed down the food.

Silence descended over the dim room, broken only by Ren's grunts and gulps. After some time, Denys stood and returned to where El remained seated, eyes locked on the door before turning to her.

"Ellana," he said, reaching to touch her shoulder.

She flinched away, frowning, not removing her eyes from the door.

"Ellana," he said more firmly, leaning in front of her face so she had no choice but to meet his dark eyes. They were blood-shot, exhausted. He seemed... broken.

He don't deserve your pity, she told herself. She sniffed indignantly. "What?"

Denys pursed his lips. "I want you to know, I- I am so sorry. I never meant for this to happen. You must believe me."

"Denys, if that were true, you'd never've told Ashford 'bout my necklace. That's 'ow he found out 'bout me havin' this- this—"

"Madness." Denys's lips tightened. "I wanted Ashford to agree for us to help you. There have been too many deaths. Too many losses. I wanted us to find a cure this time."

El frowned. "Too many deaths? You mean...?"

"Yes."

Her mouth dropped open. "You fuckin' *knew?*"

Denys flinched as though slapped. "El, it is not so simple. Ashford and I... Well, I—"

The door burst open and Ashford stood in the doorway, a black pouch clasped in his hands. She watched him walk in, strut-ting and proud. He seemed... triumphant. Confident.

This ain't good.

"Ashford, wait! Ashford, I— Oh." Suddenly, Beth was there, taking in the room. "El!" she cried, running over and scooping her into a hug. "Oh, I thought I'd lost you. I was sure he had—"

"This is all rather touching, but I shall have to insist on you two separating. Now." Ashford snapped his fingers impatiently. "Denys, the door, please."

Despite what Denys had said to her, he followed Ashford's command—though didn't lock the door as he usually would, El noted. She glanced at Ashford; he hadn't noticed.

"It is as well we're all here. Perhaps you'll take some notes, Elizabetha. Do you have your notebook?" He snorted with derision. "It was fun watching you both, believing you could solve such a mystery. And look where we are! Aren't you both so *clever*. You really did it." There was a tinge of madness to the way he spoke, an unhinged glint in his eyes.

"Did you bring the necklace?" El asked. Beth's hand rested on her shoulder, and she took great strength from it.

"I did." He held the pouch up.

"Remember what I said, Ashford. You want anythin' from me, I'll need that necklace back."

"You know, I had planned to give it to you. I'm a man of my word. A man of honor." As he spoke, he revealed the EtherStone necklace.

"You 'ave no honor, Ashford. You're a killer," she spat.

He ignored her. "I've been reminded my mission must come first. That the tests I had hoped to carry out here were... selfish."

"Reminded?" Beth asked. "Mission? Ashford, you aren't making sense. Reminded by *who?*"

Placing the necklace in his pocket, Ashford met his wife's eyes. "The EtherFather, of course."

El looked up at Beth; her friend's lips were downturned, brow furrowed.

"Ashford, the EtherFather... talks to you? In your mind?" Beth asked.

He snorted derisively. "Who else would give me such an important mission?"

Beth's voice remained soft and full of kindness; El admired her for being able to maintain such compassion in the face of evil. "Don't you see? Ashford, you've killed those whose minds have been overcome with madness. The very same madness that consumes you."

"Silence!" he cried.

Beth flinched and El took her hand, squeezing it.

"I am *not* like them," Ashford insisted, a hint of desperation in his voice. "I am saving Alpinside. I am saving *all of us!* The loss of a few whores is really no loss."

At the door, Denys watched the scene unfold, stony-faced and silent. El wondered how much of this he'd already known and how much he was learning now.

"What d'you want from me, Ashford?" El asked.

He met her gaze. "Your life. The mission will be complete then. He has promised, when you are dead, it is over. You are the final pawn."

"No!" Beth sobbed.

"El!" Ren called, rattling his chains. "Don't hurt my sister, you-you fuckin' monster!"

"It's time this was finished. All of it." El released Beth's hand and stood, placing herself between her friend and Ashford. "Do whatever you want wi' me. Just let Ren an' Beth go."

"No, El," Beth whispered.

El felt a hand on her back but didn't look back at Beth, afraid she might waiver if she did.

Ashford frowned, shaking his head. "You make the mistake of believing you have any power here. It's out of my hands now. I tried to keep you alive a little longer." A sad smile flitted across his lips. "Even if it was an attempt to strengthen my connection to Him, He doesn't care for such concerns. He can wait no longer."

"Ashford, please," Beth said, pushing past El. "The EtherFather is *not* speaking to you. There is no mission." She grasped his arm, trying to pull his attention towards her. "Please, Ashford. If there's any of the man I loved left within you, *please* listen to me."

He barely seemed to acknowledge her words, his face an emotionless mask. "You do not know of what you speak, Elizabetha," he said coolly. "You would risk the whole of Estra for a Scrubber. You are not the woman I believed you to be."

He shoved her aside and she fell to the ground. Before El had a chance to go to her, she was being slammed back into the chair. She lashed out, thrashing her arms and kicking her legs, but it was no use. Ashford was freakishly strong, his expression unmoving, his eyes blank.

As he knelt to strap her arms and legs down, he called to Denys, "Remove Beth and Ren."

"No!" Ren and Beth shouted in unison.

"I will be obeyed!" Ashford snarled, turning to face them. El noted the flash of red in his eyes. "Denys, get them out of here before I fucking kill them all."

Denys shuffled forward, first releasing Ren. With one hand clasped round Ren's forearm, he leaned down to pull Beth up. "Come with me," he said quietly.

Ren stared at El, his eyes glossy.

She bit her lip, determined not to cry, and nodded at her brother. "Go on, Ren. Beth'll look after you."

As Ren was led away by Denys, she swallowed back a cry of despair. Beth gave her one final, tear-filled look before the door was closed.

Ashford's back remained to El, his shoulders hunched. He let out a deep, weary exhale, and, to her surprise, when he faced her once more, tears glistened on his cheeks. "I did not ask to be chosen. I did not ask for this."

After all this man had done, El found it difficult to summon any sympathy. "Those women din't ask to be killed. They were unwell an' you was their doctor. You was meant t' save 'em, not murder 'em. Not t' mention the others you killed 'cos they was in the wrong place at the wrong time."

Ashford pulled out a kerchief and dabbed at his cheeks. "I see you still don't understand the nature of what I do. Of *why* I do it." He narrowed his eyes. "I must ask before I kill you, how do you not know you are connected to the EtherMother? Surely you know of Her schemes; surely you've been given your own mission?"

"Mission? There's no *mission*. But I 'ave been asked for help. To free those who've been imprisoned against their will." She met his eyes. "By the EtherFather."

"Lies!" Ashford rushed at her, his face leering above hers, lips peeled back over his teeth. "The EtherMother seeks to overturn the EtherFather, to take what is His and—"

"Her? No. *They*. The EtherMother is many. Everyone who's ever lived an' died finds peace with the EtherMother, your mother an' father included. That's 'ow it should be, anyway, but the Ether-Father stopped that." As El spoke, she attempted to reach into the pocket of Ashford's waistcoat. She was able to brush the outside of the pocket and feel the weight of the necklace within.

Ashford's face contorted with rage, and he jerked backwards, hands clenching into fists. "What mockery is this? How dare you try to make me believe my parents would have *anything* to do with the corrupt power who seeks to twist your mind. The EtherFa-ther rewards His loyal followers. My parents are with Him. No. You're wrong." With an eerie calmness, he punched her in the face. "You are a filthy whore, just like the others. A disgusting servant of the EtherMother who would see this whole kingdom undone." He delicately wiped the blood from his knuckles.

El sucked at the re-opened cut on her lip, tasting iron. "If you really believe all o' that, you're fuckin' madder than any of us. Do what you must wi' me; it's useless arguin' with a madman."

"I'm not mad, Ellana. I've more clarity than ever; I am doing the EtherFather's work." With a resigned sigh, he pulled the knife from the sheath at his belt. "I won't enjoy this."

A strange sense of peace settled over El as he moved closer, almost in slow motion. She focused on the pocket from which she must retrieve the necklace if she had any hope of living. She stretched her arm within its binding, the leather straps digging into her skin.

Ashford held the knife at chest level. His eyes glowed that awful red, his lips were peeled back, his face a contorted mask of evil.

El grimaced at the pain in her wrist but kept reaching. As Ashford lifted the blade to her throat, she knew there was no hope.

She was going to die.

She closed her eyes and laid her head back, so tired, so sick of fighting. Blade met skin. She slowed her breathing, swallowed back a scream.

I'm sorry, Ren. Look after 'im, Beth.

Suddenly, the door crashed open.

El's eyes flew open. *Denys.*

He charged towards Ashford, knocking him to the ground. Though the pressure of the knife had lifted, El wasn't unscathed; there was a burning slice from where she'd been nicked. She barely paid it any heed as she twisted in the chair to watch.

Denys was atop Ashford, pinning him in place. The blade was close by, glinting in the dim light of the flickering gaslamp. Ashford writhed and struggled, growling and screeching.

Denys slammed his hands down against Ashford's wrists, shouting, "Stop this! Please, Ashford. Stop."

Ashford calmed, limbs stilling, though his breathing was still ragged. "Denys," he said, voice quivering, "you know I can't. He'll simply choose another. His mission must be completed. I must do this, my friend. I cannot stop. Don't ask it of me."

Ashford began to sob, his head shaking from side to side as he repeated those words over and over.

El could only watch helplessly. She wondered when the madness had fully taken Ashford, how long he'd lived with the voice in his head.

Denys's mouth was downturned, his lips trembling. "Ashford." He leaned down, touching his forehead to his Companion's. "My love. I'm sorry I didn't stop you sooner. I was too afraid to lose you. But this has gone too far. Too many have lost their lives. I'm here to pull you back from the abyss of— Agh!"

Ashford had freed his right knee and driven it into Denys's gut. As Denys slumped, Ashford lurched to his feet, lunging for the knife.

"Denys," El called, "the necklace, in his pocket! Get it for me."

Ashford had the knife, though he stumbled as he worked to get himself fully upright.

They were running out of time.

"Now, Denys!" El pleaded.

Getting to his knees, Denys launched himself at Ashford's legs and pulled him down. Ashford hit the floor with a loud *crack*.

Blood streamed from Ashford's nostrils. He kicked out at Denys. "Denys, stop or I will kill you. You will leave me no choice."

Ignoring the kicks battering his head and arms, Denys crawled up Ashford's body, grabbing at his clothes. "You will not kill anyone else," he said through gritted teeth. "I will—" He grabbed for Ashford's pocket, pulling out the necklace. "—make sure of it."

Denys stood, treading on Ashford as he leapt for El, thrusting the necklace into her hand. Then he was unbuckling her arm, placing himself between her and Ashford.

"Very well," Ashford said, face unreadable. "You *both* shall die."

El didn't look at him, instead squeezing the necklace in her hand. "Help me," she cried. "Help me!"

Ashford swiped out at Denys with the knife. Denys cried out, then was pushed aside by Ashford. He fell to the floor beside her chair, clutching his arm. El looked up to find Ashford above her. His eyes were the worst she'd ever seen them; dark red, full of rage. His mouth was set in a hard line.

She scrunched her eyes shut, brandishing the necklace at Ashford. *Please, please, please,* she prayed.

A blinding light pierced through her eyelids and the necklace vibrated so hard she almost dropped it.

"You have been misguided, Ashford Branton." A voice—no, many voices—spoke. "Stop this now or face the consequences."

Ashford let out a crazed laugh. "You cannot stop me, heathen! Sorceress! Manipulator!" His eyes lit with a manic glare. "Your last whore dies now."

"No, Ashford!" Denys wailed.

Ashford lurched at El, the knife brandished. As the Ether-Stone necklace pulsed with a final glaring light, he stabbed out, screaming as the necklace touched his chest. Falling silent, he collapsed backwards onto the floor. At the same time, the Ether-Stone in her Ma's necklace shattered.

El let out a choked laugh of relief, twisting to check Ashford was at the very least unconscious. As she did so, a fiery pain shot through her body, from her shoulder to her groin. She glanced down.

The knife protruded from the left side of her chest, close to her armpit.

"No," she whispered.

"El, don't move," Denys said gently, coming to kneel at her side, clasping her hand.

"Denys, you saved me," she croaked, then noticed the bleeding wound on his left arm. "Oh—y-you're hurt."

"Shh, shh. I'm fine, just a small cut. Save your energy." He examined the knife. "We need to get you to a doctor."

El laughed, then winced, then coughed. "You *are* a doctor."

Denys's eyes met hers. "This is beyond my skillset. And I never was good with blood."

She choked back another laugh as he stroked her cheek. It was soothing. Her eyelids drooped.

"No, no," he said. "Stay awake, El." He undid the remaining straps. "I'm going to fetch Beth and Ren. Please stay awake."

El exhaled weakly. "Not goin' anywhere."

Denys hurried for the door.

As soon as he'd left, El let out a sigh and closed her eyes. With the darkness, the pain ebbed away.

❦

THE PAIN IN HER CHEST HAD BEEN EXCRUCIATING. HOT, SHARP, fiery.

But then there had been peace, so warm and comforting that she never wanted to leave.

"Ellana," said a voice, soft and all too familiar. "Ellana, it's time, my love."

"El, wake up," came Denys's voice.

Her body was gently shaken.

"El!" That was Beth. "Is that a knife? Oh, by the Mother! Denys, you have to do something!"

"El, don't leave me," Ren pleaded. "I can't lose you too."

She drifted, floated, melted towards the soft voice beckoning her.

"Come to me, my darling."

A sharp, repulsive scent tinged her nostrils. She gasped, jolting awake, then cried out in pain at the abominable throb in her chest.

She blinked, hand searching for a familiar touch. "Ren? Beth?"

Ren was at her side in an instant. "I'm 'ere."

His touch was so warm.

"She's shiverin'! That's not— That can't be good, can it?"

El blinked and it was Deny's face above hers, not Ren's. His dark skin shone with sweat, his eyes wide with panic.

"El, listen to me. There's no time to fetch anyone else. I'm going to remove the knife. I- I think I can save you." His lips quivered as he smiled at her. "There are- there are tools here. I have to try."

"Denys, you already saved me," she whispered. When he didn't respond, she wondered if she had actually spoken the words aloud.

"Bring that lantern over here, Beth, and hold it steady." He let out a long, shuddering breath, clearly steeling himself. "Old gods, guide me."

He yanked upwards. When the knife came away, El was near blinded with agony. The warm pulse of her own blood flowed across her chest and cascaded down her side.

"We must staunch the flow, quickly," Denys said methodically.

"Those cloths, Beth. Now." Hands pressed on her chest, slipping, crushing. "Please, please."

"Hold on, El." Beth's voice trembled.

"Shit," Denys muttered. "Shit, I was never any— Fuck!"

El blinked and Denys was replaced by Ren, though there was still a hand pressing into her wound.

"El," Ren whispered, tears dripping down his cheeks, "please, don't leave me."

"Sorry, Ren," she managed to say, iron bubbling in her throat.

He laid his head on her shoulder, his body shaking with sobs.

She wanted to give him something to remember her by but didn't know what she could offer. Then she remembered the necklace, or what remained of it, still in her hand. With a great deal of effort, she lifted her arm and pushed it towards her brother. "Take it," she said. "Ma's. Yours, Ren. Take it."

"I'll look after it for you," he said. "Just 'til you're better."

"A'right, Ren."

Time seemed to dip and blur, and it was increasingly hard to keep her eyes open. At first, she'd been aware of the warmth of the blood gushing from the wound, soaking her dress, dripping to the floor. Now, it felt like nothing, provided no heat. It was becoming harder to breathe by the second. El was losing awareness of her body, the pain. A blessing, she reckoned.

Then the light came, blinding in intensity, pure white. It divided into the orbs she'd seen before, welcoming in their peaceful, pulsing glow. El was overcome with calm. She smiled, might've even laughed.

In the distance, Ren's voice echoed. "El?"

She tried to speak; her lips wouldn't obey. She wanted to reach for him, but her body ignored the command.

"Hold on, El. We're getting help." Beth. Her friend. The only true friend she'd ever had.

"We did it," she wanted to say. "We solved it. We stopped the Stalker." She had no strength to speak.

"El, I'm so sorry. I really thought I could— Oh, gods, no." Denys's voice turned to sobs.

"Ellana," the voice again.

It tugged at her mind, a voice from her past, from a time when everything had been better, simpler, easier. A time before the Stalker, before Beth, before Ren, even.

"My El, my beautiful girl."

"*Ma?*" She could've cried. Perhaps she *was* crying. Usually, El would've stopped herself from such an open display of emotion, but it no longer seemed to matter. Nothing seemed to matter. "You're 'ere, Ma."

"Yes, El, I'm here. You did it. You saved us. You freed us. Now, we can take back what is ours. We can stop the EtherFather's oppressive reign."

"I... I did that?" El said—or perhaps she simply thought it.

"You can let go, my love. You can let go."

"What 'bout Ren?" she asked. "I can't leave 'im."

There was a long breath, a sad sigh. "I know it is hard, my love, but you must. He will be looked after."

For the first time in her life, El was selfish, thinking only of herself, and let out one last breath before drifting to join the orbs.

PART V
THE AFTERMATH

Evil Killer Unmasked

The identity of the Scrubbers' Stalker, the evil killer who has so cruelly taken the lives of so many of our friends and neighbors, has been revealed. Ashford Branton, the nobleman who posed as a doctor to choose his unsuspecting victims, has been unmasked by none other than his wife, Elizabetha Branton. Her Companion, Ellana Stone, whose life was unfortunately taken as the last of the cruel murderer's victims, assisted her in unveiling his identity.

--The Workers' Tribune

Funeral Finally Held for Disgraced Nobleman

The delayed funeral was finally held on Friday for Lord Ashford Branton, the young nobleman whose wedding to Lady Elizabetha Branton (nee Estamore) was, not so long ago, the talk of Alpinside. This tragedy is mired in mystery, for his untimely death was apparently linked to the murders that have blighted our fair city this past year. Some even spoke of Lord Branton himself being involved in the vicious killings—though this reporter finds that hard to believe, given his good name and the medical expertise that he so generously shared with the poorer folk in the Workers' District. Amidst such rumors, few turned out to honor the late Lord Branton, whose estate now passes to his widow, Lady Branton. It is unclear at this time whether Lady Branton will continue her husband's business affairs given the speculation around her husband's identity as the Stalker. Furthermore, the disruption to the EtherStone mines that occurred coincidentally on the same night as Lord Branton's death has caused increased tensions in Alpinside, with many concerned for what their collapse might mean for our beloved city's future.

--The Alpinside Affair

Shamed Nobles Flee Alpinside

Following the death of Lord Ashford Branton and the collapse of
the EtherStone mines, several nobles have left Alpinside and
retreated to their estates elsewhere in Estra. Lord Landrum and
Lady Oren Estamore following the deaths of their son, Edward—
who succumbed to a mysterious illness—and their wed-son, Lord
Branton, were reported to be distraught, and have retreated to
their countryside manor to deal with their grief. Speaking to this
reporter, they advised they did not know when they might return
to Alpinside and asked for privacy at this difficult time. Lord
Artavius Aberforth, one time friend and business partner to Lord
Estamore, devastated by the loss of his family's mines,
disappeared not long after the night of the collapse. This reporter
has been unable to reach him for comment.

-- The Alpinside Journal

EPILOGUE
THE SACRIFICE

In the weeks awaiting Ashford's funeral—delayed to allow a full investigation by the City Guard—Beth found she cared little for the increasing gossip around her. Though she longed for her parents' support, she'd come to understand why they could not remain in Alpinside. They had, after all, lost their child. Not so long ago, she'd learned what it meant to fear such a thing.

With Ren and Denys by her side, she'd watched as her husband's body was burned, a hand resting on her belly. Could it be considered a blessing to bear the child of a man such as Ashford? She didn't know, yet she knew El's sacrifice wouldn't be in vain. Change was coming to Alpinside, to Estra. It already had, starting the night of Ashford's death, with the sudden collapse of the EtherStone mines. It was only a matter of time before everyone would notice the retreat of the EtherFather and the succession of the EtherMother.

And Beth had work to do.

"Stay with me," she'd said to Denys on the morning of Ashford's funeral, and she'd meant it.

"I will," he'd replied, though he had been unable to meet her gaze.

Now, some four weeks since that day, she stood with Denys by the window of the reception room, watching Ren play in the manor gardens. The boy was as unaware of their conversation, as he was unaware of Denys's true involvement in all that had transpired. Beth would do all she could to protect and take care of Ren, as she'd promised El. She looked up at Denys. Though he had remained with her, he had been often confined to his study and bedchamber. Now that he had ventured out to join her, she knew she must speak frankly.

She cleared her throat. "Help me rebuild under the guidance of the EtherMother."

He clasped his hands, perhaps to stop them from fumbling nervously. "Beth, after all I've done—after what I *allowed* to happen, how can you want me to stay? Those poor folk, the young women and their families. And Edward... I should have done more to—"

"Hush," Beth said. "Edward was a troubled man, much as it pained me to accept the truth of what he did. He is at peace now." She watched Denys for a long moment, taking in his bloodshot eyes and sunken cheeks. "You loved him. Ashford."

Denys's mouth gaped open. "Beth, I—"

"I see the hole his death has left in you." She placed a hand to her stomach, imagining her child responding within the cocoon of her womb, tiny as they still were. "He had a way of making his love intoxicating. And you were at his mercy for much longer than I. I don't know what he said to convince you to hide the extent of his madness—whether he even needed to say anything —but I don't believe you could've stopped him if you tried. He cared for you, *loved* you, but I believe he would've killed you if you'd stood in his way." She lifted her chin, just as she'd seen El do so many times. "I forgive you, Denys."

Denys let out a sobbing gasp, a hand flying to his mouth. "Beth, I don't- I don't deserve your forgiveness."

She looked at him. "And yet you have it. The EtherMother guides me. We must do what we can to spread the word. The

EtherFather's power is draining rapidly, yet tendrils of His control remain. The city is in chaos and there are those who will try to take advantage of the situation. We must act quickly. I have already waited longer than I should have." She placed a hand on his shoulder. "I need you, Denys. Please."

He exhaled, his breath clouding on the window. "I don't know if I can. I know you asked me to stay but... I've thought of leaving. Returning to the Southern Isles. Finding what remains of my family."

Ren's grinning face appeared on the other side of the glass. He waved at them, his childish play briefly pushing aside the grief that had weighed upon him since his sister's death.

Denys chuckled lightly. "He has El's spirit."

"He does," Beth said. "Remember what she sacrificed for us, Denys. Please. Do this for her, if not me."

Denys snorted. "Oh, Beth." He slowly reached over and squeezed her hand, pulling away as quickly as he could. "I would do it for you, too. Without you and El, I wouldn't have come to my senses. I will spend a lifetime trying to make amends."

"Without Ashford, none of us would be here. Daisy, Delilah, Rosie, Penny and Reggie, Lissie, Davyd, and Stephyn." She swallowed. "Ellana. All these people lost their lives. Let us not allow that to have been for nothing. Let us do this for them, Denys."

Denys nodded curtly. "For them." He flashed her a smile, full of unspoken words, his dark eyes brightening for the first time in weeks. "Yes, for them."

Beth looked towards the sky. *For you, El. For you.*

ABOUT THE AUTHOR

Lucy A. McLaren is a fantasy author and professional counsellor, passionate about writing dark fantasy stories that include a realistic representation and exploration of mental health issues. She is a lifelong fan of fantasy stories, and enjoys reading, writing, watching and playing them. When not writing, she can be found spending time with her husband and attempting (largely unsuccessfully) to wrangle her son.

www.ingramcontent.com/pod-product-compliance
Lightning Source LLC
Chambersburg PA
CBHW020014120726
47903CB00004B/1277